"You asked yesterday if I had any questions. Well, I do."

Ava looked up to see Scott standing in the doorway.

"Hi," he said, not moving into the room. "I didn't realize this was your studio. I was just walking by and I saw you working. Then I remembered what you'd said about questions."

"Questions?"

"About the tile-making process." He took a notebook from his pocket. "How do you actually make them?"

She glanced at him long enough to tell that he wasn't here to talk about tiles. He wanted to know more about her mother's disappearance. Fine. If he wasn't going to come clean, she'd make him pay the price. She launched into a detailed explanation of paint pigments, moved on to glazes and anything else she could think of to throw into her m̲o̲n̲o̲l̲o̲g̲u̲e̲. When she saw his eyes ̲s̲t̲a̲r̲t̲ ̲t̲o̲ ̲g̲l̲a̲z̲e̲ ̲o̲v̲e̲r̲, she ran a̲n̲ dissertation o̲n̲ ̲_̲_̲_̲_̲.

"That's the sho̲_̲_̲_̲_̲ ̲_̲_̲_̲_̲ ̲_̲_̲_̲_̲ enty minutes later.

"Interesting," he ̲_̲_̲_̲_̲

"You stopped taking notes about fifteen minutes ago," Ava said. "And *interesting* is one of those words people use when they can't think of anything else to say."

He looked at her for a full five seconds. "Interesting."

Dear Reader,

I'm sure most of you have felt that tug of nostaglia when you return to places you knew as a child. I know I have. For me, it's a wistful feeling, a yearning to recapture something that seems as elusive as smoke. I've found that it's equally impossible to explain. No one but me really understands exactly how magical the lights along the seafront in Ramsgate, Kent, seemed when I was fifteen and in love— or imagined I was. Or, except for my sister, the specific taste of ice cream from Stonelees, a dairy that opened only during the summer. A few years ago, I went back to England and took that same walk—the ice cream parlor had long gone. Some things had changed, others were as I remembered them, but the magic wasn't there. I couldn't— no matter how hard I tried—feel the way I had at fifteen.

For Ava, the heroine of *Suspicion*, the childhood that she and her twin sister, Ingrid, spent on the island of Santa Catalina, twenty-two miles off the Southern California coast (didn't the Beachboys say it was twenty-six?—they were wrong) was an enchanted time full of wonder and promise. After her husband dies early in their marriage, and a few years later her mother mysteriously drowns, Ava begins to wonder how much of her past was truly as idyllic as she recalls, and to what extent her memories have been colored by what she wants to believe....

I love to hear from readers. Please visit my Web site at janicemacdonald.net and let me know how you enjoyed this book.

Janice Macdonald

P.S. If you ever visit Southern California, take the Catalina Express over to Avalon. It truly is a magical place, no matter how old you are.

Suspicion

Janice Macdonald

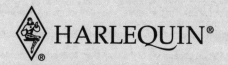

HARLEQUIN®

TORONTO • NEW YORK • LONDÓN
AMSTERDAM • PARIS • SYDNEY • HAMBURG
STOCKHOLM • ATHENS • TOKYO • MILAN • MADRID
PRAGUE • WARSAW • BUDAPEST • AUCKLAND

ISBN 0-373-71157-3

SUSPICION

Copyright © 2003 by Janice Macdonald.

All rights reserved. Except for use in any review, the reproduction or utilization of this work in whole or in part in any form by any electronic, mechanical or other means, now known or hereafter invented, including xerography, photocopying and recording, or in any information storage or retrieval system, is forbidden without the written permission of the publisher, Harlequin Enterprises Limited, 225 Duncan Mill Road, Don Mills, Ontario, Canada M3B 3K9.

All characters in this book have no existence outside the imagination of the author and have no relation whatsoever to anyone bearing the same name or names. They are not even distantly inspired by any individual known or unknown to the author, and all incidents are pure invention.

This edition published by arrangement with Harlequin Books S.A.

® and TM are trademarks of the publisher. Trademarks indicated with ® are registered in the United States Patent and Trademark Office, the Canadian Trade Marks Office and in other countries.

Visit us at www.eHarlequin.com

Printed in U.S.A.

To Carolyn, who always lets me sing "Pineapple Princess."

Acknowledgments:

I'd like to thank Deanna Shiew of C & S Ceramics & Crafts
in Muskogee, Oklahoma, for all the details she provided
on the tile-making process. If there are any errors in
description, they are mine alone. Deanna was truly
a tireless and invaluable source of information.

Thanks also to www.cataromance.com. The e-mail loop and
the willingness of its members to offer their expertise on an
absolutely amazing range of topics is truly a writer's boon.

CHAPTER ONE

"I KEEP HAVING this dream. I'm looking down into the water and I can see my mother's face staring up at me...." Ava Lynsky held the fingertips of her left hand in the palm of her right and squeezed hard. Her skin felt numb and icy-cold, her chest hurt. "And then it isn't her. It's me or my sister, and every time we come up to the surface, something pushes us down again."

"Something?" the therapist asked.

"A hand."

"Do you know whose hand it is?"

Ava didn't answer. Through the tinted windows she could see the small square structure of Avalon Municipal Hospital through a clearing of eucalyptus trees. Her father was one of two Catalina Island physicians on staff there. She imagined him looking through the windows to see her sitting in a psychologist's office. Could imagine the mixture of incredulity and contempt on his face. *Neurotic,* he would say. *Can't stand neurotic women.*

"Ava."

She looked at the therapist. "Hmm?"

"Whose hand is it?"

Ava shook her head. "I don't know."

"When did you start having these dreams?"

"They started after my mother..." She couldn't seem to finish.

"After your mother *died,*" the therapist said.

The word reverberated in Ava's head, clanged like a bell,

louder and louder. She hugged herself, hands tucked under her arms, pressing down hard. Her heart felt swollen in her chest. "It's been three months now. I stay up most of the night because I dread going to sleep. I can't work. I've started a dozen different things and they're all awful and I've got this new commission and I'm scared to death."

"What do you think the dream represents?"

She looked at the therapist, a cool, thin-faced woman from the mainland sitting upright in her chair, hands folded neatly in her lap. She wore brown linen slacks and a cream silk blouse.

"Ava, whose hand is pushing you down?"

Ava shook her head. The silence lengthened, began to feel unbearable. She had an insane urge to scream. An ear-shattering scream like a siren, bouncing off the walls, bringing everyone outside to see what had happened. The therapist had brown hair, cut close to her head. She seemed so... Ava tried to think of a word. Controlled. Yes, that was it. Ava glanced around the room. Two of the plastic slats on the miniblinds were twisted, the framed print on the wall was a Matisse, a bridge and trees, all green and wavery like an underwater scene. God, she couldn't stand the silence. Her chest was bursting, the scream welling up inside her. *Help me.*

"Ava, our time's up." The therapist stood and moved to her desk. "I'll be here on the island again next Monday." She opened a black appointment book and smiled at Ava. "Does this time work for you?"

"Yes," Ava said, then, "Uh, actually, no." She smiled so that the therapist wouldn't take this personally. "I think I just need to figure things out for myself."

The therapist eyed her for a moment. "Well, you have my number." She took a business card from a black plastic holder on the desk. "My after-hours number is there, too."

SCOTT CAMPBELL sat under one of the woven umbrellas at the Descanso Beach Club and tried not to feel irritated that

Ava Lynsky was now ten minutes late for their ten-thirty interview. There were worse places to wait for someone to show up. He glanced around the sun-splashed patio just to make sure he hadn't missed her. He'd never met Ava Lynsky, but she'd described herself when she called to set up the interview. "Long black hair and..." She'd laughed. "Some people say I look kind of like Andie MacDowell."

Scott glanced at his watch again. Flipped open his notebook, drew a square and then another interlocking square. On the way to interview her, he'd paid a quick visit to the Catalina Historical Society. Back in the mid 1880s the Lynskys had briefly held deed to the island. Later, after it changed hands again, Samuel Lynsky had been partners in the Santa Catalina Island Company. By the time chewing-gum magnate William Wrigley bought the island in 1919, Lynsky and his growing family were involved in just about every aspect of Catalina commerce, from silver and zinc mining to hotel construction and steamship transportation.

Ava Lynsky was an artist. Decorative tiles, she'd told him. His notion of tiles was the type sold in boxes in the flooring department of home-improvement stores; he had no idea what decorative tiles were, but apparently she had a gallery full of them. She'd called to arrange publicity for an upcoming reception. The purpose of today's interview was to give him some background.

He was more interested in the death of her mother. Three months ago, Diana and Sam Lynsky III had boarded their twenty-six-foot Columbia, *Ramblin' On,* and set out for a sail to mark their fortieth wedding anniversary. They'd eaten lunch around noon and then Sam Lynsky, recovering from a bout of flu, had taken a nap in the aft cabin. When he awoke an hour or so later, he told sheriff's deputies later that day, his wife was gone. A land-and-sea search turned up no sign of the body, and although the L.A. County Sheriff's Department had not officially closed the case, the consensus was that Diana Lynsky had drowned.

Ava's father was a local pediatrician, a cofounder of the island's small municipal hospital and something of a local legend. As the father of a fourteen-year-old daughter, Ellie, whose behavior of late invariably left him scratching his head, Scott was particularly interested in the child-rearing book Lynsky had written. *Dr. Sam's Unorthodox, Iconoclastic and Occasionally Hilarious Guide to Child Raising* was prominently displayed in the local bookstore.

Sam Lynsky had offered to take him on a tour of the island that afternoon, and Scott planned to use the opportunity to find out what child-rearing advice the doctor might have. The prospect of Ellie's upcoming visit filled him with an equal mix of dread and anticipation. Anger at himself, too. Where along the way had he lost touch with what made his daughter tick?

Twelve minutes late now. Scott clasped his hands behind his head and thought about the story he'd written a year or so ago. A honeymoon couple on a Bahamian cruise. A moonlit stroll on the deck, no one else around. She'd lost her balance, the distraught bridegroom said. A week later, the groom was charged with her murder. Such things happened.

He'd had it with crime and grime, though. Ten days ago he'd done his final interview for the *Los Angeles Times*. A profile of a homeless poet. He'd spent an entire day on skid row getting background. And now he was living on Santa Catalina, the new publisher and editor of the island's weekly newspaper. A new life for him and, he secretly hoped, for Ellie, although he wasn't naive enough to suppose his ex-wife would relinquish their daughter without a struggle.

He banished thoughts of Laura to the back of his mind

and gazed out at the shimmering horizon. Santa Catalina
Island, a submerged mountain range, twenty-one miles long
and eight miles wide at its widest point. The island was
mostly unpopulated except for the two-square-mile town of
Avalon, where three thousand people lived year around and
about ten thousand during the summer. Santa Catalina,
twenty-two miles off the coast of California and, as the
brochures promised, "A world away from the smog, traffic
and fast-paced life of the mainland."

Scott stretched his legs, which still bore the pallor of his
former life, led mostly indoors. After two days on Catalina,
he'd given up dressing as he had at the *Times*. The blazers
and dress shirts were gone. He wore jeans to the council
meetings, and the rest of the time it was Bermuda shorts
and one of the ten polo shirts he'd found for fifty cents
each at a Salvation Army thrift shop in Glendale.

Out in the harbor one of the high-speed catamarans that
traversed the stretch of water between the island and the
mainland was churning huge arcs of foaming wake as it
plowed past the art deco roof of the Casino carrying yet
another boatload of camera-snapping, luggage-toting tourists into Avalon.

"Scott."

He turned. Ava Lynsky looked more like Snow White
than Andie McDowell, he decided. Porcelain skin, red lips
and a lot of black curly hair, barely contained by a red
bandanna tied peasant-style around her head. She wore a
yellow sundress and held the leash of a white poodle the
size of a small donkey. The poodle wore a red-and-blue
cape.

The dog looked at Scott and growled.

"Henri. Be nice." Ava Lynsky grabbed the dog's cape
in one hand and pushed at his rump with the other. "Sit,
like a good boy." She smiled at Scott. "Am I late?"

"Fourteen minutes," he said. "Traffic?"

She stared at him.

"I'm being facetious," he said. Avalon restricted the number of cars on the island. Golf carts, bicycles and scooters were the preferred means of transportation. His first day on Catalina he'd walked through the entire town in fifteen minutes. "Shall we?" he said.

"Oh, my God, *Ava!*" A woman in a tropical-colored sarong broke loose from a nearby table to wrap Ava in an enthusiastic embrace. "Sweetie." She stood back to peer into Ava's face. "How *are* you?"

"Peachy." Ava smiled. "Fantastic."

"Really?" The woman looked doubtful. "Really, really?"

"Absolutely." Ava nodded at Scott. "This is Scott Campbell, the *Argonaut's*—"

"New editor." The woman clutched Scott's arm and beamed at Ava. "This is such a wonderful girl and I just *know* the sun's going to start shining for her again. All the stormy weather's over, sweetie. From now on it's rainbows and sunshine. And look at that ring." She grabbed Ava's left hand. "Have you set the date yet?"

"Probably next summer. After I've finished the project I'm working on."

"And you're doing better?" Again she peered into Ava's face. "Doing okay?"

"Have you been ill?" Scott asked after the woman left.

"Of course not." Her face tinged a pale pink, she removed a pair of sunglasses, a leather-bound portfolio and a bag of potato chips from a red canvas bag. She slipped on the sunglasses, set the portfolio on the table and ripped open the bag of chips. "I could eat my elbow," she said.

Scott opened his notebook.

"Don't write that down." She held out the bag. "Help yourself."

"No thanks."

She took a chip, adjusted her sunglasses, glanced down at the dog. Smiled across the table at Scott. "Okay, let's talk about my work," she finally said. "What do you know about Catalina tiles?"

"Nothing," Scott said.

"Well, hand-painted tiles are a Catalina tradition." She dipped into the bag of chips again. "They're wonderful. Incredible jewel-like colors. You'll see them all over Avalon. There's a beautiful example right in the center of town, the Sombrero Fountain. And the Casino has an exquisite tiled mural of a mermaid in the foyer. You might want to take a look."

"These are pieces you painted?"

"No." Her strained expression suggested the stupidity of the question. "Those are historic tiles. The tiles I paint are mostly used in private homes. My theme is the magic and wonder of childhood." She crossed her legs. "A reflection, you might say, of my own childhood."

Elbows on the table, Scott regarded her for a moment. She had a tiny fleck of potato chip in the bow of her lip. He debated whether to mention it and decided against it. "Your own childhood was magical?"

"Oh, absolutely." She smiled. "Idyllic. My twin sister and I had Shetland ponies and our own Boston Whalers to sail around the bay. Ingrid's was red, mine was blue. My father called us the twin princesses of Catalina. He and my mother were the king and queen. Anything we wanted, we could have by stamping our little feet."

Scott thought of his own daughter. Pictured her stamping her foot to demand that her parents quit acting like selfish geeks and get over themselves. Pretty much the essence of his last conversation with her.

"It's hard for mainlanders to understand," Ava said, "but there's a magic to life here on the island."

"And is it still that way for you?" He'd opened her

portfolio and now glanced up from a picture of tiles embedded into the low wall of a children's playground—starfish and shells, a child's beach bucket, an ice-cream cone, a bright yellow sun. He waved a hand to take in the picture-postcard views of blue ocean all around them. The impressive diamond on her left hand. "It all looks pretty good to me."

Eyes hidden behind dark glasses, she smiled again. Her left shoe wobbled precariously from her toe. "Of course it is."

He glanced down at his notes. "I had a question about your mother's accident—"

"We're here to talk about hand-painted tiles," she said. "Do you have any other questions?"

He didn't and she replaced her portfolio in the canvas bag, tossed her potato-chip bag in the trash, picked up the dog's leash and bid him a terse goodbye. Scott watched her until she disappeared behind the Casino. If she'd been any more brittle and uptight, he thought, she'd shatter completely. He briefly considered going after her, then decided that Ava Lynsky's emotional well-being wasn't his concern. Besides, his ex-wife had taught him all he needed to know about dealing with neurotic, stressed-out women. It was an exercise in futility.

SOMEHOW SHE'D MADE IT through the interview with Scott Campbell. With blood pulsing in her head, Ava walked around to the back of the Casino, where tourists seldom ventured, and stood against the wall, breathing hard as if she'd just run a race. Henri whimpered at her side, licked her fingers.

"I'll be okay, Henri. Give me a minute. I'll be okay." Her face felt hot and damp her fingertips numb. Her heart was thundering again the way it had in the therapist's office. She opened her eyes. A man in a Hawaiian shirt and a straw hat appeared over by the railing. He stood watching the water. With the back of her hand, she swiped at the tears streaming down her face. "I'm okay," she told herself. "I'm okay. I'm okay. I'm okay."

"Happened again, huh?" Ingrid asked when Ava met her on the narrow strip of town beach ten minutes later. "Did you see the therapist this morning?"

Ava pulled her knees to her chin, wrapped her arms around them. They were sitting on a patch of empty sand amidst the brightly colored towels spread out all around them. The breeze off the ocean blew strands of hair across her mouth; the mingled aromas of coconut oil and waffle cones drifted from Olaf's ice-cream stand.

"I don't like her," Ava said. "Do you want to get an ice cream?"

"I just had an apple." Ingrid pinched Ava's arm. "Oink."

"Thank you," Ava said. "I needed that."

"Sorry, that was hateful. I didn't mean—"

"Forget it. It's not like I don't know myself. Every time I squeeze into my jeans, I can hear the way Mom nagged about my *avoir du pois*. I guess she thought it was more tactful to tell me I was fat in French."

"What about those antidepressants you were taking after Rob died? Maybe they'd help. Do you still have some?"

"No." Last night, unable to sleep, she'd torn her bathroom cabinets and drawers apart looking for the pills prescribed after her husband's death three years ago. She'd stuck the mostly full bottle in the medicine cabinet and pretty much forgotten about it until the dreams started. But the bottle had disappeared, and she had no idea what happened to it. She opened her mouth to tell Ingrid, then found she didn't want to talk about it. "I don't need them," she said. "I'll be fine."

"If they stop the panic attacks, Ava—"

"I'm going to move," Ava said. "I think the problem is living in Dad's house. When I'm not there, I can kind of imagine that Mom just forgot to call."

Ingrid sighed.

"I know," Ava said. "I'm just telling you how it is. Remember how wrapped up she used to get in her projects? Days would go by and then I'd finally call her and she'd have no idea how long it had been. That's what it seems like now, as long as I'm not up at the house being reminded of everything."

"Yeah, Mom would give an absentminded professor a run for his money." Ingrid smiled. "Remember that time she paid for gas and drove off without pumping any? I was there when she called to say she'd run out up by the hospital. Dad just shook his head."

"Yeah, well…" Ava threw a rock for Henri and watched as he ran down to the water, white floppy ears catching in the breeze. *I'm not happy,* Diana's voice said. *I haven't been for some time.* She squeezed her eyes shut and the voice went away. "If I just kind of think of her that way…"

"It's called denial," Ingrid said.

Ava shrugged. "I only know I feel worse at the house. I can't walk up the hill without looking up and seeing Mom on the balcony, or lie in bed and not hear her singing downstairs…"

Ingrid laughed. "That alone would be reason enough to move. Mom's singing, I mean."

Ava glanced at her sister and they both started laughing. In a sudden rush of feeling, Ava put her arm around Ingrid's shoulders and pulled her close. They sat there for a moment, toes dug into the sand, united in the bond of shared memories. Two thirty-four-year-old women, slightly built, with blue eyes, pale skin and thick black hair. Ava's was long and curly, Ingrid wore hers in a spiky bob. They were two parts of a whole, Ava thought. Even if they lived on different continents, she felt sure she would instinctively know if Ingrid was ever in trouble.

"'Pineapple Princess they call me,'" Ingrid sang in Diana's off-key voice. "'Pineapple Princess, I love you, you're the only girl for me-hee—'"

Ava punched her arm. "Stop."

"'Someday we will get married,'" Ingrid warbled, "'and I'll be your Pineapple Quee-een.'"

"Ingrid, shut up," Ava said. "The lifeguard thinks you're insane."

"Let him," Ingrid said. "So where are you going to move? Wait, I already know. Grandma's old cottage."

Ava stared at her. "I only saw the For Rent sign this morning."

Ingrid shrugged. "You've only mentioned the cottage a dozen times before. It just figures. What does Ed think of the idea?"

Ava watched the glint of her diamond in the sunlight and realized with a pang of guilt she hadn't even considered her fiancé's possible reaction, but since he'd been waging a vigorous campaign to have her move in with him, he was hardly likely to be thrilled about the idea. "I haven't told him yet." She dug her toes into the sand. "I'm meeting Lil at two. She's going to take me up there. Want to go?"

"I can't. I'm giving a riding lesson to a bunch of Breatheasy kids. Hopefully Dad won't want to go along to make sure they don't start wheezing or something."

"Ingrid," Ava said reprovingly, "he's a doctor, for God's sake. The kids have asthma—of course he'd go along. That's why parents send their kids to the camp." She watched a couple of small boys, all coltish limbs and salt-dulled hair, kick sprays of sand into the air. After a moment they settled down to work, faces intent as they arranged pebbles into fantasy castles, held together with

wet sand carefully dripped from plastic beach shovels.
"You and Dad need to work things out," she said. "You
can't stay mad at him forever."

"What's to work out? I think he's a two-faced phony
and he thinks I'm beyond hope. *I* can live with it." She
stretched out her legs. "So how'd the interview with the
Argonaut guy go? I forget his name."

"Scott Campbell." Ava pulled a face. "He didn't like
me, I could tell. Plus, I was a bitch."

"A bitch." Ingrid grinned. "You?"

"I couldn't help it. Something about him just set me off.
I know he didn't give a damn about hand-painted tile. He
wanted to talk about Mom."

"Reporters are like those pigs that sniff out truffles,"
Ingrid said. "They get a whiff of something wrong and
they keep rooting until they dig it out."

"But there *is* nothing wrong," Ava said. "A boating
accident isn't sexy, that's all. They'd rather hear that Dad
pushed her out of the boat or that she wanted to end it all.
They start asking all these casual little questions. 'Now,
your parents were married forty years,'" she said, mimick-
ing a reporter's impartial tone. "'Must have been a happy
marriage.' And you know damn well that's not what they're
thinking."

"So what's he like?"

"Mr. *L.A. Times?*" Ava shrugged. "Kind of preppy-
looking. All Gap and Eddie Bauer. Chambray shirt, cotton
this and natural fiber that. Wire-rimmed glasses. Condescending."

"Cute?"

"I didn't notice."

"Liar."

"Cute. He kind of looks like Rob."

"Please say you didn't tell him the 'twin princesses'
story," Ingrid said.

"Of course I did," Ava said. "Why wouldn't I?"

"Because it's so damn misleading." Ingrid shook her head. "So you told him about the Boston Whalers, too?"

"And the Shetland ponies."

Ingrid groaned.

"Well, it's true," Ava protested.

"It's also true that Dad was always so busy being St. Sam to everyone on the island that he never had time for us or Mom."

"Mom didn't feel that way." Ava felt her heart speed up. "She *was* happy. I know she was."

"You don't know. No one really knew what was going on in Mom's head."

"Ingrid—"

"No, I'm sick of you always painting this fantasy world. Did you tell this reporter that throwing money at us was Dad's way of making up for all the things he didn't do? Did you talk about how it was always his family who ended up paying for his generous impulses?"

"That's *your* perception," Ava said. "You're still angry at Dad because of Quicksilver—"

"Quicksilver." Ingrid hooted. "God, how could I have thought I was in love with a guy called Quicksilver? He was such a jerk."

"See?" Ava said, eager to redeem their father in Ingrid's eyes. "Dad was right."

"Maybe he was right that the guy was a jerk, but Dad stepped over the line by booting him off the island. Dad's like some kind of benign dictator. He needs to learn he can't go around orchestrating everyone's lives." Ingrid wrapped her arms around Henri's neck. "By the way, did you find those papers yet?"

"I tried to look last night," Ava said. "But you know how Mom's study is. There's so much stuff everywhere.

Books and magazines all over the place, stacks of papers—''

"She had these diaries," Ingrid said. "They had red
covers—''

"I know, Ingrid." Ava felt a surge of irritation. "You've
only mentioned it half a dozen times already. If it's so
damn important, *you* look for them. Ask Dad to get them
for you."

"Right," Ingrid said. "The day I ask Dad for anything
will be the day I walk to the mainland."

AN HOUR LATER Ava could still feel Ingrid's anger, like a
blanket weighing her down. She was standing on the deck
of the old bougainvillea-draped cottage that had once be-
longed to her grandmother and taking deep breaths to stay
calm. She didn't want to deal with Ingrid's anger at their
father, or Scott Campbell's condescending smirk, or her
own bad dreams and panic attacks. All she wanted was to
feel peaceful again. Peaceful and safe.

"I really want to rent this place, Lil," she told her friend
from Lil's Lovely Island Real Estate. "Actually, I'd like to
buy it. I want to move in today, though. Henri would, too,
right, Henri?"

Henri's tail thumped and he gazed up at Ava in much
the same way Ava gazed at pints of rum-raisin ice cream.
Liquid-eyed, drooling slightly. Henri had been her mother's
dog and wasn't coping very well, either. After Diana's accident, his nonstop howling had driven her father to distraction. Either keep the dog with her, he'd said, or it was
going to the pound. Ava felt a very strong bond with Henri.

"What's your dad going to think about you living here,
then?" Lil asked in the Eliza Doolittle accent that thirty
years of living on Catalina had done little to change. "He'll
be all alone in that big house of his, won't he?"

"Oh, he'll be fine," Ava said, already gearing up for her

father's resistance. After Rob died, at her parents' urging, she'd sold the house she'd bought with Rob and moved back home. "Right after my mother…after the accident, he needed me there, but he's fine now. Busy. You know my dad, he's always on the go. Up at the hospital, running the asthma camp. Busy, busy."

God, she was starting to babble. She took a breath. Henri sat so close to her leg she could feel his warmth, and she reached down to tangle her fingers in the curls on his head. *My father's fine,* she thought. *I need to save myself.* And she felt she could do it up here in this cottage, which nestled like an overgrown shrub in the scrub-covered hillside on Middle Terrace Road. Up here, the sun was soft and filtered, and the breeze from the ocean rustled the leaves of the eucalyptus that sheltered the cottage.

Up here she'd get her life back together again. The dreams would stop and she would be able to work. Up here where, like a bird in a nest, she could see all of Avalon spread out below. The familiar sites that were part of the tapestry of her life: the Casino's round red roof, the boats in the harbor, the Catalina Express on its daily runs to and from the mainland. The play of light and shadow. Nothing had changed and yet everything had changed. Up here maybe she could make some sense of it all.

Lil seemed dubious about the cottage's charms.

"Mind that rotted bit in the wood, luv," she said. "Catch your heel in that and you'll fall head over teapot into the brambles. Need to replace the whole thing, I should think."

Ava glanced down at the worn wood. The deck wouldn't be all she'd have to replace, she suspected. In the twelve years since her grandmother died, the cottage had changed hands a number of times, and with each new owner it looked a little more forlorn. Now it was for rent again, which meant she could move in right away. But she really wanted to *buy* it and bring it back to life. Mend the house and mend herself and Henri.

"I'm afraid you'll be buying a headache." Lil delved into her shoulder bag and pulled out a candy, which she unwrapped and threw to Henri. He caught it in his mouth, dropped it on the deck and barked at it. "All right." She shot him a reproving look. "Don't make a song and dance of it—it's just a sweetie. Honestly, Ava, you don't want this house."

Ava smiled. "Honestly I do."

"There's a lovely little house on Marilla that I just listed. Let me take you there."

"I want this one." She heard herself tell Scott Campbell the Catalina-princess story about stamping her foot to get what she wanted. Now she wished she hadn't. He didn't like her. But so what? Scott Campbell was the least of her concerns.

"The Marilla house has a lovely kitchen," Lil persisted. "All modern. You'd love it."

"Lil, I want this one," Ava said again. "Let's go back in."

Lil followed her back into the cottage. The living room was small and square, roughly the size of the pantry in her father's house, half the size of the guest bathroom in her fiancé's oceanfront condo. For a moment she pictured Ed and her father—the pair tended to see eye to eye about most things—standing in the tiny room, incredulous looks on their faces. She shut out the image, walked over to the fireplace and crouched down in front of it.

"See these?" She traced her finger over the bright, blue-glazed tiles that surrounded the hearth. Every fourth tile was a vividly painted scene of activity. Under yellow suns or silver moons, stick-figure girls and boys played ball, fished, flew kites or lay tucked in bed reading a book. "I was ten when I painted these," she told Lil. "My grandmother had a wood-burning kiln out back, and I molded the clay, painted the tiles, glazed them, the works. That's pretty much how I got started.''

Lil bent to take a closer look. ''Clever girl. They're lovely. Like little rays of sunshine.''

''See that one with the kite? Ingrid and I got kites for Christmas one year, and our dad took us down to the beach to fly them. The sky was this brilliant blue the way it gets in December after a rain, and our kites were red, and I think Ingrid was wearing yellow shorts. But we were racing and laughing and watching the kites high up in the sky... I was trying to capture that feeling.''

''You did, luv.'' Lil glanced at the door. ''Well, then, shall we go?''

''This house has all kinds of good memories,'' Ava said, reluctant to leave. ''When Ingrid and I were little, our grandma would bring us out here and we'd watch the boats down in the harbor and she'd tell us about steamships and Charlie Chaplin and movie stars who came over. Happy memories.''

''Sometimes it would be nice to go back, wouldn't it?'' Lil's smile was wistful. ''I often think that. And then I say to myself, silly old fool, 'course it wasn't that much better than it is these days. All you do is remember the good and forget the not-so-good.''

''Maybe.''

'''Course you're young yet. You probably still remember everything like it was yesterday.'' She patted Ava's arm, then delved into her bag again. ''Here, have a sweetie. Make you feel better. Good for your throat, too. Helps my voice, I always say.''

Ava took the candy. When she and Rob were married, Lil had sung ''Ave Maria'' at the wedding. She'd sung again at Rob's funeral. ''I'll Remember You.'' God, she was going to cry. ''Lil, please don't look at me like that, okay? I'm fine, I really am. If I buy this place, I'll be so busy fixing it up I won't have time to be sad.''

"Well, if you've made up your mind, I don't suppose there's much I can say.''

Ava smiled. "Exactly.''

"On the bright side, though, I looked up your horoscope this morning. I like to do that before I show a house. You'd be surprised how many times it's steered me into a new direction. Like the time I was showing a gentleman this property up on Chimes Hill Road and his horoscope said, '"Not a good day for scaling new heights.' Well, if that isn't telling you something. I immediately rescheduled for the next day.''

"You sold it?''

"I did. You know what his horoscope said the day we closed escrow? 'A new start will prove beneficial.' Listen, love, I just know things are going to start looking up for you. I feel it right here.'' She tapped her chest. "The sun's going to come out again, you'll see.''

I'd settle for feeling normal again, Ava thought.

"Let me go in and do a bit of exploring,'' Lil said when they were back at the real-estate office. "Place has been rented for so long I'm not sure who owns it anymore. I'll find out though, luv, and give you a ring this afternoon.''

CHAPTER TWO

SCOTT STOOD IN THE cereal aisle at Von's trying to remember whether Ellie ate Cheerios or Rice Krispies. He picked up the Cheerios, dropped the carton in the basket and then, in a fit of indecision, set it back on the shelf. Maybe she didn't even eat cereal. Why, he asked himself, hadn't he paid more attention? His ex-wife's voice supplied the answer. *Because you don't pay attention, period, Scott. You've never been there for me, and you haven't been there for Ellie for God knows how long.*

He dumped both the Cheerios and the Rice Krispies into the basket and moved on down the aisle. Things were about to change. Ellie's two-week visit wouldn't be long enough to completely mend the rift in their relationship, but it was a start. He'd spent the morning cleaning and vacuuming his apartment, bought new sheets and a set of dishes and made a list of all the things they would do while she was on Catalina—a glass-bottom-boat ride, snorkeling, horseback riding in the interior. It was going to be a good visit.

His cell phone rang as he wheeled his basket to the cash register. Laura. His ex-wife had called every day since he'd arrived on the island. Some days she called twice. Usually—within earshot of Ellie, he was certain—she'd start with a list of his various transgressions and shortcomings and then she'd put Ellie on the phone. By that time, not surprisingly, his daughter was hostile and surly.

"Ellie, I know you *want* to go to Spain," he said now. They'd had this conversation before. "But I don't have the money to send you. *I* didn't go to Europe until I'd graduated from college."

"You could afford it if you still worked at the *Times*." Ellie's voice was full of indignation. "You didn't *have* to quit."

Phone shoved between his head and shoulder, Scott unloaded the basket.

"It's not my fault you wanted to go live on some stupid island," Ellie continued.

"You're going to love it here, El." Scott tried to divert her. "It's really beautiful. We'll go swimming, snorkeling. I've already bought you a bike."

"I might not come."

His hand froze around a can of green beans. "What do you mean? It's all set up."

"Mom wants me to go to Cleveland with her to see Grandma."

He took a breath. "Is that what you want to do?"

"I don't know." She sighed. "Mom gets kind of lonely. I feel bad for her."

He finished unloading the groceries, pulled out his billfold and waited for the cashier to ring up the total. He recognized Laura's tactic, but he had little taste for making Ellie a pawn in her parents' game. Better just to back off.

"Fifty-two fifty," the cashier said.

He fished out a twenty and a ten, then realized that was all the cash he had. As he wrote out a check, he tried to remember exactly how much he had left in his checking account. The shopping expedition in preparation for Ellie's visit had pretty much blown his monthly budget.

"Listen, Ellie," he told his daughter, "I'm going to be disappointed if you don't come, but I'll leave it up to you to do what you think is best."

"Sure, Dad," she said listlessly. "Whatever."

After he'd carried the groceries to his apartment, he

headed back to the *Argonaut* and the letter he'd been trying to write to the people of Catalina. His thoughts kept drifting to Ellie and the obscure feeling that by not insisting she come to Catalina, instead of accompanying her mother to Cleveland, he'd somehow let her down.

More trouble still was the vague sense of relief he felt now that the trip was in doubt. While he loved Ellie unreservedly, the fear of not being able to pull things off and failing somehow to make her happy was a weight on his shoulders. He got up from the desk, poured a mug of coffee and sat down again. She'd told him once that he "sucked" as a dad and maybe she was right. Retreat and distance came easily to him, a little too easily. Qualities that probably didn't do much to reassure his daughter.

He looked up from his musings to see Ava Lynsky standing in the doorway. She looked different, though, her hair or something. It took him a moment to realize it wasn't Ava. Actually, she looked like a less-vivid version of Ava. Same build, same fine bone structure, but her hair was short and choppy, and in contrast to Ava's Snow White coloring, this woman had the tanned complexion of someone who spent a lot of time outdoors. Her feet were clad in hiking boots and she wore jeans and a sleeveless cotton shirt.

She glanced around the cramped offices of the *Catalina Island Argonaut,* where undelivered stacks of last week's newspaper vied for space with the mountain bike he'd just acquired, the small brown fridge where the previous publisher had kept her peppermint schnapps and a precarious mountain of boxes still to be unpacked.

"So you're the new publisher, huh?" She stuck out her hand. "Ingrid Lynsky. You met my sister this morning. My father asked me to pass on a message to you. He's supposed to give you a tour this afternoon?"

"At four," Scott said.

"Don't look for him before five," Ingrid said. "My father overcommits. If he has enough time in the day to do four things, he'll try to squeeze in six. Everybody is inconvenienced, but hey, that's Dr. Sam for you.''

Scott scratched his ear. He could still hear Ellie telling him he sucked. "You're not a member of the Dr. Sam fan club?" he asked Ingrid. "I thought everyone on Catalina subscribed to it."

Ingrid laughed. "Oh, did I give you the wrong impression? I'm sorry. Dr. Sam's a saint. Most people have to take a boat to the mainland. My father can walk."

Scott looked at her.

Ingrid looked straight back at him, her gaze steady and unflinching. "Anyway," she said, "just so you know, he'll be late."

''HOPE YOU'RE NOT expecting to make any money with that paper,'' Sam Lynsky said as he pulled his Jeep back onto the road. He'd breezed into Scott's office at five-thirty with a convoluted tale about being stopped a dozen times as he tried to get away from the hospital and everyone wanting a minute of his time. "The *Argonaut*'s never turned a profit in forty years. How come you bought it?"

"Escape," Scott said before he had time to think about it. "Things on the mainland were getting ugly."

Dr. Sam rounded the curve of Abalone Point and headed toward Pebbly Beach. "No family?"

"Divorced." Scott glanced at the doctor, a youthful-looking sixty-year-old with white hair curling from under a red baseball cap, neat mustache and a clear blue steady-eyed gaze. "I have a fourteen-year-old daughter."

"You going to make enough to get by?"

"I'm counting on the newspaper to provide some revenue." He'd seen the publisher's account books. Maybe not much by Lynsky's standards, but he could get by. "And I've got some freelance assignments lined up."

He rested an arm on the window ledge. If his head weren't full of Ellie, he'd enjoy this tour, he thought as they turned onto Wrigley Terrace Road. Avalon Bay was behind them now, and the grey-green mountains that ringed Catalina filled the view through the windshield. The wind off the ocean felt bracing.

"That's the old William Wrigley home up there on your left." Lynsky waved his arm at a palatial white structure nestled in the hills. "Built in the 1920s as a summer home. Before that the Wrigleys would come over in June and stay at the St. Catherine's Hotel. The story goes, Mrs. Wrigley woke up one morning and said, 'I would like to live there.' It's a hotel these days, but when I was a boy… Hold on."

Scott grabbed the Jeep's roll bar as Lynsky executed a sudden hairpin curve. The doctor's driving was a tad hair-raising.

Lynsky glanced at Scott and laughed. "You think that's bad? In my great-grandfather's days, before the Bannings started building real roads, they'd run stage coaches from Avalon over to the Isthmus. Six horses, galloping down the summit, hooves flying. Wooden wheels." He shook his head. "We're too soft these days. Want everything too easy. Where's the challenge? Where's the spirit? You said you're divorced?"

"Right."

"How long were you married?"

"Fifteen years."

"I was married," Dr. Sam said, "nearly forty years. Not a natural state, though, marriage. Society forces you into it, but it's not natural. Used to have a collection of toilet paper until my wife got rid of it. Toilet paper from every country I ever visited and barf bags, empty, of course, from every flight I ever took. She threw them all out. Sorry I ever got married," he said.

"Wouldn't do it again, huh?"

"'Thus grief still treads upon the heels of pleasure...'"
Lynsky steered the Jeep across a stretch of brush-filled terrain. "'Married in haste, we may repent at leisure.'"

Lynsky careered around a bend, sending Scott slamming
into the passenger door. He gave up on trying to take notes.
Between the doctor's driving, his nonstop monologue and
conversational threads introduced, then left dangling, he felt
disoriented. Now the harbor was a dizzying drop-off to his
left and they were hurtling along a mountainous ridge road,
then down a canyon and up again to a view of the Pacific
spread out like a blue silk sheet far below.

"Congreve." Lynsky stopped the Jeep and they both
climbed out and stood at the edge of the cliff, looking out.
"*The Old Bachelor*. He also wrote, 'I could find it in my
heart to marry thee, purely to be rid of thee.'"

Scott decided to mull that over later. The vista below
him was one he'd seen in the postcard racks in town. The
glittering ocean, the yellow wildflowers that dotted the
steep slopes, the landmark red roof of the Casino and the
familiar white bulk of the high-speed Catalina Express.
What the postcards didn't capture was the dusty sun-
warmed smell of sage and eucalyptus, the subdued hush of
waves, the cries of seabirds.

"Won't find a more beautiful place anywhere else on
earth," Lynsky said after a while. "You look at the mainland over there—" he gestured at the faint bluish outline
of the Southern California coastline "—and feel pretty
damn lucky you're over here."

Scott nodded. He'd mailed a postcard to Ellie that morning. After he'd dropped it off at the post office, though, it
had occurred to him that picturesque scenery was unlikely
to be a selling point to a teenage girl whose notion of paradise right now was all about shopping malls and cosmetic
counters.

"There're a lot of good people on the island," Lynsky

said after they were back on the road again. "Most of them, in fact. We're a fairly law-abiding lot. A tourist now and then who has a few too many Wicky Whackers or Margaritas and starts making a nuisance of himself, that's about the worst of it."

"Suits me," Scott said.

"You're daughter's fourteen, you said?" The doctor turned to look at him. "Difficult age. Suddenly you're not a hero anymore and you can't do a thing that's right."

Scott watched palms and eucalyptus and other low scrubby trees he couldn't name fly past as the Jeep tore down another canyon. *Tell me about it,* he thought.

"Of course, I say that and my daughters are thirty-four and we still don't see eye to eye. Ava's doing okay." Lynsky wiggled a hand. "Lost her husband three years ago, but she's engaged to a fine man now. Attorney here in town. Got a few things in her own life to work out, but Ed's good for her."

Scott recalled Ava's telling him about stamping her foot to get what she wanted and felt a stab of sympathy for the fiancé.

"Ingrid, Ava's twin, has taken a vow of poverty," Lynsky was saying. "Doesn't believe in working for a living. Dropped out of medical school with one year left to go. She's quite content to live on whatever she grows—lettuce and beets, she tells me, but who knows what else. Lives behind some horse stables on the other side of the island." He shook his head. "I can't figure her out."

Scott felt vaguely defeated. If Dr. Samuel Lynsky living on an idyllic island, loved by everyone—a man who'd actually written a book on raising children—had problematic relationships with his daughters, what were his own odds? He wanted to ask the doctor what went wrong. What would he do differently?

They were headed back into town now, Dr. Sam nimbly

maneuvering the Jeep through narrow streets of equally narrow houses that rose in tiers from the harbor, dodging the ubiquitous golf carts, most of them driven by tourists who rented them from stands along the seafront.

"Las Casitas over there—" Lynsky nodded at a development of pink, adobe-style cottages "—used to be housing for the island's workers." He leaned an elbow on the window frame. "Don't get the wrong impression about what I just said. Ingrid's okay. Ava is, too. Diana's death hit them both pretty hard." He looked at Scott. "You know about that?"

"A boating accident, I heard."

"Three months ago. Took the boat out for a sail. Bad timing all around. I was getting over flu, and Diana had been having dizzy spells. I went below to take a nap, and when I woke up she was gone." Lynsky pulled off his cap by the brim, replaced it a moment later. "Coast Guard, helicopters. Everyone out there looking for her. Nothing."

"I'm sorry," Scott said. The words seemed inadequate, but he'd never been very good at offering condolences. "How are you managing?"

"*I'm* fine." Lynsky pinched his midriff. "Overdosed on casseroles for a while. People couldn't do enough. Still can't. Lot of talk about creating some kind of garden in Diana's name, inlaid tiles, that sort of thing. The mayor's asked Ava to design it." He glanced at Scott. "You've met Ava?"

"This morning. She showed me some of her work."

"Paints decorative tiles. Catalina tiles are world-famous. Ava refuses to even discuss any kind of memorial. Since Diana died we can't spend two minutes together without a battle." He cleared his throat. "Body's never been found—that's part of the problem. Good chance it never will, I've been told. Meanwhile, life has to go on."

"Difficult to find closure, I would imagine," Scott said,

then cringed at the words. *Closure.* One of those pop psychology terms people say that mean absolutely nothing. Tie everything up in a neat little package and then move on. Lynsky pulled up outside the *Argonaut* office, and Scott grabbed his canvas backpack from the floor behind him and stuck out his hand. "Thanks for the tour, Dr. Lynsky."

"Got a business deal for you," Lynsky said. "You might as well accept, because you're not going to support yourself with that paper, I don't care what old Aggie Broadbent told you about the thing turning a profit. She just wanted to unload it."

Scott watched the doctor leaf through a manila folder of papers he'd removed from under the front seat.

"You know much about the Lynsky family?" Sam asked, still riffling through papers.

"Some. I stopped by the Island Historical Society yesterday."

"So you probably know my family owned this island years ago. Not for long. It changed hands a few times before it was deeded to the state around 1900. Diana was putting everything into a book before she died. I want it finished." Lynsky stuck the folder back under the seat. "Need to sort through her papers before you see them, but if you're interested, the book should solve your money problems. What do you think?"

"Sounds interesting," Scott said. "What do your daughters think about it?"

"They don't know anything about it," Lynsky said. "And I don't know that they need to. They get their hands on Diana's papers and it'll be yak-yak-yak. Stirring up things that don't need to be stirred up, and the book will never get written."

"Won't they want to see the papers?"

"You want to write this thing or not?"

"I'm just asking," Scott said.

"You let me deal with my daughters," Sam said. "You do a good job with the book, they'll be thrilled. A year from now, they'll have forgotten all about the papers." He fished under the seat, produced another file. "I'm going to give you a check right now," he said. "Just to get things going."

"Hold on a minute, Dr. Lynsky." Things were moving a little too fast. "You don't want to talk about this some more, see some samples of my writing?"

"Nah." Lynsky was scrawling his name across the check in a bold black hand. "And it's Sam." He held out the check. "You worked for the *L.A. Times.* That's good enough for me."

Scott ignored the check. "I'd like to think things over first."

"Suit yourself." Lynsky dropped the check on Scott's knee. "Might as well deposit this while you're doing your thinking. It'll tide you over when the advertising drops off. Meet me for breakfast at the Beehive tomorrow. Around eight-thirty. I'll bring some things to get you started."

"YOU SITTING DOWN?" Lil asked Ava later that afternoon when she called with the information on the cottage. "Guess who the owner turned out to be?"

"No idea," Ava said.

"Your dad," Lil said. "Seems he bought it back a few years ago, no idea what he intended to do with it. It'll make things easier for you, I should think."

Not necessarily, Ava thought as she walked up to the hospital to see her father. A volunteer in a pink smock was sorting through a stack of *National Geographic* magazines when Ava poked her head around the door of the hospital auxiliary office.

"Your father?" she said. "Let me think a minute. I saw him early this morning making rounds and then…" She paused and smiled. "You know your dad—doing ten things at the same time. Now what was it he said he had to do? Something about dropping by the *Argonaut*…"

"If he comes back in the next hour or so, please tell him I need to talk to him. I've got some things to do in town, so I'll meet him back here."

"All right, honey, I'll tell him." The volunteer peered at Ava. "You doing better?"

"Fine, thanks," Ava said. Maybe she'd just get a billboard made up. *Don't ask. I'm fine. Fantastic. Never been better.*

"Keep busy. That's the best thing you can do."

"Absolutely," Ava agreed.

"Bring that dog of yours back. Everyone got such a kick out of him in that cape. It's so heartwarming to see how animals raise people's spirits."

Ava smiled. Henri was a participant in the Pets Are Therapy program. For an hour every week Henri was stroked, petted and fussed over by the half a dozen or so hospice patients. They fed him treats, rolled balls across the floor and laughed at his shameless grandstanding. At the end of the hour, the patients looked happy, Henri seemed happy, and as Ava walked him back into town, she always felt…well, happier.

"How's your sister?" The volunteer's smile had cooled slightly. "Still living out by the horse stables?"

"Ingrid's fine, too." Tomorrow, she would try to go through the whole day without using the word fine. "She's happy working with the horses, not dealing with people all the time. Listen, I need to get going."

"Sure, honey." The volunteer gave Ava a quick hug. "Take care, sweetie."

As she left the hospital and walked down Avalon Canyon Road into town, Ava considered the merits of Ingrid's solitary existence. No need for constant reassurance or pre-

tending to be something you weren't. If Ingrid felt morose
or out of sorts, she just dug in her garden or rode horses
until she was in the mood for human contact again.

Hands in the pockets of her denim jacket, Ava turned
onto Sumner—past the tiny house and summer rentals that
had once been tent sites owned by her grandfather—and
onto Crescent, now thronged with tourists disembarking
from the Catalina Express.

She stopped to look at a dress in the window of Island
Fashions, a clingy pistachio-colored shift that would look
great if she could lose the ten pounds she'd gained in the
past two months. *A minute on the lips, forever on the hips.*
Diana's voice, taunting her. *You should see me now, Mom,*
she thought. In the window she could see the reflected parade of passersby. A small stout man separated himself
from the rest. He'd spotted her.

Too late to pretend she hadn't seen him, she turned to
smile at the mayor of Avalon. A sixtyish man in a tropical
shirt, with a bald head and plump pink face and chins that
dissolved into his neck. A sweetheart, but she couldn't look
at him without thinking of a melting ice-cream cone.

"…so hard for you," he was saying now. "The council
thought that one of your beautiful art pieces would be a
fitting tribute to your mother." He patted her arm and made
room for a couple of straw-hatted tourists. "No pressure,
though. We'd never want to do that. How you doing, anyway, honey?"

"Fine. Busy of course."

"Well, that's good." His eyes lingered on her for a moment. "You know Muriel was just saying this morning—
she runs the grief-counseling program at the hospital, you
know—anyway, she was saying that all most people really
need is someone to listen to them."

Ava kept smiling. "It's great that they have someone as
dedicated as Muriel."

"She's a good listener," the mayor said. "A real good listener."

"Tell her I said hi," Ava said.

"Will do. And, Ava, you take care now. And when you're ready to think about that piece for your mother, bless her soul, you just give me a call."

"Right," Ava said. She crossed the road and walked along the seafront, killing time until she returned to the hospital to meet her father. A crowd of little girls in pigtails and Crayola-colored clothes were giggling and hitting each other with their backpacks. She caught the eye of one of them and winked. She kept walking, past the signs hawking rides in glass-bottom boats, past Olaf's ice-cream store, past the guides hawking tours of the Casino and Jeep excursions into the interior. It was hard to walk through Avalon without running into someone she knew, but she'd discovered that if she kept her head down people were sometimes reluctant to approach her.

Which suited her just fine. Anything to avoid The Look. People had started treating her differently after Rob died. They'd smile and chat, but there was a new solicitousness in their voices. A caution, as though they were dealing with a convalescent who might relapse. They'd peer into her eyes as though to make sure someone was really there. Now, since her mother's death, it was happening again.

She hated it. They meant well, but she hated it. Either she avoided people completely or, when that wasn't possible, she became so impossibly bright and chipper that she was always expecting someone to rap her on the head and say, "Knock it off. We know you're hurting. Just admit it."

But she couldn't. Instead, she'd breeze around doing her happier-than-thou schtick until she couldn't stand herself anymore. Then she'd go home, wrap herself up in an old afghan her grandmother had knitted, pig out on whatever

was on hand—amazingly, ice cream was always on hand—
and fall asleep watching a cheesy movie on late-night TV.
Then wake up hours later, screaming because she'd seen
her mother's face again staring up at her from beneath the
water. *I'm not happy, Ava. I haven't been for some time.*

BACK AT THE HOSPITAL, she found her father in his small
office, just off the main corridor, waiting for the next patient. Dr. Sam Lynsky III wore a gold paper crown and a
white lab coat over jeans.

"That place was falling apart when your grandmother
had it," he said after she told him about the cottage. "It
needs to be torn down."

"I can fix it up." Ava folded her arms over her chest,
ready to do battle. "Don't give me a hard time about it,
Dad. What's it to you if I want to live there?"

"Ava, I am rattling around in a two-million-dollar property that was and still is your home. It's lonely and un-
welcoming and far too large, and I'd like nothing more than
to come home in the evening to my daughter's company—
both my daughters, but I realize that's asking too much. I
can't imagine how it could be a question of privacy, but—"

"It's full of Mom," Ava blurted, exactly the kind of
reasoning she hadn't intended to use. "Maybe it doesn't
bother you, Dad. Maybe you're getting on just fine without
her, but I can't take it."

"Ava." Sam leaned back in his chair. "Your inability
to deal with your mother's death is hardly a plausible reason to buy a ramshackle piece of property. At some point,
you'll need to accept what happened. In the meantime,
there are any number of other houses on the island."

"Maybe so," Ava said. "But I want that one."

"Jerry the pharmacist is going to sell his place." Sam
had emptied a canvas briefcase onto the consulting-room

floor. "Got the information in here somewhere... Oh, here's something you might be interested in." He tossed a brochure at Ava.

Ava glanced at the glossy ad for a Los Angeles gallery. "Dad, what does this have to do with Grandma's cottage?"

"Nothing. Just pointing out the sort of marketing you need to do. Never going to get anywhere painting three tiles a week. Need to think big."

Ava fumed inwardly. Her father kept digging, papers flying all around him. He wasn't a large man, but with his extravagant gestures and nonstop barrage of words, he always seemed to make a room feel too small.

"Jerry's house would be a smart buy," he said. "Now where did I put that piece of paper?"

He continued to shuffle through papers as he told her what a wise investment the pharmacist's house would be. Her father had bought and sold plenty of real estate in his life, and he could be quite persuasive on financial matters. In fact, as she listened to him, she found herself thinking that maybe the pharmacist's house was indeed the way to go. On the verge of saying she'd take a look, she stopped herself. Sam eventually wore everyone down. This time he wouldn't prevail.

"Dad, just give me an answer on the cottage. I don't feel like sitting here while you turn everything upside down. Lil said I could move in—"

"Hold on a minute." He stopped to examine a piece of paper. "Asthma Foundation holding some fancy-schmancy conference in L.A. Waste of time and money. What they should do—"

"I don't give a damn what they should do." In one move Ava scooped up all his papers and shoved them back in the bag. "I want Grandma's cottage."

"How are you going to pay for it?"

"I have money." She felt her face color. She knew, as

her father certainly did, that she had money from Rob's insurance and in her trust fund. Although work was picking up, her commissions were by no means steady and she barely scraped by on what she made.

"Big commission?"

"Dammit, Dad, why do you have to make everything so difficult? The place is empty, I could move in tonight and rent it until the buy closes." She saw him wavering. "Come on. I really want the cottage."

"A lesson in life," her father said, "is that we don't always get what we want."

The intercom on his desk buzzed to indicate a patient was waiting. "I'll let you know," he said. "I might decide to tear the place down."

Ava left, slamming the door behind her, and walked back down the hill into town. He'd let her have the place, she knew that, but not before he'd made a huge and unnecessary production of it. Not so long ago she'd loved him so unreservedly it frightened her. Lately everything he did irritated her. And then she'd feel guilty. Guilt and irritation, an endless seesaw. And the irony was that all he was doing, all he'd ever done, was be himself. How her mother had stood it for forty years, she had no idea.

CHAPTER THREE

"DR. SAM?" The waitress at the Beehive smiled at Scott.
"No, haven't seen him this morning. Kind of early yet. He
doesn't usually come in till later."

Scott glanced at his watch. Lynsky had said eight-thirty,
and it was now nearly nine. He ordered coffee and decided
to give the doctor another fifteen minutes. The check Lynsky had given him the day before was still on his desk, but
Ellie had asked him again about the school trip to Spain.
When he called her tonight, it would be terrific to tell her
she could go.

"Here you are." The waitress set a cup down in front
of him. "The thing with Dr. Sam is, you never know from
one minute to the next what he's going to do." She chuck-
led. "Just part of the guy's charm, I guess."

By nine-fifteen, the doctor still hadn't arrived, and Scott
walked back to the *Argonaut* and began writing a piece
about an upcoming fishing tournament. He'd just finished
it when his phone rang.

"You can run but you can't hide," Mark, his former
colleague from the *Times* said. "Listen, Carolyn and I had
a big bust-up—"

"Jeez, let me alert the national media." Scott's younger
sister, Carolyn had been dating Mark for a year, most of it
marked by big bust-ups. The surprise was that they'd even
gotten together in the first place. Carolyn, whose favorite
color was black, was deep into the club scene. Mark, when
he wasn't chasing a story or reading a book, was writing a

police-procedural novel, which he hoped to sell for enough money to allow him to leave the *Times*. He was an introvert; Carolyn craved excitement. They fought about everything. "So what was it this time? She got a tattoo you didn't like?"

"Close. She's dyed her hair orange. God, I tell you. I thought burgundy was bad. Listen, I could use a change of scenery. Feel like having a house guest for a day or so?"

MARK CAUGHT THE ten-fifteen Catalina Express from Long Beach, and Scott met him at the pier; by noon, they were eating fried fish and chips at a white plastic table on the patio of the Casino Dock Café, looking out at a scene that Ava might have painted. To their left the terra-cotta roof of the Casino; below them Avalon's version of a traffic jam—kayaks, dinghies and fishing boats, leaving, arriving, or just tooling around.

"Well, sure, I'd *rather* be stuck in traffic on the Golden State Freeway, stressed out because I was late for the mayor's press briefing." Scott emptied the rest of a pitcher of beer into their glasses. "I mean, this is pretty damn hard to take."

It was all impossibly picturesque. The wheeling gulls, the sparkling blue ocean and, just for a touch of color, a chugging red Harbor Patrol boat. So beautiful that, although he couldn't drop the note of mockery when he spoke to Mark about his new life, he suspected deep down that he'd already succumbed to the island's legendary spell. Now if he could just work things out with Ellie.

"So has your brain turned to mush yet?" Mark asked. "I mean, this is idyllic and all that, but…where's the grit?"

"It's everywhere," Scott said. "Garden club chicanery. A tourist in a gorilla suit terrorizing women on the pier. Graffiti-covered golf carts outside Von's. Lobster poaching. I tell you, I can't keep up with it."

"Seriously."

Scott drank some beer, pushed his chair back from the table and thought about Sam Lynsky's proposal. Any number of reasons could have prevented the doctor from keeping their appointment, but he was beginning to wonder if Lynsky might just have been spewing a bunch of hot air. He frowned down at the food on his plate and decided to run the whole thing past Mark.

"A few months before I came here, a woman drowned, or at least it looked like a drowning, out on the bay," he said. "Her husband's family is old and well connected—at one time they practically owned Catalina. The husband is a pediatrician to just about every kid on the island. Eccentric, but the town practically worships him. I've never heard a critical word."

Mark grinned. "And God knows, you've tried to find one."

"That's the old me," he said. "The new me yearns for truth, justice, beauty and goodness. Not necessarily in that order." A joke, so he'd seem less serious about it than he really was. It came easy, the role of cynical observer. "Anyway, this is apparently a golden family. Beautiful daughters—twins. One's a local artist. The other one manages a riding stable on the other side of the island."

Mark's grin broadened. "Available?"

Scott looked at him. "The artist's engaged. I don't know about the other one. The artist's—" he hesitated "—a princess. High-strung, high-maintenance. Some poor guy's locked himself into a lifetime of trouble. Kind of like Laura, only with money."

"I take it you've met her."

"Yep. And immediately got off on the wrong foot." He shook his head, remembering. "Anyway, moving on, Lynsky and his wife had gone for a sail around the island.

While Lynsky was taking a nap belowdecks, his wife apparently fell overboard.''

"And the husband didn't hear anything?''

"He says he woke up and found her gone. There was a massive search, but the body hasn't been found. All the usual angles were checked out. No recent insurance policies, no domestic disharmony. Nothing to suggest it was anything but an accident.''

Mark drank some beer. "And?''

"I don't know. There's something about Lynsky. A little too jocular when he talks about his wife, maybe. Which wouldn't matter, except he's asked me to write his family history.'' A waitress in red shorts dropped a check on the table, smiled and sashayed off. Scott watched until she'd disappeared into the restaurant. "He's offered me access to his wife's papers. Diaries, letters, that sort of thing. Offered me more to write it than I made in a year at the *Times*, and frankly, I could use the money.''

"So…what? You're conflicted?''

"Kind of. Maybe it's all this.'' He nodded out at the sparkling bay. "Okay, maybe I'm just perverse. Maybe there's something about perfection I can't deal with, but I just have this gut feeling that there's something…ugly beneath the surface.''

His expression skeptical, Mark grabbed the check from under Scott's credit card. "Too much time on your hands, pal. It doesn't sound like anything to me. If no-one else sees anything suspicious about it, I wouldn't go around turning over rocks. Take the money and do the damn book. You're over here in paradise. Don't screw with it.''

"DAD'S JUST DOING his power trip,'' Ingrid said after she'd called Ava to find out what was happening with the cottage and learned that Sam still hadn't decided about selling it. "What you need to do is pretend you don't want it, then he'll lose interest because he doesn't have anything to hold over you.''

"I know.'' Ava was sitting at the worktable in her studio, doing what she'd done every day for the past two months—putting in time without actually producing anything. Hours passed spent in blank staring. And then at night, the dreams. "I just hate playing his damn game. Why is it so hard for him to understand that the cottage might help me get myself together?''

"He understands okay. That's the whole point. But what you need is less important to him than his power trip.''

Ava wiped her forehead with the back of her hand. It disturbed her that Ingrid could make their father sound so Machiavellian. To anyone but Ingrid she'd vigorously defend him and, even to Ingrid, her first inclination was always to rush to his defense, but Ingrid's words were like moths nibbling away at the fabric of what she believed her life to be. Holes kept appearing. She'd patch them with denial, weave the cloth together with words and smiles until no one else could see the holes, but she knew they were there. *I'm not happy, Ava. I haven't been for some time.*

"Maybe I'll just tell him I've found something else.'' She leafed through a book of sketches, searching for inspiration. When she looked up, Scott Campbell was standing in the doorway. "I've got to go,'' she told Ingrid. "I'll call you later.''

"Hi.'' Scott hadn't moved from the doorway. "I didn't realize this was your studio. I was just walking by and I saw you working.''

"*Trying* to work.''

"Am I interrupting?''

"Not really.'' She got up from the stool and then couldn't think of what to do, so she sat back down again. Something about him made her feel awkward. Mostly, she suspected, because she'd always been drawn to the type.

Average height and weight, a touch on the scrawny side, perhaps. Slightly bookish with his round rimless glasses and blue chambray shirt. Fine, even features. Curly dark hair. Quizzical, sardonic, probably given to brooding silences. Probably subscribed to the *New York Times*—delivery cost more in California, but the book supplement was worth it—preferred merlot to chardonnay, listened to NPR and thought *American Beauty* was a brilliant film. He really did look like Rob.

"Is it distracting working here?" he asked. "Being visible from the street?"

"I can usually block out distractions." She glanced around the storefront studio she'd worked in for the past year. "When people see me working, they don't just drop in."

"I can leave."

"I didn't mean you."

"Well, I know how it is to be interrupted in the middle of a thought."

"I haven't had a whole lot of thoughts lately." Her face went warm. Why the hell had she said that? "About work, I mean. I'm…I've had other things on my mind. Actually, I'll be moving soon. I'm buying my grandmother's cottage and there's a porch in the back that will make a perfect studio. I can just stumble out of bed and start working."

"Pretty convenient," he said.

He looked genuinely interested, as though she'd actually said something, not babbled like an idiot. She folded her arms, unfolded them. Stuck an elbow on the worktable, propped her head in her hand and tried to look bored. Better than looking flustered and awkward. *Coffee.* Did she have any? No. He had an athlete's body. Not an ounce of fat. Unlike her own fleshy roll constricted now by the waistband of her jeans. Her hand was going numb.

"Anyway," he said, "you asked yesterday if I had any questions and now I realize I do."

"Questions?"

"About the tile-making process." He took a notebook from his pocket, flipped the through the pages. "How do you actually make tiles?"

She glanced at him briefly, long enough to tell her that he wasn't really here to talk about tiles. Fine, if he wasn't going to come clean, she'd make him pay the price. "The short answer is, you mix the clay, roll it out, mold it, fire it in one of those kilns over there, dry it for a few days, then glaze it several times and fire it again," she said. "Painting them is another process."

"So—"

"Exactly." She launched into a detailed explanation of paint pigments, moved on to glazes and firing techniques and anything else she could think of to throw into the monologue. When she saw his eyes begin to glass over, she began a dissertation on paint pigments. "That's a very short and simplistic answer," she said some twenty minutes later, "and I'm sure you must have dozens of questions."

"What I—"

"Did I mention that the tiles are mixed with two different kinds of clay?"

"Twice."

Only a touch embarrassed, she plowed on, anyway. "But I probably didn't explain that it's the glazing that gives them the really brilliant colors. Glazing and firing and more glazing and the heat's turned up and they develop this hard brilliance."

"My daughter would find this interesting," he said.

"Unlike her father?"

"On the contrary." He had his back to the shop window, a hand casually resting on the edge of her worktable. "I've been following your advice and checking out the installations around town. Right outside my office, there's a tiled mural of a girl riding a whale.''

"Designed after a 1950s-era postcard made to advertise the big tuna that used to be caught in Catalina,'' Ava said in the tour-guide voice she used during the weekly art walks she conducted. "Three children commissioned it to celebrate the anniversary of their mother's birth.''

"Interesting,'' he said.

"You stopped taking notes about twenty minutes ago,'' she said. "And *interesting* is one of those words people use when they can't think of anything else to say.''

He looked at her for a full five seconds. "Interesting.''

HOURS LATER HER FACE STILL burned every time she replayed the exchange. Screw him, she finally decided. It wasn't as if she didn't already have enough on her mind. Like her father still giving her the runaround on the cottage. That night, she packed an overnight bag, put Henri in her Land Rover and drove across the island to Ingrid's. The following morning, she called Sam on her cell phone. When he continued to waffle, she left Henri at Ingrid's, drove back to Avalon and tried to work. Thursday night she checked into the Bay View Hotel. Friday morning she ran into her father when she stopped at Von's to pick up food for Henri.

"About the cottage, Dad,'' she began.

"We'll go and have a look at it. Don't even know if it's safe for you to live there. Deck's rotting, roof leaks.''

"I told you, I'll get it fixed.''

"I want to see it first,'' he said. "Come on. Jeep's outside. Just have a couple of things to do and we'll go look at the place.''

Two hours later they were barreling across the interior, Sam rambling on about a species of cactus he wanted to show her. "Never seen anything like it growing here before," he said. "You'll be amazed. Just can't remember exactly where I saw it."

Eventually he gave up searching and they headed back into town. The wind pressed her back into the seat as Sam whipped the Jeep around the curve of Pebbly Beach Road. Maybe Ingrid was right. Maybe the cottage wasn't worth the headache of dealing with Sam. Maybe she should have Lil show her the place on Marilla. Sam was driving and gesticulating and rambling on about this and that. *You don't listen to Sam,* she reflected. *He's background noise.*

"The purpose of this little expedition," she reminded him, "was to see the cottage. If we're not going to do that, just let me off in town. I've got Henri locked up in the studio. I need to get back to feed him."

"Aaah." Sam waved her protest away. "That dog's not going to starve. Do him good to lose a few pounds, anyway. Damn." He looked across Ava at the blue waters of the bay. "I'd like to get another Catalina marathon organized next year. No reason why it couldn't be done again. The English Channel at its narrowest point is the same width as the Catalina Channel. Twenty-two miles. I could see reinstating the George Young Spirit of Catalina Award. He's the guy—"

"Who swam it in 1927," Ava interrupted. "Do you have any idea how many times you've told me that?"

"What was his time?"

"Fifteen hours and forty-six minutes." She'd committed the facts to memory when she was about ten. "And in 1952 Florence Chadwick beat his time by nearly two hours. I need to get back, Dad. Forget about the cottage, okay? I'm not interested anymore—"

"Sure you are. You've always wanted that place. There's a Dumpster around here somewhere." He drove slowly, checking the side of the road. "I saw it this morning. Someone dumped a whole load of lumber. Just what I need for the deck.''

"So I *can* have the cottage?''

"Makes no sense, but if that's what you want to do… Need to fix that deck, though.''

"I can *buy* the damn wood.''

"Why waste good money?'' He brought the Jeep to a screeching halt in the middle of the street. "There it is. See the wood sticking out?''

"Dad, you can't stop here,'' Ava protested, but he was out of the car, the top half of his body already disappearing into the Dumpster. Through the sideview mirror, she could see a white van, and behind that a golf cart. Neither vehicle could move until the Jeep made way. Drivers would recognize her father's car, though, and wait patiently, because that was Dr. Sam for you. She glanced again at the mirror— four cars behind them now. Over at the Dumpster, she could see her father's tanned legs beneath a pair of tattered paisley Bermuda shorts. She slid over to the driver's seat and drove the Jeep to the side of the road.

The other cars trickled past, the drivers sending jaunty waves. Through the windshield, to her left, the Bay View Hotel and, next to it, the *Argonaut* office, where Scott Campbell was probably sitting at his computer making condescending observations about small-town life.

Her father yelled something from the Dumpster.

Ava glanced at her watch. Five. She tipped her head back against the seat rest, closed her eyes. Her head was a giant gourdlike thing, crammed to the bursting point with…stuff. One tap and it would all come pouring out. Orange emotional goo, seeds of doubt, stringy bits of memory…

"Ava.'' Her father appeared at the passenger window. "Are you deaf or something? How come you moved the car? I need you to help me haul out the wood. It's good

stuff. I'll be able to do the whole deck and the handrail."
He started back toward the Dumpster. "Come on."

Ava sighed and got out of the car. Somehow it always
ended up being Sam's agenda. "Five minutes, Dad, and
then I'm going to walk."

"This won't take five minutes." He gestured at the
Dumpster. "Okay, we can do this two ways. I'll help you
climb in and you can hand the wood to me, or I'll get in
there, but you'll have to give me a boost—"

"Dad…" Ava held her hands to her face for a moment.
Her heart was hammering so hard she felt dizzy. She took
a deep breath and eyed the rusty Dumpster, brimming over
with mattresses and cardboard cartons. "I don't want to go
climbing in Dumpsters."

"Fine, I'll do it." He started shimmying up the side.
"While we're standing here yakking, we might as well unload it." He threw a piece of wood at her. "Here, you start
stacking it as I hand it to you."

Exasperated, she took the wood, set it on the sidewalk
and reached for the piece he held out to her. "It doesn't
matter what *I* have to do or what anyone else wants to do.
It's always your damn agenda first, isn't it?"

"Fine." He slid down to the sidewalk, brushed dust off
his shorts. "Go feed the dog or whatever it is you have to
do that's so important. I'll do this by myself. It didn't seem
like a whole lot to ask, but obviously I was wrong."

"Dad…" He'd started walking toward the Jeep with an
armful of wood and she grabbed his arm. "Why does it
have to be this way?"

He pulled away, tossed the bundle of wood in the back
of the Jeep and started back to the Dumpster. "Go. Leave."

"No." She stood in the middle of the sidewalk glaring
at him. "Why, Dad? Why does everything always have to
be so damn black and white? Why just for once, can't you
compromise?"

A muscle worked in his jaw. "I don't want to stand here debating it."

"Dad." She watched him climb into the Jeep and start stacking the wood. "Just talk to me. Please."

"Leave me alone," he said. "You sound just like your mother."

EVEN FROM A FEW YARDS distant, Scott could see that Ava Lynsky was not happy. He'd finished his beer on the hotel patio and was heading to the *Argonaut* office when he glanced up the road to see a Jeep blocking traffic. He thought he recognized the Jeep and the driver. By the time he reached it, the Jeep was on the side of the road, and Ava, in an oversize white T-shirt, black leggings and running shoes, seemed close to tears.

"Can I help?" he asked.

She looked at him. "Oh, no, we're fine." She pushed her hair back with her hand. "Dumpster diving is a Lynsky family favorite. Promotes bonding and understanding. I could be home working, feeding my dog, anything. But no…" Her voice cracked. "Sorry." She flashed him a bright smile. "Enthusiasm. Sometimes it just carries me away."

"Hey, Scott," Sam Lynsky called from the Jeep. "Just in time. All kinds of good wood in here that's just what I need to rebuild Ava's deck. She doesn't want to get her clothes dirty, but—"

"Go to hell, Dad." Hands fisted at her sides, Ava glared at Sam. "Just go to hell. I don't need you to rebuild my deck. I don't need you for anything."

Scott stood rooted on the spot for a minute. Ava had stormed off down the road and Sam was back at the Dumpster for more wood. It took him less than ten minutes to help Sam, now all cheery affability, load the rest of the wood into the Jeep and inquire casually about Ava's address. "Need to get together to talk about that book," Lynsky said as he drove off. "Remind me the next time you see me."

Ava hadn't gone far. As he started back to the *Argonaut* office, Scott glanced over his shoulder at the small triangular park squeezed into a piece of land between the St. Catherine's Hotel and the newspaper office. Last week he'd taken his laptop out there to write, inspired by the views of the bay just across the road. Now Ava sat on a bench there, her back to the street, shoulders hunched. He stood at the edge of the park for a moment, then walked the few yards across the grass.

"Ava."

She turned. Her eyes were red, her lips dry and chapped. Behind her, steep cliffs brushed clear blue sky.

"Hi," she said.

"Are you okay?"

"Fine."

"I can leave you alone. If I'm intruding—"

"It depends," she said. "You have this sympathetic look on your face. If that's why you're here, then yes, you are intruding. Sympathy is not an acceptable reason for you being here."

"Being unsympathetic is my specialty." He sat on the bench. "Ask my ex-wife."

Her eyes flickered over his face as though she was assimilating this new information. "About my father," she said after a moment. "Pay no attention to what you just saw. Contrary to how it may look, I'm not mad at him. He's—" she spread her hands "—very determined. He doesn't trust anybody's work but his own. That's what he was getting the lumber for."

"Must keep him quite busy. Do-it-yourself projects. A medical practice. And he has an asthma camp, too, right? I think I read something about it in a back issue."

"Camp Breatheasy. Kids from all over the country come here to participate. You should do a story on it."

"I will." He watched her face. "You must be quite proud of your father."

She looked directly at him. "I am."

He felt reproved somehow, as if she'd just told him that she knew why he'd really come over to talk to her and he'd disappointed her by showing his cards. He cast around for something to say and found it in the bench they were sitting on. A tiled inset in the back of the bench was painted with a scene of young woman playing a piano amidst a setting of vibrantly colored tropical plants. "Come and Celebrate with the Girl of Our Dreams," the painted inscription said.

"By the way," he told Ava. "I'm still checking out examples of hand-painted tiles. I noticed this one a few days ago."

Ava traced a brilliant red hibiscus on the corner of the mural. "Commissioned by a man to celebrate his marriage. They came to Avalon on a visit and married a few years later at the Wrigley Memorial. She died several years ago."

"You probably know everything there is to know about this island," he said.

"Maybe not *everything*. It's a small island, though. I've spent thirty-four years on it."

"Ever lived anywhere else?"

"Nope."

"Ever wanted to?"

"Not really. It would be like leaving a house you've lived in forever. Everywhere I go, there's an association or a memory."

"A Pollyanna Princess living on her enchanted island."

Her expression darkened. "A cynical outsider, determined to turn over stones."

He'd offended her again. He drew a breath. "What I meant was that even though I haven't lived here very long,

I appreciate the island's appeal. This morning when I was walking to the office, I looked out at the water and I could see the mainland. It did seem like another world. I can imagine it would be easy to feel as though fate had blessed you somehow. Although I know your personal loss—''

''Which is really what you're here to talk about, isn't it?''

''Not at all.''

''Of course it is. Just like you casually dropped by the studio to talk about tile-making. Please. Okay, get your notebook out. My mother didn't accidentally fall overboard and drown. My father pushed her. At least, I think that's what happened. It could be suicide, of course. Or maybe she staged her disappearance—''

''I'm sorry, I didn't mean—''

''Yes, you did mean. You're exactly like everyone else in the damn media. You sit there thinking that I'll fall for your fake friendliness, that I'm just going to pour my heart out. Well, sorry to disappoint you, but it's not my day for pouring.''

IF SCOTT USED too much force to open the front door, which he tended to do because it frequently stuck, it would fly open and hit an ugly green velour chair. It was a bad location for the chair, but the room was little larger than a closet and already crammed with an orange sofa. Tonight, the sofa was occupied by his sister, Carolyn, who was curled like a pretzel around Mark. They both sprung apart like characters in a sitcom when Scott burst in. Carolyn wore black combat boots and the kind of cotton housedress his mother used to wear. Her hair, shorter than his, was the approximate color of a tangerine. The last time Scott saw her it had been lime-green.

''Surprise,'' she said. ''I got fired.''

Scott picked up the day's mail from the coffee table.

"The surprise would be if you managed *not* to get fired."
Until now she'd worked—for brief periods—at vintage-
clothing stores in Pasadena and Los Angeles while she ma-
jored in theater at Glendale Community College. Carolyn
was twenty-four and always just on the verge of getting her
act together. Sometimes Scott felt as though he had *two*
daughters.

"Since Mark's staying with you," Carolyn said, "I figured I might as well be here, too. Don't look so horrified.
I can cook and clean and if you just happen to get any
action, I'll make myself scarce. 'Course, Mark has to come
with me."

Later, as they sat around the table eating the enchiladas
Carolyn fixed, Scott described his exchange with Ava Lynsky. After managing to offend her yet again, he'd ambled
back to the office. But he'd thought about Ava on and off
for the rest of the day. He still felt mostly sympathy for the
fiancé, but something about her intrigued him.

Carolyn wasn't impressed. "If you want my opinion,
she's hiding something. No one would get that bent out of
shape if everything was okay."

"Nah." Mark shook his head. "Sounds to me like she's
just a brat." He looked at Scott. "Didn't you say the
daughters were princesses? That's probably how she is with
anyone who isn't in her social class. She probably got a
bunch of media calls after the mother died, and reporters
are just part of the unwashed masses."

"Okay, I've got it." Carolyn leaned forward, lowering
her voice to a conspiratorial whisper. "Maybe *she* killed
her mother. And she's trying to pass it off as an accident.
Next she'll off the father, then the sister. And then, ta-da,
the princess collects all the money."

Scott and Mark both grinned. Scott tossed a tortilla chip
at his sister.

"Bet you," she said. "Three hundred dollars says I'm right."

"Three hundred dollars would pay half of what you owe me for the clunker you conned me into buying for you," Scott said. "And then there's the fifty-dollar phone bill I paid—"

"I'll wash dishes." She climbed onto Mark's lap, put her arm around his neck. "Seriously, can't you see it? Murder on Catalina," she said. "Tune in tomorrow to learn who gets snuffed next."

"Carolyn missed her calling, don't you think?" Mark asked Scott. "She should be writing movie scripts."

CHAPTER FOUR

"You look a little tired tonight, sweetheart," Ava's fiancé, Ed Wynn, told her as they dined on trout amadine at the Catalina Yacht Club. "Are you feeling under the weather?"

"No, Ed." She smiled brightly. "I'm fine. Fine, fine, fine." A week now since she'd first seen the cottage and her father was still holding out. A week of alternating nights at Ingrid's and the Bay View. But she was fine. Fine, peachy-keen, Jim Dandy fine. Tomorrow, she decided, she would spend the entire day without using the word.

Ed did not seem reassured. "Are you taking the multi-vitamins I bought you?"

"Religiously. I just have a bunch of things to do. In fact, maybe we could make this an early night."

"Absolutely." He helped her on with her coat and they waved and smiled to all the people they knew who were also dining at the yacht club. "I'm concerned about you," he said as they walked out into the night. "What you need is a little TLC. A back rub, a warm fire. A little brandy."

She felt a pang of guilt. She hadn't told Ed about the cottage yet. Either he'd be disappointed that she wanted to move into a place of her own, instead of into his luxurious home, or recognize how much she wanted the place and offer to intervene with Sam. Both prospects filled her with a dull sense of resignation. Ed was a truly good man, she was always telling herself—and then she'd wonder why she *was* always telling herself.

"It sounds wonderful," she told him, "but I think I need an early night."

"Suit yourself," he said amiably. "By the way, I meant to ask you. What do you think of the new *Argonaut* editor? You've met him, I assume."

"A couple of times." She willed herself not to blush at the mention of Scott Campbell's name. Since the last embarrassing interlude at the park, she'd taken an alternative route into town to avoid walking past the newspaper office. "I doubt he'll last long."

"My thoughts exactly. I met him at the Conservancy board meeting yesterday. A mainlander with an attitude." He reached to adjust the coat she'd thrown over her shoulders. "Will your father be home, do you think?"

"I don't know." She stopped walking. "I'm not staying there tonight, Ed. I've been staying at the Bay View for the last few days."

His brow furrowed. "What on earth for?"

"It's just temporary…"

"How does your father feel about that?"

Her shoulders tensed under his arm. "It's *my* decision. I was going to wait until I knew for sure before I told you, but I want to buy my grandmother's cottage. My dad still owns it and…we're just working out the details." She could see Ed gearing up for a discussion and she cut it short. "Look, I really am tired. Thanks for dinner. I'll talk to you tomorrow, okay?"

"WHAT TIME DID DAD SAY he'd be here?" Ingrid asked Ava the next day over a plate of chili fries at the Beehive. "Just so I can leave before he arrives."

"Noon," Ava said. "Which means one at the earliest."

They were sitting in the Beehive's window booth, which everyone on Catalina knew was Dr. Sam's unofficial consulting room. Three or four days a week, he dispensed medical advice, scribbled prescriptions and offered up political opinion and social commentary over the luncheon special. It didn't seem that long ago, Ava reflected, since the days when Diana would send her or Ingrid down to the Beehive to remind their father he had patients in his real office. "I guess I should be glad he's not sitting in a bar somewhere," Diana used to say, "but just once in a while, couldn't he even *pretend* to be conventional?"

"All right, girls. More tea?" Shirley, the Beehive owner, poured from a plastic pitcher, molded to look like cut glass. "Your dad joining you?"

"Supposed to be," Ava said.

"Don't hold your breath," Ingrid said.

Shirley stuck a pen into her henna-red beehive and fixed Ingrid with a look. "When you going back to medical school?"

"Never."

"You're breaking your father's heart. All those plans he had for you. Going into practice together…"

"Those were *his* plans." Ingrid dipped a French fry in the chili and bit into it. "I'm happy with my life."

With a shake of her head at Ingrid, Shirley addressed Ava. "How *you* doin' hon?"

Ava smiled brightly. "Fine. Terrific."

She watched Shirley make her way to the row of chrome and red-vinyl stools that lined the counter, stopping at the end stool to whisper in the ear of a gray-haired woman whose face took on the rapt look of someone receiving juicy gossip. Shirley and the Beehive were inextricably linked. Years ago Shirley had been a *HeeHaw* Honey. Black-and-white photos of her on the *HeeHaw* set, in pigtails and gingham, her front tooth blacked out, hung on the wall above the cash register.

"So what's going on with the cottage?" Ingrid asked.

"Same old, same old. Dad's going to let me have it, but

first he has to do his thing with it. I'm about ready to say to hell with it."

"Which is why I won't play his game." Ingrid shook her head. "I'd love to use some of my trust fund to buy the stables, but I'd burn the whole place down before I asked Dad about it." With her fork, she poked at the diced onion on the chili. "Do you ever think how weird it is that no one ever picks up on the difference between the lovable, eccentric Dr. Sam and the stubborn, contentious—"

"Dogmatic," Ava said. She'd heard Ingrid ask the question a dozen times. "Don't forget dogmatic."

"I'm serious. No one has any idea what he's really like."

Ava leaned her head back against the booth. She didn't feel like talking about Sam. In truth, he was somewhere between both versions.

"I mean nothing's changed for him since Mom died," Ingrid said. "Nothing about her being gone stops him from chopping wood up at the camp, or seeing patients, or tearing around in the Jeep, or doing whatever he damn well feels like doing. Sometimes I want to tap him on the shoulder and ask if he's aware Mom's not around anymore."

"Tomorrow's her birthday," Ava said. *Would have been.* Referring to Diana in the past tense was something she hadn't quite mastered. She drank some water, set the glass down.

"Hey." Ingrid tapped a French fry against Ava's hand. "Where are you?"

"Right here. I'm fine," she said when Ingrid kept peering at her. "I was just thinking about the birthday cake we made her last year."

"Coconut," Ingrid said.

"No, lemon. We squeezed fresh lemon into the frosting. You don't remember that?"

"I remember coconut," Ingrid said. "And I remember she had a headache."

"She always got a headache when we had birthdays and celebrations," Ava said. "Like when Rob and I got engaged. Mom wanted that big party and I just knew she'd get a migraine."

Ingrid laughed. "I even remember filling a plastic bag with ice to take in to her. Uh-oh," she suddenly said. "Did Mr. *L.A. Times* just walk in?"

"Did he?" Ava ducked her head. "I don't want to talk to him. Pretend you didn't see him."

"He's with some girl. Oh, my God, you should see her hair. It's orange, bright orange. And she's wearing army boots."

Ava picked up the menu and raised her eyes just long enough to see Scott smile at the orange-haired girl. She returned to the menu, the image of him burned into her brain. Neat, preppy, controlled. Khakis and a greenish-gray polo shirt. He probably looked neat, preppy and controlled in bed stark naked.

"Not that I give a damn," she told Ingrid. "But the Tangerine Temptress doesn't exactly seem like his type." She downed a glass of water, ate the last French fry and glanced at her watch. "Look's like Dad flaked out. Maybe what I should really do is take the next boat back to the mainland and start a new life."

"Before you do," Ingrid said, "be sure to ask Dad about Mom's diaries. I want to see them."

ON THE EVENING OF Ava Lynsky's exhibit, Scott stood with Carolyn in a corner of the gallery watching guests in summery clothes chat and mill about while juggling glasses of white wine and paper plates. The music wafting softly over the subdued buzz of talk and laughter was classical—Chopin maybe, but he wouldn't bet money on it. Spring flowers in straw baskets and raffia-tied mason jars bloomed on every surface, including a white-covered buffet table at the end of the room.

He hadn't seen Ava since their conversation in the park and would have forgotten about the event altogether if the waitress at the Beehive hadn't mentioned it when he stopped in for breakfast that morning. He hadn't seen Sam Lynsky, either, or heard anything more about the book. He'd told Ellie the trip to Spain was a no-go. She'd told him she hated him.

"I don't know about you," Carolyn whispered now, "but I feel about as conspicuous as a stripper in church."

"You wanted to come."

"Yeah, well, there was nothing on TV."

He shot her a glance. Mark had returned to L.A. and Carolyn was decked out in full club-scene regalia. Ring in her left nostril, short flouncy black skirt, bomber jacket, black fishnet stockings and combat boots. She'd also furnished his ensemble for the evening: a shirt the approximate color of cow dung, khaki-olive according to Carolyn, and some pants that made him feel like a gangster from a 1920s movie, but that, Carolyn assured him, looked "very West Side."

Possibly not the appropriate sartorial note for a Catalina soirée, but assimilation didn't happen overnight.

Carolyn tapped a black-painted finger against her arm. "I swear to God, if that old bag in the pink muumuu gives me one more look, I'm going to go over and rip that damn flowerpot thing off her head."

"Ignore her. She's—" Scott hesitated, already anticipating his sister's reaction "—president of the Catalina Chow Chatters," he said sotto voce. Carolyn's predictable hoot drew a few glances in their direction and he shot her a warning look. "Keep it down. She'll think we're laughing at her."

"Hey, I *am* laughing at her. This whole scene's hilarious,

I swear to God.'' Her usual expression of terminal ennui, an essential club-scene accessory was gone, in its place a broad grin. ''Catalina Chow Chatters. What the hell is that all about?''

''They meet once a week to chat about their chows,'' he said, straight-faced. ''She has two chows, Charley and Charmaine.'' He elbowed Carolyn in the ribs. ''Behave yourself. I did a story on her last week. She was quite... charming.''

''Oh, God, Scott.'' Carolyn shook her head. ''Please don't tell me they serve chow mein.''

''Chocolate-chip cupcakes.'' He felt himself losing the battle not to grin. ''Okay, knock it off. Everybody is looking at us.''

''The hell with them,'' Carolyn said. ''You know what? I was never a huge fan of your ex-wife, but she was right about one thing. You were crazy to give up your job at the *Times*. I mean seriously, how long can you get up every morning and write this kind of garbage? You're going to go stark-raving nuts.''

''Well, it's not all like that. There are...meatier stories.''

''Name one.''

He thought of Diana Lynsky. ''I can't.''

''I give it six months.''

''We'll see.''

Carolyn went off to browse the buffet table and he went off to browse Ava Lynsky's artwork, two dozen or so tile installations, hung at eye-level and illuminated by recessed ceiling lights: several views of Avalon Harbor, white yachts and blue water; an elaborate dwelling with a cone-shaped roof, nestled into a green hillside—the caption beneath it read The Holly Hill House; renderings of brown seals on white rocks, smiling kids in yellow kayaks, a shaggy-headed buffalo traipsing through long grass.

''Did you know there were buffalo on Catalina?'' he

asked Carolyn when they'd returned to their corner, Carolyn with a yellow paper plate of deviled eggs and small open-face sandwiches.

"Buffalo?" With her teeth, she removed an olive from whipped golden yolk, swallowed it and shrugged. "I can't honestly say I've stayed awake nights wondering."

"I didn't know until last week." Scott took one of the sandwiches, paper-thin cucumber slices artistically aligned with strips of red pepper. "Someone from the Conservancy called the paper to suggest I do a piece about the buffalo. I thought it was a joke."

"Speaking of meatier stories," Carolyn said.

Scott ignored her. "Years ago some Hollywood types doing a film about Zane Grey brought over fourteen of them. Now the offspring roam through the interior, doing...whatever buffaloes do."

"So did you write about them?"

"Not yet. Too many other hot stories going on. The garden club's electing a new president tomorrow." He let a moment pass. "Daisy Summers, I kid you not."

"Like I said, I give you six months. Maybe three."

Scott said nothing. He'd just spotted Ava again, talking now to the president of the Catalina Island Improvement Association, a woman he'd been introduced to his first day here and who had immediately listed the articles she wanted to see in the *Argonaut*. At that moment he'd had his first serious doubt about leaving L.A. He watched Ava. Her white sundress seemed to gleam against her tanned arms and shoulders.

"So is that the artist?" Carolyn asked. "The one with the black curls?"

"Yep."

Carolyn smiled. "Ah."

Scott shot her a look, "Ah, what?"

Carolyn kept smiling. "Just, ah."

"What the hell is that supposed to mean?"

"I just figured out the real reason we're hanging out with a bunch of yahoos drinking cheap wine and chowing down on egg salad."

"The real reason we're here," Scott said, still watching Ava Lynsky and wondering whether the tall geek with the crewcut in whose ear she was whispering was the fiancé, "is…" The geek had just whirled Ava around and was lifting the hair off the back off her neck, fiddling with something back there and causing Scott to lose his train of thought.

"Quit drooling," Carolyn said.

"Don't be absurd," Scott said.

"Actually, I think she's kind of witchy-looking," Carolyn said.

"Exotic," Scott said.

"If you're going to go put the make on her, do it now," Carolyn said. "I'm getting bored."

"I'm not going to put the make on her," Scott said. "I just need to talk to her."

"Whatever," Carolyn said.

Scott shot her another look, composed his features as he headed over to talk to Ava Lynsky, who was listening to the island-improvement woman but watching him as he moved through the crowd. He tried not to notice that his pulse had sped up.

"MY GOODNESS," AVA SMILED at Scott. "A representative from the fourth estate. This must be a bigger occasion than I thought."

"You summoned me," he reminded her. "I'd be remiss in my duties if I neglected to cover Avalon's cultural scene. Particularly one as glittering as this."

"That is *so* kind of you," Ava said. "I can't tell you how flattered I am."

"The pleasure is all mine," he said.

"You've taken a look around?" she asked. "Tried some of our delicious refreshments?"

"Made an absolute pig of myself," he said. "Everything's...divine."

Jerk, Ava thought, and turned to the president of the Catalina Island Improvement Association who had been shooting glances like Ping-Pong balls between herself and Scott. "You've met Scott Campbell, haven't you? Aren't you just thrilled to have a former *L.A. Times* reporter over here in Avalon covering our little goings-on?"

"Yes, well—" Doris gave him a measured look "—we'll see. I'm sure you'll find no shortage of exciting things to write about," she said with a frosty smile. "Now if you'll excuse me, I need to get a little plate of goodies for my husband. He's over there just salivating for some of those scrumptious-looking Swedish meatballs."

Ava watched Doris head for the buffet table and wished Scott Campbell would just go away. She'd spotted him as soon as he walked into the gallery—all urban and hip with his orange-haired girlfriend—and tried to ignore him. Tried unsuccessfully to ignore him. What really irritated her was the way the two of them had just kept to themselves, off in the corner, whispering and laughing as though they found the whole scene quaint and amusing.

"Well—" she tried to remember where she'd left her wineglass "—are you finding plenty to write about?"

"Still finding my way around. Meeting people, that sort of thing. I met your sister a few days ago. And your father was kind enough to give me a tour of the island."

"How nice." Reminded of her father, whose latest delaying tactic was the cottage's leaking roof, Ava felt her cordial mask slip. Her head was aching, and while she hadn't expected Ingrid to show up for the reception, she was a little hurt that her father hadn't put in an appearance. She felt surly, tired and not in the mood for social chitchat.

"We seem to have gotten off on the wrong foot," he said, "and I wanted to suggest we start over."

"But you're on the trail of a story, right? Driven, dogged, persistent. That's the way reporters are, isn't it? Not that I've had a lot of experience with hard-bitten reporters, of course, here in my sunny island paradise."

"Look, could we knock this off?"

"Knock what off?"

"Come on." He nodded toward the bar, where glasses of white and red wine were arranged in little rows. "Let me get you a drink."

"I have one." She glanced around. "Somewhere."

"Have another one."

"No, thank you. One glass is my limit."

"Talk to me while I have one."

"Talk to you about what?"

"Anything."

"Look." She folded her arms across her chest. "I really can't think of anything I want to say to you. But thank you so much for attending my humble little event. I didn't prepare any press kits, but if you'd like one, I can pull something together." She touched his arm. "And now I really need to go and mingle."

An hour later Ava checked in for another night at the Bay View. She was still annoyed at Sam and his newest delaying tactic. It was late April and the island probably wouldn't see rain again till November at the earliest. She'd figured out his strategy. If he inconvenienced her enough, she'd give up and return home. The strategy would fail; she could hold out for as long as he could. When hotel living got too expensive, there was always Ingrid's couch and the campground at Two Harbors on the other side of the island. She ignored the curious glance from the clerk at the front desk—a weekend busboy at Camp Breath-easy—signed the register and went up to her room.

The following morning she was eating breakfast in the hotel dining room when Scott Campbell walked in. A decent night's sleep, coffee and a well-made omelet could do wonders for the disposition, and feeling slightly embarrassed by her churlish behavior the night before, she smiled at him. He came over to her table.

"Okay, *I'm* here," he said, "because the hotel manager gives me a deal on breakfast." He nodded in the direction of the *Argonaut* office, a few yards down the street. "It's convenient and a whole lot better than what I would make for myself."

"Which would be?"

He grinned. "What would I make for breakfast? Nothing that required cooking, I can assure you of that."

"If you'd like to join me…" Divorced, definitely. Used to a wife cooking for him. Orange-haired girlfriend was his first foray into dating. He'd learn to become more discriminating. "By the way, I apologize for my…bratty behavior last night. And while I'm dishing out apologies, I might as well add one for that little scene in the park."

"Forget it," he said. "I just figured that was the way princesses behaved. Not having had a whole lot of experience with them myself."

"Can we drop the princess stuff?"

"The p-word will never pass my lips again."

She smiled, but suddenly felt very conscious of the two of them sitting across the table from each other. Outside the window, boats were moored in the harbor. Early-morning sunlight glinted off the water, and the small square of beach was filling with towels and umbrellas. It occurred to her that anyone seeing them sitting here might assume they'd spent the night together.

"So what brought you to Catalina?" she asked. "And don't say the boat—it's an old joke."

"Your father asked me the same thing." He glanced around for a waiter, then looked at Ava. "Hold on a second, I'll go tell Benjamin I'm here. I eat the same thing every day."

Ava drank some coffee and watched Scott as he went off to look for the hotel manager. Cute, definitely cute. Ed's face swam into view and she felt a stab of guilt. *Just looking. No harm in that, right?*

"So where were we?" Scott asked after the waiter had set down a plate of scrambled eggs and ham. "You were telling me about your work."

She'd been stirring creamer into her coffee and she glanced up at him. "No, we weren't, but it's sweet of you pretend you're interested."

"Let's cut this stuff out, okay? I am interested. I just don't know very much about—"

"Tiles." She smiled. "I lead an art tour every week from the Casino. I discuss some of the tile installations around town. It's quite informative. You should come by."

"I'll do that," he said.

"So why are you here in Catalina?"

He scratched the back of his neck. "Escape from reality."

"Meaning?"

Obviously uncomfortable, he frowned down at his coffee. "It's kind of hard to explain. I was at the *Times* for twelve years, nearly thirteen, and I guess I'd grown pretty cynical. Not a whole lot of illusions anymore. I didn't think much could shock me." He looked up, met her eyes for a moment. "This probably isn't very good breakfast conversation."

Ava glanced around at the almost empty dining room. It

was still early for most tourists. "I don't mind if you don't."

"A horrible crime happened in the house right next door to mine. An elderly widow—my daughter thought of her as her grandmother—was raped and murdered in her bedroom. Ellie was devastated, of course. After that, she had all kinds of behavior problems."

"Is she here with you now?"

"Well, it didn't quite turn out that way. I thought it would be a good thing to move her to a different environment, but my wife disagreed. And since she's a whole lot closer to Ellie than I am…no one's fault but my own. I'm here and she's not." He paused. "I haven't given up, though. Ultimately I hope Ellie will decide to come over."

"You like it here?"

He smiled. "What's not to like? I'd been covering crime and living in traffic. Now I write about fishing tournaments and swim in the ocean every day." He buttered a slice of toast. "It's more than that, though. I guess the joy seemed to go out of life. I couldn't shake my depression. I could work, but there was this insidious gloom. I started to feel that I'd never be happy again or have any reason to hope."

Ava had stopped eating as he spoke. She'd almost stopped breathing. She understood so completely what he'd described that she felt herself almost gaping. She drank some water, pushed her plate aside. When she looked up, he was watching her. "It's sounds trite to say I know what you mean," she said. "But I do."

He nodded. "Yeah, I imagine you do."

"It always seemed like we led this magical existence. My mother used to say how fortunate we were. Telling us we were the luckiest people alive to be living here in all this beauty."

"You thought so, too?"

"Absolutely. One year for Christmas, she'd had one of

those glass balls—you know the kind you turn over to make
the snow fall?—specially made with four tiny figures inside. Ava and Ingrid and Diana and Sam. All palm trees
and sunshine and sparkle. After her accident I felt as if the
island had…betrayed me. It's so beautiful, but it's as
though something dark and horrible is lurking beneath the
surface and…'' Embarrassed, she stopped. ''I'm sorry. I
hate people who can't wait to plunge in with their own
stories.''

''I don't think that's what you did,'' he said. ''I just felt
you understood.''

''So now you're here and…?''

''I want my daughter here and I want to feel optimistic
again. I want to believe that people are essentially good
and decent. I used to believe that. I hope I can do it again.''

Elbows on the table, chin propped in her hand, Ava met
his eyes across the table. Neither of them spoke. *I want to
tell you that I feel this incredible bond,* she thought. *It's so
strong it frightens me. I want to unleash all the things I
have locked up inside.* Moments passed. She smiled at him.
''Thank you for the company. I should probably get going.
Work to do.''

''Yeah.'' He took some bills from his wallet, set them
on the table. ''My treat,'' he said when she started to open
her purse. ''It was nice talking to you, Ava.''

CHAPTER FIVE

"To be perfectly honest with you, it's a tad…over the top." Scott looked up from the restaurant review he'd just skimmed to its author, who'd been waiting outside the *Argonaut* office when he returned from breakfast with Ava, and was now waiting anxiously for his response. "Maybe you could tone it down just a little?"

"Agatha never had any problems with my reviews," Harriet Smith said. "Agatha always said my writing was lyrical."

"Well, it does have a certain…" Stumped for a word, he shook his head. "But let me read one paragraph aloud and you tell me if you see places we could work on."

"Go right ahead." Harriet settled into one of the chairs behind his desk, her expression expectant. "I'm listening."

"'My taste buds positively squealing with joy and anticipation,'" he read, "'I surveyed the menu, literally torn between the scrumptious wedge of succulent iceberg lettuce smothered with velvety ranch dressing and generous strips of almost-clucking chicken breast, or the sturdy but mouth-watering meat loaf à la Mediterranean with its darling side of tiny glistening baby carrots.'"

"Oh, my." Harriet smiled. "It *does* sound delicious. My mouth is watering just listening to you." She tapped the review with one red-painted fingernail. "You run it just as it is. I guarantee the Beehive will be turning people away." She winked at Scott. "Agatha would run it on the front page."

After she left, Scott returned to the letter he was still trying to compose to the residents of Avalon. A pattern to his workweek was beginning to emerge. Mondays were mostly editing the stories for the next edition. Tuesdays he laid out the paper and e-mailed the copy to a mainland press. Wednesdays, assuming fog didn't ground the plane, the newspapers were flown over from the mainland and delivered. Thursdays he started thinking about pieces for the next week's issue, Fridays he got serious. Saturdays and Sundays he wrote, and the whole thing started over again on Monday.

Convincing Agatha Broadbent of his suitability to take over her baby, as she called the fifty-year-old tabloid, hadn't been easy. He was a mainlander and an *L.A. Times* reporter to boot. "People here on the island don't want muckraking," she'd warned him over gin and tonics at the Catalina Country Club, the first of half-a-dozen similar exchanges needed to convince her of his suitability. "They only have to turn on the TV to get that. No muckraking and no doom and gloom. If you've got that in mind, you're the wrong man for the job."

He went back to his desk and sat there for fifteen minutes staring at the blank screen and wondering whether Ava Lynsky was happily engaged. After another ten minutes he still had no answer, so he unpacked some boxes, made fresh coffee and carried it back to the window, where he spent ten more minutes staring across the road at the palm trees and the boats in the bay and another boatload of tourists coming into town.

Lynsky's check was still uncashed. The doctor had said nothing more about the book, and now Scott thought about Lynsky's telling him not to mention the book proposal to Ava or Ingrid. He pictured Ava's face as she'd sat across the table this morning. Thought about Ellie's last phone call in which she'd claimed she didn't care about Spain now, but there was this really great computer and her old one sucked. He drank another cup of coffee. He thought about Ava Lynsky's diamond ring.

Back at the desk once more, he tried to focus on the next week's issue. When the phone rang, he was flipping through old issues of the *Argonaut*. Agatha Broadbent had been compulsive about saving each issue. Forty years of Avalon history, filed in heavy black albums, a new one every year, arranged on shelves in what had once been the paste-up room. He ignored the first few rings and went on flipping through the pages. On the fourth ring he decided it might be Ellie.

"It's all over with me and Donald," his ex-wife, Laura, said without preamble. "He's a jerk."

"Where's Ellie?"

"At a friend's house."

"Did she decide about coming over here?"

"She said to tell you she's not coming." A pause. "She wants us to get back together. I mean it, Scott, that's all she talks about. 'I want you and Daddy to be in the same house,' she told me last night—"

"Laura…" Scott interrupted, but it was like trying to hold back the tide. As she rattled on, he puzzled as he often did about what exactly he'd been thinking fifteen years ago when he and Laura exchanged vows in a wedding that, for all he knew, the Scaramellis were still paying off. As far as he could recall, he hadn't been thinking, period. It was as though he'd sleepwalked onto the tracks of a huge tulle-and-lace-covered freight train roaring down the track. By the time he roused himself sufficiently to jump out of the way, it was too late. Laura, a fragile-looking blonde who walked with dainty, tentative steps as if she wanted to make sure she made no sound, could put her foot down with formidable finality.

"Our marriage wasn't any walk in the park for me, either," she was saying now. "I can tell you that. You made me feel lonely, Scott. You weren't there for me. Don was. Except that I see now what a jerk he was and..." Her voice broke. "I'm standing here making that stuffed manicotti you like. It's dumb, I know. It's not like you're going to eat any of it, but it made me think of when I used to spend hours making it for you. Not that I'm trying to make you feel guilty or anything..."

"Laura why should *I* feel guilty?" Feeling guilty, anyway, a legacy from his mother who played guilt like a finely tuned instrument, Scott held the phone between his ear and shoulder as he flipped through the pages of Avalon history. Now Laura was telling him all the reasons he *should* feel guilty, which he'd learned so often he could jump ahead, mentally reciting them before she did. Laura had this little-girl voice that had entranced him when he first met her and that he now thought of as wheedling.

"I miss you, Scott."

"You miss the *idea* of me," he corrected her.

"Huh?"

"The perfect husband, the happy marriage, picket fences, all that stuff." Scott turned a page. Dr. Sam Lynsky and a teenage Ava smiled up at him. Ava wore a frothy gown; Lynsky looked uncomfortable in a tuxedo. A father-daughter dance at Avalon High. He turned to look at the date on the album's spine—1984. He opened an older album and flipped through the pages, stopping at a picture of Ava and Ingrid. All black curls and gap-toothed smiles, they were blowing out seven candles on their birthday cake amidst a crowd of grinning children while the grown-ups looked on.

"Catalina's Twin Princesses," the caption read. "Little Ava and Ingrid celebrate with their parents, Sam and Diana." For their birthday that year, Ava and Ingrid got their own Shetland ponies.

"Perfect husband." Laura was still laughing as though she'd heard the world's funniest joke. "Don't make me laugh."

"Then…it's probably a dumb question, Laura, but why the hell do you want us to get back together again?"

"For Ellie," Laura said. "And because, despite everything," she said in a little-girl voice, "I still love you."

"Come on, Laura—"

"Can't you at least try? If we worked at it—"

"We have worked at it."

"You're running away, you know. You think taking off to Catalina is going to solve your problems, but it's not." Her voice rose. "You're selfish, Scott. Okay, so Don turned out to be a jerk, but three million—that's what he made in real estate last year. And now he's bought a time share on Maui. And you? You give up a good job at the *Times* to buy some run-down newspaper. So Don paid me a little attention. He likes good restaurants, Scott. He always valet-parks the car. He knows what women need. Have you ever done that once, Scott? Think about that for a minute." A pause. "You don't have an answer, do you? You know why? Because you can't be honest about your emotions. You're a cold man, that's all I have to say about it. Cold, selfish and stingy."

Scott heard the click of a disconnect and hung up the phone. He went on flipping through the albums. Ingrid and Ava rowing their new Boston Whalers around Catalina Harbor. "Not spoiled," Sam Lynsky said in the accompanying story, "just indulged. Isn't that what children are for?" More albums, more pictures. Ava and Ingrid, the tennis champions, the Girl Scouts, the high-school graduates. By the time he opened the page to Ava on her wedding day, he began to feel a little voyeuristic. He closed the book, returned it to the shelf, then picked up the phone and dialed Laura's number.

"Look," he said. "Have Ellie call me tomorrow."

Laura hung up on him again.

He put his elbows on the desk, held his head in his hands. He wanted to hear Ellie tell him what *she* wanted. Not Laura's version. He tried to imagine what he'd do if Ellie told him that she did indeed want her parents back together again. Maybe he should ask Dr. Sam if that was an appropriate sacrifice to make. Consumed by guilt for all his failings as a father, real and imaginary, he took his checkbook from the desk drawer, wrote a check for two hundred dollars, scribbled "Love, Dad" on a yellow Post-it note and addressed an envelope to Ellie. It didn't make him feel a whole lot better.

"UH-OH," CAROLYN SAID when Scott got home that night. "Someone's in a bad mood.

"I'm not in a bad mood." He stood for a moment in the blue smoky air blinking as though he'd just walked into bright sunshine. "When did you get back?" he asked Mark. "Don't you have a job to do?"

"About an hour ago," Mark said. "Couldn't resist the lure of the island. Plus," he added, "Carolyn said I could hang out here."

"That's generous of you, Carolyn." Scott looked at his sister in funereal black, her army-boot-clad feet up on the coffee table amidst a clutter of dishes and beer bottles and an overflowing ashtray, which hadn't been there when he left that morning. "Would you also like to pay the rent when it comes due?"

"Pooper," Carolyn said. "After you dragged me to that boring reception thing, you could at least be nice." She looked at Mark. "Scott's mad because some witchy-looking artist gave him the brush-off in front of everyone."

"Carolyn, shut the hell up." Scott carried an overflowing ashtray into the kitchen and dumped the contents in the trash. "And don't smoke in the house. I think I might have mentioned it a couple of hundred times."

"Really, Scott," Carolyn said after he'd stomped around the house, ostentatiously cleaning surfaces and opening windows. "Is it just the smoke?"

"No, it's everything," Scott said, dropping into a chair. "It's slipped Laura's mind that she wanted the damn divorce. Now she's calling me twice a day about every trivial thing that comes into her head." He was venting, but he needed to. "The whole time we were married, her family complained that I wasn't doing this to make Laura happy, I wasn't doing that to make Laura happy. *Nothing* made Laura happy. So now we're divorced and she's still not happy."

"Screw her," Carolyn said. "That's *her* problem."

"Except that she's dragging Ellie into the middle of it."

"How come you married her, anyway?" Mark asked. "I could never understand that. I mean she's pretty, but she always struck me as kind of whiny."

"Because Scott's a sucker for helpless women." Carolyn swept aside Scott's protest with a wave of her arm. "It's true." She looked at Mark. "Laura's this fragile, wispy little thing who looks as though she'd have a heart attack if you said boo to her. Big blue eyes, blond curls and this little-girl voice. It was game over the minute he first laid eyes on her."

"I have an idea." Scott was now tired of talking about his ex-wife. "Let's analyze Carolyn's life."

"What?" Carolyn was all feigned innocence. She looked at Mark. "You should have seen this artist Scott was coming on to last night. Talk about high maintenance."

Scott got to his feet, scooped Carolyn up in his arms, opened the door with one hand, put her outside, then closed and locked it. He leaned against it and grinned at Mark.

"Let me in!" Carolyn pleaded. "I have something interesting to tell you!"

"I don't want to hear it."

"While you were talking to the artist, I had an interesting conversation with some old geezer who had an affair with her mother."

Scott opened the door.

Carolyn studied him and cupped her chin in one hand. "Hmm. Do I want to tell you the rest of the story, or do I not?"

Scott moved to pick her up again.

"Okay." She squealed, laughing as she tried to dodge him. "Quit it, Scott, I'll tell you. This guy was going on about how the real artistic talent in the Lynsky family was Diana. Kept rambling on about what a tragedy and a loss to the art world. Greatest photographer since Ansell Adams, according to him."

"What did he look like?"

"Professor type. Pens in his shirt pocket, absentminded-looking."

"How do you know he was having an affair with her?"

Her lips curved. "Women have a sense for that sort of thing. Just like I could tell the way you went sniffing after the artist that you weren't going over there to talk about oil paints."

"WHERE WERE YOU last night?" Ava's father asked when he dropped by her studio. "I stayed up till nearly midnight. I remember, because I'd just finished this interesting article in the *New Yorker*. Bet you didn't know that Fire Island—"

"I stayed at a hotel. Same as I did the night before and the night before that." Ava dipped a brush into a pot of yellow paint and focused on color. Color was an essential element of the tiles she designed. Catalina colors: vibrant blues, reds, greens and yellows, inspired by the island's natural scenery. She set the brush down and turned to look at her father. Wisps of white hair sprung out from the edges of a red baseball cap that bore a log-cabin logo and the words "Kids Breathe Easier At Camp Breatheasy." His turquoise T-shirt read "I'm A Party Waiting To Happen."

She would not ask him about the cottage.

"I made spaghetti for dinner." Sam regarded Henri, sleeping in a patch of sunshine by Ava's feet. "Dog does nothing but sleep," he said. "Damn thing should be out pulling sleds, earning his keep."

"Leave Henri alone. He's a slumbering prince."

Sam rolled his eyes. "I kept waiting for you to show up."

"Just like I kept waiting for you to show up at my reception." She sat back to look at the piece she'd just painted. "Life's tough, huh?"

"I was busy," he said. "Something came up at the hospital." He poured himself a coffee from the pot on the end of her workbench. "New nurse just started last week. She'd been living in Long Beach. Wanted to get away from the rat race. *Blaaagh.*" He spluttered the coffee he'd just tasted. "What is this stuff? Tastes like perfume? *Uggh, blaagghh.*"

Ava shook her head. Henri roused from his slumber, eyed Sam who was bent double, one hand clutched dramatically to his throat, pretending to choke.

"It's vanilla hazelnut," Ava said, "and I like it."

"Vanilla hazelnut," Sam scoffed as he emptied the cup into the sink. "What's wrong with plain-Jane coffee? Why does everyone have to gimmick everything up? Just like your mother. 'Give me a plain pork chop,' I was always telling her, but no, she had to fancy things up with sour cream and gravy and God knows what. One time she gave me one with melted cheese. Gruyere. *Blaaagh.* Waste of good cheese. Did you happen to see the mayor last night?

I wanted to talk to him about getting another Catalina marathon organized next year. How come you don't keep any plain coffee—''

"Dad, shut up." Ava set her paintbrush down. "You're driving me nuts."

Sam smiled genially. "It's good for you. Builds character. Better talk to Jerry the pharmacist about his place. Won't be on the market long—someone'll snap it up. He's going back to the mainland, engaged to a girl in Glendale, or is it Burbank? No, Glendale, because she works in the Galleria, big wedding. Probably won't last six months. Jerry—"

"*Dad!*" Ava jumped up from the stool. Sam was flipping through a book on glazing. She snatched it out of his hands. "I am not buying Jerry's house."

Slouched against the wall now, arms folded across his chest, Sam regarded her for a moment. "You're going to waste money staying in hotels?"

She straightened her shoulders. "I might. I need somewhere I can think."

Sam scratched the back of his neck. "What's stopping you? *I* can think anywhere. First I ever heard about needing a special place to think."

"Live and learn, Dad."

"I'll find you a place to think. Why does it have to be that place?"

"It doesn't. I don't care about the cottage," she lied. "I've found something else."

"All you're doing is distracting yourself." The humor gone from his face, Sam nudged a piece of loose flooring with his toe. "What you need to do is face your fears, not run from them."

"I'm *not* running from them. I'm trying to deal with them. I *want* to deal with them. This is my way of doing it. Maybe it isn't your way, but it's *mine*."

"I'd have to fix that deck," Sam said. "The roof. One of the window frames in the back is rotting. Last time I saw that place, you could hardly get through the door for all the dust and cobwebs."

"Do whatever you want, Dad. I told you, I've found something else."

"Damn waste of money," he said. "You should look at the pharmacist's house."

Ava took a breath. "If you mention the pharmacist's house again, I'm going to hit you."

"You're stubborn," he said. "You and Ingrid are both stubborn. You're like your mother. Who's going to help you move? Don't come asking me to do this or that. I don't have time."

"I don't need you to help me. I do know a few people on the island." She glanced at the dog. "I'll strap some stuff on Henri's back."

He sighed loudly. "You do your best with your kids, raise them in a good home, make sure they have everything—"

"Dad. This has nothing to do with *you*."

"You're sure that's the place you want?"

"No. How many times do I have to tell you? I've found something else."

"The pharmacist—"

"Dad."

"I'll stop by the real-estate office on my way up to the hospital. Tell Lil to draw up the papers."

BY FOUR THE FOLLOWING afternoon, Ava had rounded up some helpers, her sister included, to move her kiln and art equipment from the rented studio in town to the glassed-in porch at the back of the cottage. Lil's husband had hauled over a mattress and some boxes from her father's garage and told her to call him when she was ready for him to bring the rest. By five, she'd washed the windows, swept the floors and was thinking about paint colors.

The kitchen, a small narrow box with yellowing paint and flimsy laminated wood cabinets was less than inspiring right now, but the end wall had a recessed arch that could be painted a vibrant color. Pumpkin, maybe. If she put up shelves, it would make a great backdrop for her dishes.

She stood in the middle of the room hugging herself. *Mine,* she thought. *Mine. Whatever I do here will be a reflection of me alone.* It seemed an incredible thought. As a child, the colors of her bedroom had been determined by Diana. As a new wife, she'd demurred to Rob. "But this place is me," she told Henri. "And if I want to paint it purple with yellow polka dots, that's my decision. I'm emancipated, Henri," she said, suddenly giddy. "Yahoo!"

"I'm going to have a painting party tomorrow," she told Ingrid a few minutes later. "Free beer and pizza. Wear old clothes."

"Who else is coming?"

"Anyone else I can drag in. Spread the word."

"YOU GOING TO BE at Ava's party?" Shirley asked Scott when he dropped in at the Beehive for coffee late the next morning.

"My invitation must have got lost in the mail," Scott said. "I didn't know about it."

"Hey, you're not on the mainland," Shirley said. "We don't stand on ceremony. Just drop by around noon. Bring your girlfriend."

"I don't have a girlfriend."

"What about that girl with the orange hair you brought in here the other day?"

"My sister," Scott said.

"Oh. I thought she didn't look like your type. Well, bring her, too."

NOON'S KIND OF A WEIRD time for a party," Carolyn said as they walked up the steps to Ava Lynsky's house. "Do I look okay?"

"Black satin's always in style," Scott said.

"Jeez, Scott," Carolyn muttered five minutes later. "How come you didn't tell me what kind of party this was?"

"Because I didn't know." Across the room packed with a dozen or so people in overalls and paint-spattered clothes, he could see Ava halfway up a stepladder. A brush in one hand, she was carefully applying mustard-colored paint to the top of the wall. She glanced over, saw him and dropped the paintbrush.

"Uh-oh," Carolyn muttered. "Someone's in *luuuuv*."

"Shut up," Scott hissed as Ava descended the ladder, "or I'll tell Mark you wet your pants when you took your driver's test."

"Big deal. I was scared to death."

"Hey." Ava shot Carolyn a quick glance, then smiled at Scott. "Nice to see you."

"You, too." He introduced Carolyn, who quickly headed off to check out the open pizza boxes on a table across the room. "Shirley didn't mention this was a painting party."

"It was kind of impromptu," Ava said. "But I'm glad you're here."

"Just give me a paintbrush," Scott said, "and I'll get started."

She flicked her eyes over his Ralph Lauren polo shirt. "You're kind of overdressed. Come on."

He followed her into the bedroom, empty but for a double mattress, and watched as she dug through various boxes piled in the corner. She wore blue jeans and a red tank top. As she moved her arms, her bra strap slid down her shoulder.

"Somewhere in here I've got some old T-shirts that I keep meaning to drop off at the Goodwill." She pulled one from the box. "Here."

Scott glanced at the shirt she'd handed him. Emblazoned across the front were the words "I Brake For Garage Sales."

"Do you?" he asked.

"Absolutely."

"You never know what you're going to find."

"Which is part of the fun."

"The excitement of the unknown."

Ava licked her bottom lip. "Yeah."

"Well…got that paintbrush?"

"Paintbrush." She shook her head as if to clear it. "Paintbrush."

SAM DIDN'T MAKE the party, but he stopped by that evening, toolbox in hand.

"Private Sam reporting for duty." He saluted. "No task too menial."

Ava folded her arms and tried for a stern tone. "I distinctly remember saying I didn't need your help."

"Did you?" He stepped past her into the newly painted living room. "Missed a spot there. Up there by the ceiling, too. If you were smart, you'd stay at home until you got everything finished."

"Well, I guess I'm not smart, then, because I'm staying here. This happens to be home. My home. I have a mattress in the bedroom. Henri's sleeping on it right now."

"Makes no sense," Sam said. "What you need to do—"

"Dad." She flattened her palm against his chest. "Out."

Five minutes later he called her on her cell phone.

"What are you and Ed doing tomorrow night?"

"I have no idea. Why?"

"I've got a taste for stroganoff. Thought I'd have the two of you up for dinner. The new guy at the *Argonaut*, too. What's his name? Todd? Matt? Something with one syllable. Thought I'd call Ingrid, too. Time we patched things up.''

"Scott. And you haven't spoken to Ingrid since Mom…'' *Died,* the therapist's voice said. *Died. DIED.* Ava drew a breath. "I'm all for you and Ingrid working things out, but a dinner with a reporter doesn't exactly seem like the place to do it.''

"I didn't invite him as a reporter," Sam said. "I invited him up as a guy who seems a bit lonely and would appreciate a home-cooked meal.''

"Dad—" Ava clutched at her hair "—sometimes you're so damn naive I think it has to be an act.'' Either that or arrogance. If Dr. Sam had decided it was a social invitation, obviously it must be a social invitation. "You don't know him. He's a stranger. All your stuff with Ingrid—''

"Stranger?'' Stranger wasn't a word in Sam's vocabulary. "What's strange about him? Seems like a nice enough guy to me. Went to UCLA, but I don't hold that against him. Kind of lonely. Doesn't know anyone here.''

Ava thought about Scott Campbell being lonely. Lately she'd been thinking a lot about Scott Campbell. She'd also thought of how none of her clothes fit her properly these days, and her hair was completely out of control.

"What do you need for stroganoff besides beef?'' Sam asked.

"God, Dad,'' Ava groaned. "Please don't tell me *you're* planning to make the stroganoff.'' Her father's cooking efforts were the stuff of family legend. Barbecued chicken raw beneath the burnt black skin, stews with thick layers of congealed grease. The silence on the line told her what she'd already suspected. "I'm not coming up to cook stroganoff,'' she said. "I've got too much to do.''

"Ah, come on. Stroganoff. How difficult can that be? You brown some beef—''

Grrr. "You are the most infuriating—"

"Beef and what else?"

"Sour cream." She tried to think. "Dammit, Dad. You're not suckering me into this. If you want company, *you* cook. Anyway, I'm on a diet. I don't want to eat stroganoff."

"Fine. The rest of us can eat stroganoff. I'm up at the hospital right now. Jason Scadding broke his leg in three places—you remember Jason? Cute little kid, big glasses? Mother works part-time at the Beehive. Do me a favor and stop by the *Argonaut* office. Tell Steve about seven."

"It's Scott, Dad. Why can't *you* just call him?"

"Because it's more personal to ask him in person. If you're too busy, tell me and I'll go down there myself. Don't know how I'm going to find the time, got a million and one things to do, but—"

"Yeah, yeah, yeah. Okay, I'll go by. But only because you finally saw the light regarding the cottage. I'm rewarding you, Dad, for good behavior."

After her father left, Ava tried to finish the tile she'd been painting, but her concentration was shot. Arguing with her father wore her down. She imagined herself relaying the conversation to Ingrid. "He invites Scott," she'd say, "and that's that. If I pushed it, he'd finally get irritated with the whole thing, fling his hands up and say that if I didn't want Scott there, then I'd better go and uninvite him. Of course, he knows I'd be too embarrassed to do that, so he wins by default." And Ingrid would say, "I don't know how you stand him."

She cleaned her brushes and closed up the studio. And then remembered she would see Scott Campbell again. Back inside, she peered at her face in the mirror above the workbench. Not reassuring. And that was *above* the waist. No stroganoff, she decided. She bent at the waist, let her hair flop all around, straightened and dug a lipstick from her bag.

Her cell phone rang again.

"Not to bug you or anything, but have you asked Dad about Mom's diaries yet?" Ingrid wanted to know.

"I keep forgetting."

"Dammit, Ava. It's not like I haven't asked you a dozen times."

"And it's not like I haven't had a million other things on my mind." She told Ingrid about the cottage and about Sam's dinner tomorrow night and considered whether to tell her about the feeling of connection she'd had with Scott at breakfast the other day, then decided it wasn't something she could describe over the phone. "He'd like you to be there."

"He can ask me himself."

"Well, he will, Ingrid," Ava said. "He wants to work things out, he told me."

"Whatever," Ingrid said. "Anyway, I'm not going."

"Can't you at least try with Dad? You can't stay holed up with your grudges forever."

"Maybe you can't," Ingrid said. "I can. Listen, if you're going to be up at the house tonight, just go through Mom's study, okay? I know it's a mess, but see if you can find the diaries. And tell Scott I said hi. I told you I met him, right?"

"He mentioned it." Ava felt her face go warm. "What d'you think of him?"

"He seems okay. I was only there a minute. He looks like Rob."

HE DOES, AVA THOUGHT LATER that day as she and Henri stood in the *Argonaut* office waiting for Scott to get off the phone. Chair tilted back, arms folded across his chest. Navy polo shirt, red horseman logo. Preppy, inscrutable and very much in control—exactly opposite of the way *she* felt. It was the little glasses, she decided. They gave him a smartest-guy-in-the-class look that, combined with his I've-seen-it-all-but-surprise-me-anyway expression, she could find maddening. Except she didn't. Not maddening at all.

The phone kept ringing. He'd punch one button, excuse himself to the caller to answer the other line, shoot her an exasperated look, punch another button. So the orange-haired girl was his sister. She'd felt surprisingly happy to hear it. The girl hadn't really seemed like his type. Too…out there. He shifted the phone to his other ear, took his glasses off and rubbed his eyes.

"Laura," he was saying, "give me a break, okay?" And then, "Ellie, honey, listen. There's nothing wrong with the computer you have now." A pause. "Well, maybe you don't *need* to play video games." Another pause and then he hung up the phone.

He looked at Ava. "Sorry."

"PHEW." ELLIE'S VOICE still in his ear, Scott came around to where Ava stood. Ava and the poodle, who was enthusiastically sniffing and pawing at the boxes as though they contained a few pounds of sausages and maybe a stray cat or two. "I'm sorry," he said again. "Family matters. My daughter's fourteen. She's decided that if I'm not *the* worst father in the world, I'm pretty close. And my ex-wife's only too glad to encourage that view."

"I was a monster at fourteen," Ava said.

"I thought you were a princess."

"I thought we agreed to drop that."

"You're right, we did." Given her dark coloring, if he'd had to guess the color of her eyes, he'd have said brown. In fact, they were a very pale blue. He added it to the list of things about Ava Lynsky that intrigued him. "I'd like to think that Ellie will look back on her childhood and see it as a happy time," he said. "Right now that's kind of hard to imagine."

"What's going on with her coming over here?"

He sighed. "Not a whole lot."

"What's the problem?"

"She wants my wife and me to get back together, and she's kind of tying that possibility to the visit."

"Making you feel guilty as hell, I bet."

"Yep. And then I compensate by spending money I don't have."

"Big mistake," she said. "Either you're there for her or you're not. Money won't solve the problem."

Scott watched her watching the dog and wondered about her childhood. Were the Shetland ponies and Boston Whalers Lynsky's form of guilt abatement? She looked up and caught his gaze.

"Hi, Scott." She smiled. "Nice to see you again."

"Nice to see you, too. You, too, Henri," he said with a glance at the poodle.

"So what were you like at fourteen?" Ava asked.

"A dweeb."

She looked amused. "Yeah, I bet."

"Thank you." He wasn't sure what to make of her comment. "And your clue was…?"

"Oh, just an air about you. Don't be offended. It's actually quite attractive. You're probably responsible, conscientious and kind to your mother."

"Thank you," he said again. "I guess."

"Oh, it was definitely a compliment." She cocked her head to one side. "Pat Metheny."

His mind still partly on Ellie, it took him a moment to realize that she was talking about the music on the CD player. "Right," he said. "You like jazz?"

"Some of it. I was married to a jazz enthusiast. He liked the more experimental stuff. I like saxophone. Moody, bluesy things that make you feel as though you're sort of wallowing in sensuality.''

He smiled and pictured sensual wallowing.

''You're into experimental?'' she asked.

''Music?''

She folded her arms across her chest. ''Music.''

''The opposite. I'm a wallower, too. I just hadn't heard it described that way.''

''Henri.'' She snapped her fingers at the poodle. ''Get over here.''

The poodle ignored her and Scott glanced over to see Henri devour a half-eaten cheeseburger from his desk. Laura had called just as he'd bitten into it.

''Sorry,'' Ava said.

''Don't worry about it.''

''Actually, I was coming to invite you to dinner Saturday night,'' she said. ''Well, technically, my father is inviting you to dinner.''

''But you'll be there?'' he asked.

''Yes,'' Ava said. ''With Ed. My fiancé.''

CHAPTER SIX

ED DID NOT UNDERSTAND about the cottage. The phone cradled between her head and shoulder, Ava lay flat on the mattress, still the only piece of furniture in the cottage, listening to Ed tell her all the reasons she'd made a nonsensical decision and why she needed to call her real-estate agent first thing in the morning and cancel the contract.

"I can appreciate that it might be painful to live at your father's house," he said, "but you could move in with me."

"I know, Ed, thank you." Ed had been talking about her moving in with him ever since she'd accepted his ring nearly six months ago. "I need to...I don't know, be on my own for a while."

Even with just a few of her things scattered around, the cottage already felt like her own. She'd set up the coffeemaker in the kitchen, lit a couple of candles, and Henri was stretched out contentedly beside her.

On the phone Ed was now telling her about his latest case. Ed the corporate attorney. Ed whom she'd agreed to marry next summer. Ed had been Rob's law partner and a constant source of strength after Rob died. Gratitude turned into affection and then one evening they were talking about marriage. It was like watching a movie, and dozing off during a transitional scene. You wake up and wonder what happened. But now was not the time to bring up doubts she'd been having lately. Trouble was, it *never* seemed the time.

Not that she didn't love Ed, of course, it was just… She stuck up her left leg and studied the chipped Raisin Red paint on her toenails. In her ear, Ed's voice droned on, as familiar and soothing as warm milk. Scott Campbell was neither familiar nor particularly soothing, but she realized that she was looking forward to seeing him again tomorrow. She wondered about his fourteen-year-old daughter. Did she pour out her problems to him? Today he'd seemed a little distracted. A dweeb, he'd called himself. She smiled at the thought. He was definitely no dweeb.

Now Ed was going on at very great length about torts, which made her think of gooey cakes and the fact that she was more than a little hungry. She yawned. Although he was incredibly sweet, Ed could be somewhat stuffy and long-winded.

"And how are things going with you?" he finally asked.

As succinctly as possible, since Ed appreciated brevity even if he didn't practice it himself, Ava told him about the interview the day before with the *Argonaut* editor, the reception and Sam's invitation to dinner.

"I'll have to give you an answer on that later," he said. The sound of papers being shuffled suggested he was multitasking. It was a discipline he preached until she wanted to scream. She pictured him in his book-lined office. Gold-rimmed reading glasses, lamplight on his gray-flecked hair. "I think I scheduled something that I managed not to write down." More paper rustling. "And what else is going on?"

"Henri ate the editor's cheeseburger," she said. "Scott Campbell, that's his name. I stopped in at the *Argonaut* to give him a message from my dad." She rolled onto her stomach and wondered why the hell she was telling this to Ed who not only wouldn't care, but wasn't even listening. She trudged on, anyway. "Scott was eating a cheeseburger and Henri took it right off the desk." More papers shuffling. "He likes Pat Metheny, Scott, I mean, not Henri.

He's into this wallowing sort of jazz, that stuff you always call indulgent.''

"Sorry?"

"I was talking about jazz.'' She heard a veritable gale of paper rustling. "Are you even listening?''

"Of course I'm listening. What about Pat Metheny? Did you buy a new recording?''

Ava took a deep breath. Ed had a lot on his mind. She sat back down on the bed. *Ed, I'm considering my entertainment options for this evening. I can't decide between galloping through the Avalon stark naked on the back of a buffalo, or a few hours of unbridled passion with Scott Campbell. Any thoughts, my darling?*

"My mother invited us to dinner next week,'' Ed said. "She's making a beef tenderloin. I wish you would learn to make the sauce the way she does. I'm not sure if it's a Bernaise or—''

"Ed—'' still cradling the phone, Ava got to her feet, unzipped her jeans, stepped out of them, then undid the buttons on her shirt ''—do you ever wonder…well, that maybe we don't really *see* each other anymore?''

"See each other? I have no idea what you're talking about.''

"I mean, maybe we know each other so well there's no…no…''

"No what?''

"No…surprises.''

Ed laughed. "I'd say that was a good thing. Who wants surprises, anyway? I certainly don't and I think that would be the last thing you'd want.

"I guess you're right.'' She thought about standing in her bedroom with Scott talking about the excitement of the unknown. Thinking for a moment that he'd been about to kiss her. Feeling disappointed when he hadn't. "It's just that…''

"Just that what? Finish your sentences, darling. You know how it irritates me when you drift off like that. Are you all right? Did you ever make that therapy appointment?"

"Yes, but I'm not going back. I'm fine. Everything's fine. Listen, Ed…" She wanted to say she loved him, but the words wouldn't come. Through the silence on the line, she felt him waiting. "It's just…" On the edge of tears, she shook her head to clear it. "I'm just tired again. I'll call you tomorrow, okay?"

She hung up, walked into the bathroom and sat on the edge of the tub. What was it about Ed that sometimes made her feel a little… Damn, even in her head, she couldn't finish her sentences. She ran water into the tub, went back into the living room and found some bath oil in one of the boxes. While the tub filled, she brought a candle into the bedroom and poured herself a glass of merlot. Talking to Ed just now, she'd had this unsettling sensation of a large glass jar being placed over her head.

As she climbed into the tub, she glanced down at the ring on her finger, pulled it off and set it on the sink.

THAT NIGHT SHE HAD the dream again, which was depressing because it meant that maybe the cottage wasn't the solution, after all. "Life can get very complex, Henri," she said to the dog who'd burrowed under the blankets on the bed. "On the one hand you realize you need love and support. On the other you push it away because you don't want to be seen as needy."

Henri sighed.

"Think about it, okay?" She dug into her canvas sack for one of his peanut-flavored biscuits and a chocolate bar for herself. Breakfast. "It's a pretty profound concept."

She spent the rest of the morning working on the house. At noon the carpenter dropped by to give her an estimate on fixing the deck. He'd been in her high-school English class. Married now, like almost all her contemporaries, he had three children and a modernized duplex with swing sets and a basketball hoop. She was waiting for him when his truck pulled up at the bottom of the hill. Even before he reached the front door, she could see the baffled look on his face.

"Yeah, sure I can fix the deck." He scratched his head. "But I gotta tell you, Ava, this place is gonna need a lot of work."

"That's fine." She gave him her Pollyanna Princess smile. "I'll feel more of a personal investment in it."

He grinned. "Try financial investment." And then he gave her The Look. "So you doing okay, Ava? Susie says she never sees you at the gym these days."

Suddenly she felt depressed again. He hadn't actually looked at her body when he said that, but it was pretty clear what he was hinting at. All she wanted now was for him to leave, but she pasted on another smile and said, "Oh God, Bill, I'm so busy these days. Too much work, I tell you. Good for Susie, though. She's always been so disciplined."

"Yeah." He smiled, his thoughts clearly elsewhere. "Listen, Ava, don't be a stranger. Come and have dinner with us one night. Susie would love to see you. We haven't seen you since…well since your Mom—"

"Right," Ava said quickly. "Okay, tell Susie I said hi."

She held her breath until he'd reached the bottom of the hill and then she sat down on the mattress in the bedroom and slowly breathed in and out until her heart stopped racing.

Later that day Lil called. "All settled in, luv?"

"Getting there."

"That's good. Feeling better, are you?"

"I'm fine, Lil. Really. What's up?"

"Oh just some papers I need to have you sign. Could you come by the house at half-past three tomorrow? I'll have them all ready."

SCOTT WAS SPRAWLED on the living-room floor of the stucco box on Claressa, the phone melded to his ear, his back against the orange-and-brown striped monster of a couch. His eyes were closed, mostly so he could avoid speculating about the possible origins of various stains on the matted gold carpeting, but also because his ex-wife's lengthy list of reasons as to why he'd been a less-than-perfect husband had a curiously sleep-inducing effect.

By the time she'd moved on to his inability to boil water, his head was sagging on his chest. He shook himself awake, listened to Laura for a little longer, told her the kitchen stove had gone up in flames and hung up. Knowing his cooking ability, she probably believed him.

Hands pillowed behind his head, he stretched out on the carpet. Carolyn and Mark had gone into town to play pool; he'd declined their invitation to go along.

He stared up at the water spot on the ceiling. If Ellie came to live with him, he'd have to find another place to live. This apartment, a tan stucco box shoehorned between a duplex and an apartment building, was cramped and hideous, to boot. A wrought-iron balcony just big enough for a canvas chair and hibachi, a "barely there" kitchen and a living room with a sofa bed. His bedroom looked out on an alley, and if he left the windows open, he could hear the sounds of his neighbors' domestic discord.

Still, except for missing Ellie, he felt good about his move to the island. He liked the fact that he could easily travel the entire town on foot. From the *Argonaut*'s office located at one end of Avalon's crescent-shaped bay, he could stop for an ice cream at Olaf's in the center of town and still reach the Casino on the other end of the bay in less time than he used to spend stuck in traffic on the Golden State Freeway.

His daughter was the cloud on the horizon. Laura was always available to talk, but Ellie was invariably out or asleep. He suspected that his ex-wife was playing games. When the phone rang again, he thought maybe she was calling back to ask about the kitchen.

"'Allo, Scott?" a voice with an English accent said. "Lil Langtry with Lovely Island Real Estate. I'm having a little housewarming party for Ava Lynsky tomorrow. You know Ava, don't you? Nice girl, had some bad luck, though. Anyway, she's buying her granny's little cottage. Bring your camera, all right? It'll be a nice story for the newspaper."

"HEY, I DID A SEARCH on Diana Lynsky," Mark said when he and Carolyn got home. "Just for the hell of it. The *Times* archives had a couple of interesting items. Before she married Lynsky, Diana was engaged to some guy in Long Beach."

Scott, at the counter shoveling sugar into a mug of instant coffee, turned to look at Mark. "Yeah? So?"

"Okay, the *Times* ran an engagement picture. It's, what, forty-five years or so ago, but Carolyn saw it. She swears the guy in the picture is the same one she saw at that reception last week."

Scott shrugged. "Maybe he stayed in contact with her."

"Yeah, who knows?" Mark popped open a beer. "Anything new on the book?"

"Not a word."

"Maybe the guy's just a flake. Comes on all strong, gives you a check and then nothing." He grinned. "You should cash the damn check—that would get his attention."

"I'd like to," Scott said. "It would pay a few bills."

"I have another theory. I figured it out while I was in

the shower.'' Carolyn appeared in the kitchen doorway in a yellow terry-cloth bathrobe, her head wrapped in a towel. ''Diana Lynsky isn't dead. She staged her disappearance so she could go and live with the professor dude, her only true love.''

Scott looked at Mark and shook his head. ''Do you have any Hollywood contacts? We have a brilliant mind languishing away here.''

THE NEXT DAY HE ARRIVED ten minutes early for Ava's surprise party. When he stepped into Lil Langtry's living room, he had the disorienting sensation that he'd entered a time-travel capsule. One minute he'd been out in the Catalina sunshine, knocking at the door of a Spanish-style bungalow with dwarf orange trees in the front yard, and the next he was in a front parlor being served from a Spode teapot. From the coronation china on the sideboard to the framed photos of the Queen above the sideboard, this was a house in which Britannia clearly ruled. It was all he could do to keep his jaw from dropping.

''First one 'ere, you are.'' Lil wiped her hands on the front of an apron decorated with picture postcard views of England's Lake District. Beneath it she wore a pleated tartan skirt and an emerald-green twin set. Her iron-gray hair looked newly permed. ''Did you bring your camera?''

''Yep.'' He still hadn't quite adjusted to being both reporter and photographer and had actually left without it, then had to go back and dig it out and find film. Pictures, he was discovering, went a long way to make up for the shortage of anything really newsworthy to write about. Yesterday, though, the tourist in the gorilla costume had struck again. A camper reported him swinging from the trees at the Two Harbors campground. Possibly next week's front-page story.

"Cup of tea?" Lil cocked her head at him. "It's just made."

"Thanks."

"Milk and sugar?"

"Just sugar, thanks."

"There y'are. Don't spill it now." Lil held out a translucent china cup and saucer decorated with pink floribunda roses. "Have a sausage roll. I just made them this morning, and the pastry's lovely and flaky, if I do say so myself. Enjoying Catalina, are you?"

"Yeah, it's great," Scott said. "What's not to like?"

"My thoughts exactly," Lil said. "How long we been here, Len?" She glanced over at her husband, whose face was hidden behind a copy of the *Daily Mirror*. "Thirty years, isn't it? Nodded off," she told Scott. "He does that. Well, we'd never go back, would we, Len?"

Scott looked at Len, or what he could see of Len. The newspaper headline read Diana Not Really Dead. For a fraction of a second, Scott imagined the reference was to Diana Lynsky.

"In the market for a home?" Lil asked. "You married? Kiddies?"

"I'm renting right now, but if my daughter comes to live with me, which I'm hoping she will, I might be looking for something."

Lil, watching him intently, suddenly got up and took the newspaper from her husband's hands. "Look at Scott," she commanded. "Who does he remind you of?"

Len peered at Scott over the tops of his glasses. "I dunno. Looks a bit like that...what's 'is name, that chap on *Home Improvement*."

"Oh, he does not." Lil flapped her hand. "He looks like Ava's Rob. Even had little glasses like you, he did, poor thing. He *died*." She mouthed as though someone might be in the next room listening. "Terrible tragedy for her it was. Thank God she's found a nice young man. Ingrid's single, though. You said you were divorced?''

"Don't start that." Len rolled his eyes at Scott. "Right matchmaker, she is. Can't stand the thought of anyone being single. No matter that they might be happy as a lark that way, she won't have it.''

"I'm trying to find someone nice for Dr. Sam," Lil said. "Bit soon yet, though. Still, maybe next year. And like I said, there's Ingrid, except that girl's married to her bloody horses.'' She stood and peered through the lace curtains, "Oh, good, here's Joan, my new assistant. She wasn't sure she'd be here. Female problems. Shift over, Scott. Don't take up the whole couch.''

Scott moved to the end of the couch and for the next ten minutes or so, smiled and answered when he was spoken to but generally tuned out as the room filled up with people.

"Shh, everyone, here she is.'' Lil had peeked through the lace curtains. "Ooh good, she's got her dad and Ingrid with her. All right, she's coming up the path now. Just about to knock on the door. One. Two. Three. Everyone together now...

"Surprise!"

AVA BLINKED. AT LEAST HALF the island was packed into Lil's living room, all clapping and cheering. Scott, down on one knee, camera aimed up at her face, winked.

Sam had an arm around her shoulders, Ingrid was whispering something she couldn't hear over the noise of the crowd, and Lil was steering her over to the couch.

"Right then.'' Lil glanced at Scott, still taking pictures. "That's enough of that. You go sit on the couch next to Ava. No, not down that end, right next to her. Come on, put your arm around her. You sit on his other side, Ingrid. Now give me your camera, Scott. I'll take a picture of all of you.''

"Just following orders," Scott said as he draped his arm across Ava's shoulders.

"I always admire guys who can take orders," Ava said. "Especially from women."

"Smile," Lil commanded. "Say cheese."

"Say sex," Shirley from the Beehive called. "That's always good for a smile."

"Sex," Ava said, thinking about Scott.

"My father's watching you like a hawk," Ingrid muttered, then leaned across Scott to talk to Ava. "Check out Dad watching Scott. He's trying to be casual, but he's about ready to toss Scott out on his ear."

"I tend to have that effect on fathers," Scott said. "One look at me and they lock up their daughters." He turned his head slightly to look at Ava. "Are you still eating breakfast at the Bay View?"

"Not since I saw you there." She was intensely aware of the weight of Scott's arm, the press of his thigh against her own. "How about you?"

"No. I've decided I like the Beehive's breakfast better."

"The Beehive does a fantastic spinach omelet," she said.

"I'll have to try it."

"You should." People were milling all around them, chatting and laughing, porcelain cups and saucers chinking, but Scott's close proximity, his eyes on her face as they talked, gave her sense of intimacy. The thought made her face warm.

"Has your dog stolen any more cheeseburgers lately?" he asked.

"No, he's being pretty good these days."

"Big dog," Scott said. "He probably eats a lot."

"You wouldn't believe it," Ava said.

"I used to have a German shepherd," Scott said. "He ate like a horse."

"Henri goes through dog biscuits like crazy—"

"God, you guys," Ingrid said loudly, "If this conversation gets any more scintillating, I'm going to start snoring. I thought I'd wait to see if you started comparing dog-food brands and then I decided life's too short. Kick it up a notch, huh?"

"Your sister's bored," Scott said. "What can we do to liven things up?"

"Pretty much anything," Ingrid said.

Ava winked at Scott. "Don't tell her about the skinny-dipping thing."

"I won't," he said, "if you don't mention the night of passion under the counter at the Beehive."

"Come on, you two." Lil shoved a plate of small frosted cakes between Ava and Scott. "You can make goo-goo eyes later."

"Hey, Scott, you going to sit there talking to those girls all day?" Sam called. "Thought you were supposed to be a reporter."

"I've been summoned," he said with a glance at Ava.

"Have a cake," Lil said.

"I've already had one," Ava said. "I'm watching my weight."

"Watching your weight? You be careful. I was just saying to Len the other day, you young girls always trying to slim, it's not healthy, is it? Come on, everybody, eat up. There's lots more treacle tarts and shortbread, and I've got scones with strawberry jam and clotted cream. Come on, eat up. We're not opening presents till the food's all gone."

"I can't believe you said that," Ingrid said after Lil had left with her cakes.

"I am. I've gained ten pounds."

"I mean what you said to Scott about skinny-dipping."

"Oh, that." Ava picked a cake crumb from her lap. "Actually I can't believe I said it myself."

"He has a girlfriend with orange hair," Ingrid said.

"She's not his girlfriend," Ava said. "Besides, I have a fiancé."

AVA LYNSKY HAS a fiancé, Scott reminded himself as he left the party and walked back to the *Argonaut* office. *And you already have more than enough complications in your life.* He poured coffee and sat down at the computer to make another stab at the introductory letter he wanted to write to the people of Catalina. Of course, with three issues already out it was hardly introductory anymore. Two hours later, with nothing to show for his efforts, he closed up the office and wandered next door to the conveniently located bar of the Bay View. He'd hoped Sam Lynsky might mention the book during the party, but the doctor hadn't said a word.

Inside the darkened hotel bar, he ordered a beer and took it out to the patio. If nothing else, he decided as dusk fell, it was a pleasant way to spend the evening. *Sure it's pleasant,* he heard Laura's voice in his head. *Why wouldn't it be? You're escaping all your responsibilities.*

From inside the hotel, he could hear the Eagles singing "Hotel California," and then Benjamin, the hotel manager, appeared on the patio, placed another cold one on the table and held out a fork impaled with a piece of steaming, mahogany-colored meat.

"Taste," he said. "Divine, no?"

"Fantastic," Scott said, chewing the beef.

Benjamin smiled happily and folded his soft pink hands over the white-aproned bulge of his considerable midsection. An aging queen, he was so swishy and theatrical with his spun-gold toupee and exclamatory sighs that Scott suspected at first the guy was putting him on. But under the schtick Scott had discovered that Benjamin was a shrewd judge of character, knowledgeable about the island and an entertaining source of local gossip. "If I don't know personally," he'd assured Scott, "I can find out who does.

Just ask.'' In addition, he was an excellent cook who traipsed over to the *Argonaut* several times a day to have Scott taste this or that.

Scott had decided Ellie would like Benjamin. He realized that lately he'd taken to deciding on people that way. Seeing them through his daughter's cool gaze and making a judgment. Unfortunately *he* was the one who didn't pass muster. He drank some beer and watched a passing blonde in red Capri pants. She looked up and waved at the hotel manager.

''Hi, Deanna.'' Benjamin trilled. ''How's every little thing in your world?''

''Peachy keen.'' She fluttered her fingers at him.

''Husband's having an affair with Betsy, the gal who manages the Surf Shack,'' Benjamin muttered to Scott. ''She should dump him, but oh, well. You know what they say on the island. You don't get divorced, you just wait your turn. Marriageable pool is small,'' he explained.

Which made Scott think of Ava, whom he'd been thinking about on and off for several days now. He drank some beer and tried for a casual tone. ''What do you know about Ava Lynsky?''

Benjamin eyed him suspiciously. ''Are you married?''

''Not anymore.''

''Looking for a serious relationship?''

''No.''

''But you're interested in Ava?''

''Jeez.'' Scott rolled his eyes. ''I was just asking, okay?''

''She's engaged to an attorney here in town,'' Ben said. ''And don't get any ideas or her father will kill you. Dr. Sam looks like a pussycat, but let me tell you when it comes to his daughters…'' He shook his head. ''My oh my. A few years back, Ingrid took up with a mainlander who didn't meet Dr. Sam's specifications. The good doctor chased the poor fellow off the island.''

"But he approves of the attorney?" Scott asked, hoping to be contradicted.

"Of course. The guy comes from a family almost as old as the Lynskys. Her husband was a nice fellow, too. Rob." He shot a glance at Scott. "Looked a little like you."

"That's cheering," Scott said, reflecting on the idea of Ava of the dark curls and red lips as a young widow. "How'd he die?"

"Brain aneurysm. Huge wedding at the country club, everyone on the island was there. The next I heard he was dead. Poor thing, she's overdue for a break from tragedy."

"So Diana's death must have been quite a shock, huh?" Scott said.

"I'll say." Benjamin tapped Scott's arm. "First there were all these whispers about suicide. Diana was unhappy, Diana drank too much, Diana was... Well, bless her heart, she was a bit..." He twirled a finger beside his forehead. "Feet not always firmly planted, if you know what I mean."

"What about the marriage? Did she and Sam Lynsky get along?"

"They seemed to," Benjamin said. "The gossip didn't start until after she died. Until then, they were the golden couple." He paused for a moment. "Well, except for the fight at the country club. From what I hear it was quite something. She actually poured a drink over his head. Dr. Sam hustled her off home in a hurry, but it had tongues wagging, I can tell you."

"What did she look like?"

"Brittle. Very, very thin. Polite, but distant. Masses of dark hair like Ava, but more...flamboyant. Artsy-looking, I suppose. Not exactly the type you'd picture for Dr. Sam. Ask anyone on the island and you probably won't hear a negative word about her, but I'm not sure anyone really knew her that well."

"Did she work?"

"Volunteered at the hospital, gave tours of the Casino. I heard she was once quite the budding photographer, exhibited her work in L.A. and San Francisco, but that was years ago."

"She hadn't done anything recently?"

"Not that I know of. Like I said, she kind of kept to herself." He leaned forward. "I have a friend over on the mainland," he said in a hushed tone, "who swears to God he saw Diana Lynsky last week in Long Beach having dinner at Captain Jack's."

Scott looked at Benjamin. "Credible?"

"Who knows?" The hotel manager shrugged. "Same fellow also swore he saw Mother Theresa drink a gin and tonic at the yacht club…"

CHAPTER SEVEN

DAY AFTER THE PARTY, Ava sat on an upholstered chair in the lofty dining room of her father's home talking to Ingrid on her cell phone. High above her head, a narrow balcony looked out over the massive carved dinner table. Diana had once employed a string quartet to play from the balcony during an elegant dinner party. As children, Ava and Ingrid, in gold paper crowns and velvet bedspreads around their shoulders, had used it to stage their own performances.

Ava was trying to persuade Ingrid to come to dinner. "Dad would really like it. I thought Ed was coming, but he has a meeting, so it's just me and Scott—"

"Cozy," Ingrid said.

"I'm not interested in Scott."

"Bull."

"Ingrid, I love Ed."

"No, you don't. He's a security blanket. You're too scared to let go."

"That's not true," Ava said. "Look, I moved into the cottage. I could have gone to live with Ed, like he wants me to, but I got my own place."

"That's a start," Ingrid conceded. "Next you return the ring."

Ava chewed her thumbnail. The idea that her relationship with Ed was based more on security than real love bothered her. Still she had noticed that her mood whenever she was with him lately hovered between irritation and claustrophobia. Ingrid was saying something else about Scott Campbell.

"...and you said he was condescending."

"I said he *seemed* condescending."

"Yeah, well, after you told him the Catalina Princess story. What do you expect?"

Ava got up and walked into the kitchen, pushing both Scott Campbell and Ed to the back of her mind. "Come on, Ing. We'll make the stroganoff and something really yummy for dessert. Maybe bread pudding with whiskey sauce."

"*You* make bread pudding with whiskey sauce," Ingrid said. "If Scott Campbell's being nice, it's because he's after a story. He's probably figured out that Dad offed Mom or something—"

"*Ingrid.*" Ava had pulled open the fridge to check the contents. She closed the door. "For God's sake. What's wrong with you?"

"Oh, quit taking everything so seriously," Ingrid said.

"Maybe I don't have your sense of humor, but what you just said doesn't strike me as very funny."

"Don't tell me it's never crossed your mind that Dad just got pissed off with Mom about something."

"No, it hasn't actually." Ava walked through the house as she talked, trying not to get caught up in her sister's mood. Ingrid didn't mean what she was saying. She was like their father, sometimes just throwing things out to get a reaction. In the hallway, Ava sat at the foot of the stairs and said nothing as Ingrid offered examples of Sam's temper to bolster her theory.

"So he yelled at Mom for forgetting to feed the parrot?" she said, finally interrupting Ingrid's tirade. "That doesn't make him a murderer. And it obviously didn't cross anyone else's mind. Not even anyone in the sheriff's department."

"Well, of course not. Who would suspect St. Sam?"

"Ingrid, shut up." Ava felt herself losing the battle to stay calm. "Just because you're always mad at him—"

"I'm not mad at *him* anymore. He's just who he is. It just irritates me that everybody is so suckered in by him."

"Can we talk about something else?"

"Sure. Let's talk about your panic attacks."

Ava frowned. "What about them?"

"It just hit me last night. You've got the same kind of thoughts I have about what happened to Mom, but you've just suppressed them. Now they're all coming out in the panic attacks and the nightmares."

"That's crazy," Ava said. "You need to deal with your anger at Dad, Ingrid. I'm not kidding. You can't really believe—"

"I don't know *what* I believe," Ingrid said. "I just know I can't quite choke down the official version. Which is one of the reasons I want to look through Mom's diaries. Maybe it would answer some questions."

"Then why don't *you* get the damn things, instead of bugging me about them?"

"Because I don't want to deal with Dad and I didn't think you would make such a big deal about getting some stupid diaries."

"I'm not making a big deal. I've had other things to do. Look, just come over tonight." Ava walked back to the kitchen. "We'll get the diaries and cook and talk. Come on, Ing."

"I'm not in the mood for playing nicey-nice," Ingrid said. "That's your thing."

"Okay, here's the deal," Ava said. "If you don't come over here, I'm not looking for Mom's diaries."

"Go to hell, then," Ingrid said, and hung up.

Ava stood for a moment, shoulders hunched, clasping her arms. The kitchen felt empty and cold. Her parents had bought the house above the historic Zane Grey pueblo for its views of the harbor. Ventilated by a breeze off the ocean, it was cool even in the summer. Now in late April, it felt frigid. The kitchen looked different, too, cleaned up somehow. Diana had been an indifferent housekeeper at best. "It's so damn boring," she would say. "I can always think of a million things I'd rather do. Besides, your father doesn't really notice."

Ava glanced around the large airy room. Late-afternoon sunlight slanted on blue ceramic counter tiles. The walls of the house were so thick no outside sound came in. She noticed this as though for the first time and wondered whether she'd always been aware of it and had just forgotten. When they all lived there, when Diana was alive, the house had seemed full of sound.

The vinegars were gone, she suddenly realized. The numerous bottles of flavored vinegar—balsamic, raspberry, vinegars infused with various herbs—the long, slender, dark-green bottle of olive oil. Gone, too, the stoneware jars of wooden spoons and kitchen implements; the blender and the bread machine that her mother kept out on display. No dishes in the sink, dish drainer empty except for two salad bowls and a wineglass.

It was all so quiet. So clean. Cold and unaccountably on edge, Ava found herself glancing over her shoulder as she moved about the room. Down at the far end was the huge brick fireplace that Diana had preferred to the stove for cooking on in the winter. It was always gushing out huge black clouds of billowing smoke that wafted upstairs and set off the alarms. Sam would shake his head and ask why he needed to remind Diana *every* year that the chimney needed to be swept out occasionally.

On the wall next to the fireplace, slightly smoke-grimed, were Diana's cookbooks. Two shelves of them jammed in between stacks of *Bon Appetit* and *Gourmet* magazines, yellowing copies of the newspaper food sections, overflowing binders and manila folders. The faded red gingham cover of a *Better Homes and Gardens* on the top shelf, a *Fannie Farmer* and the *New York Times Cookbook,* which Diana had considered the ultimate authority.

Crammed on the lower shelf were Junior league cookbooks, thin paperbacks on casseroles and canning, a glossy picture encyclopedia of cake baking and then the foreign cuisines: Catalan, Singapore, *Mastering the Art of French Cooking, Volumes I and II;* a book of Italian pasta; Japanese, Indian.

Diana hadn't just cooked from these books, she'd *escaped* into them. Ava touched the spine of a Russian cookbook, *Please to the Table.* She and Ingrid had both loved the title. As children, they would bow and sweep away imaginary crumbs and, in Russian accents, bid Diana to the table. The sight of Diana as Madame Olga, shawl around her shoulders and knitted tea cozy pulled over her hair, always reduced them into fits of helpless laughter. With a scratchy vinyl record of *Doctor Zhivago* playing in the background, Diana would solemnly command, ''Blini. *Feeled* with caviar and smoked fish. Or *vill* it be *vild* mushrooms? Caviar, definitely. And flavored vodka to drink.''

They'd play the game for hours, coming up with ever more imaginative fillings for the blini, but eventually the animation would leave Diana's face and she'd take off the shawl and the tea cozy. ''Phooey, back to reality,'' she'd say. ''Your father will be home any minute and I promised I'd attack the cobwebs today.''

Ava bent to pick up a newspaper cutting that had fluttered to the floor. A recipe for pasta primavera. She took down an Italian cookbook, opened the front cover. Inside were more clippings, notes in her mother's handwriting, supermarket coupons, recipe cards. ''You should organize this stuff,'' she used to tell Diana ''How can you even find anything in here?'' But Diana had just smiled. ''Oh, sweetheart, there's an element of surprise in coming across something you didn't expect. It's much more fun that way. I hate predictability.''

Something, somewhere in the house creaked, and Ava felt her heart jump. God, this was ridiculous. She was scared in her own house, well, not her house any longer. The house she'd grown up in. The house she could navigate blindfolded. She glanced at the recipe card still in her hand. On the blank side, Diana had written, ''Darling this is the hardest thing…''

Ava stared at it now. A scrawl on the back of a recipe for gnocchi. What was the hardest thing? Who was Diana writing to? It could mean anything. Ingrid had put some weird thought in her head that made everything seem…sinister. The kitchen, of all the rooms in the house, the one that seemed most full of Diana. Empty now, scrubbed clean. And yet she could almost feel her mother's presence. Diana might have just gone out to the garden to pick vegetables.

Not quite unaware of what she was doing, Ava started over to the window that looked out on to the raised beds where Diana grew herbs and summer vegetables, then stopped herself. Okay, this thinking was as crazy as Ingrid's. She shoved the card back in the cookbook. If Ingrid wanted the damn diaries so badly…

Her sandals clattering on the wood, Ava ran upstairs. The room Diana had used as an office was down the far end of a long balcony that ran the length of the second floor. Stationed at intervals along the expanse of dark wood floor were massive and ornately carved gargoyles and artifacts her parents had collected during their travels and that figured prominently in the childhood stories she and Ingrid would make up.

Most frightening was a seven-foot *ropero* cabinet with angels carved into the door panels. As a child, she'd been convinced that monsters lurked inside. Now as she approached Diana's room, she averted her eyes, filled with an absurd fear that a door would fall open to reveal her mother inside.

Her hand on the doorknob, Ava paused to take a breath. Then she opened the door.

The room looked exactly as it had when her mother was alive. For a moment Ava stood perfectly still thinking about how she would describe it to a stranger. Like all the rooms in the house, this one had soaring ceilings and tall chapel-like windows at one end. Along one wall, an elegant eighteenth-century hand-painted screen; more gargoyles and carved pieces were scattered here and there.

In the middle was a massive slab of marble that Diana had used as a desk, the top of it barely visible beneath the blizzard of papers, magazines and books. Atop all this, jars of pencils, boxes of paints, a huge blue *papier-mâché* pig and, incongruously, what looked like a brand-new electric mixer.

Beside the desk, beneath the desk, covering every inch of floor all around the desk were items of clothing: a black mohair shawl, a single white sock, a black sweater. More paper in boxes, white mostly, strewn haphazardly, scrawled upon in various-colored ink, wadded into balls, stained with brown splotches, folded into quarters, torn into scraps. Sam used to joke that burglars could break into the house and ransack Diana's study and no one would ever know. Certainly no one would know now.

Ava took another breath, then gingerly took a few steps across the paper carpet to a file cabinet. The top two drawers were open and overflowing with more paper. The bottom one was closed. She pulled it open. More paper. She picked up a piece from the floor. On it, Diana had written. "Weighed 134 yesterday. Must cut down on calorie intake tomorrow."

Ava left the room and closed the door. Let Ingrid search for what she was looking for herself.

AN HOUR LATER, with dinner under way and Sarah Vaughan singing on the stereo—one of Sam's collection—Ava had pretty much recovered from the spooky sensation that had gripped her earlier. In future she decided she'd avoid discussing Sam or Diana with Ingrid. The dreams and panic attacks were difficult enough without hearing Ingrid's whacky theories. She still felt disappointed that the cottage hadn't entirely stopped the dreams, but maybe it just took time.

Meanwhile, she felt only slightly guilty about looking forward to seeing Scott Campbell again. After all, she had invited Ed; he'd chosen not to come. She lifted the lid of the pan in which the meat was simmering, removed a piece between her thumb and forefinger and popped it into her mouth.

Henri, sitting at her feet, barked.

"Sorry." She reached for another piece, dropped it to him.

"I kind of like this Henri, you know that? Making dinner for someone besides you and me." She'd tried to cook for Ed, but he was a picky eater and had a weak stomach, to boot. He'd insisted on so many restrictions that after a few attempts, she'd given up altogether.

Cooking was one of the things she missed after Rob died. She'd leave the studio about four, come home and start dinner so that when he walked in, the house would be filled with tantalizing aromas. And she always lit candles, had music going on the stereo. Diana had teased her unmercifully about "nesting."

Except for Rob's twelve-year-old daughter, who had taken an instant and violent dislike to her, Ava loved the brief time she'd spent as Rob's wife. Loved wheeling the shopping cart around Von's, buying his favorite extra-sharp cheddar, a bag of bow-tie pasta, a jar of artichoke hearts. And she'd plan their meals as she shopped, sautéed mushrooms to go with the New York steak she'd just put in the basket, eggs for Sunday morning's omelet, whipping cream for the tiramisu, a special treat for their one-month anniversary.

She glanced at the clock. Ten minutes to go. Buttered noodles with the stroganoff, she decided, and a green salad. She opened the fridge. Where was her father? He'd dropped by briefly, then disappeared with some rambling explanation that halfway through she'd stopped listening to and promised he'd be back in plenty of time for dinner.

Which she didn't believe for a moment. Okay, hand cupped to her chin, she stood at the stove thinking. Not that it mattered how Scott Campbell saw her, but it wouldn't hurt to fix herself up a little. She opened the door to let Henri outside, then on an impulse, ran upstairs to her old room and began sliding hangers along the bar in the closet looking for something to wear.

Big white shirt she'd forgotten all about. She stripped off her sweater, slipped on the shirt and made a face at her reflection in the dresser mirror. *Blah.* She tied the ends of the shirt, peered at the results. Not bad. She turned sideways, untied the shirt. It hung, wrinkled now, over her jeans. *Dammit.* She ripped off the shirt, started sliding hangers again. Nothing fit. Downstairs, she heard Henri barking. She pulled on a red nightshirt and ran down to investigate.

As HE WALKED TO THE LYNSKYS' for dinner, Scott mentally listed all the things conspiring to prevent his new life from being quite the paradise he'd hoped to find. Ellie topped the list, of course. Immediately below Ellie was an assortment of other money concerns, all of which could be relieved by Sam Lynsky's funding.

Surprisingly high on the list was a kind of restless loneliness. Surprising because with Carolyn and Mark occupying the living room, he'd hardly had a moment alone since he arrived on Catalina. But it was a specific kind of loneliness, one that, when he allowed himself to dwell on it, inevitably offered Ava Lynsky as the only solution. Her engagement ring was yet another problem.

He headed up Chimes Hill Road. The mast lights on the boats in the harbor were just beginning to punctuate the dark-blue evening sky. Visible from the town below, Sam Lynsky's house was a white, three-story Spanish-style home, high on a bluff above the pueblo where the author Zane Grey once lived and wrote. Scott didn't know a whole lot about Catalina home prices, but he'd lived in California long enough to know that any place with an ocean view was automatically several million.

Even modest homes, if they looked out on crashing waves or picturesque coves, commanded astronomical prices, and Sam Lynsky's house was not modest. The pair of heavy carved front doors looked like the sort of entrance he'd seen on village churches in Mexico; in fact, the whole place reminded him of the palatial villas he'd seen in the hills above Mexico City. Definitely not modest, but not ostentatious, either. Still, if he knew nothing else about the occupants, he'd feel pretty confident that they hadn't had to cut grocery coupons to send their kids to college. Or maybe they had.

"Millionaires know how to save money," his ex-wife used to say as *she* cut grocery coupons. "That's why they're millionaires."

Scott rang again. He'd brought wine, both red and white because he'd forgotten to ask and he had no idea what went with stroganoff, and a bunch of plastic-wrapped yellow tulips he'd picked up in Von's. The tulips were now giving him second thoughts. Technically Dr. Sam had extended the invitation, but he'd been thinking of Ava when he bought the flowers and couldn't decide whether they struck the right note. And what *was* the note? *I have absolutely no interest in you and these seemed pretty impersonal.* Or *I'm too entangled in a messy divorce and custody issues to even think of dating and you're not available, anyway, but you kind of intrigue me.*

He turned his back to the door and looked out past descending terraces vibrant with crimson and purple bougainvillea and lush tropical plants he couldn't even begin to name to the bay where the sun was just beginning to set.

One summer when he was a boy he'd spent a weekend over here. His parents had rented a vacation cottage, a place about the size of the one he now lived in. He and Carolyn and their father would leave early in the morning with fishing poles, the air damp and cool, misty clouds hanging over the mountains. In the evening his mother would cook the fish they'd caught. It seemed a million years ago, he thought, his mind back on Ellie, and so infinitely simpler than life today.

He rang the bell again. This time he heard movement inside. A dog barked. And then the door was flung open and Ava stood there looking faintly irked and wearing a long, red tartan shirt. Her legs and feet were bare, her toenails the same color as her shirt. Beside her, on its haunches, sat the poodle he'd met earlier—he'd forgotten its name. It barked, a decibel higher than a jet taking off at close proximity, then disappeared into the house.

"You're early," Ava said.

Scott glanced at his watch. "You said seven, I thought. It's ten after."

"Humor me," she said. "I can't find anything to wear."

"Actually, what you're wearing looks fine, but—" he

glanced at his watch again "—you're right, I am early. Want me to take a walk?"

The dog reappeared and sat again at Ava's feet. Something lacy and white dangled from its mouth. Ava bent to look. Her black hair had divided into two glossy sections, falling on either side of her head and exposing the back of her neck. Scott shifted the flowers and wine to the other hand. Ava was prying the dog's jaws apart.

"*Henri*. Dammit, that's my underwear." She grabbed it from his mouth and looked at Scott. "He used to live in this house, but he doesn't like being back here, so he's acting out. He just dug up my mother's vegetable garden. A huge bone he buried God knows how long ago. Bad boy." She wagged her finger at him. "Go find your chew toy."

"I can come back," Scott said.

"If you don't mind chaos…"

"I live with it on a daily basis."

She closed the door behind him and took the flowers. "Tulips." She smiled. "I love tulips."

"Good."

"No, really, I'm not just being polite. I *love* them." With the flowers crooked in one arm, she pulled away the cellophane. "See how waxy and perfect the petals are? It always amazes me that they just…grow. I mean, they look more like someone sculpted them."

He smiled.

"Okay." She rewrapped the flowers. "I saw that look. You think I'm nuts, don't you?"

"Not at all." He remembered Laura's blasé acceptance of the dozen hothouse roses he'd bought for her last birthday. Ava's obvious pleasure was both endearing and surprising. If he'd thought about her likely response beforehand, he'd have pegged her for blasé. "I'm glad you like them," he said.

"I love them." She turned and glanced over her shoulder. "Come on. You can talk to me while I finish dinner."

As he followed her through what seemed like an endless maze of rooms, he had an impression of vast airy spaces, terra-cotta tiles and vibrant colors, a wall of deep cobalt-blue, an expanse of Chinese-yellow. Light flooded in through windows that commanded views of the glittering bay and sage-green mountains. The views seemed as much a part of the decor as the striking art on the walls. What kept it from looking like something out of an interior-decorating magazine—and in his view made it more interesting—was the sheer volume of...stuff.

He did a quick inventory as Ava stopped to pick up a book that the dog, circling and barking and clicking across the tiled floors had knocked from a table. Four ornate bird-cages, sans birds, atop a long library table that stood next to a rattan umbrella stand crammed with an assortment of tattered-looking umbrellas. A dollhouse, the doors and windows flung open as though a child had just finished playing. Fringed shawls and blankets draped over chair backs and tabletops, books everywhere—stacked, shelved and leaning in precarious mountains against the walls.

"Amazing house," Scott said. "Incredible, really. Do you ever get lost in it?"

She smiled. "I've had time to learn the layout. My sister and I were born here. There was no obstetrician on the island at the time and my mother was supposed to go over to the mainland for her last month, but we fooled her by arriving early, so my father delivered us. Right upstairs in their bedroom."

"Who's the collector?"

"All of us. The truly weird stuff is...was my mother's. My father is the biggest accumulator, but we all have this genetic predisposition to amass stuff. Once something gets misplaced in this house, that's it. You'll never find it again.''

He followed her into the dining room, roughly the size of his entire apartment. More books stacked at one end of a massive wooden table set with plates and napkins in primary colors, piled onto the seats of several of the dozen or so high-backed chairs drawn up around the table. Something drew his eye up to a balcony two-thirds of the way up the wall. Ava had followed his glance.

''It's for playing *Romeo and Juliette*,'' she said.

''Is that what you used to do?''

''Sometimes. But I didn't like them dying, so we rewrote the ending to make it happier.''

''You and Ingrid?''

''And anyone else we could rope in. Mostly, though, we were the stars.''

He glanced up again, picturing an eight-year-old Ava with long black curls playing to the audience below. Ingrid's image was harder to conjure. He wondered if Ingrid ever resented her more vibrant twin. ''Will your sister be here tonight?'' he asked.

''No.'' Ava watched the dog snap at a fly. ''I wanted her to come, but…Ingrid's not big on social stuff. Anyway, my father said he'd be back before seven, which means it will be eight at least before he shows. Dinner's essentially ready, so if you're hungry, just say so.''

''I don't mind waiting for your father.''

''No one ever does.''

She'd stepped out onto a rustic wooden deck that led off from the dining room, and he followed her. They stood for a few moments looking at Avalon, spread out below them, the palm trees and the small shops, the endless parade of tourists. He was thinking about the way Ava's mouth had tightened when she mentioned her father, the way her voice had sounded like Ingrid's. He watched a lighted mast out in the bay. He felt like an archaeologist just beginning to produce interesting artifacts from a dig. Ava's voice interrupted his musings.

"Beer? Glass of wine? Tea? Coffee?"

He was still holding the brown paper sack with the wine he'd brought. He held it out to her. "Red and white—I didn't know which."

"I had you pegged for red," she said, taking the sack.

"You're right," he said. "But I didn't know about you." He sat down on a chair made from strips of woven leather. There were four of the chairs on the desk grouped around a small circular table. The sun was burnt orange and low in the sky, the lights of homes bright punctuation marks extending up into the shadowy blackness of the hills. He could hear far-off sounds, music faintly, waves breaking. Ava sat opposite him, her feet up on the chair, arms wrapped around her knees. She was still wearing the red shirt. He liked her for not rushing off to change.

"Did you resolve things with your daughter?" she asked.

"My daughter…" He'd forgotten that she'd been in the office while he was talking to Ellie. "No, not really. It's an ongoing saga."

Ava got up and returned minutes later with two heavy, green-stemmed wineglasses. She handed one to him and took a sip from the other one. A moment later she disappeared into the house again and returned with a lighted candle, which she set on the table between them.

"You can see my cottage from here," she said. "It's almost directly across the bay from where we're sitting." With her wineglass she gestured at the darkened hills. "One street above the *Argonaut* office, up on Middle Crescent."

"Where did you live before that?"

"Right here. I moved back after my husband died,

but…it's difficult to be here. Too many memories, that sort of thing." She drank some wine. "Where do *you* live?"

He'd been watching the play of candlelight on her face. "In a beige stucco box on Claressa."

"Canvas City." She held her wineglass in both hands, as though warming them on a mug of coffee. "Around the turn of the century, the Bannings pitched tent housing all along Claressa and Catalina for summer visitors. My father has pictures of them in the family album. They were pretty comfortable—beds, chairs, even electricity and maids to clean up."

"My apartment is considerably less grand. If my daughter comes to live with me, I'll have to look for something else."

"How old are you?"

"Thirty-eight."

"So you were only twenty-four when your daughter was born. Was it difficult?"

"Being a father, you mean? It still is."

"My father says the same thing." She drank some wine. "What's the hardest part?"

A moth circled the pool of light around the candle. Scott followed its movement as he spoke. "Figuring out the difference between what she truly needs to be happy and well-adjusted and what she wants."

Ava grinned. "Does she twist you around her little finger?"

"She's pretty good at making me feel guilty."

"She lives with her mother?"

"Right now. We just have a few things to work out."

"Like you and her mother getting back together?"

He nodded. "That's pretty much what it comes down to. Laura's convinced it could work if I try hard enough. It won't—we've already been through the trying-harder phase—but neither Laura nor Ellie can quite accept it."

"Don't let them talk you into doing something you don't believe in," she said. "Living a lie never makes anyone happy."

He looked at Ava for a moment. It sounded like an opening, but he'd already managed to offend her enough times that he wasn't taking any chances. He let the remark go and filtered through his brain for a land-mine free topic. Ava spared him with a question of her own. What happened with his marriage? she wanted to know.

"You wouldn't rather talk about...the economy? Art? The Catalina Chow Chatters?"

"No."

"It probably broke up because I didn't pay enough attention. I just expected it to sputter along. When it started to break down, I did pay it more attention, but by that time the...engine was blown." Ava looked amused. "Well, it's a guy kind of explanation," he said.

"So why didn't you pay attention in the first place?"

"I don't know. Or I do, I guess. We should never have got married."

"But then if you hadn't married your wife, Ellie wouldn't be Ellie."

"True."

"So what are you going to do? Go on letting Ellie think there's some hope you and her mother will get back together?"

"No. We need to have a talk. If I can't get her to visit, I may go back next weekend. I guess I've been trying to avoid a showdown." He drank some wine. More discussion of his domestic problems had all the appeal of a root canal, but he kept discarding alternative topics as too incendiary.

"The *Times* sent me to Mexico City two years ago," he said, confident he'd found something safe. "A piece about the assassination of a local politician." A sudden wariness in Ava's face made him move quickly to his point. "Tiled building fronts,'' he said. ''I noticed them on a lot of the old buildings. One place was completely covered with blue-and-white tiles. It had all this ornate plaster—''

''The Wedding Cake House,'' she said. ''Hand-painted, twice-fired, tin-glazed ceramic tiles. They were brought to Mexico from Talavera, Spain. Blue and white were the predominant colors, but green, yellow and red were also popular. Quit pretending you want to talk about my art.''

''I thought we already established this,'' he said. ''I do.''

''Liar.''

''I don't want to offend you. Not that I'm *not* interested in tiles—''

''But you'd rather dig around for dirt.''

Irritated suddenly, he set his wineglass on the table. ''Listen, Ava. We can talk about whatever you want to talk about. If it's art, that's fine. I don't know a whole lot about it, but I'm always interested in learning. If you want to talk about other things, that's fine, too. But I'm not going to sit here censoring everything I say for fear of upsetting you. Your father asked me to dinner and that's why I'm here. Period.''

''Sorry. I asked for that.''

He waved away her apology. ''I just wanted to establish some ground rules.''

''Ask me anything.''

''You won't toss your wine in my face?''

''I promise.''

''So.'' He glanced at her diamond. ''You're engaged to a wonderful man—''

''My father told you that?''

''Your father and a couple of other people in town.''

She laughed, but one ankle was moving and her fingers whitened around the stem of her glass. ''You go around Avalon asking about me?''

''Absolutely. I collar complete strangers on the street and

say, "'Tell me everything you know about Ava Lynsky.' And they tell me she's wonderful, warm, a brilliant artist—"

"Stop. You were going to say Catalina Princess."

"So, anyway, Talevara tiles come from Spain, huh?"

"Sorry again. It's actually Ingrid's fault. She says reporters were like pigs digging for truffles and—"

"You heard me oink."

"No, I don't think of you that way. Really. I like you and that's the truth. Actually you kind of remind me of Rob. My husband. He died—"

"Ava!" Sam Lynsky bellowed from inside the house. "Dinner ready?"

CHAPTER EIGHT

"DAD." AVA FELT AS IF she were emerging from a daze. She came in from the deck and now, blinking in the bright light of the kitchen, she looked pointedly at the clock, then at her father. He pulled the blue nylon parka he was wearing up over his head and threw it onto a chair. His turquoise T-shirt said "St. Anne's Maternity Home." She eyed it for a moment, the slightly scooped neck, the generous cut, and shook her head.

"What?" Sam said.

"It's a maternity shirt, Dad." Scott had just entered the kitchen, too, and she caught his look of amusement. Her father, emptying a brown paper sack of oranges into a blue enamel bowl he'd set on the counter, seemed unperturbed. "He does it to get attention," she said to Scott.

"I do not," her father said. "It's a perfectly functional shirt that I picked up at the auxiliary thrift store for ten cents. You'd prefer it if I spent twenty-five or thirty dollars on a Ralph Lauren? Where's Ed?"

"He had a business meeting." Sam's glance had taken in her nightshirt and the wineglass in her hand, and as though he'd caught her doing something she shouldn't, she felt compelled to offer an explanation. "Scott came early and we got talking and—"

"Where is that thrift store?" Scott broke in. "I've been looking for one. I thought I'd have to go back to L.A. to stock up on shirts."

Ava folded her arms across her chest and fixed Scott with

a look. Earlier, checking him out—and very definitely liking what she saw—she'd noted the Eddie Bauer logo above the back pocket of his jeans, the small red polo player on his cotton shirt. She nodded at his shirt. "That doesn't exactly say thrift store."

"Fifty cents," Scott said. "Pants were a dollar twenty-five."

Ava shook her head. Her father, grinning broadly as if he'd won the lottery and found a new best friend, to boot, was over at the refrigerator pulling out beer. Scott, also looking pretty content, sat backward on one of the chairs, arms resting on the top. He winked at Ava. She looked away, got very busy reheating the stroganoff.

It was kind of scary how good this felt. The kitchen, warm with the savory aroma of simmering beef; her father telling Scott now about the Anita O'Day album he'd found just the other day; and Scott countering with a find of his own: a Dave Brubeck he'd been searching for. If Scott hadn't been there, she and Sam would be bickering about something or other: Sam's rolling in at eight, when he'd said seven; her cottage and its state of disrepair. Everything would feel cold and tense and sad with Diana's presence floating restlessly about them. Ava took a tub of sour cream from the fridge and stirred it into the sauce. Right now she couldn't feel Diana, and the thought disturbed her.

Her father and Scott were still talking thrift shops when she turned from the stove to see Scott watching her. He smiled and she felt a rush of warmth up the sides of her neck. Conscious suddenly of her bare legs, she excused herself, tore up the stairs and threw on the white shirt she'd discarded earlier, pulled on her jeans. It would be very easy to fall into something with Scott—bed for starters. She felt...sensitized, erotic. She imagined feeding him strips of beef, his tongue on her fingers.

"Ava," Sam called from downstairs, "you've got two

hungry men down here. Any minute now, I'm going to microwave that frozen rabbit."

"I'll be right there." Still buttoning the shirt, she raced down the stairs, stood at the bottom for a moment to catch her breath and push her hair around. "My father's been threatening me with that damn rabbit," she told Scott as she walked into the kitchen. "He got it on sale in Von's and it grosses me out. I am not going to cook it," she told her father, "so you might as well get rid of it."

"*I'll* cook it," Sam said.

"What's wrong with rabbit?" Scott asked. "My grand-mother was from Germany. She used to make *hasenpfeffer*. It was great."

"Rabbit stew," Sam smacked his lips. "You got the recipe for it?"

"I don't need a recipe." Scott tapped his forehead. "It's up here."

"Great," Sam said. "Come over one night and we'll have it for dinner."

"That's a deal," Scott grinned at Ava. "Want to join us?"

"No, thank you." She looked sternly from one man to the other. "You two are a very bad combination. And you—" she stuck her finger in Scott's chest "—are not allowed to encourage him."

THE FOLLOWING MORNING Ed stopped by, as he always did on Saturday mornings, to take her out for lunch. Ava wasn't ready. She'd awoken around seven from an erotic dream about Scott, thrown on jeans and a work shirt and was deep into organizing the space in her studio when Ed knocked at the front door.

"Did you forget?" he asked.

She raked her fingers through her hair. "Kind of. I've been putting stuff away and…" With a sweep of her arm at the still-minimally-furnished living room, she smiled at him. "What do you think?"

Ed folded his arms across his chest. Sunlight glinted on his smooth blond hair. "It's small," he said. "Are you sure you'll have enough room?"

"Small. That's all you can say?"

He peered at her. "Are you in a bad mood for some reason?"

"I wasn't."

"Well, Ava, this house was your decision. I didn't feel it was a wise one and I'm sure your father had plenty of reservations."

"This has nothing to do with my father."

"My point exactly. It's *your* decision, but you can hardly expect unbridled enthusiasm for what you've done." He glanced at his watch. "You'd better go and shower. I told my mother we'd drop by—"

"Ed don't *tell* me to go and shower. I think I can figure out whether I need a shower. I'm not..." She stopped. "Would you mind if I didn't go with you? I've got a lot to do and I could really use the time."

Ed looked at her as if she'd suggested a quick trip to the moon. "Where's your ring?" he finally asked.

She glanced down at her left hand. "I took it off last night when I washed."

"Where is it now?"

"On the bathroom sink, I guess. I'll get it." In the bathroom, she found the ring and brought it back to show him. "Look." She slipped it back on her finger. "Happy?"

He tipped his finger under her chin. "It's not an issue of whether *I'm* happy, Ava. It's whether *you're* happy."

"I honestly don't know how I feel," she said before she had time to change her mind. "But when I think about us getting married, it's like this door slams."

Ed frowned. "Have you discussed this with the therapist?"

"No." She glanced down at the ring. Her heart had started racing, but if she didn't do this now, she never would. With one quick move, she twisted the ring off again and held it out to him. "You're terrific and wonderful and I love you, but you deserve more."

Ed looked momentarily confused, but quickly rallied. "I haven't the faintest idea what you're talking about, but let's discuss this when you're thinking more clearly."

She looked at him. Had he always been this condescending and…paternalistic? "My thinking is fine, Ed." *I'm just ready to toss out my security blanket,* she thought.

SCOTT SPENT SUNDAY morning cycling across the rugged interior of the island. Sunday evening he cleaned his apartment, had two long and generally positive telephone conversations with Ellie and spent a couple of hours lining up stories for next week's issue. Monday morning he called Ava to suggest that the art program she taught at Camp Breatheasy would make an interesting feature. Ava had sounded pleased to hear from him and said she was teaching a class that afternoon.

Now as he stood at the back of the large wooden crafts cabin, watching her hold up sepia-tone pictures of the Catalina Pottery Plant, he found it necessary to remind himself that he was here to do a story. He'd get distracted by her face. The sharp, longish nose, the red mouth smiling now, the tumble of black hair. She was clearly enjoying herself, her expression animated as she moved about the cabin, answering questions, handing around adobe bricks for the kids to see.

They were all seated on the floor, listening attentively but clearly eager to get their hands in the tub of red clay that Ava had promised them they would turn into designs of their choosing. Henri, who apparently went everywhere Ava went, seemed less enthralled and was slumbering in a patch of sunshine. Ellie would like Henri, Scott thought. She might even like Ava, too. He glanced at her left hand. *The diamond was gone.*

"Artists have been making tiles on Catalina since the 1920s," Ava was telling the kids. "And the story of how they came to discover the clay is quite interesting. Does anyone know who William Wrigley was?"

"He invented chewing gum," a boy called out.

Ava smiled. "Well, I'm not sure he actually invented it, but one rainy day, Mr. Wrigley and another man were out driving around the Avalon golf course when their cart got stuck in the clay. As they tried to free it, one of the men noticed that the clay was a kind of adobe. Who can tell me what adobe is used for?"

Scott dragged his thoughts away from Ava's ringless left hand, flipped his notebook open and recorded her answer. The clay had been used for Catalina's growing building needs, including the red tiles of the Casino, she said. He found himself interested despite the distraction of glancing up occasionally to catch Ava looking directly at him. He made a mental note to take a tour of the Casino.

"The clay had exactly the right texture and flexibility to make ceramic products," Ava told the children, "and soon many talented ceramic artisans came to Catalina to design decorative tile and pottery. The tiles were distinctive for their incredible jewel-like colors, green, red and blue. Today, you can see examples of their work all over the island, embedded in walls, stairways, planter boxes."

"I saw a mermaid," a small girl called out, "in the Casino."

"Exactly." Ava smiled. "That's a great example. The benches along Casino Walk also have some beautiful hand-painted tiles with scenes of Catalina. Another one I'm sure you've all seen is the Sombrero Fountain, which was designed in the mid 1930s.''

She glanced across the heads of the children to look directly at Scott again, and he vaguely recalled her mentioning the fountain when he'd interviewed her at the Descanso Beach Club. His interest in tiles had taken a quantum leap since then. He scribbled ''Sombrero Fountain,'' planning to add it to his list of things to check out. He'd actually noticed it already, mostly because it sat right in the middle of Crescent, almost opposite the Pleasure Pier, and everyone had been clicking cameras at it. The benches hadn't registered.

''Where can I see some of your work?'' he asked after Ava had given the kids blocks of clay to mold.

''Mostly in my studio right now. I've got a huge commission that's nearly due, and so far all I've done is discard things and tear out my hair.''

''That's happened to me on occasion,'' he said. ''It's called being blocked.''

Ava looked at him. ''How do you deal with it?''

''A lot of staring into space. Unless I have a deadline, in which case I just plow on and hope something comes from it all.''

''So far that hasn't worked for me.''

''Blocks sometimes happen for a reason. Something's happening on a subconscious level that's screwing up the creative process. If you can figure out what the problem is, it might unblock you.''

Her eyes turned wary.

''I'm not saying that's happening with you, I'm just saying…'' He scratched the back of his neck. Clearly he'd taken yet another land-mined-filled route. ''Tiles,'' he said. ''Tell me everything you know.''

She poked her finger at his chest.

''What?'' he asked.

"It must be hell trying to hold a conversation with me."

"It has its challenges."

"Sorry."

"You're forgiven."

She glanced at the dog, who was engaged in a vigorous cleaning of his nether regions, then looked out the window at a couple of kids playing tag. "My father was asking about you this morning. I told him you were coming up here to do a story, and he said you might as well stick around for the campfire tonight."

"Will you be here?"

A smile played around her mouth. "Actually it's my night to cook dinner. I do volunteer kitchen duty at the camp once a week." She started gathering up the sepia pictures spread out across the table. "See you."

HER FACE WARM, Ava headed over to the camp infirmary to look for her father. Scott had smiled his inscrutable smile and gone off to take pictures of kids headed for a field trip. She told herself not to think about him. Abandoning the security blanket didn't mean abandoning caution entirely. Sam wasn't in the infirmary and no one had seen him.

In the modern, low-beamed kitchen cabin, all chrome-plated industrial appliances and granite counters, she kneaded a small mountain of bread dough into submission. While the bread was rising, she poured herself a diet soda and carried it out to the patch of grass in the center of the camp where a couple of kids were throwing balls for Henri. The fifteen cabins were grouped in a clearing on ten acres of gently sloping scrub oak and toyon. She'd been a freshman at UCLA, her first extended time away from Catalina, when her father had built the first cabin on land his grandfather left him. The following year, he'd built a lodge with a dining hall, shower and toilet facilities, a boat shed and, in the midst of a stand of gray-green eucalyptus, an arts-and-crafts center.

By the time she graduated and returned to the island, parents of asthmatic children from all over the country, were angling to send their kids to Camp Breatheasy to swim, sail and fish in the clear waters of the coves at the base of the camp, ride horses and participate in evening sing-alongs while learning from the legendary Dr. Sam how to effectively manage their asthma.

Ingrid had once planned to join their father in practice—and then he'd intervened in her relationship with a guy from the mainland and she'd dropped out of medical school and barely spoken a civil word to her father since. Ava was thinking about this when her cell phone rang. Ingrid, of course. It happened so often, this telepathy, that it hardly seemed remarkable anymore.

"Mom's study is all locked up," Ingrid said. "I went over there this morning and the door was bolted."

"Bolted? There wasn't even a lock on it before."

"Well, there is now. You didn't notice it when you were there last?"

"No. The door was closed, but I don't remember seeing a bolt." Ava lay back on the grass, feeling suddenly beleaguered. Three nights now since she'd had the dream and no panic attack for a while, but it was there, she could feel it. Something dark and frightening, lying in wait to catch her unawares.

"Did you check with Dad?" she asked Ingrid, already knowing the answer.

"Would you, Ava? Please? If I ask him, I'll sound all suspicious and there's no way he'd ever tell me what's going on."

"D'you ever think that's because there *is* nothing going on?" Ava said. "You know Dad, he probably just found an old bolt and decided to use it on Mom's office. He could just as easily have bolted the kitchen or one of the bed-rooms.''

''I think it's weird,'' Ingrid said.

''I gave Ed his ring back,'' Ava said.

''It's taken you long enough. The guy at the *Argonaut?*''

''No.'' She picked at her nail. ''Of course not.''

Ingrid sighed. ''I don't know why you even bother trying to lie to me. You know damn well I can read your mind. Even over the phone.''

Ava grinned.

''But don't make more problems for yourself. It's kind of naive to think the *Argonaut* guy isn't just looking for a story…''

INGRID'S COMMENT PUT AVA in a bad mood for the rest of the afternoon. Her mood didn't improve when she discovered the kitchen cabin was out of detergent for the dishwasher and Sam hadn't reordered. She could already hear his voice when she told him they were out. *''Damn dishwashers. What's wrong with washing dishes by hand, anyway? Your mother used to run it half-full. If you had to pay the water bill, I'd tell her…''*

From there, her thoughts drifted to what Ingrid had said about Diana's study being bolted. Ingrid was paranoid, she decided. Sam had always been the way he was right now. Always finding odd things that he had no particular use for. Invariably they'd end up in the house, where Diana would eventually pitch them. Ingrid needed to get a grip. An image of the clean and tidy kitchen counters in the big house flashed across her mind. As if she was there now, she recalled the weird sense she'd had in the house last week.

Damn Ingrid and her suspicions. She wasn't about to buy into them. She strode off to the infirmary.

Sam still wasn't there.

Tension clawed at her shoulders. She called for Henri

and they walked down the hillside from the camp, followed a trail for a mile or so, then climbed back up the hill. Deep in thought, she approached the camp, ducked beneath a stand of massive palms and started for the kitchen cabin. Almost hidden beneath the spreading branches of a giant palm, she spotted a couple deep in conversation.

Henri, on the scent of something, had taken off across the field. The pair didn't look up as she passed. In a brief glance Ava registered the woman's long dark hair and bare white knees. Shadows hid the man's face. As she pushed open the heavy wooden door of the cabin, something made her look back at the couple. The man, who had turned and was looking now toward the cabin, was her father.

Inside the kitchen cabin, Henri back at her side, Ava breathed very slowly. If she kept breathing very slowly and focused on her breathing, she could stop the panic rising now like a tide inside her. She fixed her eyes on the edge of the counter. God, she couldn't breathe! Her heart was racing and she couldn't breathe and the walls were shrinking and she wanted to run from the cabin. *Breathe,* she told herself. *Breathe, breathe, breathe.*

By the time her father burst into the kitchen nearly thirty minutes later, his face wreathed in smiles, eyes and cheeks bright, she'd got two pies into the oven and the panic attack under control. Sam wore old jeans and a black T-shirt that read "Look Who Turned 30." About the age, it occurred to her, of the woman she'd just seen him with.

A low, simmering anger made her heart race again. She wanted to hurl accusations, pound on his chest, scream at him. Everything would change if she did. Pent-up resentment, unacknowledged grudges would spill out, forever poisoning their relationship. Unable to look him in the eye, she grabbed a sponge and wiped the counter.

"Hi, Princess. Hi, lazy beast." He nudged Henri with his toe, then looked at Ava. "What's cooking?"

"Pies." She did her best to ignore her father as he tore around the kitchen. A wave of perpetual motion, he pulled open the oven door, scraped a spatula around a bowl of chocolate filling, returned to the stove to lift the lid of a saucepan. He huffed and puffed and chattered and sang, interrupting himself to issue a string of run-on questions. "Can we make something special for the sing-along tonight? What about s'mores? Did you order maraschino cherries? Did you talk to Ingrid? Did the pharmacist call? Did you invite Steve to dinner?"

"Scott."

"Steve. Scott. Knew it had one syllable. Did he sit in on your class? Think I'll rope him into helping build the new cabin. He could use the money. Is Ed coming? Where did I leave—"

"Ed's not coming," she snapped. "And I'm sure Scott doesn't need you to worry about his finances."

Sam was either ignoring her or he hadn't heard. He continued his storm around the kitchen, singing and yakking until she couldn't stand it any longer.

"Dad, for God's sake—"

"Heard a good thing about you today," he said. His smile broadened as he launched into a tale of how, earlier in the day, he'd overheard a couple of tourists admiring the tiled mural on a restaurant in town and how excited they'd been to learn from him that the artist was his daughter. "Can you tell that I'm just a little proud of you?"

Ava felt herself teetering between the urge to scream and pound on his chest and the equally strong impulse to fling her arms around his neck and tell him she loved him no matter what. She did neither. Outside, she could hear the voices of counselors herding kids into the dining hall. She glanced up at the clock on the wall. Dinner wasn't for twenty-five minutes. After that Sam would be caught up in the whirl of evening activities. She leaned her back against the counter, watched as he dragged a five-gallon drum of ice cream from the bottom drawer of the industrial freezer.

"Dad, what the hell are you doing?"

"Making banana splits. The kids have been asking for them."

"*Before* dinner?"

"Why not? What's wrong with having dessert first? Makes life more exciting."

"I made pies for dessert."

"Pie and ice cream. What's wrong with that?"

Ava took a deep breath. "How come you locked up Mom's study?"

He looked at her. "Why are you bringing that up now?"

"Because I want to know. Mom's got some things we…I'd like to look at. Boxes of photos, papers."

"Ingrid put you up to this?"

"No one put me up to anything." Simmering anger threatened to boil over. "I have a right to look through Mom's things. Ingrid and I both do. You're not the damn palace guard."

"I don't have time to get them for you right now."

"I don't need you to get them for me. I need the key."

"I don't have it."

"Where is it?"

"I'll find it."

"Dammit, Dad." Ava ground her teeth. "Why does everything have to be so difficult with you?"

"What's difficult?"

"Everything about you. Just tell me where the key is and let's drop it, okay?"

"I want to go through her papers myself before you and Ingrid start pawing through them."

"Well, what's taking you so long? It's been three months, for God's sake."

"Haven't had time. You want to take over my practice?

See patients? Run the camp? Oversee the volunteer staff? Chop wood, clear brush?''

"You could, of course, just hire more help," Ava said.

"We've been over this before," Sam said. "Hired help would destroy the spirit. No family feeling. Everyone complaining about overtime and benefits. If you're too busy to help out, just say so. I don't want some halfhearted effort—''

"We're not talking about *my* schedule, Dad. I'm not the one who's too busy to find a damn key." She leaned against the counter. "You seemed to have plenty of time today. Who was that woman you were talking to, anyway?" In the beat of silence she watched her father calmly scooping out ice cream and putting it into a line of small plastic bowls he'd set out across the counter. Her heart was beating so hard it made her voice shake. "You were so engrossed you didn't even notice me, did you?"

The smile had gone, but he went on filling the dishes. "I thought I asked you to order more maraschino cherries. We were out last time I looked."

Rage swept through her like a brushfire. Fueled by his implacability, its intensity stunned her. In an instant she was in front of him, in his face, her whole body shaking. For a second she considered grabbing the scoop from him, hurling it across the room.

"Goddammit, Dad, don't I deserve an answer? Mom's only been gone three months and you're sitting in a damn park with some woman my age, maybe younger, and you're so wrapped up in each other, a bomb could have gone off."

Without a word, he crossed to the refrigerator and pulled the door open. His back to her, he peered inside the shelves, moving jars and bottles around. "Write down maraschino cherries," he said over his shoulder. "It's not a banana split without maraschino cherries."

LYNSKY FINALLY MENTIONED the book again. Scott had been in the dining hall waiting for the kids to file through the chow line before he filled his own plate. Lynsky had squeezed his shoulder and asked to be reminded about some papers he wanted to give Scott. "You'll need them for the biography," the doctor had said. Before Scott could respond, Lynsky was gone, and there hadn't been another chance to talk to him.

Now, sitting cross-legged around the campfire watching Dr. Sam entertain the kids, Scott felt a reluctant admiration for the man. The young campers obviously adored him and the feeling was mutual. Lynsky was in his element, leading the kids in song as he doled out sacks of popcorn. His hands wrapped around a mug of hot chocolate, Scott watched sparks from the fire shoot high into the dark sky. Something about Lynsky reminded him of his own father. Same exuberant enthusiasm, even the same hyperkinetic verbal style. He'd been twelve when his father died—too concerned about being seen as childish to openly grieve, but watching Lynsky now, he realized the void that was left in his life.

On the other side of the circle, the doctor, his face red in the fire's glow, had launched into a story about how as a boy he'd helped his father build a roping arena for the horses the family kept on their ranch in the island's mountainous interior. Scott watched the kids watching the doctor, their expressions rapt. Lynsky's nonstop avalanche of words, the arm waving and gesticulation, all seemed to swell his presence, giving him a larger-than-life quality that made him as entertaining to watch as to listen to.

"Anyone want to guess what we needed to spread on the ground for the horses to run on?" Lynsky asked. The kids started calling out their answers. "Grass?" "Leaves?" "Concrete?" "Buffalo dung?" At that, all the kids went, "Ewww." "Sand," a little kid in a Camp Breatheasy baseball hat called out.

Smiling widely, Lynsky looked around at the gathered faces. "Who said that? Give him a double order of popcorn. Never mind, I'll do it." Groaning theatrically, he raised himself off the ground, grabbed a bag of popcorn from a wicker basket and made a sweeping bow as he presented it to the grinning boy. "Very good, that's *exactly* what we used. Sand. And you know where we had to get the sand from?"

"The beach!" the kids yelled in unison.

Lynsky slapped his forehead in mock frustration. "Hey, you guys are too smart. That's *exactly* where we had to get it from. We had to drive big trucks down to the beach at Two Harbors, shovel in the sand—" he pantomimed hauling heavy shovels of sand "—then drive it *all* back." Another theatrical groan. "It was hard, hard work, let me tell you."

A woman next to Scott, who'd been smiling as widely as the young campers, leaned over to bring her face close to Scott's ear. "Isn't he amazing? I swear to God, I've never seen anyone like him with kids."

Scott nodded, still half listening to Lynsky describe a roundup of wild horses from the interior of the island. Just as he started to raise his hand to ask how the horses came to the island—he'd decided it wasn't fair for adults just to butt in—Lynsky explained that they were descendants of horses left behind by Spanish explorers.

"He's like, I don't know, totally in touch with what it's like to be a kid," the woman was whispering. "I mean, when he's with kids, it's like he's a kid himself."

Scott waited until Lynsky had wrapped up his story and the counselors were herding the kids toward the horseshoe of cabins on the far side of the field before he turned to look at the woman. "You have a child here?"

"Yeah, that's her over there. Courtney." She pointed to a girl whose long blond hair flew around her face as she dodged behind a tree, laughing and trying to escape the counselor's outstretched arm. "A year ago she couldn't walk across the room without needing her puffer. Dr. Sam's done wonders with her. I swear the man's a saint."

Scott asked the woman her name and jotted it down in his notebook, then pulled himself to his feet. "Saint" might have been pushing it a bit, he thought as he brushed shredded bark off his jeans, but in the evening he'd spent at the camp, talking to parents, listening to Lynsky describe his work with asthmatic children, he had a better understanding of why the residents of Avalon held the doctor in such high regard. In fact, as Scott headed over to the golf cart for the ride back into town, he was already thinking about the book's first chapter. Tomorrow, he decided, he would call Lynsky to set up an appointment to iron out details.

CHAPTER NINE

WITH HENRI AT HER HEELS, Ava carried a plastic bag of garbage from the kitchen to the Dumpster at the back of the camp and tried to decide whether to walk to Ingrid's— six miles over rough interior terrain—and spend the night there, or find someone to drive her back into Avalon. She'd driven up with her father, but was in no mood to ride back with him. As she heaved the trash into the Dumpster, she remembered that Sam had invited Scott to stay for the campfire.

She ran back to the kitchen cabin, grabbed her purse and went to look for him. The counselors were attempting to get the kids into their cabins, and she spotted her father piggy-backing a blond-haired boy. The boy was laughing and thumping Sam's back and urging him forward. Ava ducked around a tree, clicked her fingers at the dog, who'd gone off to investigate a stump, and headed over to the parking area. Her father's battered Jeep was parked there and, next to it, a yellow golf cart, where Scott sat in the driver's seat, an open notebook on his knee. Head bent, he was so engrossed in whatever he was writing that he didn't hear her approach.

She came up beside him. He wore a red Camp Breath-easy T-shirt he hadn't had on earlier. The shirt surprised her somehow. She would have expected him to remain aloof, but here he was, already in her father's entourage. Or maybe she was just feeling surly.

"Boo!"

"Hey." His eyes widened and he closed the notebook. "What's up?"

"Henri and I need a ride back into town."

"Sure." He patted the passenger seat. "Hop in. I wondered where you'd got to. I thought you'd be at the campfire."

Disconcerted by the swift little thrill at the thought of Scott thinking about her, she climbed into the cart. Henri jumped in after her, sitting bolt upright on the seat and taking up so much room that she was pushed over to Scott's side. With one arm around the dog and the other over the back of Scott's seat, she held on as he maneuvered the vehicle around the steep curves of Old Stage Road.

"Do you ever get lost out here?" Scott asked.

She shook her head. "I've lived here forever, remember? Anyway, this is the only road through the interior. It cuts across the island, Avalon on one end and Two Harbors on the other, which if you've never been there is the most fantastic camping spot in the world." Self-conscious suddenly, she glanced at him again. "I only sound as though I work for the Chamber of Commerce."

"Maybe you would give me an insider's tour of Catalina sometime," he said after a while. "So far, all I've seen is the tourist stuff—the Casino, the Botanical Gardens, the Holly Street House—"

"Which a man by the name of Peter Gano built for his fiancée," Ava said. "But she refused to leave her society friends in Pasadena, so he spent the rest of his life living there alone. Her loss, I say."

"I bet you know dozens of trivia like that."

"It might be trivia to you," she said, "but it's—"

"Part of your heritage."

She smiled. This felt good, she decided. Good to be bumping along the road with him, a crescent moon overhead, the night air on her face cooling the anger inside.

Good to feel the little charge that flickered like a current between them. "Did you know there's no gambling in the Casino?" she asked, perky as a tour guide.

"Actually, I did. Casino is an Italian word for…a place of entertainment or something?"

"Very good. You obviously read the brochures. That's *exactly* what it means."

"You sounded *exactly* like your father just then," he said.

"Hmm." Ava's smile faded. "Rubs off, I guess."

"It wasn't a criticism, Ava." He glanced at her. "So where were you tonight? Working?"

"Cooking, cleaning," she said. *Working off the anger at my father.* "My mother used to do most of the cooking. I'm just filling in until he figures out how to replace her." An image of her father talking to the woman tonight flashed across her brain. She saw the woman's white knees. Maybe he'd been auditioning for a replacement.

"Your father's quite a character," Scott said. "He's got a real knack with the kids. He's teaching them, but he never talks down or lectures, and he's clearly having a great time into the bargain."

Ava curled her fingers in Henri's curly coat. She was not in the mood to hear tributes to her father. For a while they lurched along the rutted road in silence. Every so often the cart's headlights caught a pair of bright eyes in the scrub, or the swift movement of an animal darting across the road.

"So how do you like Catalina so far?" she finally asked.

"Interesting. I still wake up every morning with the feeling that I'm on an extended trip to Disneyland."

"Well, you said you wanted to feel optimistic again," she said, remembering their conversation over breakfast. "Disneyland is supposed to be the happiest place on earth, right?"

He grinned, his teeth white in the darkness. "That's illusion. I'm looking for the real thing."

"How would you know if you found it?"

He shrugged. "Don't know." A pause. "What about you?"

Her arm across the back of Scott's seat was going numb. "I'm already deliriously happy."

Scott turned his head to look at her. "Why don't you drop that crap, Ava?"

She removed her arm from the back of his seat. "Drop what crap?"

"The arch, guarded stuff. I've had…seven, eight conversations with you, and only once did I get the sense that I was seeing the real you."

"You've actually counted the number of conversations we've had?" She couldn't decide whether this pleased or alarmed her. "And what? You made notes afterward?"

"No notes. I'm just intrigued. You paint this idyllic image of your life, but I get the feeling that you don't believe it yourself."

"You're a reporter." Her mood took a sharp downturn. "Let me tell you a little bit about what it's like to be on the other side. After my mother's accident, we probably had five calls from reporters on the mainland wanting to know if she was happy, if my father beat her, if they owed money, if she was suicidal, if she staged her own disappearance. On and on. No one seems able to accept that it was an accident."

"But if you're satisfied it was an accident—"

"See, that's exactly what I mean. You have that tone in your voice."

"I apologize for the tone," he said.

"Skip it. I keep getting caught off guard by you, and then something jerks me back to reality. You're looking for a story, the more bizarre the better. You don't care that my parents were childhood sweethearts. That there was never anyone else for either of them. That they were planning a second honeymoon to Greece. There's no drama in that, is there.''

''You have a problem, you know that?''

''Right, a problem with you. I knew guys like you at UCLA. Cynical, think you've seen it all. Incapable of believing that happy marriages actually exist or that people really can be content and well-adjusted. It goes against your jaded version of things, doesn't it? Well, let me tell you something. If you spend your life lifting rocks, you're going to uncover a bunch of worms. It's pretty much a given.'' Embarrassed by her outburst, she fumbled around on the dashboard. *Who exactly am I trying to convince?*

Scott swerved to avoid a rut. ''Your fiancé decided not to come, then?''

She glanced down at her bare ring finger, then decided now wasn't the moment to announce her broken engagement. ''It kind of looks that way, doesn't it?''

''And he didn't come to dinner at your father's, either.''

''And your daughter would like you and your ex-wife to get back together.'' Henri had slumped into a sleeping heap across her lap. She shifted her knees slightly under him. ''If I want to be psychoanalyzed, I'll seek professional help. Likewise, if I feel the need to discuss my private life with a reporter, I'll add your name to the list. I have to warn you, though, you're facing stiff competition.''

After that they bumped along in silence.

''Where do I drop you?'' Scott asked as they drove into town.

''Right here's fine.'' As Scott brought the golf cart to a stop, she grabbed Henri's collar to stop him from jumping out. ''I can walk the rest of the way. She climbed out and glanced briefly back at him. Thank you for the ride.''

''You're welcome, Ava,'' he said, and drove off.

AFTER THAT FIASCO, Scott made it a point to avoid Ava. Not easy in a small town like Avalon, and the fact that he didn't run into her made him suspect she was doing a little avoiding of her own. Maybe it was best. Unless they tiptoed around, exchanging superficialities, something that didn't interest him, he was bound to upset her. But for days after the ride, she stayed a constant presence in his brain. Impossible not to think about her or to sort out his conflicted feelings.

One afternoon he found Carolyn and Mark in their usual spot on the couch. They provided a convenient sounding board. Carolyn had a new theory.

"Okay, this is a good one," she said. "See, Ava really believes her mother committed suicide. She's scared that if you dig around enough, you'll come to the same conclusion, and all the stuff about how happy the mother was will turn out to be a bunch of hoo-ha."

He shrugged, got a beer from the fridge and slumped down in front of the TV. Carolyn waved her hand in front of his face.

"Hey. Look at me."

"What?"

"Quit moping about her."

He brushed her hand away. "I'm not."

"She's a princess."

"Knock it off, okay?"

"You don't need another princess." Carolyn sat on the arm of his chair. "Plus, this one has money. You can't afford her."

"I can't afford you, either," he said.

She punched his arm. "Jerk. I'm going to get a job. I'm just waiting for an employer who will appreciate my unique qualities."

Scott glanced at Mark, who was grinning broadly. "So

in other words, you're going to be freeloading here for the foreseeable future.''

''Hey, Scott, maybe you should marry this Ava chick,'' Mark said. ''Think of it as helping out your needy family.''

''Hey, cool,'' Carolyn said. ''You could write a book about it, Mark. The Princess and the Paupers.''

Scott shook his head at her, finished his beer and went to bed. He could come up with any number of reasons Ava Lynsky was not relationship material, but it had taken every bit of effort he could muster not to apologize and suggest that they stop somewhere for a drink and talk things over. He'd had to drive away quickly before he changed his mind. Plus, he'd felt like a hypocritical jerk—still did—grilling her when his own life was hardly a textbook example of harmonious adjustment.

But after a week of battling to keep his distance, he gave up the fight. Around ten o'clock he walked into town and called her from the pay phone in the lobby of the Bay View Hotel. Her voice sounded sleepy, or maybe she'd been crying, he couldn't tell.

''I'm sitting at a bar watching a party of tourists get slowly drunker,'' he said. ''There's a game on the TV over the bar that I couldn't care less about, I'm bored to death with my own company, and I thought maybe you'd take pity on me and join me for a drink. I've never had a drink with a real live Catalina Princess before.''

''She no longer exists,'' Ava said.

''Were you asleep?''

''No.''

''So?''

''Right now I don't think I'd be very good company,'' she said.

''I'll take my chances,'' he said. ''If you're not, I'll make you pay for your own drink.'' Silence on the line. ''Are you okay? Sorry, I forgot you don't like that question, but really, are you? Can I do anything?''

"No," she said. "Thank you."

"How's the work going?" Maybe she just wanted him to get off the phone and leave her alone, but he sensed something was wrong and it made him push on. "Did you get unblocked?" He heard a long sigh. "Ava?"

"I'm fine. Really."

He didn't believe her. On the other hand, he didn't know her. Maybe she *was* fine.

"Listen, Ava," he said, "I realize that you know absolutely everyone and you've probably got more friends than you know what to do with and I'm just an obnoxious reporter—"

"Stop. I'm the one who needs to apologize for the other night. I'm sorry, really. I should probably lock myself away until I figure out how to deal with people."

"Might be kind of drastic."

"I don't think so."

"Well, if you find yourself in need of someone to talk to, I hope very much you'll think of me."

"Thank you," she said. "You're very sweet."

"Promise?"

"Yes."

And so he went back to the bar, dropped some change on the table where he'd been drinking and set out along Crescent, restless and unhappy. Something about Ava tugged at him and refused to let go. Attractive, privileged, a talented artist whose vibrant work spoke of joyful, uncomplicated happiness, and yet he sensed a disconnect. Ava Lynsky wasn't who she appeared to be. He could tell himself it wasn't his concern, that he had more than enough to deal with in his own life, but his thoughts always returned to her.

The air was cool, the sky a deep midnight-blue. Out in

the harbor, the mast lights twinkled like rows of fireflies, and the Pleasure Pier, which during the day was a garish shade between green and turquoise, stretched out dark and enticing, the glow from small kiosks mirrored in the black water below.

At the El Encanto, a plaza of shops and souvenir stands where Mariachi bands played on the weekends, he slowed to look at the Sombrero Fountain. It stood in the middle of the traffic circle, a circular planter filled with pansies, their color almost black in the streetlight, splashing a plume of water from a bowl-shaped centerpiece. He wanted to take a closer look at the painted tiles, but two girls, probably in their late teens, were sitting on the edge, talking together. One of them looked up and smiled as he approached. He kept on walking. He'd look at the tiles another time.

Restless and, he suddenly realized, ravenous, he returned home and foraged in the fridge for food. Lunch had been a dish of squid risotto that Benjamin had brought over for him to sample.

"Should I put this on the menu?" The hotel manager had asked. He'd been wearing a navy-and-white-striped apron with "Harrod's" printed across the front. "Is it perhaps a touch too…daring?"

"No and yes," Scott had said. After Benjamin left, he'd dumped the mostly uneaten risotto into the trash can under his desk.

The fridge was empty but for a six-pack and an opened can of chili, which sported an impressive green fur coat. Carolyn and Mark had returned to the mainland—for good, Carolyn said. He wasn't holding his breath. In the pantry he found six cans of beef stew and eight boxes of macaroni-and-cheese bought on sale at Von's. He boiled the noodles, stirred in the powdered cheese and wondered how he'd manage if Ellie did come to live with him. He made a mental note to check for an evening cooking class. Maybe he and Ellie could take it together.

The next morning he had a visit from his former in-laws.

The Scaramellis had taken the seven-thirty boat from the mainland and were waiting outside the *Argonaut* office when he arrived for work. Gina, his ex-mother-in-law, wore a purple nylon windbreaker, similarly colored glass earrings and an expression that said she meant business. His one-time brother-in-law, Vinnie, wore a black muscle shirt, running shorts and yellow aviator glasses pushed up on his forehead.

"Laura would kill us if she knew we were here," Gina Scaramelli said, sitting down on the chair in front of Scott's desk. "But someone needs to get things sorted out. Laura's miserable, Scott. It's about time you two stopped behaving like children and worked out your problems."

"My sister still loves you," Vinnie said. "She wants you to come home. So does Ellie."

"Absolutely," Gina agreed. "On the phone this morning she said, 'Grandma, please tell Daddy I want him to come home.'"

"I am home," Scott said. "And Ellie knows she can come here and live with me. That was the original plan."

"You're escaping," Vinnie said. "You got some romantic idea about living on an island and leaving all your responsibilities behind. Well, it won't work."

"We're concerned," Gina said. "No matter what happened between you and Laura, you're still family in our eyes and we worry."

"Well, don't." Scott said. "I'm happy. This is what I want."

Gina rolled her eyes. "For this you give up a good-paying job at the *L.A. Times?* I bet you don't even have health insurance."

Beyond Gina's shoulder, Scott could see out through the

window to the dock where passengers were already starting to board the nine-thirty Catalina Express back to the mainland. "Nine-fifteen," he said. "If you're not at the front of the line, you won't get a window seat."

"We've got time," Gina said. "Worse comes to worst, we'll catch the next boat."

The front door opened and Ava walked in. Scott smiled, forgetting the Scaramellis for a moment, struck by how pleased he was to see her.

She glanced uncertainly at Gina and Vinnie, then looked at Scott. "I brought you some brochures. In case you want to learn a little more about the island. And it was sweet of you to call last night. Sorry I was such a dud, but maybe some other time, okay?"

"Great." He got up, walked around the desk and tripped over Vinnie's outstretched feet. Straightening, he caught Vinnie looking at Ava, openmouthed and all but panting. Gina was giving Ava the narrow-eyed look of someone who'd just put two and two together. He ignored them both. "Thanks," he told Ava. "I appreciate it."

"You're welcome." She fluttered her fingers at him. "See you."

He pulled open the door for her. "Take care."

"You, too," she said with a parting smile over her shoulder.

"Too much eye makeup," Gina said when Scott was back behind his desk again. "And she could lose a few pounds. Did you see how tight those jeans were?"

Vinnie grinned at Scott, then ducked as Gina backhanded him.

Scott, on the verge of a vigorous defense, kept his mouth shut.

"Pigs. Men are all pigs. Your wife's wasting away to skin and bones, and look at you. You're sleeping with her, right? You should be ashamed of yourself. Every night

Laura's crying her eyes out.'' She elbowed Vinnie. ''Tell Scott how your sister sleeps with their wedding picture under her pillow.''

''Laura's your wife.'' Vinnie pushed his yellow aviator glasses higher up on his head, scratched at the hairy expanse of chest above his muscle shirt. ''You shouldn't be running around with other women.''

''Laura's my *ex*-wife.'' Scott resented having to defend himself, but he didn't want them taking back garbage to Ellie—which they probably would anyway. ''The divorce is final. What I do is with my life now is none of your business.''

''Well,'' Gina said. ''Excuse *me*.''

Scott drank some cold coffee from a cup printed with ''World's Greatest Dad''—Ellie's birthday gift to him last year—and started to open the morning mail. The first envelope contained a press release from the Catalina Chow Chatters. ''Welcome to Catalina,'' someone had scrawled in the margin. ''Come to our Thursday chat about chows. The most lovable dogs on the face of the earth!!!''

''Well, listen, you guys,'' he told Gina and Vinnie, ''I have work to do. There's a boat at noon…''

''Where's a place we can get a bite to eat around here?'' Gina had her hands folded across her purse. ''No offense, but that coffee you made tasted just like mud. And if I don't get something in my stomach, my blood sugar's going to drop, and we all know what that means. Tell him, Vinnie.'' She elbowed her son. ''Tell him how I nearly passed out the other day. Where's the little girls' room, Scotty?''

''So, hey.'' Vinnie waited until his mother had left the room and leaned across the desk to leer at Scott. ''You got something going with that babe?''

AFTER SHE'D MADE herself look like an idiot by dropping off tourist brochures for Scott—like he couldn't just pick them up himself if he wanted to—Ava stopped in at the Beehive to meet Ingrid for lunch. They were sitting at the counter on the red-and-chrome swivel stools and she was picking at a salad—she really wanted comfort food, say, an ortega chili-cheeseburger, but she was trying to be good—and tuning in and out of Ingrid's rant about their father. Mostly out, because it wasn't anything she hadn't heard before and also because she really wanted to talk about Scott.

"Dad just drives me nuts," Ingrid was saying. "I'm doing what you said, trying to patch things up. And I just asked him if he still thought about Mom very often. That's it. I mean, it took an effort to even pick up the phone to call him—"

"Which you wouldn't have done except for the key," Ava said. "Not that I'm defending him or anything."

"You're always defending him." Ingrid sipped her iced tea through a straw. "Anyway, he goes on and on about how he doesn't have time to sit around feeling sorry for himself and maybe he'd appreciate a little help up at the camp. Why can't he hire someone? It's not like he can't afford it, but no, he's so damn stubborn. He'd rather make us feel guilty."

"About the diaries," Ava said. "He called this morning. He said he'd leave the key on the rack in the kitchen." She drank some water. Her heart had started racing again. She took a paper napkin from the dispenser, set the glass in the middle of it. "Listen, Ingrid, can we not talk about this right now? I feel as though it's all I ever think about."

"Well, you're the only person I can let off steam to. Everyone else thinks Dad's this saint. He's all smiles and aw-shucks until something doesn't go his way, and then… By the way, I noticed Dad's cleaned the kitchen. *And* he's not wearing his wedding ring."

"Hey," the guy on the stool to Ava's left said, leaning close. "We gotta stop meeting like this."

Ava turned slightly and he grinned as if he knew her. Yellow aviator glasses pushed up on his forehead, gold chains, a muscle top, hairy shoulders and rubber flip-flops. A dude.

"Excuse me?"

"You and me. About forty-five minutes ago. You were down there to see Scott."

"Oh, right." She'd been vaguely aware of two other people in the office. Mostly she'd seen only Scott. "Hi," she said.

He stuck out his hand. "Vinnie Scaramelli. So are you and Scott like…" He waggled his eyebrows. "I mean, not to get personal or anything, but he's kinda already got a wife and…"

Ingrid, on the stool to her right, had stopped midrant to listen.

Ava drank some tea and addressed her sister. "Anyway, you were saying?"

The dude leaned across Ava to speak to Ingrid. "So you girls both live here, huh?"

"Yes." Ava said, thinking about Scott having a wife.

The dude leaned closer. "So, like, you know all the hot spots?"

"Sorry, I don't." Down at the end of the counter, Ava watched Shirley drop some change into the pocket of her apron—striped brown and yellow like her bumblebee earrings. The dude was going on about rum drinks and how some places served cheap rum that gave him a hangover and she wondered how he could possibly imagine she cared. She couldn't quite picture Scott drinking rum with the dude.

"Maybe Dad's got a girlfriend," Ingrid said. "Maybe she cleaned up the kitchen."

"They say Luau Larry's a cool place," the dude said. "This buddy of mine says they do some kind of drink, Wicky Wacker, I think it's called. Last time he was over here, he drank them till he passed out." He leaned closer. "So what do *you* do for fun?"

Ava gave him another blank look and was about to suggest to Ingrid that they leave when Ingrid announced that she was feeling kind of nostalgic for an ortega chili-cheese burger. The dude was grinning at her, waiting for an answer. She couldn't remember the question.

"Ah, come on," he said. "You don't look like the type to sit home playing solitaire. You like dancing? Getting crazy?"

Okay, he was asking for it. "Actually, I ride buffalo," she said.

Ingrid laughed aloud. To her left, the dude grinned as though he hadn't heard properly. "Say what?"

"I like to ride buffalo through the interior of the island."

"You ride buffalo?"

"We both do," Ingrid said.

"Side-saddle, preferably," Ava said, almost enjoying herself now. "And stark naked if the weather's warm enough."

"It creates…a certain bonding," Ingrid said.

"Yeah, right." His face lit in a slow grin. "So listen, you girls got boyfriends or anything?"

"I'm madly in love with a buffalo herder," Ava said.

"Buffalo herder." The dude looked skeptical. "Get outta here."

"His name is Bill," Ingrid said. "And he becomes insanely jealous if Ava so much as looks at another man."

The dude said something Ava didn't quite catch.

"Excuse me?" she said.

"You are full of it, you know that?"

"It's one of the occupational hazards of hanging around buffalo," Ava said.

"That and the smell," Ingrid said.

"I mean it. You are two seriously weird chicks."

Ava smiled. "Thank you. We work hard at it."

The dude threw some bills down on the counter. "You think you're hot stuff, don't you?"

Ava glanced around, just to confirm he meant her and Ingrid and not some other hot stuff who might have just wandered up. "Us?"

"Both of you. You have one hell of an attitude. Scott needs his head examined if he's got something going with you. Let me tell *you* something, lady." He looked directly at Ava. "You're not even good-looking. Come on, Ma," he said to the small dark-haired woman to his left. "Get your butt in gear and we'll make the next boat."

"So Scott's married?" Ingrid asked after the dude had left.

PREDICTABLY THE SCARAMELLIS' account of their visit to Catalina quickly made it back to Laura and Ellie. Scott had been in the shower thinking about Ava and trying not to think about the Scaramellis when the phone rang. He grabbed a towel, wrapped it around his waist and ran dripping to the nightstand. It was Ellie calling from Laura's cell phone. Her voice sounded strange, muffled somehow. "Your voice sounds funny, El," he told her.

"Thanks, Dad. Maybe it's because I'm standing in some stupid gas station and there's all these bums looking at me."

"Where's your mom?" Scott asked, instantly alarmed. "She's not there with you?"

"Yeah, she's here. She went to buy a soda."

"Get in the car and lock the door until she gets back."

"Dad, I'm not a baby."

"Get in the car, El," he said, picturing bums leering at his daughter.

Ellie sighed. "Okay. I'm in the car, the doors are locked. Now can we talk about what I want to talk about?"

"Talk."

"Grandma said you have a girlfriend."

He hesitated for a split second. "Grandma's wrong."

"You sure?"

"Positive."

"Okay, because I have everything all figured out, and if you had a girlfriend, it would screw up everything. Now listen, Dad, and don't say a word until I'm through, okay?"

"Okay."

"Catalina sounds really cool. I got all the postcards you sent."

"It is, Ellie. You'd—"

"Da-ad. I told you not to say anything until I'm finished."

"Sorry."

"Okay, here's what I think. And don't say anything. You like it in Catalina and I'm pretty sure I'd like it. Glendale's getting really gross, all this graffiti everywhere, and my friend Chelsea's moving to Oxnard, so I'm really bummed about that, but I'm going to stay with her for two weeks this summer. Mom said I can take the train, which would be way cool."

With the phone held between his ear and shoulder, Scott toweled off, took some clean underwear from the drawer and didn't interrupt as Ellie moved on to Chelsea's brother Damian, who was also way, *way* cool. He sat on the bed.

"El," he prompted. "You said you had everything figured out?"

"That's what I was getting to, Dad. Mom said she wants to make a new start and I was thinking wouldn't it be way cool if she came to Catalina to live, too— I said don't say anything, Dad…"

CHAPTER TEN

BETWEEN THE DUDE'S COMMENT that Scott had a wife and Scott's comment that she was arch and guarded, Ava had decided to ban Scott from her thoughts. Wife or ex-wife, something about his life suggested unfinished business, and she had more than enough unfinished business in her own life. For starters the looming deadline on her work-in-progress.

She sat at her worktable tracing the outline of a single lupine onto a small square clay tile trying to achieve a Zen-like focus on what she was doing. It wasn't working. The colors looked dull and muddy; her father's voice jangled in her head; last night she'd had the dream again; and every time she went into the bedroom, she saw Scott on the day of the painting party talking about the excitement of the unknown.

She picked up the phone, dialed the *Argonaut,* heard one ring and hung up. Scott wasn't the solution. In the kitchen she picked at the crumbs on the edge of the pan of brownies she'd baked at some ungodly hour this morning after the dream had left her unable to sleep. The truly frustrating part about the creative process was that you couldn't sit down and just command it to happen. *Big project? Needs to be finished yesterday? Tough. I'm not in the mood.* The creative muse simply didn't give a damn.

Two days and she'd done nothing but discard the tiles she'd started to paint. *Figure out what's bothering you,* Scott had said. She laughed. As though she only had to come up with one thing and, presto, the creative juices would flow again. Even when she consciously tried to figure things out, it was like trying to remember a song. The elusive fragment of a tune, a word or two. Enough to hover tantalizingly as you tried to identify it, but not enough for an answer.

She picked up the paintbrush again. Ten minutes and two discarded tiles later, the phone rang. Her father.

"You have a rotted plank on your deck. I'm coming over to fix it."

"I'm trying to work, Dad." She shifted the phone to the other ear. "And while I've got you, what's the deal with the key? Ingrid and I went over to the house and it wasn't on the rack."

"I thought I put it there."

"Well, you didn't. And, Dad, Ingrid's driving me nuts about the damn diaries. Could you please either leave the door unlocked or leave the key. We're coming over tonight."

"I won't be there."

"Fine, leave the key."

"You don't want your deck fixed?"

"Not right now."

"I'm busy. I might not have time to do it when you're ready."

"I'll hire someone to do it."

"Why waste good money? Need to make a list of the other things that need to be fixed. If you'd bought the pharmacist's house like I told you, I wouldn't have all this work to do. Damn house isn't fit for you to live in. It's dangerous. You got a hammer? Five-inch nails? Never mind, I'll bring 'em—"

"I'm busy, I already told you."

"You can work while I'm there."

"No, I can't."

"Well, then, it'll have to be when I get the time to do it."

"Terrific. Bye, Dad." She took a breath, picked up the tile she'd been working on, inspected it for even a hint of something redeemable. Nothing. She tossed it in the galvanized trash can at the side of her table, depressingly half-full of discarded tiles. If her father saw the discarded tiles, he'd rescue them.

Same with food. Once at the camp, she'd thrown away several dozen sandwiches with curling edges left over from the previous day's buffet. He'd rescued them from the trash and eaten them for his lunch the next day. "Can't stand waste," he'd always say as he devoured mushy black bananas, or sulfurous-smelling cheese. Her mother claimed he'd regularly inspect the garbage cans to make sure she hadn't thrown out anything that was still edible. "Edible by his standards," Diana would say with her familiar little smile of amused tolerance.

Ava pushed Sam to the back of her mind. For reassurance that she could actually paint, she studied the row of completed tiles on a shelf above the worktable. Each tile was painted with a different flower or shrub found on the island. St. Catherine's lace, larkspur, lilac, all delicate and beautiful. Their perfection seemed a mockery.

She'd painted them before the accident.

She'd been sitting at her work table tracing the first of the designs commissioned by a Hollywood producer when Diana had called. "I'm not happy, darling," she'd said. "I haven't been for some time. Your father is a wonderful man and I love him dearly, but...well, I really can't go on like this."

Ava had set down the paintbrush and shifted the phone to her other ear. "Listen, Mom, I'll be right over."

"There's no need for that," Diana had said. "I don't want to interrupt your work. I'll be fine."

Now, thinking about that call, Ava remembered the surge of impatience she'd felt. Diana had a flair for dramatic announcements. Even now, Ava could still remember the terror she'd felt at thirteen when Diana had calmly said on Christmas Eve, "All this seasonal jollity is so depressing. I'd take an overdose if it wouldn't ruin things for everyone else."

And Diana had been prey to a range of ailments—migraines, colitis, chronic fatigue and various aches and pains that always seemed to strike her on the day before a significant event. Like the day before Ava married Rob. "I honestly can't see any purpose to my life," Diana had announced as Ava was packing for her honeymoon to Mexico City. Sam had dismissed the remark as just Diana being Diana, but her mother's words had overshadowed the honeymoon. The first night of her married life, she'd awoken thinking about Diana and called home every day just to reassure herself.

The day of Diana's phone call, Ava had set her work aside and gone over to her parents' house. Diana wasn't home, but she'd left a note pinned to the door. "Ava, my love. Gone to have lunch with the girls. Sorry to worry you, darling. But please don't fret. No doubt it's hormones or something."

When she'd called Diana that evening, her mother had given her bright theatrical laugh. "Oh, sweetheart, I *told* you not to worry. Everything is fine. Daddy's here and we're talking about our anniversary tomorrow. Can you believe it will be forty years? We're going to take the boat out for a little sail and have a picnic lunch. Won't that be fun? And Daddy said he has a surprise for me."

After the accident the sheriff's deputy questioned both her and Ingrid. No, they'd both assured him, their mother was happy. Ingrid claimed afterward that she'd still been in shock during the questioning, and if she'd thought about it some more, she might have had a different response.

Their father, too, had assured the deputy that his wife was the happiest woman on Catalina, and if there was any doubt about it, the deputy could ask anyone on the island.

Ava had said nothing about Diana's threats. Given Diana's penchant for drama, she wasn't even sure whether *threat* was the right word. Diana *hadn't* taken her own life. Diana was terrified of water. Sam used to tease her about never learning to swim. The reason she hadn't learned, Diana had once confided to Ava, was fear of putting her face underwater. Once, she'd slipped and fallen into the shallow end of the pool. She'd emerged sputtering and hyperventilating, refusing to go into the pool again.

Ava got up from the stool, began to pace the small house. An edge of desperation made her heart pound. She went from the studio into the living room, where Henri, asleep in a patch of sun, woke to eye her briefly, then doze off again. Back in the kitchen she stopped pretending she wasn't going to finish the whole damn pan of brownies and took them out to the deck—the rotted deck that Sam had been going to fix for her but probably wouldn't now because she'd hurt his feelings—and sat with her back up against the sun-warmed wood of the house.

Money had never been an issue; between trust funds and insurance payments after Rob's death, she need never work at all. But relying on money she hadn't earned herself seemed a cop-out somehow, an indication that she wasn't really her own person. The money sat untouched in a variety of accounts she only thought about when her broker called to brief her.

She'd been barely supporting herself on steady, but mostly small, commissions when the Hollywood producer called. He'd seen her work in a magazine profile on emerging California artists. Once a frequent visitor to the island, he seldom had time to visit anymore and wanted something to remind him of Catalina. He'd hired her to design an outdoor tile carpet for the pool area of his Malibu home. The botanical tiles would form a border around a stylized view of Avalon Bay and the Casino.

"You've finally hit the big time," Diana had said when Ava had called to tell her about the new project. "Designing for celebrities, imagine!" And then, "Oh, darling, it's hard not to be the tiniest little bit envious. I used to have talent. Instead, I got married and had children." Still, they'd all toasted Ava with champagne over dinner at the yacht club, her parents and Ingrid. It was the last time they'd all been together as a family.

A week later, Ava had picked up the phone to hear Sam tell her that Diana had fallen overboard, and divers and the Coast Guard were out looking for her. All the preoccupations that usually stopped her from working were nothing compared to the loss of Diana. The idea that her mother was unhappy enough to throw herself into the ocean was so inconceivable and terrifying, she honestly didn't know whether she could live with it.

God. She held her face in her hands. She wasn't even a fourth of the way through the project. Every morning she'd unlock the front door of her studio, gather her implements and sit down to start painting. Within ten minutes she'd be nearly weeping in frustration. Sometimes she'd grit her teeth and just paint, anyway, but every brush stroke looked dull and insipid. The spirit, the inspiration had vanished.

And so had the brownies.

The phone rang again.

"Hey there, Ava," an unfamiliar voice said. "Just checking on the status of your work-in-progress. How's it coming along?"

Ava swallowed. It had taken her a moment to identify

the caller. "Hi, Adam," she greeted the Hollywood producer. "It's...coming along just fine."

"Good. Still looking to have it finished by the end of the month?"

"Absolutely."

"Good. Good. Got a documentary-film crew coming to do a piece on me. I want to have the piece up and installed. Make a nice backdrop. Good exposure for you, too. I'll try to work your name into the interview."

"Great, Adam." Her fingers were wrapped like claws around the receiver. In her peripheral vision, she could see the overflowing bin of discarded tiles. "Thank you."

After she hung up, Ava carried the empty brownie pan inside, set it down on her worktable and picked up one of the tiles. She knew if she sat here until next week, she wouldn't produce an acceptable tile. Come on, Henri." She nudged him with her toe. "We're going for a little ride."

THE SUN WAS SINKING below the horizon as Ava steered her Land Rover through Hog's Back Gate and onto Old Stage Road. Her grandfather once told her about the stage coach road that used to exist years before. Constructed largely with picks and shovels, it had skimmed over the top of mountain ridges, plunged into canyons and wound around hairpin curves, precipitating, according to the old man, the fatal heart attack of an elderly Lynsky aunt and a young wife's premature labor.

A four-wheel drive and road improvements made the journey much easier, but by the time Ava pulled onto the dusty trail that led to the horse stables and, behind the stables, Ingrid's small wooden cabin, she was thinking, as she always did, that it was time Ingrid got over her pique with their father and found a place to live in town.

As she drew up, she could see Ingrid in denim cutoffs and a green blouse sitting outside the cabin, her face illuminated by the yellow glow of an oil lamp. Her head tilted slightly to one side as Ava approached, she wore the same quizzical expression their mother used to wear.

Henri was out of the Land Rover almost before Ava had turned off the ignition, bounding across the dirt to Ingrid, who was drinking a beer. In a bowl at her feet were quartered limes, which Henri inspected and immediately devoured.

"Henri, you nutcase." Ava pulled at his head. "You don't eat limes."

"Wrong." Ingrid watched the dog. "Looks like he likes them." She looked at Ava. "Has he gained weight?"

Ava glanced at Henri. "Maybe a tad."

"Speaking of which…" Ingrid pinched Ava's waist.

"It shows, huh?"

Ingrid shrugged. "You could lose a pound or two. Want a beer?"

"Yeah. Sure." Ava flexed her fingers, clenched from the drive, and sat down on the steps. Three years ago when Ingrid had told her astounded family that she intended to live a simple life uncluttered by striving, commercial excess and rampant dishonesty, she'd failed to mention—though it hadn't taken long for everyone to find out—that she intended to share that life with an ex-surfer called Quicksilver.

Diana had been quietly appalled. Sam had asked how she planned to support herself and warned that if she expected any money from the family, including trust-fund money, she could forget it. He'd been furious, but not nearly as furious as he'd been when Ingrid had calmly informed him that she didn't intend to take a penny from her trust fund and she certainly didn't need family handouts. Quicksilver disappeared after a month or so; Ingrid claimed her father had bribed him to leave the island.

Since then, Ava's twin had pretty much stayed away

from Avalon. The family knew where she lived, Ingrid always said, so they could come and see her. Sam and Diana had never visited, Sam because he was too angry, Diana because Ingrid's new life embarrassed her. For a time, especially after she married Rob, Ava had also felt herself growing away from Ingrid. Rob had questioned his sister-in-law's willingness to scrape by on what she earned working in the stables and giving riding lessons. Transportation was a bike she'd had since high school, and she grew most of her food in the vegetable beds behind the stables. "I can manage on nothing," she'd boast.

Ingrid handed Ava a beer and a small framed picture. "Remember that? I knocked it off the shelf when I was doing my annual housecleaning this morning. Mom was so envious of you that day."

Ava glanced at the small picture. She'd just received a check for her first commission, a tiled mural on one of the restaurants in town. Diana had taken the picture of her holding the check. Now she looked at Ingrid, who had sat down on the stairs beside her. "Why would Mom be envious of me?"

"All kinds of reasons. You were probably closer to Dad than she was. You were doing the kind of work she'd always wanted to do. And then you got that big commission—"

"Which I'm now completely blocked on."

"More bad dreams?"

"Last night. It's driving me crazy, Ingrid. I'm getting scared to go to bed. I thought once I moved out of the house, I'd be okay." Her eyes filled. "I can't sleep, I can't work. I'm constantly shoving food into my mouth. I don't know what to do."

Beyond the small clearing where they sat, the darkness was shadowy with tall trees that, in daylight, she would recognize as native oaks, cottonwoods, willows and eucalyptus. Henri padded over to sniff around the perimeter of the light cast by the oil lamp for a few moments, then with a sigh dropped onto the ground by Ava's feet and dozed. "Mom was happy, wasn't she?"

Ingrid looked at her. "Apart from having to put up with Dad, you mean?"

"Come on. Quit making him sound like some kind of monster. I mean, God knows, he can be irritating." She told Ingrid about Sam wanting to fix the deck. "I love him and I appreciate all his help, but sometimes he's so damn dogmatic and unyielding and oblivious to anything else but what he wants to do."

"Sometimes?"

Ava sighed. "I know. Everything he does irritates me these days." She drank some beer, stabbed by a pang of guilt. "I mean, I know he was trying to help me, but —"

"This is what you always do," Ingrid said. "You make excuses for him. I bet you didn't even ask him to build the deck. He just took over, right?"

"Well—"

"What if Dad weren't around, Ava? You'd figure out the deck was dangerous and fix it yourself, right? Or pay someone to fix it. Big deal. Instead, Dad has to get involved and, of course, it has be done Dad's way and he can't understand why you're not willing to just pitch in and help, so now his feelings are hurt. Well, I'm sorry, but I don't feel a whole bunch of sympathy for him."

"No one's asking you to feel sympathy for him. It's just the way Dad is. I don't think he was this bad before. I think he's changed since Mom... You could try to understand. It's got to be difficult for him, too."

"Poor Daddy," Ingrid said, her tone mocking. "I'm just so mean to him." She tossed a stone into the darkness. "Every time you're reasonable and understanding, Ava, every time you make excuses for him, you undermine me—''

''I'm not undermining you. This has nothing to do with you. It's my damn deck we're talking about.'' Ava pulled on the sweatshirt she'd tied around her shoulders. Ingrid's anger was like tinder-dry brush, always on the verge of igniting. She didn't want to be angry at Sam the way Ingrid was. At her feet, Henri twitched in the throes of a doggy dream. Lucky dog. No nightmares and panic attacks haunting *his* days and nights.

''Ava, you asked me if Mom was happy,'' Ingrid said. ''I'm just saying that with the way Dad is, I don't see how she could have been.''

''If it was that bad, why would they have stayed married all these years?''

''She just blocked him out. It was that or her sanity. To be fair to Dad, though—''

''That's a novel concept.''

''To be fair to Dad, though,'' Ingrid repeated as if Ava hadn't spoken, ''if she wasn't happy, I think it was also because of what she hadn't done with her life. I'm sure that's why she envied you. That commission you got just reminded her of all the things she hadn't done with her own life.''

''But Mom had the choice.'' Ava picked up the picture again. ''She had a lot of talent—some of her photography was brilliant. She could have created a career for herself. She didn't have to be Dad's satellite.''

Ingrid sighed. ''I guess. Sometimes, though, you make decisions that seem right at the time and then you spend the rest of your life regretting them.''

''Medical school?''

''No, I'm not sorry I dropped out.'' Ingrid picked at a scab on her knee. ''Well, maybe sometimes.''

''You could go back. Dad would be thrilled.''

"Yeah, especially when I come to him for the money."

"Ingrid, if you really wanted to go back, *I'd* lend you the money."

Ingrid grinned. "Miss Moneybags. I guess there's something to be said for being left a wealthy young widow, huh? Thanks, though. I appreciate the offer."

"Think about it," Ava said. "It would be horrible to look back when you're fifty or sixty and hate the life you've chosen for yourself." She set her bottle down on the step. "Okay, this is going to sound bizarre, but what if Mom felt that way? What if she isn't really dead? What if she just decided she'd had it with the life she had and she wanted to start again?"

Ingrid said nothing for a moment, just frowned at the beer bottle in her hand. "Maybe she put something in Dad's drink to make him sleep," she finally said. "Arranged for someone to pick her up. And now she's a…belly dancer in Hollywood."

Ava laughed, despite herself. "You don't think much of that theory, huh?"

"Not the belly-dancer part. If she's alive and living on the mainland, someone would have seen her. The Sheriff's Department would have figured it out." She put her arm around Ava's shoulders. "Kind of a…comforting thought, though, huh?"

"Or another version of denial. It's easier to take than my dream of her in the water."

"But think about it, Ava. If she really had just run away, it would mean she'd written us out of her life. Wouldn't that be kind of hard to deal with? It would be for me. Anyway, if she wanted a new life, why wouldn't she just get a divorce?"

"Maybe she didn't want to deal with Dad." Having voiced her theory, Ava felt reluctant to abandon it. "You know Mom. She could be kind of…weird sometimes. Maybe she didn't want to go through the hassle.''

"Maybe Dad offed her.''

"Ingrid." Ava punched her sister's arm. "I know you think that kind of remark is funny, but I don't.''

Ingrid shrugged. "I'm going to hate myself for saying this, but I've honestly thought about it. I'm not talking premeditated. I'm just saying they could have had a fight. Maybe he got angry and they had a shoving match.''

"But they never fought,'' Ava said. *"I* never saw them fight.''

"But if they did, if Mom was really unhappy, maybe she wrote about it.'' Ingrid stretched out her legs, wiggled the ankles of her hiking boots. "Maybe I'm completely off target, but I need to know.''

"The diaries.''

"Exactly. I didn't want to tell you why I wanted to look at them, because you're already having bad dreams, but I just have this weird feeling.''

"What if we find out that she was never happy? What if there was a suicide note or something? It would change how we remembered everything, wouldn't it? Think about how great things were when we were growing up, like the sun was always shining and we had this perfect life…''

"Boston Whalers and Shetland ponies. The Twin Princesses of Catalina. Yeah, we'd have to revise a lot of things, I guess. But I'd rather do that than live with some kind of fairy-tale illusion.''

"Maybe.'' Ava rubbed her arms. Her fingers were numb from holding the beer bottle, and her forehead felt tight and drawn. "I think I'd rather have the illusion, but it's too late, the bubble's burst. Now I just need to figure out how to move on. If the diaries can help do that, I'll get the damn things.''

ELBOWS ON THE DESK, Scott skimmed the latest Avalon Baywatch police report looking for anything that might be

expanded into a larger story. Thursday, 11:00 p.m.: Paramedics responded to a report of an unconscious man found
lying on the sidewalk after an assault involving a beer bottle. Friday, 10:45 p.m.: An off-duty lifeguard responded to
the Descanso Beach Club's report of a 21-year-old woman
who had passed out under the table. Friday, 11:10 p.m:
Baywatch Avalon responded to a report from the Catalina
Cantina that a 42-year-old man with head pain fell to the
floor.

Nothing there, unless it was a piece about the conse-
quences of getting a skinful of Wicky Whackers, or one
too many margaritas. On an impulse, he went to the files
and leafed through back issues until he came to the report
on Diana Lynsky's disappearance. Nothing he didn't know.
Sam Lynsky had told sheriff's deputies that he'd fallen
asleep around noon. He'd reported his wife missing at
2:25 p.m.

Scott called the sheriff's station.

"You ready for the fishing trip?" the sheriff's deputy
who answered the phone asked. "Just say the word. I never
need an excuse to take the boat out."

"I'm going to take you up on it," Scott said. The deputy
had mentioned it three times now. "I'm still getting settled
in. Maybe in a week or so." He waited a moment. "Just
curious. How frequent are drownings over here?"

"About eight or nine a year," the deputy said.

"People just not familiar with the water?"

"That, and all kinds of things. If they're diving, it could
be malfunctioning equipment. Could be they've been drinking. You name it."

"The body's usually recovered?"

"Usually it surfaces," the deputy said. "Not to get too
technical, but gasses make them buoyant enough to… Then
again, a body in deep cold water might never come up.

Doesn't happen a lot, but it's not unheard of.'' He paused a moment. "Anything else?"

"That's it," Scott said. "And I'll give you a call about the fishing trip."

Through the window, he watched passengers trickle out of the steamer that had just arrived. Backpacks and overnight bags, shorts and sandals and baseball caps. Gearing up for a carefree weekend. The sight made him restless. He locked up the office and ambled down Crescent. The window of a gift shop caught his eye and he ducked inside and bought a present for Ellie. A pair of earrings, tiny bright-blue enameled flowers—forget-me-nots, he thought.

He'd rejected Ellie's suggestion about her mother coming to Catalina. Tried to explain as gently as he could that it wouldn't work for any of them. Ellie had hung up on him and refused to talk to him since. Now he was seriously wondering whether his move to Catalina had been a mistake, after all. He could probably get his job back at the *Times,* pick up the threads of his old life. The prospect filled him with a dreary gloom that seemed at odds with palm trees and sunshine and tourists in tropical clothes. He paid for the earrings and stuck the tissue-wrapped package in the back pocket of his jeans and wondered if they were really the sort of thing a fourteen-year-old would wear. *Ava would know.*

He stepped around a middle-aged couple in his-and-her Hawaiian shirts who had stopped to study a map, and entertained a fantasy about taking Ellie over to Ava's studio for a tile-making lesson. Ellie would be so charmed by Ava that she'd forget all thoughts about him working things out with Laura. "I know you'd be *much* happier with Ava, Daddy."

Dream on, he thought as he walked into the Beehive.

*And while you're at it, fantasize about what you'd do with
ten thousand extra bucks in your checking account.*

AVA LET HENRI run around the backyard of her father's
house while she waited for Ingrid to arrive so they could
go through Diana's papers. The yard was huge, almost an
acre. She used to hear Sam complain that it was too much
to take care of—but of course he wouldn't hear of hiring
a gardener.

She wandered over to the raised vegetable beds he'd built
several years ago. Every spring Diana had planted rows of
spinach and mesclun and kale, which she would compul-
sively water and tend for a couple of months until a weed
sprouted here, another there. Soon the watering days would
taper off altogether as Diana became absorbed in something
else—making marmalade, jars and jars of it that filled two
shelves of the refrigerator because Diana didn't trust the
canning process, or photography, or leading art walks
through the Casino—and Sam would start complaining
about the cobwebs and all the things that never got done.

Last summer's lettuce, still in the ground, had bolted and
spotted topknots of yellow flowers. Ava bent to yank one
out, then changed her mind. What did it matter? She sat
down on the grass, arms around her knees. Henri was digging at one of the beds, dirt flying up around him. She
called him and checked her watch.

Ingrid was ten minutes late. An image of Diana's chaotic
office flashed through her mind and she pulled herself up
off the grass. Maybe she'd just check things out herself
before Ingrid arrived.

Inside the house, she poured a glass of water at the sink
and felt again the strangeness of the kitchen. Maybe spirits
stayed trapped in a house, she mused, only making their
presence known if they needed to convey a message or
something. Lost in thought, she didn't hear her father come
in. He tapped her on the shoulder and she screamed.

CHAPTER ELEVEN

"DAMMIT, DAD! What are you doing, sneaking up on me?"

He reached over her to run water over his hands. "I walked into the house, Ava. I can do that—it's my house."

She glared at him, drying his palms on the sides of his Bermudas—orange-and-blue-striped with yellow happy faces on the blue stripes—and smiling that sweet happy smile that filled her with the schizoid urge to simultaneously hug him and slap him silly. God, she was going to cry. "I know it's your house!" she snapped.

"I was looking for you," he said. "Went by your house. Got to get that deck of yours finished so you don't break your neck. And—" he kicked his toe at the rough floor tiles "—I wanted to say I'm sorry for being me. I don't mean to upset you, but lately that's what I always seem to do. Maybe you could pass that along to Ingrid, too. Not very good at all that mushy stuff but—" a muscle worked in his jaw "—I love both you girls."

Ava felt her throat close. It was easier by far to be angry. She waved her arm at the empty counters. "How come you put all of Mom's stuff away? The breadmaker, the blender..."

"What am I going to do with them? A blender?" He shrugged. "What do you even use it for?"

"Well, God, Dad. What's next? Her cookbooks?"

"I thought you and Ingrid might want them."

She turned on him. "Why? Why can't they just stay here?"

"For one reason, I don't cook. And for another, I want to paint the kitchen."

"Just remove all traces, right?"

"Ava. The kitchen needs repainting. And your mother is dead."

"Shut up, Dad." Her heart racing now, she eyed the empty counters. If the blender had been there, she would have thrown it. "Just shut up. You think I need you to tell me that? You think I don't know? You think I..." And then she was sobbing, arms folded on the counter, her head buried. She felt Sam come up behind her, put his hands on her shoulders and squeeze.

"Come on, Princess. This isn't easy for any of us."

"Is that true, Dad?" Her voice was muffled by her arms. "It doesn't seem that difficult for you."

"Ava." He patted her back. "I'm sorry if you'd rather it had been me and not your mother. I'm sorry if you blame me somehow, if you think there's more I could have done. I'm sorry. I can think of very few occasions in your life when I couldn't step in if need be and correct whatever was troubling you. But this is one of those times. Your mother is dead and there's absolutely nothing any of us can do about it. Accept it, honey, and move on with your life."

"I need to ask you something, Dad."

"Make it quick." His apology over, he was clearly ready to move on. "I've got things to do."

She turned to look at him. "Was Mom happy?"

"Of course she was. You know she was. Ingrid been giving you her conspiracy theories?"

"*I* need to know."

He was already at the door, feeling around in his pocket

for keys. "Nothing you can do about it, anyway," he said. "So why not just tell yourself she was."

"SO WHAT'S THE HOT gossip?" Shirley set a plate of *huevos rancheros* in front of Scott, shifting aside the yellow notepad on which he'd been scribbling story ideas for next week's issue. "How about a story on me? I ever tell you I used to be a HeeHaw Honey?"

"Yeah, but I haven't heard it for a day or so," Scott said. "Refresh my memory."

"Get outta here." Shirley whacked him on the arm. "What about the time I ran into Jerry Seinfeld? You want a good story—that's gonna have the papers flying off the racks, I tell you. My hero." She clutched her hand to her heart, just below the beehive name tag pinned to her yellow cotton uniform. "Did I tell you he said I looked like—"

"Eileen Brennan?"

She feigned dismay. "I told you?"

"No. I thought you *were* Eileen Brennan."

"Get outta here," She left and returned a moment later with a coffeepot. "So how come you don't have a girlfriend, Scotty?"

"I do." He motioned for her to move closer. "Keep it quiet, but things are getting pretty serious with Britney Spears. Now if I could just accept that Jennifer Aniston is married…"

"Too young, both of 'em." She poured coffee into Scott's mug. "You know Ingrid Lynsky? Nice girl…well, a bit of a screwball, but you'd probably get along just fine with her."

"Thanks, Shirley." No need to mention that he'd been thinking pretty much nonstop about Ingrid's twin sister, Ava. Or the relief he'd felt when his ex-wife had also nixed their daughter's idea of a happy-ever-after life together on Catalina. Or the fantasy that Ava, sans her diamond ring, would maybe drop by the Beehive for breakfast and find every seat but the one opposite his empty. "But let's talk about *your* love life."

"I don't kiss and tell," Shirley said, and took the coffeepot to the next booth.

Scott scooped egg and beans onto a tortilla, rolled the thing up and took a bite, reviewing his list of article ideas. Pretty slim so far. As soon as he'd finished breakfast, he was off to the Casino to interview a former Miss Catalina on the occasion of her eightieth birthday. At noon, it was the Rotary Club Auction, where he'd shoot a few grip-and-grins for next week's Civic Spotlight Corner and, at three, the Halibut Tournament.

"If you were a good reporter," Sam Lynsky said as he dropped onto the seat opposite Scott. "Instead of sitting here stuffing your face, you'd take your camera down to the Pleasure Pier. There's a guy in a gorilla suit terrorizing the women."

"Damn." Scott grinned at Lynsky, whom he hadn't seen since the campfire. Not the Lynsky he'd been hoping to see, but he didn't mind the distraction. "It's a tough decision. If I didn't have a full plate of food in front of me—"

"Good thing I found you." Lynsky removed a manila folder from a battered black leather case. "Been meaning to talk to you about the book." He glanced briefly at Scott. "Still planning to do it, right? You'll want to look through this. Haven't gone through it myself yet, but it's articles and…God knows what else." With one finger, he flipped the folder open to reveal scraps of paper and a pile of yellowing newspaper clippings. "Got another check for you, too. Can't stop to talk about it for long—have to get up to the camp. We need to talk about costs. You charge an hourly rate? Doesn't matter, I want the book done whatever—"

"Dr. Lynsky—"

"Sam." He glanced around the restaurant. "Where's Shirley? I could eat a horse. Got a crack in one of the ceiling beams up at the camp. Need to fix it before it comes down on someone's head. That falls and…'' He drew a finger across his throat. "Know anything about insurance premiums? I tell you…''

Scott drank some coffee and, while Lynsky digressed to a rambling tale of a long-ago hunting expedition, thought about how he'd write the book. Information on earlier generations would mostly come from the Historical Society and Lynsky's own papers. Straightforward enough, and he could already envision how he'd do it—with the exception of the present generation. When he tuned back in, Sam had moved on to a Coptic-Christian bloodletting ceremony he'd encountered during a trip to Ethiopia fifteen years earlier. Scott mentally shook his head. Lynsky made him feel slightly dazed. Waiting for the man to pause was like standing on the edge of the freeway hoping for a break in the traffic before you crossed. He thought again of Benjamin's claim that Diana Lynsky had been spotted, alive and well, on the mainland, and wondered if maybe she'd just escaped.

"Nice people, the Ethiopians," Sam was saying now. "Beautiful features. Anyway, where were we? How come you haven't cashed that last check?''

"Because I hadn't decided whether to do the book.''

"Why wouldn't you want to do it?''

Scott stuck his elbows on the table. "The truth?''

"Hell, yes. No point in pussyfooting around.''

"For starters, I'm curious about your wife's death.''

"Curious how?''

"The body not surfacing.'' He watched Lynsky's face. "Someone said they'd seen her on the mainland.''

"Probably the same joker who spotted Bigfoot.''

"You don't think anything of it?''

"'Course not. Can't think why you'd even ask. If you have any doubts, call the Sheriff's Department. They'll tell you all you need to know. What else is stopping you?''

"I'd want to end up writing something I felt proud of, and I'm not sure how well we'd work together. Talking to you is kind of like getting mowed down by a truck."

Lynsky grinned. "I like that. Most people around here think I walk on water." He glanced up at Shirley, who'd stopped by the table with her coffeepot. "Right, Shirley?"

"I didn't catch what you said, Sam." Shirley poured the coffee. "But whatever it was, I agree."

"Look *I* want you to do the book," Sam said after Shirley left. "I know I go on, but life interests me. I wake up every morning, looking forward to the day ahead. Trouble is, I can't stop talking about it all. I tell myself, Sam, that's enough. Shut up, no one wants to hear your blah-blah-blah, anyway, but that's me. Do the book, okay? I'll stay out of it as much as I can." He took a tortilla from the covered warmer beside Scott's plate. "Don't mind, do you?"

"Go ahead." Scott watched the doctor spread butter on the tortilla. The man was definitely disarming. One minute he was the garrulous windbag oblivious to anything but himself; the next he'd show a flash of self-awareness that both surprised and endeared. Sam Lynsky might not be the easiest person to capture on paper, but it would be an interesting challenge.

"The way I see the book," Lynsky said as he reached for a second tortilla, "is a chapter for each generation up to the present. There's enough paper in my wife's office to cover the island. Unbelievable how much stuff she kept. Pictures, old letters. Lots of history, my family. Hers. If you can't get a story from that, you're not much of a reporter." He winked. "Just kidding."

"Have you told your daughters yet?"

"Thought I'd wait until I confirmed it with you. Soon as you tell me we're on, I'll let them know. They'll be fine with it." He scratched the back of his head. "Then again, who knows with women? I think they'll be fine with it.

You'll probably want to talk to both of them. Ingrid can be kind of difficult—you'll have to tread carefully with her. Wait until I tell you before you say anything, though. No point in courting problems.''

"And your wife? Who do I talk to about her?''

"You can look through her diaries and papers, get what you need there. Get my daughters to tell you about her. I can help, too. 'Course, Diana was always a bit of an enigma. Never quite sure what was going on in that head of hers. That's women for you, though. So how's the newspaper doing? Advertising picking up?''

"Dropping off, actually.''

"Well, Aggie kind of let the thing go to hell. Tell you what, I'll put a buzz in a few ears. Get some ads from some of the bigger places on the island.'' He grinned. "They all owe me favors. God knows how many tonsillectomies I've never billed for. Don't worry about a thing. Meet me up at the house tomorrow around six and I'll have some things to get you going on the book.'' He stood, reached for the last tortilla and rolled it up like a cigar. "And cash the damn check. Buy your daughter some new shoes.''

AVA STOOD AT THE CLOSED DOOR of Diana's study, bracing herself before she went in. Sam had just left the house when Ingrid called on the cell phone to say there'd been an accident at the stables, one of the riders had broken a leg and everything was in turmoil. She couldn't get away. Ava took a deep breath. The key wasn't on the rack as Sam had said it would be, but she figured maybe he'd left it unlocked.

The door was closed, but the padlock Ingrid mentioned was unfastened. Her hand on the ornate wrought-iron knob, Ava took another breath, delaying the moment she faced the room. A fanlight above the door cast a puddle of light at her feet. She opened the door.

All traces of her mother were gone. The long, marble-

topped table where Diana wrote letters in the small patch
of space not piled high with books, the loose sheets of
paper, the empty coffee cups and various bottles of lotion
and hand cream always uncapped, the leather armchair
where Diana once read and listened to music, the bookcase,
the pots of geraniums and vases of dried flowers, the overflowing wastebaskets. Gone.

Her immediate reaction was to call Ingrid. She did and
got no answer. She closed up the house, grabbed Henri and
walked down the hill into town. Sam knew that she and
Ingrid had wanted to go through Diana's papers. Why
would he just clear out the study and then not even mention
it? Because Sam was anything but predictable. He could
have just got it in his head to do it and that was it.

Crescent was jammed with tourists pouring off the four-
o'clock Catalina Express. Head down, preoccupied by her
thoughts, she plowed through the crowd and ran smack into
Scott Campbell.

He started laughing. "I saw you coming from way up
the street. I kept thinking, any minute she's going to look
up, but you didn't."

"You could have moved aside, of course."

"I *could* have."

Henri barked.

"*Now* you warn me." She glanced at Henri, then up at
Scott. Since he was still laughing, it was hard to keep a
straight face, anyway, and seeing him again reminded her
of what it was about him that made her heart beat a little
faster. That, and the day was warm and sunny. The bay
was a brilliant cobalt-blue, and the tangle of bougainvillea
climbing the wall behind him was the color of oranges.
Deadline be damned, she was tired of cooping herself up
in the studio being blocked and obsessing about everything.

"Please don't say something corny like we have to stop
running into each other like this," she said.

"I won't if you'll make good on your tour offer."

"Actually I didn't make the offer. You suggested it."

"You didn't agree?"

"Nope."

"I took myself on a tour last week," he said. "After I called you. I was walking back home and I stopped to look at that fountain in the center of town. I wanted to take closer look at the tiles…but a couple of girls scared me off."

"They scared you off?"

"Well, they were teenagers and they were sitting on the edge of the fountain. I thought they might see me as an old masher."

"Speaking of mashers." She told him about her encounter with the dude. "I don't think he quite knew what to make of me or Ingrid. He said you have a wife."

Scott scratched the back of his head. "Laura's family hasn't quite grasped the concept of divorce. Neither, unfortunately, has my daughter. A few days ago she called to suggest that she and her mother come to Catalina to live. She said if I really cared about her happiness, I'd want it, too."

"And?"

"I told her it wouldn't work and she hasn't spoken to me since."

She touched his arm. His smile had faded, his eyes were dark. "I'm sorry, really. What are you going to do?"

"Tomorrow, after I get this week's issue out, I'm going over to see her. It's tough, because she's a bright kid and she's so convinced that all it would take for things to work out is a little more effort on my part. She can be so persuasive I sometimes find myself wondering if maybe she's right." He shook his head. "She's not, I know that, but I want her to be happy."

"Tough being a parent, huh?"

"Tough being a good parent. Anyway…" He looked at her for a moment. "How's the new place?"

"Great."

"And work?"

"Not so great. I still can't do a damn thing."

"Maybe you just need a break from it. How about a bike ride?"

"A bike ride?"

"Fresh air, physical activity. All that good stuff."

"Now?"

"Why not?"

"Because I should work."

"You're blocked, remember?"

"*You* don't have work to do?

"I worked late last night."

Ava kept looking at him. Her arms were folded across her chest, she realized. A defensive posture. She unfolded them. "I haven't gone on a bike ride in ages."

He started walking. "Come on. There's a bike-rental place at the foot of the pier."

WITH THE DOG RUNNING along beside them, they rode for two hours. Up and down the steep trails that crisscrossed the island, through stands of scrub oak and eucalyptus. Ava, in the lead, calling out the names of plants and shrubs, offering a running commentary as they rode.

"We have vegetation here on the island you won't find anywhere else in the world," she said when they were riding abreast. "Seeds and organisms blow in on the wind, or the waves wash them in or birds bring them, and they adapt and become part of the local ecosystem." She turned to look at him. "Just like everything else that comes over from the mainland."

"Adapt or perish, huh?"

"Or go back."

"The longer I'm here, the less I want to leave."

She smiled.

"I don't even miss the traffic noise anymore."

"Rob used to say the same thing. He said he thought he'd go crazy at first, but Los Angeles got less and less appealing."

Scott steered around a rut. It had taken him a moment to recall who Rob was. "How long were you married?"

"Two years."

"How did you meet him?"

"I was volunteering at my dad's camp and Rob's daughter was one of the campers. She was eight and she had really severe asthma. Most parents just send their kids and don't see them for the next week or so, but Rob was very protective. He stayed in Avalon, at the Bay View actually, and came up to the camp every day. One night we went out to dinner and then we just started seeing more and more of each other. We got married the following year."

"Have you stayed in touch with his daughter?"

"No." She sighed. "Nicki and I got along just fine until she realized her father was more to me than just another parent. She saw me as a competitor for Rob's love. It was pretty clear how much she resented me—to the point that I sometimes wonder if our marriage would even have survived. It was pretty brutal."

"It's tough," Scott said, thinking about Ellie.

"How's your sister?"

"Fine. Well, as fine as Carolyn ever is."

"When Ingrid and I first saw her, we thought she was your girlfriend. I was watching you over the top of my menu. I called her the Tangerine Temptress."

He laughed. "Carolyn would be insulted to think she even *looked* like my type. I'm much too conventional for her."

"So she's still staying with you?"

"Kind of." He relayed the story of Carolyn's firings, her on-again-off-again relationship with Mark. "She was only six when our father died and I kind of took on the father-figure role. I'm not sure I've done a great job with that, either."

"I'm sure you've done the best you can. Maybe you're too hard on yourself. Does Carolyn manipulate you, too?"

He laughed. "Too?"

"I get the feeling your daughter probably does a pretty good job of it."

"Ellie?" He considered. "I don't think—"

"Does she sulk when she doesn't get her own way?"

"Yes, but—"

"And what do you do?"

He turned his head to smile at her. "Give in."

"See? I don't know a whole lot about *being* a parent, but I know plenty about being a daughter. Remember the foot-stamping thing? I wasn't joking."

"Do you think your father is a good parent?" Scott asked.

"I think my dad's like a benevolent dictator. He does what he believes in and if you don't agree, tough. And he's arrogant enough to really think he knows best."

"But you manipulated him?"

"Only on the little things."

"Shetland ponies?"

"They tied in with his notion of how children should be raised."

"I think with Ellie, I feel guilty for the years I spent being…distant. Too wrapped up in work. Now I'm trying to make up for it. Except that as my ex-wife points out, now I've physically distanced myself, too."

"But you want her to come over here, right? So quit beating up on yourself. Coming to Catalina was a good decision.'' She smiled at him. ''No traffic, no smog, no muggers in dark alleys.''

They both fell silent for a moment. Then, with a glance at her left hand curled around the bike's black rubber grip, he said, ''You're not wearing your ring.''

''We broke it off.''

He waited for her to elaborate, but she said nothing and they rode along in silence. With a stab of guilt, he thought about Lynsky telling him not to mention the book. One complication resolved—Lynsky's reassurance about money matters—another one looming. He watched Ava's legs, tan beneath red shorts, pumping the pedals. What if he and Ava ended up in bed together and *then* she learned about the book? And didn't want him to do it? He pushed the pedals harder, began working up speed. Ava sped up, too. Soon they were flying down canyons, stepping on the pedals to ride up hills...

''Okay, I give up.'' Ava slowed to a stop, threw her bike aside and collapsed in a patch of grass. Flat on her back, she looked up at him. ''That's the most physical exercise I've had in months.''

He stood for a moment looking down at her. Laughing, arms outstretched, black hair massed all around her head and shoulders, red mouth. The white cotton of her shirt rose and fell with her breathing. Face flushed, smiling still, she watched him. Her eyes were very blue. He saw himself kissing her, peeling away her thin clothes. And then like uninvited guests, he saw Sam Lynsky and Laura and Ellie all parading by, shooting him looks of contempt.

''Come on.'' He grabbed Ava's hand and pulled her to her feet. ''Race you back.''

They rode back down the trail, Henri running behind them with considerably less energy then he'd shown at the start. Back in town, they returned the bikes and then he walked with her up the hill to her cottage. At the steep flight of steps to the door, she stopped.

"You know, today was a lot of fun," she said.

"I enjoyed it, too."

"I'd invite you in but…"

"It's fine." A leaf had lodged in her hair. He removed it with the tips of his fingers. "I should get back."

"Listen, about your daughter…I didn't mean to stick my nose in."

"You didn't."

"I mean, it's none of my business."

"Ava—"

She smiled. "God, my legs are going to kill me in the morning."

"Good." He touched her chin. "You'll think of me."

AVA TURNED TO WAVE at Scott as he walked back down the hill, then she tore upstairs and called Ingrid. "Oh, my God, Ing, I have to tell you something. I was coming home from Dad's and I ran into Scott and we went for a bike ride and I think I'm…I can't even, I feel so incredible. It's like I don't know what to think."

"What?" Ingrid sounded surly. "I have no idea what you're talking about. Did you get the diaries?"

"No. Look, could we *please* not talk about the diaries for a minute?"

"Hello-o," Ingrid said. "I thought you decided last night that you wanted to see them."

"I do." Already, like a splash of cold water, she could feel the euphoria fading. The magic of lying in the grass looking up at Scott and knowing he was about to kiss her. Already, it was beginning to look foolish and rash, and the magic was giving way to glum resignation that nothing had really changed. She felt like Cinderella after her coach had turned back into a pumpkin. "Mom's office was cleaned out," she said. "Everything was gone. Didn't you get my message?"

"Yeah. What happened, though? Did you ask Dad?"

"He left before I found out."

"So call him."

"*You* call him, Ingrid."

"You're the one with the bad dreams."

"I know that."

"So what's the deal with Scott?"

"We just went for a bike ride." Now she didn't feel like talking about it. "No big deal."

"It didn't sound like that a few minutes ago."

"Well, it is now." She carried the phone over to the window just in time to see Sam climbing the stairs to the cottage. "Guess who's here?"

"Scott or Dad?"

"The latter."

"Call me."

"OKAY, HERE'S MY NEW, *new* theory." Carolyn sat on the dirty yellow shag carpet painting her toenails black. "Lynsky and the daughters are all in it together. Maybe he needed a whole bunch of money for...I don't know, maybe he wants to set up the artist daughter in business and so maybe—"

"Maybe you should keep your theories to yourself." Scott picked up the ashtray, carried it out to the kitchen and emptied it into the trash. He'd just walked home from Ava's and he wanted time alone to sort out his thoughts. "What happened to your permanent return to the mainland?"

Carolyn pouted. "What kind of a welcome home is that?"

"This isn't your home," Scott said. "And what's with the job you were supposed to start?"

"I did start it." Carolyn wiggled her toes. "I couldn't stand it. The owner was this big jerk who kept coming on to me."

"Lynsky called." Mark stuck a stale tortilla between the pages of the book he was reading. "He thought I was you and he went on at great length about decomposed granite, which I gather is essentially the character of the soil in his backyard. That and clay, which after a rain becomes as hard as concrete."

"It must have been a bitch digging a hole to bury his wife out there." Carolyn clasped an ankle in both hands, drew up her foot and blew on the newly applied polish. "You ought to check the place out, Scott. See if there are any fresh mounds of dirt."

Scott watched his sister paint her big toe. "What you ought to do, Carolyn," he said, "is take that foot you've just finished painting and stick it in your mouth, then leave it there."

"Thanks, Scott." She smiled at him. "I love you, too."

"Lynsky said that the hardware store is going to run a full-page ad in next week's issue," Mark went on. "And Lil's Lovely Island Real Estate wants half a page on an ongoing basis. This was right after he told me about the clay in his backyard and before he'd stopped long enough for me to tell him he wasn't talking to you."

"Yeah, he's quite the talker." Scott dropped down on the couch next to Mark. "Effective, though. I've been working on the hardware store ever since I got here. I couldn't even get a commitment to a measly eighth of a page. Apparently Lynsky's calling in favors."

"So it sounds like you're going to do the book," Mark said.

"I'm leaning that way. What else did Lynsky say?"

"Just that he had another check for you. And instead of

you going up to get the papers, he'll drop them all off at the *Argonaut* tomorrow.''

"What's this book going to be?" Carolyn asked. "A murder mystery?"

Scott looked from Carolyn to Mark, who'd picked up his book again. The title, he saw with a glance at the cover, was *How the Criminal Mind Works.*

"It's going to be a family history," he said. "And let's drop all the whacky theories, okay? I've thought about the whole thing. Lynsky might be an eccentric character, but I believe in him. I think his wife's death was an accident and I'm writing the book on that assumption. Got it? And I want to see some serious progress on looking for a job. If you're going to stay here, you're going to stop freeloading.''

"Jeez." Carolyn said. "Who have you been talking to?"

AVA WAS ARRANGING a collection of Mexican folk art on the mantelpiece. She'd just unpacked two hand-painted wooden animals, a silver picture frame and an Aztec figure from the storage box. Behind her, she could hear Sam ripping wood from a rotten window frame. For the past hour, they'd been discussing his intention to have Scott write a family history. It was why he'd packed up Diana's study, he explained, and moved everything to the attic. He planned to give Scott access to her papers. Now, just the thought of breaking this piece of news to Ingrid made Ava's head ache.

"Maybe right now isn't the time for a family book," she said. "Things are too unsettled."

"What's unsettled? *I'm* not unsettled."

Ava set a cluster of white candles of different lengths next to the picture frame and stood back to look at it. Focusing—or trying to focus on something other than Sam—

lessened the urge to throttle him. "I realize that you're the center of your own universe, Dad, but—"

"Right, I'm a terrible person. Horrible." He'd wandered into the kitchen. "Don't know why they don't tar and feather me. Shoot me in the head and be done with it. Need to do some grocery shopping," he called. "Von's has tomato juice for a dollar. I like a glass with breakfast. Out of eggs, too."

Ava got up and found him standing at the open refrigerator. She grabbed the refrigerator door and closed it. "You could at least have consulted me and Ingrid before you talked to someone about doing a book."

"Consider yourself consulted."

"After the fact."

He shrugged, his expression impatient. "If I give the papers to you two first, it'll be yak-yakking over this and over that. Everything will end up gathering dust in a box under your bed, just like your grandmother's diary. Bet you have no idea where it is, do you? You and your sister are both the same, just like your mother."

Ava felt her face go warm. She'd been given her grandmother's girlhood diary for her sixteenth birthday. It was safe, she was sure of that. But exactly where it was in all the stuff she'd accumulated over the years, she had no idea. She felt simultaneously guilty and defensive. "I have a right to go through Mom's papers," she said.

"And I have a right to see they're taken care of," he said. "I'd like a book of our family history from the time the Lynskys came to Catalina until now." His voice was slow and careful, as though he was trying to explain a complex medical regimen to a young patient. "Your mother had mentioned it several times. She was always saying you girls were too busy to be bothered with it."

"I don't remember her say—"

"I'm not laying blame. I'm just telling you the way

things are. I want the book to be something we'll all feel proud of, something you can give to your children one day. If we leave those papers in the mess they're in right now, that's never going to happen.''

"Still, you should have spoken to—''

"Aggie down at the *Argonaut* was going to write it, but then she went off to Arizona. Now I've asked Scott to do it. Being a writer and all, I think he can do a decent job. If you have a problem, you'd better talk to him about it.''

INGRID WAS, PREDICTABLY, furious when Ava called to tell her about the book. The next day Ava drove across the island, picked up Ingrid and brought her back to spend a couple of days at the cottage. By then Ingrid had calmed down enough to allow that *maybe* a family history would be okay, as long as they went through the papers before Scott did. Later that night, drinking Wicky Whackers under the thatched roof at Luau Larry's, she conceded that the book was probably a good idea.

"It's not like either of us are going to write it,'' she said.

Ava stirred the ice in her drink. "Except…what if we find a suicide note?'' Ingrid looked at her, considering. "Would we just destroy it?''

"Or what if she wrote something like, I don't know, Dad beat her up?''

"Ingrid, come on. If Dad beat her up, you think we wouldn't have known about it? Why can't we ever talk about this without you coming down on him?''

Ingrid leaned back against the booth, watching the crowd of revelers in a nearby booth. "I don't know,'' she said finally. "I hate all these thoughts I have about him. I don't even know why I have them. I just feel…antagonistic toward him. I want to tell him I love him, but I can't seem to make myself do it.''

"It's not that hard. Really.'' She thought of Scott's concerns that he'd failed as a father. "Dad did the best he could—within the limitations of being Dad. You have some good memories. You don't have to focus on the negative."

"I know, I know." Ingrid stabbed at the ice in her drink with the plastic straw. "Dad's just so impossibly bombastic and larger than life. He's like one of those figures in Macy's parade. Everyone else is awed, looking up at him bobbing above the crowd." She grinned. "I just want to let some of his air out."

"If Scott does the book, he'll have to talk to us," Ava said. "Forget about Mom's papers. Are you going to tell him all this stuff?"

"No." Ingrid shook her head. "I can't. It's okay if I bitch to you about Dad, but I can't tell anyone else how I feel." She drained her drink. "Listen, I don't want to deal with this anymore. Let's just go through Mom's papers, pull out anything that's not picture perfect and just give Scott the Pollyanna Princess stuff. Dad wins, but what else is new?"

"I don't like the feel of that," Ava said. "It makes everything a lie."

"*We're* not calling the shots, Ava. Dad is. You think if I told Scott what I really thought, any of it would end up in the book? Of course not. Dad's paying him. We'll be lucky if we even get the damn papers before Scott sees them."

"Oh, we will," Ava said. "I promise you we will."

CHAPTER TWELVE

"I'm sorry I was a brat, dad," Ellie told Scott when she called him at the *Argonaut*. "Mom doesn't want to live on Catalina, anyway. I guess I should have talked to her before I told you, huh?"

"Yeah, it might have been a good idea." Scott eyed the carton of papers Lynsky had dropped by that morning with a promise of more in the next day or two. "But listen, sweetheart, you're sure you don't want me to come over? I could be there early enough for us to catch a movie or something."

"Da-ad, I told you. I'm spending the night at Chelsea's."

"Right," Scott said. "Well, if you're sure…"

"Are your feelings hurt?"

"No, of course not." At Lynsky's insistence—and to cover the deductible on the braces Laura said Ellie needed—he'd deposited both of Lynsky's checks and he was about to tell Ellie that perhaps he could swing the new computer she wanted. Then he stopped himself. Money bought only the semblance of a clear conscience. "I love you, baby," he said. "And I want you to keep next weekend free for sure, because I'm coming over."

"Or I could come there," Ellie said.

Scott beamed. "Even better."

He'd hung up and was thinking about an interview he'd just done with an Avalon resident who claimed that the mayor was using a private helicopter to spy on residents in their backyards when Ava Lynsky walked in.

He hadn't seen her since their bike ride three days ago, and his mood, already on the upswing, improved still further. "You saved me," he said. "I was sitting here trying to frame a piece about local espionage…"

"Max Fowler," she said. "What is it this time? The mayor's using a helicopter to drop bricks on couples making out on the beach?"

"Close." He got up from the desk and came around to her. "You know this guy?"

"Everyone knows him. One of the local eccentrics. Years ago he and the mayor dated the same woman or something. The mayor married her and Max has been a nutcase ever since. Shirley down at the Beehive said Max swore to her that the mayor had secret video cameras installed in the women's shower stalls at the yacht club."

He grinned. "Nice to see you."

"You, too."

They stood for a moment. She wore a sunny yellow dress and her expression was friendly, but she'd folded her arms across her chest and seemed distracted. "Where's Henri?" he asked.

"At home. Probably devouring the mattress."

"He recovered okay from his run?"

"Yeah. He was kind of pooped the next day, but the exercise was good for him. Me, too." Her smile flickered, then died. She uncrossed her arms, pushed at her hair. "Listen, Scott, my father told me that he asked you to write our family history."

He nodded, gearing himself up. "Have a seat. Your dad mentioned it to me a few weeks ago," he said after Ava perched on one of the chairs by the desk. Shoulders straight, hands folded in her lap, she had the look of someone on a job interview. The formality about her now made it hard to imagine that he'd almost kissed her. "I'm guessing you've just found out."

"You're guessing correctly. What did you tell him?"

"When he first asked me, I told him I wanted to think about it. And then I didn't hear anything more about it until I ran into him in the Beehive a couple of days ago."

"And you told him you'd do it?"

"Essentially."

"Do you want to?"

"I'm interested. I could use the money. You're not happy with the idea?"

"It's nothing personal," she said. "I…Ingrid and I kind of resent Dad mentioning it to you before he spoke to us. The idea of a biography isn't new—my Mom had already started compiling notes. It's mostly the way Dad…" She shook her head. "He decides something and it becomes a fait accompli."

"He mentioned some papers that he wanted me to see. Your mother's—"

"Which is another thing I want to talk to you about." She leaned back in the chair, glanced around the room. "Do you have any coffee? Soda or something?"

"Sure." He got up, poured coffee from the pot he'd made earlier. "Sugar?" He set a white ceramic mug on the desk, squatted in front of a small brown refrigerator and pulled open the door. "I used the last of the creamer yesterday, but there's some flavored stuff my sister bought."

"Black's fine." She held the cup in both hands, stared into it for a moment. "Um…had you already decided to do the book when we went on the bike ride?"

"I hadn't decided. But that's not what you're really asking, is it?"

She gave him a wide-eyed look, but said nothing.

"And now you're thinking ulterior motives?" he guessed.

"I don't know." She picked at her thumbnail. "It's all kind of meshed together."

"No, it's not. Going on a bike ride with you had nothing to do with your father or the book. Nothing to do with the newspaper. Listen, this is a job. It doesn't consume my thoughts on a twenty-four-hour basis."

"But it kind of complicates things."

"Things being?"

"If we had some mad passionate affair," she said without a trace of a smile. "I wouldn't know whether I was the real attraction or you were just gathering material."

He looked at her. She was gazing intently into her cup as though the instant-coffee scum floating across the surface might reveal his true intention. He kept looking until he saw her struggling not to smile.

"Okay, maybe that sounds a tad paranoid," she said.

"Just a tad."

"That first day when you interviewed me at the Descanso Beach Club, I told Ingrid that you were condescending. I didn't like you."

"It was mutual," Scott said. "I told my friend from the *Times* that you were a spoiled rich Princess."

"Hmm. Friend from the *Times*." She set the mug down on the desk. "I could indulge in a paranoid moment."

"Don't," he said. "I do have thoughts that have nothing to do with putting things down on paper."

"I'll try to keep that in mind."

"If I try hard, I can also manage not to be condescending."

"I think I changed my mind about you that morning after the reception when we had breakfast. You said something then, and I felt this…connection. Which you kind of ruined on the ride back from camp."

"My foray into psychology? I know, I was mad at myself after that."

"Not as mad as I was at myself."

"How about we both forgive ourselves?"

"Deal." She straightened up in her chair, folded her arms again. "But back to the book…"

"Back to the book," he said.

"My sister and I had a long talk last night. We both have some questions about…certain things that the papers might answer. We'd like to look at them first. Before you go through them for the book."

"Sure. It'll be a while before I get to your part, anyway. I've got a lot of material from the Historical Society to go through."

"Great." She smiled. "I'll tell my dad."

He glanced at his watch. Nearly four. He thought about his options for the rest of the evening. Drink a beer and watch TV in his stucco box on Claressa, or drink a beer and watch TV in the corner bar. He outlined them to Ava. "Doesn't that strike you as kind of pathetic?"

"Yeah, it does. And usually I can't stand pathetic, but since you're kind of cute, I'll take pity on you. My option for the evening is taking Henri for a walk and tiling my bathroom. If you'd like to join me…"

"Give me thirty minutes to write up a quick story so that I can meet next week's deadline and I'll be right there," he said.

SHE ALMOST RAN BACK to the cottage, then tore around the place picking up and straightening. She'd inherited Diana's proclivity for disorder. During her marriage to Rob, her nonchalance toward most things domestic had baffled him. He'd draw hearts with their initials in the dust on the bedroom dresser, buy expensive orange-oil furniture polish and feather dusters. She'd finally suggested that if a spotless house was that important to him, he should clean it himself. Her mind was always racing in more interesting directions. A design she'd just finished or how to capture the quality of late-afternoon sunlight or even whether the caloric difference between sinful fettuccine Alfredo and the more virtuous tomato spaghettini was really worth the sacrifice.

"Come on, Henri, move it." She dragged a sock from under him and checked to see whether its mate was under the couch. It wasn't. The mystery of missing socks was something she pondered occasionally. Her sock drawer probably contained twenty mateless socks that she couldn't bring herself to toss out because she figured the partner had to be around somewhere. It never appeared, and the pile of single socks kept growing.

She removed an empty cottage-cheese container, *Shape* magazine, a bottle of nail polish and four pens from the top of the steamer trunk that served as the coffee table, shook out the paisley, velvet and brocade throw pillows, rearranged them at one end of the couch, surveyed them for a moment, then heaped them on the floor by the fireplace where she imagined discarded clothes, candlelight on bare skin and Scott without his glasses.

She lit candles, filled the CD player with a selection of moody jazz, heavy on the saxophone and sultry voices, dashed into the kitchen to check on wine. Some Merlot left. Would it look as though she was trying too hard if she fixed something? An appetizer. Sautéed mushrooms, except she didn't have any and it was too late to go to the store.

A quick glance told her it was almost five. Damn, she wasn't even dressed. Forget the food. In the bedroom, she pulled clothes from the closet. A pair of slim black trousers. She held them up to herself. God, who was she kidding? Ten pounds ago, maybe. Okay, from now on she was going to starve. Sweats? No, too. You didn't wear sweats until you were well into a relationship. Sweats were for cuddling up with a video and popcorn. Sweats would be nice.

She threw on an oversize shirt, held her breath while she zipped up her jeans, bent over at the waist and tossed her hair around and, finger combing the strands, went back to the kitchen to answer the phone. It was Ingrid calling from a friend's house where she'd decided to spend the night.

"Did you talk to Scott?"

"Yes." Ava hesitated. "He's coming over tonight."

"What did you tell him?"

"I just said we wanted to look through the papers before he did. He's fine with that."

"You didn't tell him why?"

"Yes, Ingrid, I spilled my guts to him." Phone cradled between her head and shoulder, she flipped through a cookbook Diana had given her. Chocolate mousse. The author of this book was always so verbose. *Give me the damn recipe and skip the chatter,* she thought. "Of course I didn't say anything."

"Because I've had another thought about Dad, and it kind of ties in to why you keep having those dreams. You know how nothing Dad does is ever his fault? It's always someone else, never—"

"Ingrid." Ava glanced at the clock. Scott would be here any minute. "Do we have to talk about this now?"

"Remember when Mom slipped on those steps by the dock? They had seaweed all over them?"

"Yeah, I remember." The steps went down into the water, the bottom three or four, submerged but visible beneath the dark murky movement of the waves. She'd always averted her eyes, not wanting to see the eerie outline beneath the lapping water. Even thinking about them now made her heart beat faster. "What about it?"

"She was carrying something Dad wanted her to bring down to the boat, and she couldn't see over the top of it and she tripped. If Dad hadn't asked her—"

"Can we talk about this some other time?"

"Dad can never accept responsibility for his behavior, that's all I'm saying. It's always someone else's fault. I was thinking, what if—"

"Ingrid." She heard the doorbell. "I've got to go."

She hung up, took a deep breath. No panic attack in more than a week and she wasn't going to have one now, but she kept seeing the water lapping at the bottom of the steps and Diana's face looking up.

"Ava." Scott put his hands on her arms. "What is it?"

Unable to even speak, she shook her head. With one hand, Scott reached over her shoulder to push the door close, then he led her to the futon couch. They sat down and he held her hand as she sat there gulping air. After a while the panic subsided and her breathing slowed. Scott's hand was still in hers and she realized they were breathing in rhythm. She felt as close and connected to him as if they'd just been through something momentous together.

"It might help to talk," Scott finally said.

SHE TALKED UNTIL HER voice was hoarse. Talked and cried and talked some more. She told him about the dreams and the panic attacks, about why she'd moved from her father's house, about not being able to work, about that last conversation with Diana. By the time she was all talked and cried out, the cottage was cold and she couldn't stop shivering. Scott wrapped a blanket around her shoulders and made her a mug of apple-cinnamon tea with honey.

"Thank you." Her hands wrapped around the mug, she smiled at him. "Really, thank you."

"Tea is actually quite easy to make."

"You know what I mean."

He tugged on a lock of her hair. "Not good to keep things bottled up inside."

"Deep down I've been scared that she took her life. I wanted reassurances from Dad and Ingrid that she was happy, even though she told me herself she wasn't. I just didn't want to believe it. I always believed we had this wonderful life, but to think that Mom was never happy…it's like everything I believed was an illusion.''

"Perfection is the illusion," Scott said. "Reality is that maybe there were some things that weren't so great, but a lot of other things that were."

"I keep thinking that if only I'd taken her seriously. I know that hand in the dream is me holding her down, instead of helping her…''

"Ava, you tried to help her. You went over to see her and she said everything was fine. You can't assume all the responsibility. Besides, maybe it *was* an accident."

She blew her nose, sipped the tea. Scott sat on the couch beside her, his features indistinct in the shadowy light from the waning day. He'd been so incredibly sweet, so exactly what she needed, that she felt teary again, but with gratitude now. She drank some more tea, looked up to find Scott watching her.

"Listen, about my situation…'' he said.

"An ex-wife.'' She drew her drew her knees up, wrapped her arms around them and looked at him. "A daughter. A sister sleeping on your couch."

"Don't forget her boyfriend.''

Chin resting on her knees, Ava smiled back at him. "A lucrative book offer from my father that you're probably not sure you should accept because you have these niggling doubts that maybe things aren't what they seem to be."

"Did I say that?''

"You're a reporter. You don't have to."

"So, bottom line, the odds are kind of stacked against us. If we were thinking of starting anything, that is.''

"Kind of looks that way, doesn't it?''

"Sure does.''

"Well…'' He reached over, grabbed her legs and pulled her onto his lap. "Let's defy the odds. Before we talk ourselves out of this entirely, I'm going to kiss you."

He did. And it was so warm and wonderful that when he drew away to take a breath, she pulled him back and they went on kissing. His hands tangled in her hair, he whispered her name, and none of the obstacles they'd come up with mattered. Nothing mattered except Scott's mouth on hers. They were still kissing when the front door opened and her father walked in.

"PRIVATE SAM REPORTING for duty." Smiling broadly and carrying a toolbox, he wore a tattered pair of red tartan Bermudas and a turquoise T-shirt that proclaimed "My Boat Rocks And So Do I."

"Have Hammer Will Travel," he said. "No task too menial." And then the scene on the couch apparently registered and his smile faded. "Hey, Steve. Thought you were coming up to get those papers."

"You were supposed to drop them off." Scott glanced at Ava who had flown off his lap as if propelled and was now staring at her father, eyes wide. He resisted the urge to put his arm around her shoulders.

"I was?" Sam scratched his head. "Could have sworn it was the other way around."

"Did it ever occur to you to knock before you barge in?" Ava asked. "Or, God forbid, call to say you're coming?"

"No." Lynsky's usually affable expression was gone. A pulse ticked in his cheek. "Don't have time to go running around looking for you, Steve. If you don't want to do the book, just say so." He walked out to the deck. "Thought I'd get this fixed," he called, his voice carrying into the living room. "Won't have time after tomorrow. Group of doctors from the Allergy Foundation coming over later. Bunch of blah-blah-blah, but they want to check out the camp."

Scott looked at Ava. Her fists were clenched, her cheeks spotted with pink. "Are you okay?" he whispered.

"Furious."

"Want me to leave?"

"Don't you dare." Out on the deck, Sam had started hammering. "I'm going to have a little talk with my father."

Scott stood at the window, watching Ava. He sensed a battle brewing that only marginally involved him. He didn't particularly want to get drawn in; he wanted to leave Ava even less. Then he saw her try to grab the hammer from Sam's hand and decided that he should be out on the deck with her.

"If this is the only time you can fix the deck," she told her father, "then forget it. I'll hire someone to do it."

Sam ignored her and went on hammering. His tools were lined up on the top of the trunk like a row of surgical instruments. He paused for a moment to glance up at Scott. "Just saw Ed. You ever meet him, Steve? Nice guy, couldn't ask for a better man for my daughter. Except he tells me she's got some cockamamie idea about breaking the engagement."

Ava made another grab at the hammer. "Go, Dad, now. I mean it."

"Come and give me a hand, Steve," Sam said as though Ava hadn't spoken. "With the two of us working, we can get this done in half the time."

"I said leave, Dad."

"Ed's from a good family. Plenty of money there." Sam hammered another nail. "You've got a daughter, right, Steve? You must know how it is. Be hard to see her waste herself on a loser. That's why I was so tickled when Ava got engaged to Ed. 'Course money's not everything, but poverty isn't pretty, either."

Scott watched Sam, down on his haunches now and

whistling as he examined a loose plank in the deck. The top of his scalp was freckled and sun-splotched. With a sudden shriek Ava hurled herself onto her father's back, grabbing his shoulders with so much force that they both toppled to the deck. Scott reached for Ava's hand, but she was already on her feet, her body poised as though to attack again.

"Leave, Dad. I mean it, just leave."

Lynsky, standing now, glanced around for his tools.

"The thing is, Steve, Ava's always had money," Sam said, his voice conversational as he repacked his toolbox. "Case in point, my daughter thinks nothing of wasting money on a handyman who's going to charge a thousand bucks for something I could do for free. But there's only so much advice you can give your children, right, Steve?"

"It's Scott, but you're absolutely right, Dr. Lynsky." Ava was white-faced and trembling in fury. Scott put his arm around her shoulders, partly to steady her but also to send her father a message. "My daughter's only fourteen, but I hope that by the time she becomes an adult, I can acknowledge her right to make her own decisions."

"Well, let's hope so." Toolbox in hand, Sam brushed past Scott and Ava and went into the house. "'Course, before that, you've got to put her through college. Pay for this, pay for that. Kids can be pretty expensive. You having any trouble getting advertisers for that paper?"

"Dammit!" Ava broke from Scott's grasp. "Out, Dad! Now."

"Ava…" Scott started to restrain her, but she'd stormed into the house. He followed her. Sam had ambled into the kitchen and was making a leisurely inspection of the fridge.

"I'm going to kill him," Ava muttered. "I'm going to put my hands around his neck and throttle him."

"You got any tomato juice?" Sam asked. "I've been

drinking it lately. Tammi got me started on it. She's the gal you saw me talking to up at the camp.''

Scott glanced at Ava and she shook her head.

''Husband's abusive, verbally and physically,'' Sam went on. ''Her folks have washed their hands of her, didn't want her to marry the guy in the first place. Anyway, what I was saying, Scott, is that Aggie found it hard to make a go of the paper and she was an islander. Just wondering how you were doing, being from over there. Sometimes folks who have lived here forever don't take kindly to mainlanders taking over local businesses. Might want to keep that in mind.''

''OKAY, HERE'S THE DEAL,'' Scott said thirty minutes later as he and Ava walked Henri up Pebbly Beach Road. ''We're going to walk and walk and talk about anything you want, except your father.'' He glanced at her. ''Deal?''

Ava shot him a glance. ''I can't even worry aloud that he's going to take revenge on you?''

''That's my problem,'' Scott said.

''But what about your daughter? You said you needed the money and—''

''Also my problem.''

''I can't rage and storm just a little more?''

''You've raged and stormed enough. The goal for the rest of the day is emotional tranquillity.''

Ava smiled. She'd changed into sweats and a fleece parka, and she hunched her shoulders inside it, feeling the soft texture of the fabric against her skin. *I could fall in love with a guy like you,* she thought.

''And no thinking about your father.''

''How would you know if I were?''

''Because I'm holding your hand and I'd feel it go tense and cold, like it did ten minutes ago.''

''You're sounding frighteningly dictatorial,'' she said.

"It's for your own good," he said.

"Which is exactly what my father always says."

The road ran between tall cliffs on one side and a pebbly sand beach on the other. Beyond the beach the ocean was flat and black. Scott took her hand and they crossed to the narrow strip of grass on the cliff side of the road. Then he backed her against the cliff wall and kissed her.

"You are a very slow learner," he said. "It's probably because you're a princess. I've heard that royalty isn't always very bright. Brains get dulled by all the pomp and ceremony."

"Shut up and kiss me again," she said. "And that's a royal command." His hands were on the cliff wall on either side of her head, his face inches from hers, and this kiss was as sensational as the last one. When he pulled away, she smiled because his glasses had fogged and she was so full of this magical, soul-mate feeling that she just wanted to hold on to him and never let go. She wanted to make love all night, talk and make love some more, eat bowls of popcorn in bed with him, snuggle under the blankets, wake up next to him in the morning.

He peered into her eyes. "What?"

"What what?"

"You're grinning like a Cheshire cat."

"I was thinking about eating popcorn in bed with you."

"While we were kissing, you were thinking about eating popcorn?"

"Well, not *while* we were kissing. But shortly after."

He kissed her again. A knee-buckling, tongue-in-the-mouth, hands-under-the-sweater kiss that went on until they were half slumped against the cliff, her hand at the belt of his jeans. Hot. Very hot. Almost hot enough to chase away the cold fear. They started walking again and she watched Henri, trotting ahead of them, his white coat almost phosphorescent in the dark night. The waves crashed and broke in strands of white foam. Ava tucked her hand in Scott's arm and pulled him close. *Hold me,* she thought. *Just hold me.*

"Popcorn sounds good," Scott said after they'd walked another hundred yards or so. "Popcorn, or grilled cheese sandwiches, or macaroni and cheese."

She looked at him.

"Comfort food," he said.

"Yum."

"First, though, I need to check my messages. The phone was ringing when we left this afternoon. God knows what newsworthy events have been going on. Maybe the Catalina Chow Chatters president has been overthrown, or buffalo have stormed Luau Larry's."

"Finding it difficult to fill the pages?" she asked.

"Difficult is an understatement."

When they got back to the newspaper office, Ava sat at Scott's desk while he played his phone messages.

"Good evening, Scott," the voice on the first message said. "This is Kathleen Tibbs. We were expecting you to cover the Halibut Tournament this afternoon. Everyone was waiting for you. What happened?"

Ava looked at Scott, who pulled a face.

"I completely forgot about it," he said.

"My fault," Ava said. "You were consoling me around that time. Kathleen is a good friend, though. Want me to go and make nice?"

"Might help. I'll let you know."

"What's this all about?" She held up a mug with a picture of a grinning Scott at a computer above the caption "2000 Pullet Surprise Winner."

He'd started to play the next message, and now he stopped and gave her distracted look. "There used to be a columnist at the *Times,* Jack Smith...something about never winning the Pulitzer prize. A few years back, one of the editors established this as a gag.''

"What did you get it for?"

"An exposé on a company that sold high-end down comforters that were actually filled with chicken feathers,'' he said, straight-faced.

They grinned at each other and Scott returned to his messages. The phone machine was on the top shelf of a bookcase, and he turned his back to her, jotting notes as he listened. Struck again by how good it felt to be with him, Ava came up behind him, wrapped her arms around his waist and dug her chin into his shoulder. "Am I distracting you?'' she asked as he tore a sheet off the message pad.

"Yeah, but don't stop.''

"Scott, this is Dr. Sam's secretary up at the hospital,'' the next voice announced. "There's an asthma presentation at the hospital Monday. Dr. Sam said you might be interested. Got some cute kids lined up. Bring your camera, he said.''

Scott turned his head to look at Ava. She still had her arms around his waist and his hair brushed the side of her face. She shrugged. Sam was off-limits tonight.

"Scott.'' A woman's voice on the machine said. "I need to talk to you. Call me.''

The voice was light and pitched high, what Ingrid would call a girlie voice. Ava had felt Scott's body tense slightly. Even without his telling her, she knew it was his ex-wife. She was suddenly consumed with curiosity about the woman. What did she look like? What was it about her that Scott had fallen in love with? Why hadn't it worked out?

"Do you want me to leave?'' she asked.

"No. I'll just be a minute.'' He went over to the desk, dialed a number. "Hi,'' he said after a moment. "I'm returning your call. I probably won't be home for the rest of the evening.'' He glanced at Ava. ''But I'll have my cell phone with me if you need to reach me.''

He hung up the phone. Ava thought of where he would be for the rest of the evening, and her body quivered in anticipation.

HE'D TOLD AVA NOT TO think or talk about her father, Scott reflected, but he wasn't doing a very good job of keeping the doctor out of his own thoughts. After Dr. Sam's performance that afternoon, he wondered about the perception the people of Avalon had about the man. Either no one had been privy to Dr. Sam's more extreme eccentricities, or the island's residents only saw what they wanted to see. But then, most of the island residents hadn't been making out with Sam Lynsky's daughter. He recalled what Benjamin had told him about Dr. Sam chasing away one of Ingrid Lynsky's suitors. Recalled, too, Lynsky's pointed remark about advertising revenue. Difficult to feel exactly sanguine about the whole thing.

On the other hand there was Ava. He'd never been given to literary flights of fancy, but Ava made him envy poets and musicians who could express themselves through art. He'd always thought of romantic love as the creation of greeting-card companies, but now he wasn't so sure. She was out in the kitchen, pulling doors open and closed. Every now and then he heard the ping of the microwave. He sat on the couch with a glass of merlot, obeying her command to stay put.

''Hungry?'' she called.

''That's the only reason I'm here.''

''Figured as much.'' She poked her head around the kitchen doorway and grinned at him. ''Warmed-over Thai One On noodles coming up. Ever eaten there? It's at the top of Metropole. If you haven't, don't. My peanut sauce is vastly superior.''

"I'll remember that." Hands pillowed behind his head, he looked around at the cottage, most of it visible from where he sat. Small and square, it had the simple lines of a child's drawing. A window on either side of the front door. A narrow hallway off the living room with two small bedrooms on either side and a shoe-box-size bathroom. And a tiny kitchen where he could see Ava at the stove.

A far cry, he thought, from her father's palatial digs. He liked her more because of it. But then, he conceded, there was very little about Ava Lynsky that didn't completely bowl him over. Which, given everything else, was more of a cause for concern than celebration.

To distract himself from his thoughts, which the wine wasn't quite managing to dull, he got up to inspect the brightly painted tiled fireplace on the far wall just as Ava reappeared from the kitchen. She speared a piece of broccoli from the container in her hand and held it to his mouth.

"There's more," she said. "I'm still heating it."

As he chewed the broccoli, he turned again to the fireplace tiles. "I really like these," he said. "They look as though a child painted them."

She smiled. "I painted them when I was about eight. Even now when I look at them, they make me feel happy."

He nodded, understanding exactly what she meant. "When Ellie was really small, just learning to walk, we were out in the yard and a neighbor's cat jumped over the fence onto our side, almost at Ellie's feet. She loved that cat and she just laughed out loud, this big squeal of joy, because she was so happy to see it. And I remember thinking, whatever else happens in her life, she's probably never going to have a moment like this of such pure, uncomplicated happiness."

"It's probably true." Her expression turned wistful. "Sad but true."

"Hey." She'd dropped onto the floor, was sitting with

her knees drawn up, her arms wrapped around them, chin propped on top. A favorite position, it seemed. If he went away, he would imagine her that way, smiling yet wistful. He sat down beside her.

"What would make you happy, Scott?" she asked.

He considered her question. "Mostly I think in terms of what would make Ellie happy. If things are going well for her, that's pretty much all I want. What about you?"

She winked. "Food."

"Oh, no." She'd moved to get up and he caught her hand. "You don't get off that easily."

"I used to think we were this perfect little family. Living on an island with palm trees and sunshine. Sort of magical, protected from the real world. I bought into it, totally. Until Rob died, I supposed on some unconscious level I believed that my life would always be that way. I guess that's why I'm such a mess right now. Now the magic's gone and I'm having bad dreams and panic attacks and waiting for the next awful thing to happen."

"It's called life, Ava. The perfect little bubble was an illusion."

"I know that." Her voice had taken on an edge. "You asked me what would make me happy and I'm trying to explain. I know it can't ever be the way it was, but I just want to feel safe again."

In an instant, she was up on her feet and back in the kitchen. He sat for a moment, then went after her. She was standing at the open refrigerator, black hair massed all around her shoulders, hiding her face. He stood behind her, wrapped his arms around her waist.

"Go away, Scott."

"Really?"

"No." A shuddering breath. "You think I'm nuts."

"'The happy highway's where I went and cannot come again,'" he said.

She drew away to look at him, began moving around the kitchen. "What's that?"

"Houseman. Don't ask me the rest. It's about the sum of what I remember from college literature courses. Essentially he's saying what Wolfe said. You can't go home. Another college tidbit."

"Where did you go to school?"

"UCLA. You?"

"USC."

"We used to say USC stood for the University of Spoiled Children."

"Thank you, Scott."

She was back at the refrigerator and he came up behind her again, touched his mouth to the back of her neck. "It's like Ellie squealing with perfect happiness when she was two years old," he said. "Not that she'll never be happy again, but it'll be a different kind of happiness."

"Ingrid and I were talking about what happens when we look back. Were we really happy? Or do we just remember it that way?"

"Probably a bit of both. So what do you think?" he asked a moment later. "If we stand here at the open refrigerator another five minutes, will more food magically appear on the shelves?"

"No." She closed the door and turned around to face him. "I've stopped believing in magic."

"All magic?"

A smile played around her mouth, and she watched his face. "Maybe not *all* magic," she said softly.

In the silence he could hear the rumble of the old refrigerator and behind them the dog noisily slurping water from its bowl. On the counter sat the white cartons of take-out food she'd heated, the air filled with pungent aromas of garlic and ginger. He kissed her for a long time, and then she took his hand and led him into the bedroom.

CHAPTER THIRTEEN

SCOTT'S JEANS WERE under the bed where she'd kicked them as she pulled off her sweatpants, and they were sprawled across the bed kissing and tearing away the rest of their clothes when his cell phone rang. Ava felt him go still. Her shirt was pulled up, her bra half-off, his mouth on her breast. The phone kept ringing.

"Damn." He sat up. "I'm sorry, Ava. I told Laura—"

"Go ahead." She lay back on the bed, pulled the sheet up to her chin. Scott rolled off her and fished under the bed for the phone. It rang once more before he found it.

He sat on the edge of the bed with his back to her. She could see the ridges of his spine. Her brain—detached from her body's hot clamoring at the sight of his naked backside—was coolly collecting information from his one-word responses.

"No," he was saying. "Nothing. Of course I would. *God.*" And then, "I've probably missed the last boat for the evening. I'll check. Call me if you hear anything."

"Ellie didn't come home from soccer practice today," he said a moment later. "She's not at her best friend's house." He was off the bed, fishing for his jeans. "Laura has no idea where else she could be." He pulled on his jeans, his shirt. "How late do the boats run?"

"The last one is eleven." The sheet clutched to her chest, feeling suddenly and inexplicably modest, she grabbed her clothes. "It's…ten till," she said with a glance

at the bedside clock. "If you hurry, you can make it." She
hesitated. "Do you want me to go with you?"

"No." He shook his head. "I'll call you."

"I'll walk you down to the dock."

"No, stay there. It's late, I don't want you walking back
by yourself."

"This is Avalon, Scott." She fastened her bra, pulled
her sweatshirt back on. "Have the police been called?"

"Yeah, but Laura said they won't do anything for
twenty-four hours." He turned to look at her, bent to kiss
her briefly on the mouth. "Stay here, Ava. Please. I'll give
you a call as soon as I hear anything."

And then he was gone.

FOR HOURS, SHE LAY AWAKE trying to figure out the dis-
quieting sense that she'd somehow been abandoned. *He has
a child,* she kept telling herself. Of course he'd leave to do
what he had to do. And of course, *she* was concerned for
Scott and his daughter. But beneath all those concerns, she
felt like a child who'd just had something snatched away.
All afternoon Scott had been there, just for her. Listening,
making tea, holding her. And now he was gone.

At two in the morning, still chasing sleep, she succumbed
to the siren song of a Dove chocolate bar, the last in a box
she'd bought just last week. A memory of Diana's voice
ran through her brain. "I may not be young or beautiful
anymore," Diana had once said. "And maybe I'm not making a splash in the art world, but I'm thinner than you."

She imagined Scott coming back, imagined lying naked
with him again, and compensated for the Dove bar with
forty-five minutes on the treadmill. When she still couldn't
sleep, she took a bubble bath and dissected every moment
of the hours she'd spent with Scott. Before he'd left, she'd
thought maybe she was falling in love with him. Thought
maybe it was mutual.

But he left to find his daughter, the rational part of her brain reminded her. Nothing else has changed. As the sun was coming up, she called Ingrid. Not surprisingly, her sister's voice sounded like someone who'd just been woken from sleep.

"Whaa…?"

"No big deal," Ava said. "Everything's okay. I just wanted to talk."

"I only talk during daylight hours," Ingrid said, and hung up.

Finally Ava gave up trying to sleep and wandered into the studio. "Within us all," she'd once read in a magazine, "is a calm center of tranquillity. Find that and you can deal with anything."

Or you could toss about sacks of concrete.

She wiped the back of her hand across her face. In the days of the Catalina Island tile-and-pottery plant, all the tiles had been made by hand from local clay. These days a lot of the artists on the island used ready-made tiles that were bought in bulk from the mainland and then painted and glazed locally. The results were fine, but she preferred the more individual, slightly quirky look of handmade tiles.

They were definitely more time-consuming. Two days ago she'd had a delivery from the mainland; one hundred two-pound boxes of slip, the material used to make the tiles. She'd stacked about half of them, one on top of the other, in the corner of her studio, an activity that allowed her to vent a considerable amount of frustration.

By noon she was exhausted and hungry. In the kitchen she found Sam polishing off the cartons of food she'd heated the night before for herself and Scott. Surprise halted her for a moment, and then a jolt of lingering anger propelled her across the room.

"*My* house, Dad. My kitchen. My refrigerator and my

food.'' She yanked the carton from his hand. ''If you can't call first, then at least damn well knock.''

''Hey, I wasn't finished with that.'' Over at the sink, he ducked his head and put his mouth under the running faucet. Then he straightened, spluttering water. ''What was it, anyway? Some hippie-dippy tofu nuts and twigs? *Blaagh.* What's wrong with real Chinese food? Plain old sweet-and-sour pork.''

Ava regarded him for a moment. ''Have you always been this way, Dad?''

He took a glass from the shelf, ran water in it and downed the contents in three loud noisy gulps, as though he'd been on the verge of dehydration. He wiped his arm across his mouth. ''Sure I have. You just didn't notice.''

''How did Mom stand it?''

He grinned cheerfully. ''Mostly she tuned me out. Ready to have me fix that deck of yours now? Or should I go outside and call first?''

''Neither.'' She folded her arms. ''If you keep barging in like this, Dad, Ingrid won't be your only daughter who no longer speaks to you.''

''You need to patch things up with Ed, instead of playing kissy-face—''

''Don't tell me what I *need* to do, Dad. You do not run my life.''

''This Steve guy's a loser. No one with a lick of common sense would have bought that damn newspaper. Nice enough guy—that's why I wanted to help him out. Probably do a good job on the book, too. That's how most writers are, head up in the clouds. Drown if someone doesn't tell them to come in out of the rain. Got a screwdriver?'' he started for the deck. ''Phillips.''

Without thinking she reached into the broom closet where she kept the toolbox he'd bought her for her eighteenth birthday. She and Ingrid both had toolboxes, could change their car tires in three minutes flat and replace a clutch. Sam had insisted on it. "No reason why women should be helpless," he would say. He'd never managed to persuade Diana, and her habit of forgetting to check the oil, or worse, insisting that she didn't know where the dipstick was supposed to go, infuriated him. The screwdriver in her hand, Ava went out to the deck where Sam had taken up where he'd left off the day before.

She tapped him on the shoulder with the screwdriver. "We need to talk, Dad."

He used the claw end of the hammer to remove a nail. "So talk."

"I want you to quit butting into my life. I want you to stop barging in unannounced." Images of yesterday's scene flashed across her brain, fueling her anger. Her voice shook. "I want you to respect my decisions and not treat me like a child. You are not God, Dad. Maybe everyone else in Avalon thinks you are, but you're not. You're an infuriating, stubborn, arrogant—"

"Brace that goes around the edge of the wood has worked loose," Sam said. On his back now, he looked up at her. "Come here. I'll show you what to do so you know if it happens again."

"Dammit, Dad." She nudged him with her foot. "Get up. Have you heard anything I've said?"

He stood, wiped his palms down the sides of his shorts— turquoise-and-yellow-striped Bermudas. "How about making me some lunch, and none of that damn tofu stuff. Always amazes me how they can mess up perfectly good food like sausage by trying to make it healthy. If you want sausage, eat sausage. Don't go complaining about the fat and calories."

Ava looked at him and counted to ten. "Tell me one thing I've just said."

"Something about me not being God, wasn't it?" He

scratched his head. "You want to buy this place, you better tell Lil to get the papers ready, pronto. Kind of got it in my mind to have it torn down. Property's worth twice as much. Could build three apartment buildings."

SCOTT WALKED TO THE SMALL park a block or so from where his ex-wife and Ellie lived to call Ava. "We found Ellie," he said. "I would have called you before, but it's been pretty chaotic. She was staying at a friend's house, a different friend. It took most of the morning to track her down."

"Is she okay?"

"Yeah." He stretched out his legs. Two joggers ran past the bench where he sat. A squirrel darted across the path. "Basically. She's not happy with life right now, though. Her mother's unhappy and Ellie's picked up the idea that somehow it's her responsibility to make things right again. I think I already told you she'd like to see us back together. I guess she figured that staying away would bring me back, and once Laura and I were together…"

"Poor kid," Ava said. "She probably remembers a time when things between you *were* fine, and she just wants it to be that way again."

"One of those illusions we were talking about yesterday," Scott said. "I don't think things were ever fine between me and Laura, but Ellie probably saw things differently."

"So what happens now?"

"I'm going to stay for a day or two, see if we can work things out."

"What about the paper while you're gone?" Ava asked. "Can I do anything?"

He grinned. "You can go up to the camp to see your father. I'm supposed to do a story up there."

"Don't get me started on him. I told him this morning that, despite what everyone else thinks, he's not God."

"How did he take it?"

"Pretty well. I don't think he believed me."

"I miss you, Ava. If it weren't for Ellie, I'd be on the boat right now."

"I miss you, too. I couldn't sleep after you left."

"Thinking lascivious thoughts?"

"That and…I'll tell you about it sometime. So how does it feel to be back on the mainland?"

"Well, I'm not exactly back under the most auspicious circumstances, but I'd have to say so far that I'd rather be in Avalon. I'm sitting here now in this park in Glendale listening to the traffic roaring past on Brand Boulevard. There's smog and congestion, and I'm remembering walking out on the pier and stopping to eat clam chowder on one of the stools outside Rosie's Fish Market. I watched a catamaran filled with scuba divers in wet suits take off across the water. The sun was warm on my back and the air smelled of fish and sunshine—"

She laughed. "Uh-oh. You're hooked."

"I think I am. I felt like a local."

"Rosie's is a Catalina institution," she said. "She and Earl came here on their honeymoon in the 1940s and they've been here ever since. She used to operate the pulley that brings the fish up to the scale to be weighed. Sea bass, swordfish, marlin."

"I want to be back there," he said.

"I want you back here," she said.

"You still have to give me the insider's tour of Catalina," he reminded her.

"Be happy to," she said. "Actually I'll give you the special tour. Camping over at Two Harbors, firelight and sage in the air and zipped-together sleeping bags."

"How often do you give that tour?"

"Never before."

"Damn, Ava," Scott said, smiling and shaking his head. As she spoke, he'd been thinking of the candlelit bedroom and the look she'd shot him as she stepped out of her pants. "I want to catch the next boat back."

AFTER SHE HUNG UP THE phone, Ava kept her hand on the receiver for a moment, grinning like a bridesmaid who's just caught the bouquet. She and Ingrid had been putting up tiles in the kitchen. As soon as Scott said hello, she'd taken the phone into the bedroom out of her sister's earshot. The source of her newfound happiness still felt a little too fragile and tentative to subject it to Ingrid's scrutiny.

Plenty of time to think about Scott tonight. She composed her features and returned to the kitchen where Ingrid was sitting on the floor reading a newspaper spread out to catch bits of the plaster they'd been scraping.

"Hey, listen to this," Ingrid said without looking up. "'Are you tired of being lonely?'" she read. "'Are you tired of meeting Mr. Wrong? Marriage-minded, sincere, financially secure guy seeks understanding woman willing to forgive a man's past mistakes and build a life together. I enjoy gourmet cooking, organic gardening, a roaring fire on rainy nights and the sound of high heels on a hardwood floor.' And—" she glanced up at Ava "—get this. 'I'm currently serving a sentence in federal prison in the state of California. Expected release 2010.'"

"What are you waiting for?" Ava picked up a tile and stood back to look at the wall they'd just finished. Completely covered with random tiles she'd collected over the years—a yellow sunburst left over from one project, a bouquet of cornflowers from another, a handful of tiles glazed in a bottle green that seemed to shimmer in the light from the window, geometric designs, botanicals—the overall ef-

fect was of a ceramic patchwork quilt that immediately
drew the eyes.

"What d'you think, Henri?" Ingrid glanced at the sleeping dog. "Couldn't you see Aunty Ing with a convict boyfriend?"

Henri opened one eye, then went back to sleep.

"Come on, it'd be great," Ingrid said. "I'd bake him
cookies and chocolate cakes and we'd drive up to the slam-
mer to see him on Saturdays. Maybe you'd meet a cute
poodle. We'll have a double wedding."

"Shh." Ava put her fingers to her lips. "He's dreaming
about a blond poodle bride. Can't you just see him, trotting
smartly down the aisle in a doggy tux?"

"High heels on a wooden floor," Ingrid said scathingly.
"See, that's the trouble with guys. It doesn't matter
whether they're trolling in singles bars or stuck behind
prison bars, they all have these totally unrealistic fantasies."

Ava wondered whether Scott had fantasies, realistic or
otherwise, of her. "You think so?"

"Absolutely." Ingrid lifted the lid of a pot on the stove
and sniffed. "Needs more hot sauce. Chili can't have too
much hot sauce." She stuck a spoon in the pot. One hand
cupped beneath it, she raised the spoon to her mouth.
"More cumin. Garlic and pepper, too."

Ava shook her head in mock exasperation. "You're just
like Mom. Anything I ever cooked, she'd always start telling me what it needed."

"Yeah, but Mom was a good cook."

"Thanks, Ingrid."

"No, I don't mean you aren't, but she was really good.
It's too bad Dad never appreciated it. I mean, you could
open a can of dog food and set it down in front of Dad and
tell him it was meat loaf and he wouldn't know the differ-

ence. But don't get me started on him. So who was that on the phone?''

"Scott Campbell." Hands on her hips, feigning intense concentration, Ava stood back to look at the wall. It did look pretty good, she decided. She'd also hung all her copper pots, tin molds, enameled pans and colanders from a rack above the stove, painted the alcove a persimmon color and arranged all her dishes on the shelves. On the windowsill above the sink, she'd filled an earthenware pot with a huge bouquet of rosemary and thyme she'd picked from her mother's garden. Running water or rinsing dishes, she'd catch the thyme's slightly honeyed scent, which always reminded her of Diana. "Remember how the place looked when Gran lived here?" she asked, trying to deflect the topic from Scott. "Kind of dark and fusty?''

"Yeah, it's a pretty amazing transformation," Ingrid said. "Kind of funky, but it's cool. So how come he's calling you at home?''

"Umm…" Ava picked up the tabasco sauce Ingrid had left on the counter. "You through with this?''

"Ava." Ingrid grabbed the tabasco. "Why is he calling you at home? What's up?''

"Nothing.''

"Tell me or I'll pour this tabasco down your throat. No wait." She peered into Ava's face. "I already know. You slept with him, huh?''

"No. You can't read *everything* I'm thinking, so quit trying." Still searching for a plausible reason for Scott's call, she brushed past Ingrid and busied herself at the stove. Ingrid came up beside her, twisted her head and stuck her face up close under Ava's nose. Ava laughed and pushed Ingrid away.

"Tell me everything, or I'll make Dad drive Scott off the island just like he did Quicksilver.''

"I like him.''

"And?"

"He's sweet and nice and understanding."

"Understanding about what?"

"Everything." She went to the fridge for a beer. "You want one?"

"Yeah." Ingrid twisted off the top of the beer Ava handed her. "So let's see… This wasn't going on last week when you came out to my place?"

"It just happened yesterday. I went to his office…" The recollection of why she'd gone to Scott's office stopped her for a moment. "Okay, I told you Dad wants him to write the family history book."

Ingrid smirked. "The family history fairy story."

Ava ignored the remark. "Anyway, Dad told Scott he could have access to Mom's papers—"

"What?" Ingrid set her beer down on the table. "After we've been asking for how many weeks? God, I can't be-lieve—"

"Yes, you can," Ava said. "We're talking about Dad. Does anything he ever does really surprise you?"

Ingrid dropped into one of the red-canvas director's chairs grouped around the table and was looking up, her expression one of angry disbelief. "It shouldn't, I know. I just keep getting this totally unrealistic hope that one day he'll actually stop pulling everyone's strings." She folded her arms across her chest. "So where do you and Scott fit into all this?"

"I told him everything. Scott, I mean. I meant to just tell him we didn't want him to do the book, at least until we'd looked through Mom's stuff, but I ended up…" She swal-lowed. "I know you and I talk, but I've never told you some of the things…"

"Like what?"

"Like…feeling I could have prevented what happened

to Mom. If I'd paid more attention to her, if I'd taken her little announcements more seriously."

Ingrid shook her head. "That's ridiculous. Why would you be any more responsible than me? Or Dad?"

Ava picked at the knee of her jeans. "I think she was closer to me. She told me things—"

"She told me things, too, Ava. Mostly she resented you."

"That's not true."

"Yes, it is. You never wanted to see it, that's all." Ingrid reached for her beer. "So you spewed your guts to Scott." She tipped back her head, drank. "A newspaper reporter."

Ava took a breath. "That has nothing to do with anything. We connected. I like him. It was like lifting a huge weight off my shoulders to talk about everything."

Ingrid drank more beer. "Did you tell him *my* theory on the accident?"

"That you think Dad pushed her? No, I didn't tell him that theory. Mostly because I think it's nuts."

"Did you tell him yours?"

"He asked me if I had questions about the way Mom died, and I told him I did. But it's funny, I feel better…easier about everything. It's like admitting my worst fears—kind of took away their power. Now I really do think it was probably an accident."

Ingrid slowly shook her head. "Amazing, the restorative powers of sex."

"Go to hell." Ava slammed her beer bottle down on the table. "Can't we talk about anything without you being so damn cynical?"

"I'm sorry." Ingrid reached over to catch Ava's hand. "I guess I'm kind of jealous that we talked and you still had all these bad feelings, but one session with Scott produces a breakthrough." Her hand still on Ava's, she grinned at her sister. "That and *I'd* like some mind-blowing sex."

Her anger not entirely abated, Ava hesitated for a moment. "Well, that hasn't happened yet," she conceded. "His ex-wife called just in the nick of time. He's got a fourteen-year-old daughter who's having some problems. She's trying to get him to go back with his ex-wife. He's not going to of course, but—"

"Uh-oh," Ingrid said. "Sounds kind of familiar. Not only does he look like Rob, he's in the same situation. I remember Mom warning you that Rob wasn't over his ex-wife yet—"

"No, it's not the same. Scott's completely over his ex-wife. And you're wrong about Mom. She practically begged me to marry Rob. She was always saying I'd never meet anyone as great as him. That was half the reason I dropped out of USC."

"I don't remember that," Ingrid said.

"Come on, you must. Rob and I had this huge fight because he didn't like going to the mainland, and Mom said it was selfish of me to expect him to. I can't believe you don't remember that."

"I must not have been there, I guess." Ingrid stuck her elbows on the table. "So where does this leave the whole book thing?"

"Kind of up in the air." Ava told Ingrid about Sam dropping by to find Scott and her on the couch. "Not that it's any of Dad's business, but he wasn't too thrilled. He made some pointed comments about the newspaper advertising revenue drying up."

"He's getting pretty good at driving away unsuitable boyfriends, isn't he?" Ingrid picked at the label of her beer bottle. "I'm not usually in the position of agreeing with Dad about anything, but I have to tell you, I think he's right this time. Scott doesn't sound like what you need in your life right now.''

"ELLIE,'' SCOTT SAID. "Can we talk?''

Ellie, on the back steps of her mother's house, held a massive Siamese cat in her arms. The cat's pale-beige fur was the approximate color of Ellie's ponytail. And, Scott realized, the cat's pale-blue eyes were also a similar shade to his daughter's. Both sets of eyes regarded him, balefully, it seemed.

Scott sat down beside Ellie. He'd been in Glendale three days now. He'd walked Ellie home from school, helped her through algebra homework and sat on her bed at night to talk. They'd resolved nothing. Laura was barely civil, Ellie was still unhappy, and while Ava had offered to cover anything urgent at the paper, unless he got back there'd be no issue next week. Given his already precarious finances, he could hardly afford a reduction in revenue. Especially now that the book deal was probably off.

"I've got to leave, El.'' He put his arm around her shoulders. "What can we do to make things better?''

Ellie rubbed her face in the cat's fur.

"El?''

"Why can't you just stay here?''

Scott drew a breath. "Ellie we've been through this so many times. It isn't the right answer for any of us. You wouldn't be happy, Mom wouldn't be happy—''

"She would be if you talked to her.'' Ellie's voice rose. "She was lonely. It's not too hard to figure out. You never talked to her—she says that all the time. She loves you, and she just wants you to talk to her sometimes.''

He leaned back against the steps. He'd spent hours talking to Ava, listening to her. Had he ever done the same thing with Laura? "Talk to me, Scott,'' she would beg. "Tell me what you're thinking. You're so far away. Where are you? Talk to me.'' And the more she'd implore him, the more he felt himself closing up. "Go ahead and write," she'd say. "It's okay. I'll be watching TV." And then he'd look up to see her standing in the doorway, waiting for him. "I thought maybe you'd want a bite of something." Or, "No, I want to wait up for you. It's no fun being alone."

But he had never loved Laura. Realizing that now, he also realized that he bore a large part of the blame for her infidelity. She'd been lonely and he'd been too self-absorbed to notice. And now his daughter was paying the price. The renewed love Laura thought she felt for him was habit and fear of being alone, he was sure of it. Yet, with all this domestic wreckage in his wake, what right did he have to blithely move on to a relationship with Ava?

"Ellie, your mother and I have had lots and lots of conversations," he said, trying to convince himself as much as his daughter. "Some of the things that went wrong for us are things you know nothing about. If we could make it work, we would, but it's not going to work and you need to understand that. Now let's talk about other things we can do that would make you feel better."

She buried her face in the cat's fur again. "I want to go back with you."

WEDNESDAY NIGHT, ED CALLED. Ava sat in her studio actually managing to make some progress on the Hollywood-producer's tile project. She peered closely at the outline of the garibaldi she'd just started to paint. The orange scales on the side of the fish had a depth of color that gave her a swift charge of pleasure. Was it too soon to celebrate? Had the block actually disappeared?

Tile was an incredible medium, she reflected as Ed told her in great length about a new plan to improve his golf game. Making the tile body was an art form in itself. The painting process was equally gratifying, each tile a small canvas on which to create a perfect miniature world. As Ed went on about slicing and birdies, she dipped her brush into burnt-orange paint and felt a satisfaction in her work that she hadn't felt for a long time. Scott had also called—just before she'd sat down to work—to tell her he was bringing Ellie back with him.

Paintbrush poised, Ava mentally played back Scott's response when she'd told him she was looking forward to meeting his daughter. It wasn't the words exactly—he'd sounded agreeable enough. But something in his voice... She shook the thought away. It would be fun. She'd teach Ellie how to make beads. They'd do girl things. Maybe Ellie would confide in her.

"...and I saw your father in town," Ed was saying. "He agrees. The past few months have been stressful for you, to say the least. But I think we need to clear up all this misunderstanding. I apologize for being preoccupied lately. I've been extremely busy at work, all sorts of things going on. I realize I've been neglecting you, failing to provide you with the necessary emotional nurturing—"

"Ed." She interrupted the flow of words. "This isn't your fault. It isn't anyone's fault. You're a terrific guy and I hope we can remain friends, but I don't want to marry you."

"Maybe what you need is a vacation. A change of scenery can help with depression."

Ava took a deep breath before she responded. "Ed, I want you to listen to me." Slim chance, she knew. "This isn't your fault. It's my decision. I feel my life changing, moving in new directions. I hope you meet someone wonderful and have a happy life. Good night, Ed."

After she hung up, she called Ingrid. No answer. Either her twin wasn't home or she wasn't answering. Probably the latter. Things had felt a little tense after she'd told Ingrid about Scott. She rinsed out the paintbrush she'd been using. Kind of like the strained phase they'd gone through when she was married to Rob. Once Ingrid got to know Scott, everything would be fine. Scott and *Ellie*. Her stomach tensed at the thought. What if Ellie didn't like her? Rob's daughter had hated her. Maybe she was just repeating past mistakes. She decided not to think about it.

CHAPTER FOURTEEN

THURSDAY AFTERNOON WAS the Casino Art Walk Tour. Ava had been conducting tours for the past three years and could recite the spiel in her sleep. *The Avalon Casino, Catalina's most famous landmark, is 140 feet in height, 178 feet in diameter, encircled at the seventy-five-foot level by a fourteen-foot-wide gallery. And at the time of its completion in 1929 was the tallest building in Los Angeles County.*

She could spew out details on the art inside, the ballroom acoustics, the length of the longest and shortest pipe (sixteen feet and one-fourth of an inch) on the full-scale pipe organ in the theater, the names of the movie stars who'd danced the night away (Clark Gable and Carole Lombard). What she couldn't do when she spotted Scott at the back of the crowd of mostly elderly tourists who stood in the bright sunshine looking expectantly at her, was focus on anything else but him. He'd called her again last night and that morning, too, told her he missed her. Told her to zip the sleeping bags together.

He winked and her heart lurched.

"Okay folks." She smiled at the group, buying time while she tried to remember whether she'd already mentioned that the theater inside the Casino was the first in the world to show talkies. "Can everyone hear me okay?"

They all nodded and smiled and assured her they could. Scott smiled. Her face went hot.

"How many of you came over on the Catalina Express?" she asked.

They raised their hands. She looked beyond them to Scott.

"What was the first building you spotted?" she asked.

"The Casino," everyone answered.

"Exactly." With a pang of guilty relief, she saw that he was by himself. She'd share him with Ellie, but first she wanted a little time alone with him. Distracted, she glanced down at the clipboard with the notes that she carried but hardly ever consulted. "Twelve stories tall," she said, "but as you'll see in a minute, only three levels. The theater right here on the ground floor, the mezzanine above that and the ballroom on the third floor."

"I know you from somewhere, honey." In the front of the group, a tiny woman with a fluff of white hair smiled at Ava. "Did you ever live in Pasadena?"

"No." Ava smiled back. "I've always lived in Avalon." She took another look at her notes. "The theater seats more than one thousand guests and still shows first-run films throughout the year." She stopped reading and addressed the little group. "Can anyone tell me the name of the first film that played here?"

"*The Iron Mask* with Douglas Fairbanks," a man dressed head to toe in tan cotton said. He nodded at the white-haired woman who thought she knew Ava. "On my honeymoon with this lovely young lady. Right now, you might say, we're having our second honeymoon. 'Course she's not nearly so frisky this time around."

Everyone laughed, except his wife who nudged him with her elbow. "Do you have a twin sister living in Pasadena?" she asked Ava.

"Actually, I do have a twin sister, but she lives here on Catalina." Ava smiled at the woman and led the group up a gently sloping ramp and into the circular ballroom. While all eyes, including Scott's, turned to the ornate ceiling that hung above them like a gigantic parasol, she turned hers to

Scott's exposed throat. Images of white-hot sex paraded across the screen of her mind. "Another first," she told the group. "When this was built, it was the largest circular ballroom in the world. My great-grandparents attended the opening-night gala."

She drew their attention to the thirty-two illuminated ceiling segments and the crystal chandelier, explained that the revolutionary use of open space inspired the design of New York's Radio City Music Hall. While the group were still craning their necks and holding cameras aloft, Scott made his way around the perimeter to where she stood.

He caught her hands, pulled her close and kissed her briefly on the mouth. "Hi," he whispered.

"Hi." She dragged her eyes away from his mouth. "You're making it hard to focus."

"What are you doing when this is over?"

"Nothing."

"Good."

He released her hands and moved to the back of the group again. Ava stared at the crowd and tried to remember what she was supposed to say. An elderly man, still gazing upward, jogged her memory. "Notice," she said, "how each of the parasol segments corresponds with the arches that circle the ballroom. And each arch has a door that leads out onto a promenade that circles the exterior of the Casino."

From the center of the ballroom, she walked over to the fan of sunlight spilling in from one of open archways and invited everyone to step outside for a view of Avalon Bay. They all smiled politely as they filed past her, obediently glancing up again at Ava's suggestion to observe the silver leaf panels and peacock-blue cornices on the promenade ceiling. All except Scott.

He took her hand again, pulled around the corner out of view and kissed her, not so briefly this time. When they parted, her body was shaking. The clipboard dangled from one hand; her other was still around his waist. If he was to guide her down to the floor and strip off her clothes, she doubted he'd get much resistance. Through the archway behind him, the ocean was a deep shimmering blue, the sunlight blindingly white.

"What are you doing here?" she asked, straight-faced. "Where's Ellie?"

"She's arriving tomorrow. There was some party she wanted to go to, so I thought I'd come and learn about the Casino."

"Enjoying it?"

"I'd rather have a personal tour."

"You're going to get one," she said. "Trust me."

"What will it cost?"

"Another kiss."

He leaned forward and kissed her on the mouth again.

"Not bad," she said. "But it hardly covers the cost of a real insider tour."

"I'll do better," he promised.

On the promenade, the group were sending glances into the ballroom. "I should get back to my tour."

"Honey?" a voice called.

Ava turned to see the white-haired woman in the archway, the sun at her back. "Come outside so Herby can get my picture with you," the woman called. "Now I know where I've seen you," she said when Ava was outside standing beside her. "Last year you gave a little talk at the Pasadena Library."

"Move to the left, girls," Herby said. "That's it. Little bit more. Good, two pretty girls. Say cheese."

"You were wearing a white skirt," the woman said after the picture was taken, "and the lady with you wore a beautiful yellow dress."

"My mother," Ava said, remembering now. It had been

a good day. Diana had insisted on a long and lavish lunch at a French restaurant and an equally extravagant shopping splurge afterward. "We had a great time," she said.

The woman was beaming, clearly relieved to have her question resolved. "Didn't I tell you, Herby?" She turned back to Ava. "I might be getting on in years, but I never forget a face. You and your mother look a lot alike. Same bone structure and all that black hair."

Ava smiled. "That's amazing. I wouldn't remember what I was wearing that day except that we took some pictures. I have one in my studio."

"Well, you both looked beautiful." The rest of the group had gone back inside to the ballroom, and the woman started to join them, then turned to Ava again. "Is your mother living in Pasadena now?"

"No." Ava shook her head. "No, she's…she doesn't."

"Because I saw her twice last week. Once in Old Town and then in the library."

Ava's breath caught. She glanced at Scott, who had followed her outside, then back at the woman. "It must have been someone who looked like her."

"I hardly ever forget a face," the woman said.

"My mother died nearly four months ago."

"Oh, honey, no." The woman's face creased in dismay. "Honey, I'm so sorry. I had no idea. I was so sure this lady was your mother. I have a memory for faces, you see, and well…" She patted Ava's arm. "Put it down to old age," she said.

"I'M OKAY," AVA INSISTED after the tour had finished. "Really, I'm okay."

Scott caught her shoulders. Beneath his hands, he could feel her shaking. He watched her face, peered into her eyes. A smile tried to make an appearance and lost. She buried her face in his neck. He put his arms around her, holding until finally she pulled away and looked at him.

"God, that was bizarre." Her face was pale, her eyes huge. "She just seemed so certain."

He kept his arms around her. This wasn't what he'd planned when he left the mainland an hour ago, but his resolution had weakened during the boat ride over, and by the time he spotted her at the Casino, had dissolved entirely. *I missed you,* was his first thought. *I have too much unfinished business to start a new relationship,* was his next thought. Ava pulled away to look at him. Her color had returned, but she still seemed shaky.

"Where's the best place in Catalina to watch the sunset?" he asked.

She took him to a restaurant on the water. Wooden deck, white tablecloths, an unobstructed view of the sun melting into an orange glow on the horizon. They ate mussels in wine sauce, which he'd privately had doubts about, but which Ava had assured him, correctly, he'd love. They clinked glasses of chardonnay and he mentally unfastened the tiny buttons on the front of her sundress.

"I missed you," she said.

"I missed you, too." He watched the play of light on the wine. When he looked up, she was watching him. "What?"

Her eyes stayed on his face. "Something's bothering you."

"No."

"Yes. Tell me."

"I feel as though I'm leading you into a morass. All the unresolved stuff with Laura, Ellie's visit. We've hardly got to know each other, but things are so tense with Ellie I know I'll need to focus all my attention on her, and I think it's asking a little too much of you just to hang in there while I—"

"Scott." She caught his hand. "Quit talking to your wineglass and look at me. Why don't you let *me* decide whether it's asking too much?"

"Because—"

"Listen, I'd like to think I've learned something from my experiences with Rob and his daughter. I understand that you need to spend time with Ellie. I would like to meet her, but only if and when you both feel comfortable with the idea."

Relieved beyond measure, he grinned at her across the table. "God, I've been rehearsing that little speech ever since I left Glendale."

"What did you think I'd do? Stamp my foot and demand that you pay me as much attention as you do Ellie?" She drank some wine. "So what are your plans while she's here?"

"The usual sightseeing stuff. I bought her a mountain bike, so I thought we could take a ride into the interior. The problem is I don't really know if that's what she'd enjoy, or whether it's just what I want to do."

"What does she like to do? Besides shopping?"

"I told you that?"

"I used to be fourteen."

"Do you have any ideas?"

"God, it's hard to even know where to start. I'll make you a list."

"Great." He hesitated. "And I do want her to meet you, Ava."

"You can bring her to my studio," she said. "We'll make beads. From clay," she said in response to his blank look. "You paint them and fire them, thread them on a string and, presto, a necklace."

"I think she'd enjoy that," he said. "She's always been good at art."

"I'd enjoy it, too."

He emptied the rest of the wine into their glasses. "More immediately, though, any idea what *I'd* enjoy?" A moment passed and he felt her bare foot trace a line up the inside of his thigh. Candlelight flickered on her face, and a smile played around her mouth. He reached under the white tablecloth and grabbed her ankle. "You got it."

THEY LEFT THE RESTAURANT and walked hand in hand down Crescent. She'd visited all the romantic European cities—Paris, Rome, Venice. Done the gondolier rides, stood on a bridge over the Seine. Either it was her small-town upbringing or the man she was with, or maybe a bit of both, but when it came to romance, Avalon was way ahead of those other places. The lights strung along the waterfront, the music and laughter from open-air cafés, the distant outline of the real world across the water.

On a whim they slipped into a club where dreamy rhythms were spilling out onto the street and a revolving silver ball on the ceiling sent sparkling mosaics of light over the heads and shoulders of dancers on the packed floor. Scott's lips brushed her neck and they moved together, oblivious to everything around them. When she thought she'd go mad with wanting him, he led her back out to the street and they walked up the hill to the cottage.

She'd hardly closed the door behind her before Scott had all the buttons of her dress undone. By the time they fell into bed, she was naked and Scott wore one sock.

"YOU LOOK INCREDIBLE in the morning light," Scott said.

Ava squinted one eye open for a moment. "Go away. No one looks incredible in the morning light."

"You do, though. If I had an ounce of artistic talent, I'd paint you just the way you look right now. Sun shining through the window—"

"And I'd stick the paintbrush up your nose." Ava kept

her eyes closed. "Please don't tell me you're one of those perky morning people. I'd have to ask you to gather your clothes and leave."

"Not perky, but reasonably cheerful. Good at making coffee, too. Want some?"

"You've just redeemed yourself." She pulled the sheet up over her head, listened to the sounds of him fishing for his clothes, zipping up his jeans. In the kitchen she heard water running, the fridge door open and close. She smiled. God, he was terrific. Not just at sex, which was also terrific, thank you very much, but everything about him.

The phone rang.

It was Ingrid. "While Dad's up at the hospital," she said, "I'm going to get Mom's papers from the attic. If we wait for him, we'll never see them. Wanna go?"

"Uh…" Ava wriggled under the sheet. "I don't think so."

"How come? We can sort through them, pack up the boxes again, and we won't have to deal with Dad yakking on about it."

From the kitchen Ava heard the clink of a spoon. "Scott's here," she said.

"Figures," Ingrid said.

"Ingrid, come on. I'm so happy." She lowered her voice. "I think maybe—"

"No, you're not in love. It's too soon."

Ava grinned at her sister's unfailing ability to know what she was going to say before she herself said the words. "Okay, but I'm definitely in like. Why don't you meet us for breakfast? The Beehive in about an hour."

"You got it."

Ava hung up. Damn, she'd meant to mention the woman at the Casino. If she hadn't been distracted by Scott, she would have called Ingrid last night. Out in the kitchen, he was whistling "Hotel California." She smiled again. Warm honey, that was what her body felt like. Soft and melting and… *Damn, she wanted him again.* In a flash, she was out of bed and in the bathroom brushing her teeth. A quick glance in the mirror wasn't reassuring, but she splashed water on her face, ran a brush through her hair and dashed back to the bedroom.

Scott returned with two coffee mugs and set them on the floor by the bed, removed his jeans and climbed in beside her. "Hey," he said.

"Hey, yourself." Her breast brushed his skin as she reached across for a mug. "If you think I enjoy having a naked man in bed with me, ministering to my every need, you're right."

"Not just any naked man, I hope."

"Oh, sure." She drank some coffee. "That's part of my morning routine, trolling down Crescent for naked men to bring back here."

"I think I've got my story for next week's issue," he said.

"Don't remind me about your occupation," she said. "Ingrid thinks I'm being naive."

"If I just had my camera with me," he said, whisking the sheet down off her body. "I'd have a great picture to go with the story."

"Except that sleeping with your interview subject wouldn't say much for your journalistic objectivity."

Scott blew into his coffee. "You're not really concerned about that, are you?"

She grinned. "Terrified."

"If I had any thoughts about writing anything negative about the Lynsky family, which I don't, I might as well kiss the newspaper goodbye. I know your father wasn't pleased to see me."

"About that…," Ava said. "If he does one thing to make your advertising drop off, he'll be sorry."

"What would you do?"

"I have all kinds of resources at my disposal," Ava said airily. "Don't worry about it."

He kissed her neck. "Thank you, but I *can* fight my own battles."

"Just don't underestimate my father's influence," she said.

"Ava." He set his cup down and leaned back against the pillow. "That woman at the casino who claims she saw your mother…"

She rolled onto her side and looked at him.

"Would it bother you to talk about it?" he asked. "If it does—"

"No, it's okay. It's been there in the back of my mind, too. The way she remembered exactly what my mother was wearing and even the color of my skirt. She just seemed so certain."

"This is the second time I've heard someone claim to have seen her," Scott said. "I wasn't sure whether to mention it to you. The manager at the Bay View said a friend of his saw her in Long Beach. He wasn't sure how much credence to give it, but—"

"Her best friend from college lives in Long Beach."

He shrugged. "It's a pretty big place."

"I know." She curled the edge of the sheet between her fingers. "Ingrid and I were just talking about this last week. That maybe she wasn't really…dead. Ingrid said it was nuts. But we were trying to decide if she'd been happy and I guess neither of us really knew. I want to believe she was, mostly because I can't stand the thought that…" She bit the inside of her mouth. "You know."

Scott put his arm around her. "We can talk about something else."

"No. It's not exactly easy to talk about. But not talking about it isn't easy, either."

"What happened after the accident, Ava?"

"They questioned all of us. My dad. Ingrid, me. Was she happy? Had there been any fights? Was there any reason to think it was anything but an accident? And of course, none of us thought it could be anything else."

"Do you ever discuss what happened with your dad?"

"Never. He won't discuss it. You know how he is—he just starts blabbering on about something else."

"What about Ingrid?"

"Ingrid thinks…" God, even to Scott she couldn't reveal Ingrid's theory. Because she didn't believe it herself, so why appear to give credence to it by repeating it? "Ingrid thinks Dad probably drove Mom up the wall, but essentially she believes it was an accident."

"Not suicide?"

"Well, I don't think she's entirely ruled that out. That was her on the phone while you were in the kitchen. She wants to look at Mom's diaries. We both do. Dad keeps finding excuses not to give them to us, which was why I came to your office—"

"And how we came to be lying in bed right now," Scott said.

She laughed. Then she turned and kissed him on the mouth. He drew her on top of him, kissed her neck, ran his hands down the sides of her body. Noises filtered up to the cottage from the street below, from the kitchen, the refrigerator's shuddering mechanical sigh. Scott flipped her over on her back, parted her thighs with his knee, and she forgot about everything. Including meeting Ingrid at the Beehive.

"Damn." Some forty-five minutes later, she untangled her legs from Scott's. "We were supposed to meet Ingrid…" She got out of bed, gathered up the jumble of clothes on the floor and tossed them on his stomach. "Pick something to wear. Preferably not my bra. I told Ingrid we'd meet her for breakfast."

"I can't." Scott sat up and separated his clothes from hers. "Ellie gets here this afternoon and I've got a ton of stuff to do."

Her clothes clutched to her stomach, Ava felt a weird little thread of something. Scott was out of bed now, pulling on his clothes, glancing around the room for anything he might have left. She forced a chipper little smile. "Want some help? Shopping, cleaning house? You name it."

He hopped on one foot to pull on a sock. "You've got your own work to do." He glanced around the room again, retrieved his watch on the floor by the bed and strapped it on. "I'll call you," he said.

"HIS DAUGHTER'S COMING," she told Ingrid fifteen minutes later as she slipped into a booth opposite her sister. "He's got things to do." She picked up a menu, feigned absorption in the list of breakfast specials. Ingrid plucked the menu away.

She scowled at Ingrid. "What?"

"So wham bam, thank you ma'am. Is that it?"

"No, of course it isn't."

Ingrid stuck her elbows on the table and peered into Ava's face.

"It isn't. I told you, he has to get ready for his daughter. He might bring Ellie by the studio. I'm going to teach her to make beads."

Ingrid smiled. "Sweet."

"Quit being so damn cynical. Why can't you just be happy for me?"

"Because I think you've been had." Ingrid stirred sugar into her coffee. "In more ways than one. Jeez, Ava, think about it. He comes on to you, gets you to spill your guts out—"

"Go to hell." Ava grabbed her purse. "I don't need this." She got up to go, but Ingrid grabbed her arm and pushed her back into the booth. "Damn you," she said after a moment. "Quit looking into my brain."

"You could save a whole bunch of time," Ingrid said, "if you just accepted that I can."

"So, do I like him?"

"Yeah, but you're scared. It's Rob all over again. The whole tug-of-war between father and kid. You tell yourself you can share, but you don't really want to."

Ava sighed. "Yeah, I guess I want to think it's terrific. I told Scott last night that I'd learned from what happened with Rob's daughter, but it's hard not to feel kind of left out. I keep telling myself nothing's changed, but deep inside it's like something has. I want to be all generous and friendly to his daughter, but—"

"You're a princess. Too bad stamping our feet doesn't get us what we want anymore, huh?"

"Let's talk about something else," Ava said. "I'm not really hungry for breakfast. Want to go and tackle Mom's papers?" As they left, she remembered the woman in the Casino the day before. "I met this woman who insists she saw Mom," she told Ingrid….

"AND WHERE WERE YOU all night?" Carolyn asked when Scott returned from Ava's.

"None of your business."

"Hmm." Carolyn, at the stove charring tortillas over a gas flame, tossed one to Mark. "What's your guess, Mark? I've got my money on the artist Scott was leering over at the reception."

"Artist, huh?"

"Yeah, too high-maintenance for Scott, though." She looked at Scott. "If you thought Laura was bad, this one—"

"Shut up, Carolyn." A spiral of blue smoke curled up from the tortilla and Scott reached over his sister's shoulder and turned off the burner. "Did you invite the fire department to eat? You'll probably need it."

"Yeah, yeah, yeah. Okay, listen. We're going to clear out of here so you and Ellie can have some time together. We're going camping at Two Harbors."

Scott looked at Mark. "You don't have a job to go back to?"

"I do," Mark said. "But that's what sick days are for, right?"

"Want an egg burrito, Scott?" Carolyn took the stack of tortillas to the table. "Not to ruin your appetite or anything, but Laura called just before you got here. She pretended she was calling to remind you what time Ellie arrives, but she was really calling to pump me for information about you. Like, did you have a girlfriend?"

Scott started clearing the counter of empty beer bottles, cheese wrappers, an open jar of salsa. He dumped the bottles in the recycle bin, stuck the salsa in the fridge and filled the dishwasher with what looked like a week's worth of plates and bowls stacked haphazardly in the sink. From the living room, the Eagles sang "Desperado."

"Turn that damn thing down," he yelled to Mark. He slammed the dishwasher closed and dragged the vacuum cleaner from the broom closet.

"What's wrong with you?" Carolyn asked.

"Apart from the fact that this place is a pigsty and my daughter will be here in two hours?" He plugged in the vacuum cleaner. It sputtered and coughed a cloud of dust. Carolyn turned it off.

"Scott." Hands on her hips, she looked at him. "Mark and I will have the house spotless by the time Ellie gets here. We'll disappear so you don't have to deal with us while she's here. Now tell me what else is wrong."

"Nothing."

"Is it the artist? That's where you were last night?"

He crouched down to inspect the vacuum-cleaner belt.
"Yeah."

"Is she going with you to meet Ellie?"

"No."

"Good. Because Laura, quote, 'doesn't want Ellie over
there if Scott's shacking up with some girl.' Fine for Laura
to shack up with someone, of course. She wasn't too wor-
ried about Ellie then, but God forbid you do the same."

"There's a difference." Scott dislodged a rubber band
from the row of bristles under the vacuum cleaner. "Laura
was still married. I'm not."

"Exactly," Carolyn said. "Hey, I'm on your side, bro.
God, she's unbelievable. What did she rack up in credit-
card debts? Thirty thousand, was it? And she had the nerve
to blame you. You made her feel lonely. Pah. What a piece
of work. And get this—"

He plugged in the vacuum again. "Drop it, okay? You're
not telling me anything I don't already know."

"No, listen, I want to tell you what she said today. She
said Ellie's mostly coming here to talk you into getting
back together again."

"Too bad, then. It'll be a wasted trip." As he carried
the vacuum into the living room, his mood grew progres-
sively bleaker, and the cozy scenes he'd pictured with Ellie
and Ava seemed like so much wishful thinking. Lost in
gloomy musing, when the phone rang ten minutes later, he
barely heard it over the noise of the vacuum.

It was Dr. Sam. "I'll be dropping some boxes of papers
by later today," he said. "Got another check for you, too.
By the way, if you're not doing anything next week, I'm
organizing a fishing trip. All local guys, doctor at the hospital, couple of the camp counselors. Ava's fiancé, Ed.
You've met Ed, right?"

CHAPTER FIFTEEN

"GOD, I DON'T BELIEVE this." Ava stared at the attic, empty but for a painted rocking horse that stood like a sentry by the trapdoor. "I know he said he'd put them up here. See." She pointed her toe at the worn patch on the floor Sam had warned her about. "That's why he didn't want us up here. He said it was dangerous."

"He's hiding something." Ingrid ran her hand over the horse's back. "It's been God knows how long since I asked him about the diaries, and he puts up one obstacle after another. There's some reason he doesn't want us to see them."

Ava watched the dust motes swirl around in a ray of sunlight coming through the small attic window. Her immediate inclination was to jump to Sam's defense, but she was growing weary of the role.

"Why was Mom's office locked when I went there?" Ingrid asked.

"And who is Beverly?"

Ingrid looked at her. "Beverly?"

"Dad said something about Beverly doing a good job of cleaning up Mom's office. I didn't tell you about that?"

"No." Ingrid hugged herself. "Something is giving me the creeps. Maybe Mom found out something about him. It's all in her diaries and she threatened to expose him. So he's got her locked up in the house somewhere until he figures out how to get rid of her."

"Ingrid, you're sick." Ava started back down the ladder.

Ingrid's theories might be farfetched, but something in the house bothered her, too. The creepy feeling she'd had in the kitchen last week, the dreams and panic attacks. She held the ladder, watching Ingrid's legs in jeans and hiking boots.

The lace of one boot had come untied and she was about to warn Ingrid when she felt a tap on her shoulder. She screamed. Ingrid, halfway down the steps, froze. With an ear-shattering scream, she hurled herself into Ava's arms and they stood there, clutching each other and trembling. The small, dark-haired woman with a dust cloth in one hand and a bottle of glass cleaner in the other looked almost as frightened as they'd been.

"I'm Beverly," she said. "I've been cleaning the house for your father. He didn't tell me you girls would be here, but since you are, do you know where he keeps the extra vacuum-cleaner bags?"

"I NEED AN ORTEGA CHILI cheeseburger," Ava said as they walked back down the hill from their father's house.

"I need a double Wicky Whacker," Ingrid said. "With extra rum."

"It's not even noon," Ava pointed out.

"An ortega chili cheeseburger would work, too."

"You and your damn theories," Ava said.

"If they're so far out," Ingrid said, "how come you were spooked, too?"

"Ingrid, if there was something in Mom's diaries that Dad didn't want us to see, why would he let Scott see them? Why would he ask Scott to write a family history?"

"Money. Dad pays him and the guy will write whatever Dad tells him to write."

"Why would he tell Scott about the diaries? Why not just hide them?"

"Maybe he doesn't plan to give Scott the diaries. Mom

had a bunch of other stuff, letters, photographs. Maybe that's all he intends to give him."

"Scott wouldn't be fooled that easily. He'd start asking questions."

Ingrid laughed. "Why would he need to? You've blabbed everything."

"Not everything," Ava protested.

"So you like him, huh?"

Ava smiled. "Kind of."

"But you're scared to death he's going to choose his daughter over you."

Ava looked at her sister. "I am not."

Ingrid tapped Ava's forehead. "I just looked inside. You are."

"I don't care, you're wrong."

"So when is she coming to paint beads?"

"We didn't talk about anything specific. In a day or two." The sense of unease she'd felt after Scott left that morning reasserted itself and she felt a pang of loss, as though Scott had walked out of her life forever.

"Hey." Ingrid punched her arm. "You never wanted to play the stepmommy role, anyway, right? Just think about how awful it was with Rob's daughter."

AT FIRST SCOTT didn't recognize Ellie. He'd arrived at the passenger terminal fifteen minutes early and felt his heart thumping as the Catalina Express appeared on the horizon. A crowd had formed around him and he'd pushed to the front of it to watch the passengers disembark. He glanced at a girl about Ellie's age, tottering on high platform sandals and lugging an enormous red duffel bag. Jet-black hair fell lankly down her back, and she wore blue jeans like a second skin on impossibly long thin legs. She waved at him.

Ellie. My God. For a moment he couldn't move. Her face was the approximate color of milk, her lips had only slightly more color, and her eyes were heavily outlined in black. He bit back a quip about Morticia Addams and hugged her. She didn't even feel like Ellie. Had he noticed the sharp shoulder blades, the bony angles last week? He held her a moment longer, searching for the familiar. And found it when she wriggled impatiently out of his grasp. Ellie had always just submitted to hugging.

"I didn't know it was you at first." He caught a strand of her hair, light brown the last time he'd seen it. "What's with this?"

She scowled. "Gee, thanks, Dad. Nice to see you, too."

"It is nice to see you, El." He grabbed the bag. "Fantastic." One arm around her shoulders, he squeezed her closer.

"I need to call Mom," she said.

He took a breath. "Can it wait till we get to my office?"

"You don't have a cell phone?"

"I do, but I forgot to charge it."

And we're off to a great start. They headed down the dock and he shot her a glance. In addition to the duffel bag, she also had a massive backpack. "Want me to take that for you as well?"

"Where's the car?"

"I don't have a car, I told you that. This is a small island—there's a waiting list to have a car." With Ellie tottering beside him, he moved through the throngs of disembarking passengers, past the placards hawking tours of the Casino, rides on glass-bottom boats and moonlight cruises, past the day-trippers and honeymooners and gaggles of chattering kids. Tension knotted his stomach and his head ached. He was so desperate for her visit to be a success that he felt he might be dooming it from sheer anxiety.

"How come you didn't rent a car?" Ellie wanted to know.

"Ellie, I know I explained all this. There are no rental cars on Catalina. The only things you can rent are bicycles, golf carts and motorcycles."

"Cool. I'd like to ride a motorcycle."

"You have to be eighteen."

She sighed. "So, like, what are we gonna do?"

"First, we're going to stop at my office. Just for a minute, though, then we'll drop your things off at the apartment and…" He glanced at her. "Then it's up to you. There are all kinds of things we could do. Ride bikes, check out the buffalo?"

"Buffalo?"

"Buffalo." Encouraged by the first glimmer of interest he'd seen, he told her everything he knew about the buffalo on the island, including the fact that the island airport sold buffalo burgers in its restaurant. Big mistake. Her face creased in revulsion.

"Oh, gross. Please don't tell me you actually ate one."

"I haven't." He revised plans for lunch. "So anyway, that's one idea. We're going to have a fun time," he said with more optimism than he felt. "There are lots of things we could do," he repeated. *I also have a friend who wants to show you how to make beads. You'll like her. She's an artist. I like her.* Later, he decided as he unlocked the front door of the *Argonaut* office. "So." He pulled open the door and waved his arm at the small front office, still crowded with boxes he'd yet to unpack. "This is it. Just like my office at the *Times,* huh?"

Ellie snorted. "Yeah, right, Dad." She shrugged the backpack from her shoulders. "I need to call Mom."

"Let me just check this first," Scott said with a glance at the blinking red light on the message machine. He grabbed a pen, pressed the play button. A chamber mixer, a guy from Toom's Plumbing who wasn't happy with the way his ad looked and Lil from Lil's Lovely Island Real

Estate telling him about a house he should see. A long, convoluted message from Carolyn about her plans for the week. He hit fast forward.

"...so I'm calling to tell you that I know without a doubt that Dr. Samuel Lynsky murdered his wife. I cannot reveal my identity; I am a public figure. I'm married and I have grown children who are also in the public eye. If all this came to light, it would be disastrous and painful for everyone involved. Diana and I were lovers for many years. It is my belief that Lynsky discovered this and killed Diana in a jealous rage."

His hand over the replay button, Scott glanced at Ellie. Caught up in the message, he'd forgotten about her for a moment. Her black-rimmed eyes wide, she looked like a little kid who'd just heard a scary bedtime story.

"Is that for real, Dad?"

INGRID HADN'T GIVEN much credence to the claim that Diana had been seen on the mainland, but Ava couldn't dismiss it entirely. Two days into Scott's visit with his daughter—it meant nothing that he hadn't even called, she kept telling herself—she sat on the bed with the Long Beach Yellow Pages on her lap.

"Detective, see Investigators," she read. She flipped the pages. "Questions? Suspicions? Doubts? Twenty-five years' experience. Background checks. Missing Persons Located. When you need to know the truth."

She flipped the book closed. The dreams were back. Last night she'd awoken screaming. She had a whole bunch of questions, suspicions and doubts, and they didn't just revolve around her mother. Twice she'd started to call Scott, but even in her head, she couldn't summon the appropriately casual, noninquisitory tone of voice, so she'd set the phone down. And, not the least of her problems, she'd made no progress on the Hollywood producer's project and the deadline was looming ever closer.

Now the bedroom was getting to her. All she could see was Scott, lying on his side with his head propped in his hand telling her she looked incredible in the morning light. *Pah.* She threw on some clothes, walked down to the gym and punched bags for thirty minutes. It helped. On her way back to the cottage—where she would paint at least three tiles today if she had to tie herself to the stool—she passed the *Argonaut.* The doors were locked.

Wham bam, thank-you ma'am. Ingrid's voice replayed in her head. Ava chewed the inside of her mouth. "Shut-up, Ingrid," she muttered. When she got back to the cottage, she found her father sitting outside on the deck with Henri finishing a half-gallon carton of fudge ripple. She hadn't seen or heard from him for several days.

"One scoop," he said in answer to her accusing look. "The dog ate the rest."

The thing to do, she decided, was act normally. If she let Sam see how she really felt right now—suspicious, angry, frustrated—he might guess correctly that it had something to do with Scott.

Henri was sitting very straight, his two front paws stiff and slightly parted. She looked at him and he barked. "Did you eat all the ice cream or is the bad man lying?" Hands on her hips, she tried to keep her expression stern, but Henri, with his white barrister-wig ears and long aristocratic nose, looked so goofy she grinned despite herself.

He barked again and jumped off the chair.

"I know, Henri," Ava said. "That Sam's a bad boy. *He* ate all the ice cream and he's blaming it on you."

Sam shook his head. "Damn dog's spoiled. He was standing on your kitchen table when I came in. Barking at me."

Ava caught Henri's jaw in her hands, kissed his wet

black nose. "You tell him it's your house and you'll stand on the kitchen table any time you feel like it." She got the red-and-blue cape she'd taken off him the night before and tied it back on. "Who's a good, good boy?"

He jumped up on the wooden bench where her father was sitting and licked Sam's face.

"Superdog," Ava said. "Leaps tall tables in a single bound."

"Saw the mayor today," Sam said. "Keeps asking me about that memorial for your mother. It's getting so I don't know what to tell him."

"Tell him you don't know," Ava said. "Tell him it's not your decision, anyway. Hey, Dad." She looked at her father, trying to keep her voice casual. "On the Casino Art Walk last week, I met this woman who said she saw Mom in Pasadena. Twice."

Sam scraped the spoon around the rim of the carton, held out the lid for Henri to lick. After a moment he got up and went inside. Ava followed him. He threw the container in the trash, rinsed the spoon under the tap.

"Did you hear what I said?"

"I heard you."

"Don't you have anything to say about it? I mean, it was pretty weird. She recognized me from when I gave a talk at the library. Remember when Mom went with me last year? This woman knew *all* the details. The clothes we were wearing, the color of Mom's hair. She said she saw Mom twice after that."

"Ava, your mother's dead," he said.

His voice was infinitely patient, as though he'd told her the same thing a dozen times before, but knew that in time she'd understand. "I'm well aware of that," she said.

"I'm not so sure you are."

"Of course I am. I just told you what this woman said."

"And you want to believe it." He was over at the window now, his back to her. "I see it in your face. I can hear it in your voice."

"It's not outside the realm of possibility. Things like that have happened."

"Ava, there is nothing to suggest that your mother is alive. Nothing. If you want me to go into graphic detail about bodies getting trapped under seaweed or—"

"Skip it, Dad." Maybe he was right. She *did* want to believe her mother was alive in Pasadena. Just as she *didn't* want to believe Scott had been using her.

"By the way," Sam said, "your mother's papers are out in the Jeep. I'll bring them up."

"TYPICAL," INGRID SAID when Ava called that night to tell her about the papers. "It's all a power play. He masks it with the congenial hoo-hah, but basically he's like a giant puppet master pulling strings and jerking everyone around. Including your boyfriend, I'm sure."

"He's not my boyfriend," Ava said.

"Uh-oh."

"Shut up, Ingrid."

"Hasn't called, huh?"

"Actually, he's here right now and we're thrashing around on the bed in frenzied lust."

"You'd probably hate me if I said I told you so."

"You're right, I would."

She hung up and looked at the phone. What would be wrong with just calling him? She picked up the phone again. What if she interrupted a meaningful father-and-daughter bonding session? Scott might not appreciate it. She set the phone down and it rang again immediately. Scott. It *would* be Scott. One, two, three, she counted the rings. On the fourth ring, she picked it up.

"'Allo, luv," Lil said. "Were you asleep?"

"No, no. Just...sitting here." Ava threw a pillow very hard against the wall. "What's up?"

"Well, I wondered if you could pop over tomorrow afternoon at four. Some papers I need you to sign. How's everything? Enjoying the cottage, are you?"

SCOTT SAT IN THE TV's flickering light, channel-surfing. Ellie had drifted off to bed around ten. For about an hour, he could hear the sounds of her music. When he went in to check, she was asleep. They'd had a good day, scuba-diving lessons, a safari tour to the other side of the island, enchiladas for dinner at a Mexican cantina in town. After the first day, when Laura had called four times, the calls had decreased. Today there had only been one call, and Ellie had said nothing more about parental reunification.

He switched off the TV and for want of anything more scintillating, balanced his checkbook. Not an activity to promote peace of mind. The paper's advertising revenue was down, Ellie's visit involved the outlay of more than he usually spent, and the landlord had raised the rent. Minor stuff.

Yesterday morning while Ellie was still sleeping, he'd listened once more to the tape of the guy claiming to be Diana Lynsky's lover. *I know without a doubt Sam Lynsky murdered his wife.* Out of Ellie's earshot, he'd played and replayed the damn thing so many times it had burned into his brain. Some crackpot, he'd told Ellie. The fact was, he didn't know. The guy could be telling the truth, or it could be one of those crank calls he used to get at the *Times*. *Elvis Presley is my father. I can prove it without a shadow of doubt.* Someone with a grudge, maybe, or determined to correct a perceived injustice, or envious or angry, or malicious or just garden-variety crazy.

He got up, went into the kitchen and got a beer from the fridge. He wasn't handling this well. Three days since he'd last seen Ava, but she was his first thought every morning, his last as he drifted off to sleep. He'd pick up the phone to call her, hear the damn voice in his head and hang up. They'd spent hours hashing over Diana's accident. The one scenario Ava had never proposed was murder. Whether she'd considered it, he didn't know. If he called her, he'd tell her about the tape. He knew that, and it stopped him from reaching out.

And it wasn't just that. It was Ellie, too. He set the beer on the counter, rinsed off a couple of dishes in the sink. Things were tentative enough. Despite Ava's assurances, he didn't know how Ellie would react to a girlfriend in the wings. Maybe they'd hate each other on sight. Ava had already had one less-than-positive experience with a stepchild. Easier to just drift away now, spare Ellie the trauma. He was…smitten with Ava. Okay, maybe more than smitten. But as people were always telling kids, you don't always get what you want.

Happy with that excuse, Scott? Laura's voice joined the mental chorus. *It's your style, isn't it? What you always do when things get tough. Shut yourself off. Run away.*

He picked up the phone and dialed Ava's number.

SOMETIME AROUND MIDNIGHT, Ava gave up trying to sleep and went into the studio to work. She was painting in the outline of a toyon bush when the phone rang. "Your voice sounds vaguely familiar," she told Scott. "But I can't quite place it."

"I miss you."

"Clearly."

"I know I should have called—"

"Scott." She set the paintbrush down. She'd wanted to sound detached, to make him think he hadn't hurt her by not calling, but her voice had obviously come out angry. "I'm not really mad at you. Maybe I should be, but you were with your daughter, and what the hell do I know about being a parent? For all I know it's a completely time-consuming, all-engrossing activity that doesn't leave you a moment to think of anything else.''

"Were you sleeping?"

"Working."

"Working? It's after midnight."

"I don't keep conventional hours," she said airily. She'd promised him she would hang in there and she intended to keep that promise, which, no matter how good it felt to hear his voice again, didn't preclude giving him a hard time.

"Couldn't sleep?"

"No."

"Dreams?"

"Yep." She switched the phone to her other ear. "How's Ellie?"

"She seems to be enjoying herself," he said.

"And you?"

"It's great to spend time with her. The first day was kind of strained and she kept checking in with Laura, which was a little hard to take. But we're doing fine now."

"Good."

"I miss you. Really."

"I miss you, too." She was smiling into the phone now. "Despite your disappearing act."

"What are you doing tomorrow night? I thought maybe we could all go out to dinner. I want you two to meet each other."

"Why don't you both come up to the cottage? I'll make dinner and I can show Ellie the studio."

AFTER THEY HUNG UP, he'd paced the apartment, torn as to whether or not he should have mentioned the tape. Finally he decided he'd done the right thing by not telling her about it. If it was a crank call, no point in upsetting her. If not…

The next day, waiting outside the video store where Ellie was selecting a movie, he glanced at the sheriff's substation across the street. The tape was in his pocket. He peered into the video store at Ellie, her head bent over a for-sale bin, then walked across the road.

"Someone left this on my machine," he told the deputy. "You might want to play it."

The deputy looked at him for a moment, then set the tape on one side. "I'll call you if we have any questions."

Scott nodded. "Sure."

"You ready for that fishing trip yet?" the deputy asked.

"One of these days," Scott said.

Back at the video store, he collected Ellie. On the corner of Crescent and Sumner, a woman holding a little girl introduced herself, then smiled down at the child.

"Tell this man what you want him to do, sweetheart."

The child smiled shyly and ducked her head."

"Come on, sweetie. It was your idea."

"Write a story about Dr. Sam," the child trilled.

"Tell him why, though," the woman urged.

"Because he made my asthma go away," the child said. "And he's very funny."

"And he's a good man." Her eyes shining, the woman looked up at Scott. "A really, really good man."

"Who's Dr. Sam?" Ellie asked after they'd walked on down the street.

"He runs an asthma camp," Scott said. *The guy you heard about on the tape,* he thought. "So what do you want to do today?" he asked.

"Watch videos," Ellie said.

"You can watch videos at home, El."

"I know, but you asked me what *I* want to do. And that's what I want to do." She smiled up at him. "Okay, Dad?"

"Not really. There's a ton of things we haven't done yet."

"I want to watch videos. If you didn't want to hear my answer, you shouldn't have asked me."

He grinned. She had a point. "Hey, El, I have this friend who is a really good artist. She paints tiles, like the ones I showed you at the Casino—"

"Dad, you've only told me that, like, three times."

"I have?" He scratched the back of his neck. "Well, anyway, she invited us for dinner tonight."

Ellie shrugged. "Whatever."

"What's that supposed to mean?"

"Just whatever, Dad."

"You want to talk?"

"I already told you, I want to watch videos."

HE LEFT HER WATCHING videos and walked up to the hospital to tell Lynsky that he'd changed his mind about doing the book. Ava was a part of the decision, but it also wasn't worth the frustration of trying to deal with Lynsky—no matter how much he needed the money. He'd pick up some freelance assignments if things got too tough. If Lynsky hadn't murdered his wife, he was definitely a master manipulator.

"About time you showed your face," Lynsky said when Scott knocked on the consulting-room door. "When you going to get started on that book? I'd like to see it while I've still got some eyesight."

"That's what I'm here to talk to you about," Scott said.

"You ever heard of Anita O'Day?" Lynsky leaped to his feet and began searching through a stack of magazines, books and papers piled haphazardly on an upended trash can. "Like my table?" he asked, chuckling. "Found it in the Dumpster, brand-new. Fifteen, twenty dollars at the hardware store. Been to France? Market in Aix-en-

Provence has the best olives I've ever tasted in my life. Take a look at that. I'm thinking of going back there next year.''

Scott glanced at the travel magazine Lynsky had tossed him. An open-air market in Barcelona. He shook his head to clear it. Attempting to unravel Lynsky's thought processes was like reaching into a pot of cooked spaghetti. If he'd still been working at the *Times* and had no connections, emotional or any other kind, with the island, Samuel Lynsky III would have been an incredible subject for a lengthy feature article. Lynsky was still searching for God knew what when the intercom on his desk rumbled to life. A patient was on the way in.

Scott got up to leave, but Lynsky motioned for him to stay, so he pulled up a stool and faded into the background as Dr. Sam examined the boy. He watched Lynsky press the stethoscope to the boy's back. The scene had a bit of a Norman Rockwell feel about it. The boy with his skinny bare chest, huge glasses and storklike legs dangling now from an antiquated exam table, eyeing Dr. Sam with a touch of apprehension. Lynsky, all joshing affability as he checked the boy's throat. In his blue flannel shirt, faded jeans and tooled leather boots, Scott reflected, Lynsky looked nothing like the coolly clinical white-coated pediatrician he remembered from his own childhood, always a whiff of antiseptic about him.

"Armando swallowed two tin cans." Lynsky winked at Scott and moved the stethoscope around on the boy's chest. "And eight...no nine, ten, good heavens, *eleven* nails! I can hear them rattling around inside. Why did you do that, Armando? You're not happy with the food? I'll have to talk to Ava."

Armando giggled wildly. "I didn't swallow any nails," he said. "You're crazy, Dr. Sam."

"Shh." Lynsky gave the boy a warning look, then shot

a glance at Scott. "This guy's a reporter. He hears you say I'm crazy and he'll go right back and put it in next week's paper."

Armando grinned. "Everyone already knows that, Dr. Sam. And you forget lots of things."

Dr. Sam studied the boy for a moment. "Did I forget you like blueberry pancakes?"

The boy laughed gleefully. "*Yes!* You thought I liked banana."

Lynsky frowned. "Okay, did I forget that you like Tiffany Tibbs?"

"I *don't* like Tiffany Tibbs," the boy's voice was high with indignation. "She's a girl and I don't like any girls."

"Well, see? I didn't forget then, did I?" He lifted the boy off the table. "Now tell me what *you're* going to remember today."

"Use the crom…croma…" He looked up at Lynsky. "I forget what it's called."

Lynsky shadow-boxed the boy's head. "Cromolym. And you use it…"

"Every day."

"Even when…"

"Even when I'm not wheezing."

"Because…"

"Because it stops…my lungs from getting all messed up and making me really sick."

"And what else? No…"

"Rescue inhaler?"

Lynsky addressed Scott. "That's the bronchodilator. Opens the lungs so more air flows through. But it taxes the heart, so we prefer to manage the inflammation that causes attacks. That way the inhaler is less of a crutch. Asthma management's come a long way from smoking peach-tree leaves."

"Cool," the boy said. "I want to smoke peach-tree leaves."

"I love kids," Lynsky said to Scott after the boy left. "They're honest. Honest about what they're feeling. You can make them laugh, fix them up when they're hurt. No mincing around tippy-toe to find the right words that won't offend. Be yourself. Have the courage to speak up, say what's on your mind."

Scott nodded. Looking at Sam Lynsky, he found himself wanting to feel the same fondness for the doctor that everyone else on Avalon felt. And he could almost do it. Ignore the overbearing father he'd seen in Ava's cottage, forget the tape and the manipulation and see only the grandfatherly figure he'd watched by the blazing campfire, weaving tales for his wide-eyed audience. The man was frustrating and annoying—the nonstop verbal barrage, the refusal to see any agenda but his own—but beneath it all, Scott sensed an essential goodness. He pushed all that aside.

"Someone left a message claiming you murdered your wife in a jealous rage over her infidelity," he said.

Lynsky leaned back in his chair, his blue eyes level with Scott's. "And?"

"I wanted to get your reaction."

"I don't have time for this." Sam shifted his chair back. "If you think there's anything to it, take it to the police."

"I did."

"And?"

"The deputy said he'd call if he had questions."

"So. Is that it?"

"Do you know if your wife was having an affair?"

"I'll tell you what I told the sheriff's deputy after it happened. If she wasn't happy, she never said anything to me about it. If she was involved with someone, I knew nothing about it. Except for one incident at the country club when she got drunk and threw a gin and tonic at me, we never argued, and the reason for that is a fight needs a spark to set it off, and Diana and I had stopped sparking years back.''

''But you stayed together.''

''We weren't unhappy.''

''Or *you* weren't unhappy.''

''*I* wasn't unhappy. And I never saw any sign that she wasn't happy.'' Sam opened his desk drawer, closed it again. Then he folded his arms across his chest and eyed Scott. ''You still hanging around my daughter?''

''What does that have to do with anything?''

''It doesn't. I'm through with the topic of my wife. My wife's dead. But you've got a wife on the mainland who wants you back in her life again.'' He paused. ''So the detective tells me.''

Scott felt himself go very still.

''Sounds like the two of you are having a bit of a custody battle over your daughter. You want her. Your wife wants her. Not good for kids to be caught up in that kind of tug-of-war. Not good for anyone.''

''That's my business,'' Scott said.

''Well, I'm making it my business. Here's the deal. You go back to your wife, make her happy. Make your daughter happy.'' He reached into his desk and withdrew a check, which he slid over to Scott. ''This should cover your daughter's education when she's ready for college. That and a pretty good down payment on a house.''

CHAPTER SIXTEEN

AVA WAS IN THE KITCHEN whipping egg whites when Scott called. "Hold on a second." She set the mixer down, wiped her hands down the sides of her jeans and lodged the phone between her ear and shoulder. "I'm whipping up a culinary masterpiece for dessert. White chocolate soufflé with a raspberry sauce.

"Wow."

She smiled. "So what's up?"

"Nothing. I was just calling to say that I miss you and I can't wait to see you tonight, and as much as I want you to meet Ellie, I kind of wish it was just the two of us."

Ava touched her fingertip to the stiff peak of the egg whites. "We'll have our time together and it will be even better because we had to wait."

"I haven't forgotten about the camping trip and the zipped-together sleeping bags."

"Neither have I." The oven timer rang and she pulled open the door to check the chicken breasts baking in a honey and mustard sauce. The oven heat and cooking aroma wafted up like a hot wind. She closed the door. "When do you want to do it?"

"Maybe next weekend."

"Sounds good. What did Ellie say about coming here to dinner?"

He hesitated. "She was kind of...noncommittal. She didn't really want to talk about it. She'll be fine though. We just need to move slowly."

Ava murmured agreement, but Rob had said something similar about his daughter, and the memory threatened to douse the glow of anticipation at seeing Scott again. She straightened her shoulders. She'd said she would hang in and she was going to keep her word. "Hey, Scott. Tell Ellie I'm really looking forward to meeting her, okay?"

SCOTT STOOD AGAINST THE doorjamb of Ava's studio watching her show Ellie how to mold small pieces of clay into even smaller beads. Ava's face was in profile to him, her hair held back with a red scarf. Ellie stood a foot or so away, unsmiling, arms crossed. He wanted to move in and physically draw them together. The evening had been tense. Ellie, polite but distant; Ava so painfully anxious to please, his heart ached for her. He wondered what she'd say if he told her about Lynsky's bribe.

"So?" Ava smiled at Ellie. "Want to give it a try?"

Ellie glanced at him, the look on her face clearly indicating she wanted to leave. He moved closer, put his arm around Ava's shoulders and winked at his daughter. "Go ahead and try, El. You could make a bracelet or something."

She rolled her eyes. "I don't wear bracelets, Dad."

"We don't have to make beads." Ava reached for a large piece of clay. "Actually, there's all kinds of things you can make with clay. Flowers, animals, birds…"

"Ava painted the tiles on the fireplace in the living room," Scott said.

Her face pink, Ava gave a little shrug. "Well, I was only a kid, so they're kind of amateurish."

"I think they're terrific," Scott said.

"Dad, can we go home?" Ellie said. "I'm kinda tired."

"Oh, my goodness." Ava made a big show of looking at her watch. "I didn't realize it was that late. Oh, well…listen, Ellie if you want to come by tomorrow, or any time, I can give you another lesson. I have some terrific glazes and paint we can try and—''

"Thanks," Ellie said with no discernible enthusiasm. "Thank you for dinner, too."

He told Ellie he'd catch up with her, waited until she'd walked down the steps from the cottage, then put his arms around Ava's shoulders. Her eyes were brimming as she looked up at him.

"Didn't go too well, huh?"

"The chocolate thing was fantastic." A tear had spilled over and was trickling down her face. He brushed it away with his thumb. It was on the tip of his tongue to say, "I love you," but he drew her closer and they stood with their arms around each other, Ava's heart beating against his chest. He closed his eyes for a moment. When he opened them, he could see Ellie sitting at the bottom of the steps, shoulders hunched. "It's going to take time, Ava," he said softly. "It won't be easy."

"I know." She sighed. "I didn't expect her to fall all over me, but—"

"Come on." He peered into her face. "Let me see a smile."

She produced a tentative smile that left no illusions about her true feelings. "Ellie's waiting for you. I'll talk to you tomorrow, okay?"

"I JUST DON'T THINK I can deal with it," Ava told Ingrid the next day after she'd made some excuse to Scott about joining him and Ellie on a bike ride. "It's clear she resents me and it brings back all the stuff about Rob's daughter. I stood on the deck watching Scott go down the road after her...."

"Ava, you knew he had a daughter." Ingrid sat cross-legged on the floor, sorting through the boxes of Diana's papers that Sam had dropped off. "I mean, I don't want to say I told you so, but... So what are you going to do?"

"I'm going to tell him we're through." She dropped on the floor next to Ingrid. "I care about him—a lot—but I know how important his daughter is to him. I don't know if I can..."

"Compete?" Ingrid looked up from a journal she'd just opened. "That's really what it comes down to, isn't it? You want him all to yourself and if you have to share him with his daughter, it kind of ruins the picture-perfect romance."

"God, that makes me sound..."

Ingrid raised a brow. "Like a spoiled princess?"

"I hate that."

"The truth hurts."

"So what would you do?"

"I guess it would depend on how I felt about the guy. If I cared about him enough, I'd probably make the sacrifice."

"Maybe that's what I'm doing," Ava said. "I care about him enough that I don't want him to feel he has to choose between me and Ellie." She got up from the floor, went into the kitchen and grabbed a paper towel from the roll. Ellie would clearly be happier to have her father all to herself and, ultimately, Scott would probably be happier too. Tomorrow, she'd go down to the *Argonaut* to tell him.

"Ava," Ingrid called from the living room. "Listen to what Mom wrote in her diary..."

"I DON'T LIKE HER," Ellie told Scott the day after the dinner at Ava's. "And she didn't like me, I could tell. She's totally phony, acting like she's so interested in me just to impress you."

"That's not fair, El," he protested. They were at the kitchen table, eating the scrambled eggs he'd made. "Ava was trying really hard. It was kind of difficult for her, too, meeting you for the first time. If you make an attempt—"

"She was trying too hard," Ellie said. "That's what bugged me. She needs to back off, lighten up a little. Anyway, I feel bad about you being there with her when Mom's sitting home alone." She got up from the table, grabbed her backpack from the floor. "See you later, Dad. I'm going to meet Carolyn in town. We're going to do girl things." She kissed Scott on the top of the head. "Hey, Dad, I love you."

After Ellie left, Scott stayed at the table, drinking coffee, deep in thought. The sun was shining outside, but life had taken a decidedly gloomy downturn. Watching Ava try so hard—too hard, Ellie was right—to endear herself to his daughter, the surge of tenderness and love he'd felt for both of them had almost overwhelmed him. But where Ellie viewed Ava's efforts with cynicism, he knew they were genuine, motivated by her feelings for him and real desire to reach out to Ellie. He wanted both of them in his life, but could he make both of them happy?

Adding to that uncertainty, he'd stopped by the hardware store the day after Dr. Sam's bribe to talk to the owner about renewing his ad in the *Argonaut*. The owner, who'd blushed and stammered and finally confessed that he'd decided to advertise in *Island Life*. Within an hour, two other advertisers told him the same thing. He'd never even heard of *Island Life*.

"Well, it's only just started up," the pimply-faced kid behind the front counter had explained when Scott stopped by the storefront office. "Dr. Sam's real excited about it, though. He says it will give island kids jobs and they won't have to go to the mainland."

Elbows on the table, Scott surveyed the uneaten eggs on his plate and wondered what it must be like to have the kind of control Lynsky had. It couldn't happen in a big

city—there was always someone richer or more powerful—
but in a place like Avalon, Lynsky could pull the strings
and have everyone dance to his tune. Scott carried his plate
to the sink, scraped the eggs into the garbage disposal. Lynsky wouldn't chase him off the island or dictate his relationship with Ava, but the good doctor definitely wasn't
making things easier.

WITH A SIGH, AVA CLOSED the cover of the most recent of
Diana's diaries and looked at Ingrid. They were on the bed
with the papers spread out between them. The green nu-
merals on the bedside clock clicked over to three-fifteen.
They'd started sorting through the papers the night before.
Countless glasses of diet soda, two bowls of popcorn and
half a box of tissue. Ava lay back on the bed, eyes closed,
hands folded across her chest. After a moment Ingrid lay
down beside her, toes in white socks sticking up.

Ava squinted one eye open. "We look like Egyptian
mummies," she said.

"Pressed for time in our sarcopha...what's the plural of
sarcophagus?"

"Sarcophagossywassy," Ava said. "Who cares?"

"You pooped?"

"Yep. You?"

"Ditto." Ingrid sniffed. "You know what kills me? He
gave us such a hard time about getting the damn diaries
that I just knew there had to be something in them he didn't
want us to see."

"He never even bothered to look at them," Ava said.
"Obviously, or he wouldn't have let us see them. It was
just typical Dad. He just wanted something to hold over
us."

"So what's your revised view of him now?"

"I don't know if it's revised, really. It's more like I've
peeled off layers from an onion."

"I guess I didn't need to peel off so many layers," Ingrid said. "I always kind of knew the real him."

"Well, not exactly." Ava turned her head to look at her sister. "You thought he offed Mom, remember?"

"Yeah, well…"

"What amazes me is the lengths he was willing to go to get his own way," Ava said. "I mean, I know Dad's pretty oblivious to anything except what he wants, but God…"

"And how come we couldn't see how Mom really was?"

"I know." Ava pulled a tissue from the box. "She hated us. Well, me. She only resented you."

Ingrid stroked Ava's arm. "You're the talented one, Ave. You were everything she wanted to be. You were closer to Dad than I was. Plus, you had better hair."

Ava grinned and dabbed at her nose. "But she had a better figure. That picture of us all on the beach in our bathing suits? Can you believe she'd actually write on the back that I looked fat?"

"Actually, I can. Mom was always going on about weight. It's like the one thing about herself she was proud of."

"She should see me now. I've probably gained fifteen pounds in the last three months. All I do is eat."

"Mom never needed to eat," Ingrid said. "She was too filled with envy."

Ava swallowed. "I almost wish we hadn't looked at the damn things. Now when I look back, I won't be able to see anything except how bitter and unhappy she was."

"Is," Ingrid said.

Ava was silent for a moment. "We need to have a talk with Dad," she said at last.

AVA STOOD WITH HER back against the closed door of Sam's consulting room, Ingrid at her side. Dr. Samuel Lynsky III sat on a chair, pulled out from his desk and looked from one daughter to the other. A muscle worked in his jaw, otherwise he gave no outward sign that this was anything but a normal exchange.

"You girls are blowing this out of proportion. I don't have time—"

"Tough," Ingrid said. "We want answers."

"I did think your mother was happy. Always seemed happy to me. Had everything she could want, so why wouldn't she be happy?"

"Did you ever talk to her?" Ingrid asked.

"More to the point, did you ever listen to her?" Ava asked.

"Sure, I did. She was always yakking about this and that. Worms eating the tomatoes, skin on her neck sagging, someone getting a divorce. Sure, we talked all the time."

"A *real* conversation, Dad," Ava said.

"Let me tell you something, Ava. After forty years of marriage, you don't sit around having heart-to-heart conversations about feelings. That's pillow talk, the kind of thing you do when you're getting to know each other. We stopped that sort of thing years ago. Never was much for it myself, anyway."

"So you didn't really know whether Mom was happy," Ingrid said.

"Well, she wasn't crying into the pillow every night."

"Did you know she hated us?" Ingrid asked.

Sam rolled his eyes. "She didn't *hate* either of you. That's ridiculous."

Ava grabbed one of the diaries. "'March 3, 1967,'" she read. "'Last night, I just got Ava off to sleep and Ingrid started crying. Finally they were both sleeping, but then I couldn't sleep. I looked at their faces, all peaceful and quiet now, and wanted to cry. I should love them. Instead, all I feel is hate and resentment.'"

"You mother was nineteen when she wrote that," Sam said. "Listen, can we talk about—"

"She wanted an abortion," Ingrid said. "But you talked her out of it."

"She didn't know her own mind," Sam said.

"But you did." Ava crossed her arms. "So you had no idea she was in love with this guy in Long Beach?"

"I knew she used to be engaged to him, but that was before we met. She hadn't thought about him in years. Guy never had much going for him, teaches philosophy at Long Beach City College—had any brains he'd be at a university. I got my MD in the time it took him—"

"How the hell do you know she hadn't thought about him?" Ava burst out. "That's your whole problem, Dad. You think you're this omniscient—"

"So, anyway, Dad," Ingrid broke in, "she told you she wanted a divorce—"

"How about we discuss this tonight? I've got patients to see."

"Why was it so hard for you to accept?" Ingrid asked. "Why would you go to all this trouble?"

"Lynskys don't divorce. Never have. Divorce is a sign of flawed decision-making. It says you didn't know what the hell you were doing in the first place. If you're thinking straight, divorce isn't necessary. Except that anyone thinking straight wouldn't get married in the first place. Unnatural state of affairs. But then, you'd have a bunch of out-of-wedlock kids running around—"

"So the *accident* was your idea?" Ava asked.

"Well, your mother could never have dreamed it up. Took too much strategic planning. Too many details to consider. Starting with the Sheriff's Department"

"But someone *saw* her, Dad? Guess you didn't anticipate that."

Sam snorted. "You think I'm an idiot? Of course I anticipated it. She was supposed to move to New York. Bought an apartment for her. Last I heard, she'd cut off all her hair, dyed it blond and was living in Greenwich Village."

Ingrid smiled. "She lied, huh?"

"Should have listened to me. None of this would have happened." He looked at Ava. "Hard for you at first, I know that, but you'd accepted—"

"It just never stops with you, does it, Dad?" Ava said. "You really do believe you know what's best for everyone."

He laughed. "I don't *believe* it. I know. Trouble is, other people aren't so bright. What's important now is that all this never leaves this room." He looked at Ava. "Need to sign those escrow papers for that cottage. Valuable piece of property. Can't decide whether to let you have it or tear it down and put up a condo. And those horse stables." He looked at Ingrid. "Heard this big outfit on the mainland was looking to buy them. Now if you had the money to expand the place, modernize it—"

"Go to hell, Dad," Ava and Ingrid said in unison.

"We've cut the strings," Ava said. "Sell the damn property if that's what you want to do. I'll find somewhere else to live."

"Suit yourself," Sam said. "Your boyfriend won't have any problem in that regard. He's got enough money now to buy a place in Beverly Hills. 'Course, he'll have to check with his wife, see if that's where she wants to live."

"Scott?" Ava stared at him openmouthed. "You bribed Scott?"

"He's a loser, honey. An ex-wife, a daughter. His newspaper's going under. You can do a whole lot better."

THE TELEPHONE WAS RINGING when she got back to the cottage.

"Is this Ava?" a male voice asked.

"Yes."

"Deputy Joe Bowen down at the sheriff's station."

"Hey, Joe." When they were about fifteen, she and Ingrid had taken their parents' motor launch for a joyride and ran it out of gas. Joe had been dispatched to tow the boat back to the marina; years later he still teased her about the escapade. But he didn't make social calls. She took a breath. "What's up?"

"Your father's down here at the station. He asked us to call you and your sister. Divers found a body off Little Harbor." He cleared his throat. "Not sure, but the thinking is it's your mother."

"WE'RE GOING TO TAKE you out to dinner," Carolyn told Scott.

"Mostly because you don't have anything in this place to eat except boxes of macaroni-and-cheese," Ellie said.

"You told me that's what you like to eat."

"Not the box kind, Dad."

"What do I know?" They were all still standing in a little cluster at the edge of the park next to the *Argonaut.* The sun had all but disappeared behind the horizon, and a breeze off the ocean tossed the fronds on a stand of palms by the beach. From the Bay View Hotel, the thin threads of a saxophone wafted on the breeze. Scott thought about Ava. Tonight he would walk up to the cottage to talk to her.

Ellie chose the Beehive, where Shirley smiled when she spotted Scott. "Hey, handsome," she said as she led them to a booth. "Who you two-timing with now?"

"My daughter and my sister." Scott glanced across the table at Ellie. Her hair was still a dead unnatural black, but the ghoulish makeup she'd worn the day she arrived was gone and her expression was animated. That at least was positive. His thoughts returned to Ava. How, after making a hash of one marriage, could he so soon embark on another relationship, fraught with difficulties from the start, and have any hope it would turn out? He didn't see how he could. The prospect that Lynsky might take responsibility for the breakup irked him, but there wasn't much he could do about that.

"Dad!" Ellie waved her hand in front of his eyes. "Hello-o."

"I asked if you're having the usual?" Shirley winked at Ellie. "It's okay, let him go back to sleep. He's one of the locals now. I know what he wants." She slapped Scott's arm. "So when are you going to write a story about me?"

"I don't know," Scott said, feigning ignorance. "What's the story?"

"What's the story?" She slapped him again and rolled her eyes at Ellie. "Would you believe I used to be an Eileen Brennan Celebrity Lookalike?"

"Who's Eileen Brennan?" Ellie asked.

"Kids." Shirley shook her head. "So how do you like Catalina?"

"It's great," Ellie said.

"You going to come and live here?"

Ellie shot a glance at Scott. "I don't know yet. I might."

"You might?" Scott asked after Shirley had taken their orders.

"Yeah." She grinned. "I might."

"Uh-oh." Shirley had returned with three glasses of water. "D'you hear that? Third fire truck in the past five minutes. Something's going on."

Scott, still thinking about what Ellie had just said, craned his neck to look through the window. Down at the end of Crescent where the road curved up into the hills, he could see flashing red lights. He was still peering out when he heard another siren. He glanced at Ellie and Carolyn. The

Argonaut might be a newspaper in name only, but he was still its editor.

"I'm going to go check it out."

By the time he walked the half a block to the end of Crescent, four fire engines and three police cars were flashing red lights, and he could hear another siren coming down Claressa. He pushed his way through the crowd that had formed behind an area that sheriff's deputies had already cordoned off. In the staccato bursts of light, he could see fireman shining flashlights into the crumpled wreckage of a vehicle.

"Fell down from the road up there," someone said. "Probably took the curve too fast."

Scott pushed closer. The vehicle lay upended like a massive wounded animal, wheels spinning in the air. A Jeep. His mouth suddenly dry, he spotted the deputy who'd offered to take him fishing standing on the other side of the wreck, The deputy had a flashlight trained on the accident scene, and he glanced away for a second as Scott approached.

"Dr. Sam," the deputy said.

CHAPTER SEVENTEEN

THE SOUND OF LOUD knocking on the front door gradually infiltrated Ava's dream. Still groggy, she opened her eyes and reached for her robe. More knocking and then she heard Scott's voice. After the phone call from the deputy, she'd immediately called Ingrid and they'd talked for hours. Her first thought as she pulled open the door was that he'd also come to give her the news about her mother.

"I know," she said. "The sheriff's deputy told me they found her—"

"It's your dad, Ava. There's been an accident at the bottom of the hill. The ambulance is there now. I came straight up here to find you."

She stared at him, uncomprehending. His eyes were wide and dark, and she was watching them and trying to take in his words. "He's—"

"No." He put his arms around her, pulled her close. "He was sitting up, the paramedics were swarming all around him, but he was conscious."

"Oh, my God, oh, my God," she kept murmuring.

"It's going to be okay." Scott was stroking her hair. "We'll get through this. I promise."

"BIG FUSS OVER nothing." Two days after the accident, Sam sat in the hospital bed, head bandaged, left leg in traction, tubes protruding from all over his body. "Think I'm some namby-pamby who can't take a little fall?"

Ava looked at Ingrid. "I would have expected Dad to have been a little more heroic, wouldn't you?"

"Absolutely. So his car takes a tumble from the top of a hill? I figured he'd just walk away."

"Me, too," Ava said with a glance at Sam, who, despite his bravado, looked so pale and gaunt she had to look away. "I figured he'd just brush himself off, turn the car the right way up and go on his way."

"And here he is, lazing around in some hospital bed eating Jell-O and custard."

Ava shook her head. "Guess that proves he's mortal, after all."

"Don't." Ingrid held her hands to her ears. "I'm not sure I can deal with it."

"Yak-yak-yak," Sam said. "Why don't the two of you go off and torment someone else and leave a poor suffering man alone?"

"Suffering." Ava feigned amazement. "D'you hear that? He admits he's suffering."

Sam grimaced as he reached for the water glass on his bedside table, and Ingrid jumped up to help him. Obviously exerted by the effort, he drank the water and lay back against the pillow. "I lied to you girls," he said. "Guess I did think I could play God. Always seemed to me that if people just let me handle things, we'd all be a lot better off. Your mother must have swallowed sleeping pills before she jumped overboard. Found an empty bottle floating near the boat and another one on the cabin floor."

Ava leaned back in the chair. Next to her, Ingrid sat very still, her fingertips over her mouth. Sam's eyes were closed, his chest rising and falling beneath the thin cotton hospital gown. She heard the low hum of his monitor, the soft tread of feet in the corridor outside the room.

"You kept asking if she was happy, Ava. And she was, some of the time. Lot of times, she wasn't. It was me, I recognize that. I'm not an easy man to live with and, God knows, she tried. Talked a few times about leaving, this professor in Long Beach. But *I* loved her. Don't know what I'd have done if she left…''

"Dad." His voice had trailed off and Ava placed her hand on his arm. "You can tell us this later."

He smiled weakly. "Only reason I'm telling you now is they got me cooped up here. Might as well get some things off my chest. Once I'm out of here, I won't have time for yakkety-yakking. Tell you what, you ask me questions and I'll tell you what you want to know."

Ingrid brought her knees up, wrapped her arms around them and rested her chin on them. She gazed at Sam. "You drive me absolutely nuts, Dad," she said after a moment. "Really, if you weren't lying in a hospital bed, I'd hit you."

Sam's smile broadened. "And your question is?"

"My question is…" She got up from the chair and began pacing the room. "Well, first, why should we believe you? What proof do we have about the pills?"

"Ingrid, wait." Ava looked at Sam. "Dad, were they Mom's pills?"

"Of course they…" He winced as he shifted in the bed. "No."

"They were mine, weren't they?"

He nodded. "Dated right after Rob died."

Ingrid, over at the window, stared at Ava. "How did you know that?"

"Because when I started having panic attacks, I looked for them one night and they were gone."

"So you knew Mom had them?"

"Of course not. I just couldn't find them and I put it out of my mind until right now."

Sam reached his hand out to Ava. "You were having a

hard enough time, honey. If I'd told you she'd taken your pills, you'd have started blaming yourself.''

''But Mom wrote that stuff in her journal about starting a new life.'' Arms folded across her chest, head bowed, Ingrid paced the room. ''Until they found her, I bought that whole story. What if they hadn't found her? Were you going to go on letting us believe that?''

He shrugged. ''You girls seemed to want to believe that version—''

''I didn't,'' Ingrid protested.

''I did,'' Ava said.

''I know you did.'' Sam turned his head on the pillow to look at her. ''I saw your face when you were telling me about that woman at the Casino thinking she'd seen your mother. You wanted to believe it and I wanted it for you.''

Ava folded her hands behind her neck, suddenly exhausted. Catalina's Twin Princesses, he'd always said. *Stamp your foot and you can have anything you want.* She got up from the chair, leaned over her father and kissed his cheek. ''Get some sleep, Dad.''

''I DON'T EVEN KNOW where to start,'' Ava told Ingrid as they walked into town from the hospital. ''I feel as though someone's put my brain in a blender.''

''Want to go have a Whicky-Whacker?'' Ingrid asked. ''I need to do some processing and I want something to take away the edge.''

''I need some time before I try to sort it all out,'' Ava said. ''Anyway, Scott and Ellie are up at the cottage cooking dinner. Join us.''

Ingrid shot her a sideways glance. ''Hey, I want to take back all the bad stuff I said about him. He's been pretty terrific with all that's been going on the last few days.''

Ava smiled. ''I think so.''

''So things are going okay with his daughter?''

"I haven't seen her since she came to dinner. I'm sure nothing's really changed there. I just meant he's been really supportive."

"A good friend," Ingrid said.

"Exactly."

Ingrid punched her arm. "Liar."

This time, she didn't try to deny it. Before the news about Diana, before Sam's accident, she'd intended to tell Scott exactly that—that they could be friends, but anything more was out of the question. After the accident things were so chaotic there'd been no chance to talk, and he'd been so terrific that when the thought about ending things drifted to the forefront of her mind, she pushed it away. But nothing had really changed. The memory of Ellie's sullen hostility that night at dinner, her own strained efforts. At worst, she'd end up coming between Scott and his daughter; at best she'd be the resented stepmother.

"I think I'll take a rain check on dinner," Ingrid said when they reached the cottage. "I've been thinking that it's time I finally got serious about things. I'm going to talk to Dad about going back to med school."

"What?"

"Yep. I want to be a doctor more than I want to punish Dad by not doing what he's always wanted me to do."

"Ingrid." Ava grabbed her sister in spontaneous hug. "That's fantastic. God, I'm stunned. When did you decide that?"

"After the accident. When I thought Dad might die."

"MY DAD HAD TO GO into town to get something." Ellie stood at the stove, her face flushed, a tea towel tucked around her waist. "But you arrived at just the right moment. He wants to make that chocolate thing you made for us and he thinks he knows how to do it, but I know he doesn't."

"My dad's exactly the same way," Ava said. "You should see him try to make stroganoff." She rolled her eyes. "Let me tell you—"

"It's a guy thing," Ellie said with all the wisdom of her fourteen years. "You can't tell them anything."

Ava grinned, picturing herself relaying this to Scott. The kitchen was warm from the oven, the counter taken over by dinner preparations. An opened can of peaches stood next to the blender, which was filled with something pale green. Lettuce leaves, orange peel and a large bag of carrots shared space with a litter of eggshells and a package of Italian sausage still in the wrapper. Henri sat at Ellie's feet, alert to any delectables that might fall his way. When Ava attempted a guess at the menu, nothing came to mind.

"Your kitchen is *so* cool. Especially this wall." Ellie waved a hand at the patchwork quilt of tiles. "When I have a house, I want it to be just like this."

"Thank you," Ava said, genuinely pleased. The sullen girl of the previous visit had vanished. They might not be ready for heart-to-heart discussions yet, but since the accident, Ava had noticed a definite softening in Ellie's attitude toward her. To be honest, Ellie was probably responding to a change in her as well. She felt less intense, less desperate to make a good impression on Scott's daughter. As she cleared off the table, another thought made her smile. Sam—although unintentionally—had brought this change about. "Jeez, Dad," she imagined herself telling him. "Driving off a cliff to get our attention is kind of dramatic, but I think it might just have worked. Although I don't want you to make a habit of it." She looked at Ellie. "This cottage has always been a happy place for me. My grandma lived here, and I have a lot of good memories."

"Bet it didn't look like this, though?"

"No. The cottage is me now, but I can feel my

grandma's spirit here.'' Still elated by Ingrid's news, by knowing finally about Diana, by how surprisingly good and natural it seemed to have Scott's daughter in the kitchen, she felt, as clearly as if a switch had been pulled, a swift and sudden sense of coming back into the light again. The worst was over, and whatever happened now she could come through it whole.

''So how's your dad?''

''Doing better. He doesn't like being cooped up in bed. It kind of takes away his power.''

''But he'll be okay?''

''Yeah. He'll probably be impossible to get along with until he's back to his old self again, but then, he's always been impossible to get along with.''

Ellie smiled conspiratorially, as though to say she knew all about impossible fathers. ''But you love him?''

''Of course I do.'' Ellie's face was so wide-eyed and anxious Ava wanted to hug her. ''He's not perfect, but who is?'' She pulled down *Sinful Soufflés* and began flipping through the pages. ''So do we have the eggs separated and whipped?''

''Not yet.'' Ellie studied the egg cupped in her hand. ''My mom is always ragging on my dad. I mean, not that he's perfect or anything, but he's not as bad as she says he is. The thing is, though, I hear her so much that I start believing her and then I say mean things to him, too.''

''You know what, though? I bet he understands.'' Ava found a bowl and set it on the counter. She thought about Sam's face as Ingrid had leaned down to kiss him. For all of their father's blustering, the estrangement with Ingrid had taken its toll. She would have loved to be in the room when Ingrid told him about going back to medical school. ''I bet he'd be really happy to hear you tell him that.''

''You think so? I feel like such a terrible person sometimes.''

Ava watched her for a moment. Brow furrowed, she was still cradling the egg, turning it over and over in her palm. Ellie, dragged into the middle of her parents' drama, had no illusions about their happiness. Sam and Diana had probably been just as mismatched and unhappy, but they'd shielded their daughters from reality. Both courses had taken their tolls. Impulsively, Ava gently took the egg from Ellie and gave her a quick hug. "Listen, kiddo, I'm still kind of stumbling along myself, but if you want to talk about dads or whatever, I'm here."

"Thanks, Ava. I'm sorry I was so awful last week."

Ava grinned. "Hey, I knew what to expect. Your dad says you were a horrible brat."

Ellie grinned. "He did not."

"You're right, he didn't." Ava handed the egg back Ellie. "You know all about separating these?"

"Sure." Ellie tapped the egg with a fork, then gingerly pried the shell apart. The yolk broke, trickled yellow into the white. "I guess I'm not too good at it," she said. "I don't do much cooking."

"Watch." Ava showed her how to separate the egg. "It's pretty easy once you get the hang of it." She stood to the side, watching as Ellie finished the eggs, then reached into the pantry cupboard for the rest of the bar of white chocolate she'd used before. As she started grating it, she thought again of Diana. She, Ava, had probably been just about Ellie's age when she really began to take notice of what Diana did in the kitchen. The memory filled her with a wistful sort of longing, that brought a sting of tears in her eyes.

"Look." Ellie stood back to show Ava the frothy mountain of egg whites she'd whipped. "Now what?"

"Now we melt some chocolate."

"Cool. In the microwave?"

"No, a double boiler, and you can find one in that cabinet next to the sink."

"This is kind of fun," Ellie said as she clattered around in the assortment of cooking pans under the stove. "My mom mostly makes frozen stuff, so we don't have things like—" she held up a scalloped tin ring "—this. What is it?"

"Its belongs to a tart pan. There's another piece of it in there somewhere."

"Can you make pavlova?"

"Pavlova?" Ava looked at her, surprised the girl would know about such a relatively exotic dessert. "Sure."

"My best friend's mother is from Australia and she made it for Chelsea's birthday. It was so-o-o good."

Ava mentally reviewed the list of ingredients. "Want to make it?"

"We're already making the soufflé thing."

"Hey, what's wrong with two desserts?"

Ellie grinned. "Cool."

SCOTT RETURNED WITH bottles of chardonnay and merlot to find Ellie and Ava in the kitchen so engrossed in conversation that they didn't hear him walk in. He stood for a moment in the doorway. Ava, a tea towel slung over her shoulder, was slicing kiwi fruit, Ellie at her side. His daughter's head was lowered, her face in three-quarter profile to him, but she appeared to be listening intently.

"...and the thing is, sometimes you want to believe something so badly it's almost like you can make it true if you try hard enough," Ava was saying.

"Exactly." Ellie picked up a slice of fruit. "I wanted my mom and dad to get back together even though I knew they weren't happy together. I just kind of ignored that, though. Is that how it was with your mom and dad?"

"Pretty much." Ava moved from the counter and saw Scott. "Hey, how long have you been standing there?"

"Long enough to hear all your darkest deepest secrets." He moved closer. "Sounds like you two are solving all the world's problems."

"The world's problems are easy to solve." Ava shot him a glance. "Now we're working on what to do about men. I don't think there's any solution to that."

"Hey Dad, Ava's teaching me to cook so maybe we can have something to eat besides macaroni and cheese." Hands on her hips, Ellie surveyed the platter of sliced fruit. "What else do we need to do, Ava?"

"Not a whole lot. We won't finish the soufflé until we're ready to eat, so right now you can just kick back and wait."

"I saw Carolyn in town just now," Scott told Ellie. "She's rented some Rollerblades and—"

"Rollerblades?"

"From that place on Crescent. She's trying them out along Casino Way."

"She is?" Ellie's expression reflected rapid thinking. "Ava. Do we have about an hour before dinner?"

"Yeah, but you're supposed to be the chef." Ava said.

"I know." Ellie smiled slyly. "But I figured all your talk about Rollerblades was a hint to get me out of the place so you guys can be alone for a while. Anyway, everything is in the oven." She looked at Scott. "Behave yourself and don't let anything burn. I'll be back in an hour."

After Ellie left, they took glasses of wine out to the deck. There were two chairs out there now, low-slung green canvas, and several pots of trailing geraniums. The splintered board that had precipitated the skirmish between Ava and Sam the day Lynsky had arrived unannounced to find him with Ava had been replaced. The new wood looked raw and unfinished amidst the other weathered boards. Ava set her glass down, then dropped into a chair. Scott sat down beside her.

"Cheers." He raised his glass, waited as she lifted hers. "To…"

"To…" She clinked her glass against his. "To…health and happiness."

"Health and happiness," he repeated. If nothing else, it was safe.

"I enjoyed talking to Ellie," she said. "I don't know what happened, but all of a sudden we just clicked. It was great."

"She was having a good time, too, I could tell just by looking at the two of you."

"Any talk about her staying permanently?"

"I think we're just going to take it slowly. Laura seems to have finally accepted the way things are." He leaned his head back, gazed out at the blue waters of the bay. Out on the horizon, as if on cue, the familiar white form of the Catalina Express, growing larger as it steamed toward the harbor. He caught Ava's hand, swung it between them. "Hi."

She turned her head to look at him. "Hi."

For a few moments neither of them spoke again. He thought of his barely-making-it newspaper, the unresolved bits and pieces of his life, all the reasons he should give her the it's-been-terrific-but speech he'd intended to deliver before Sam's accident.

"I love you," he said.

She squeezed his hand. "I love you, too." And then she was out of the chair and on his lap, her face buried in his neck. "I do, Scott." She pulled away to look at him. "You've been terrific. I just wanted you to know that."

"I promised you we'd get through it all," he said. "And we did."

"I don't think I could have done it without you," she said.

"Sure you could." He watched her face for a moment. "You're a lot stronger than you think you are."

"Thank you." She kissed him, softly at first and then with her hands in his hair, her mouth open against his lips. "I have to tell you something," she said when they finally pulled apart. "Before my dad's accident…"

"You were going to give me the it's-been-terrific-but speech."

"How did you know that?"

"After that dinner with Ellie…" He shrugged. "Actually, I had a similar speech planned for you."

"Because of Ellie?"

"That was one reason."

"Tell me another."

"I can't exactly promise you a fairy-tale life."

"I don't want any more fairy tales, Scott. Right now, just knowing you love me is enough."

He caught her hands in his face. "You've got that," he said.

TWO WEEKS AFTER Sam was released from the hospital, Ava, Ingrid and Sam held an outdoor hilltop memorial service for Diana on the grounds just below the old Wrigley mansion. Scott felt a trickle of sweat beneath his suit jacket. It was unseasonably hot for May, and they'd all hiked up the path to gaze out at the picture-postcard view of Avalon, framed by yellow wildflowers and blue Pacific. Diana's favorite spot on Catalina, Ava had explained.

Scott had pushed Sam, still confined to a wheelchair, up the hill with Sam protesting all the while that he didn't know why everyone was treating him like an invalid and he was about ready to rip off the damn cast, let the leg heal by itself, which it would, anyway. "Ignore him, Scott,"

Ava had said loudly enough for her father to hear. "He's not calling the shots anymore."

As one lifelong friend after another got up to eulogize a woman who, Scott suspected, none of them had really known, he glanced at Ava. Dark glasses hid her eyes, but he suspected she had a tight rein on her emotions. Ingrid, at her side, was crying openly. Next to her, Sam had bowed his head and might, if Scott didn't know better, be napping. Twice, he caught the doctor swiping at his eyes. Such a short time since he'd arrived on Catalina to first hear about the mythical Lynskys. Now he felt inextricably entwined in their lives.

Afterward, Ava and Ingrid led the procession back down the hill to the reception at the Casino Ballroom. As Scott pushed the uncharacteristically quiet Dr. Sam, he could see Carolyn and Mark, hand in hand, Carolyn's orange spiky hair bobbing like a beacon above the somberly dressed crowd. When he'd told his sister about Ingrid's intention to return to medical school, she'd immediately applied for and got the stable-hand job. The following day, she and Mark—who'd quit the *Times* to write full time—had moved into the small house behind the stables. Not exactly upward mobility, Scott reflected, but she and Mark were both ecstatic.

"That newspaper of yours folded yet?" Sam broke his silence to ask.

"It wasn't doing that well before the competition," Scott said. "Now it's pretty much moribund."

"Competition?" Lynsky scratched his head, then laughed. "Right. *Island Life.* Couldn't think what you meant for a minute. Ah, don't worry about that. One issue was enough. Too much damn work. Give me the names of businesses who dropped you and I'll make sure they buy full-page ads in your paper."

Scott steered the wheelchair past a throng of elderly

women who'd stepped aside and were smiling and wiggling their fingers at the good doctor as he was wheeled by. Lynsky might have had a setback, Scott thought with amusement, but he hadn't stopped pulling strings.

"You still seeing my daughter?"

"Which one?"

"Which one. You know damn well which one."

"I love her," Scott said.

"Planning to marry her?"

"Not for a while. We've both got a lot of things going on in our lives. Eventually, though."

"Thought I asked you to stay away from her."

"You did," Scott said. "I ignored you."

"You know that's been happening to me a lot lately," Lynsky said. "People paying no attention to what I'm saying. Think maybe I'm losing my touch?"

"Could be it's just time to let go of the reins," Scott said.

Lynsky roared. "You're okay, Scott. Got some strange ideas, but you're okay."

AVA COULDN'T REMEMBER how many people the Casino Ballroom was supposed to hold. It was part of her spiel, but she couldn't remember. Right now the place was jammed, bursting at the seams with people. If she fainted, her body would remain upright, propped between backs and shoulders. People kept hugging her. Patting her face and peering into her eyes, handing her plates of food she set down as soon as they moved away, thrusting plastic glasses into her hand. She could see Ingrid standing under the chandelier, nodding her head. "Your mother was a good person," someone was no doubt telling Ingrid. "A sweet woman." The tears welled up again. Through the blur, she looked past the throng to the balcony and the blue strip of ocean.

A man was standing out there, his back to her. She began to work her way toward him. "Scott."

He turned and saw her, he held out his arms. "Come here."

She laid one cheek against his shoulder, against the unfamiliar feel of his suit jacket. She felt the sun, warm on the other side of her face. Scott kept his arms around her, one hand stroking her back. "I just want to stay like this forever," she said. "Okay?"

He pulled her even closer. "For as long as you like," he said.

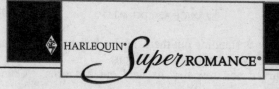

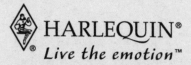

HARLEQUIN®
INTRIGUE®

Our unique brand of high-caliber romantic suspense just cannot be contained. And to meet our readers' demands, Harlequin Intrigue is expanding its publishing schedule to include **SIX** breathtaking titles every month!

Check out the new lineup in October!

MORE variety.
MORE pulse-pounding excitement.
MORE of your favorite authors and series.

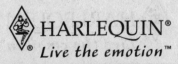

HARLEQUIN®
Live the emotion™

Visit us at www.tryIntrigue.com   HI4TO6T

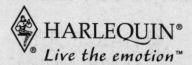

✂

Your opinion is important to us! Please take a few moments to share your thoughts with us about your experiences with Harlequin and Silhouette books. Your comments will be very useful in ensuring that we deliver books you love to read.
Please take a few minutes to complete the questionnaire, then send it to us at the address below.

Send your completed questionnaires to:
Harlequin/Silhouette Reader Survey, P.O. Box 9046, Buffalo, NY 14269-9046

---

1. As you may know, there are many different lines under the Harlequin and Silhouette brands. Each of the lines is listed below. Please check the box that most represents your reading habit for each line.

Line	Currently read this line	Do not read this line	Not sure if I read this line
Harlequin American Romance	❏	❏	❏
Harlequin Duets	❏	❏	❏
Harlequin Romance	❏	❏	❏
Harlequin Historicals	❏	❏	❏
Harlequin Superromance	❏	❏	❏
Harlequin Intrigue	❏	❏	❏
Harlequin Presents	❏	❏	❏
Harlequin Temptation	❏	❏	❏
Harlequin Blaze	❏	❏	❏
Silhouette Special Edition	❏	❏	❏
Silhouette Romance	❏	❏	❏
Silhouette Intimate Moments	❏	❏	❏
Silhouette Desire	❏	❏	❏

2. Which of the following best describes why you bought *this book?* One answer only, please.

the picture on the cover	❏	the title	❏
the author	❏	the line is one I read often	❏
part of a miniseries	❏	saw an ad in another book	❏
saw an ad in a magazine/newsletter	❏	a friend told me about it	❏
I borrowed/was given this book	❏	other: _____	❏

3. Where did you buy *this book?* One answer only, please.

at Barnes & Noble	❏	at a grocery store	❏
at Waldenbooks	❏	at a drugstore	❏
at Borders	❏	on eHarlequin.com Web site	❏
at another bookstore	❏	from another Web site	❏
at Wal-Mart	❏	Harlequin/Silhouette Reader	❏
at Target	❏	Service/through the mail	
at Kmart	❏	used books from anywhere	❏
at another department store or mass merchandiser	❏	I borrowed/was given this book	❏

4. On average, how many Harlequin and Silhouette books do you buy at one time?

I buy _____ books at one time	❏
I rarely buy a book	❏

MRQ403HSR-1A

5. How many times per month do you shop for any *Harlequin and/or Silhouette* books?
One answer only, please.

1 or more times a week	❑	a few times per year	❑
1 to 3 times per month	❑	less often than once a year	❑
1 to 2 times every 3 months	❑	never	❑

6. When you think of your ideal heroine, which *one* statement describes her the best?
One answer only, please.

She's a woman who is strong-willed		She's a desirable woman	❑
She's a woman who is needed by others	❑	She's a powerful woman	❑
She's a woman who is taken care of		She's a passionate woman	❑
She's an adventurous woman		She's a sensitive woman	❑

7. The following statements describe types or genres of books that you may be
interested in reading. Pick *up to 2 types* of books that you are most interested in.

I like to read about truly romantic relationships	❑
I like to read stories that are sexy romances	❑
I like to read romantic comedies	❑
I like to read a romantic mystery/suspense	❑
I like to read about romantic adventures	❑
I like to read romance stories that involve family	❑
I like to read about a romance in times or places that I have never seen	❑
Other: _____	❑

*The following questions help us to group your answers with those readers who are
similar to you. Your answers will remain confidential.*

8. Please record your year of birth below.

19 _____

9. What is your marital status?

single ❑   married ❑   common-law ❑   widowed ❑
divorced/separated ❑

10. Do you have children 18 years of age or younger currently living at home?

yes ❑   no ❑

11. Which of the following best describes your employment status?

employed full-time or part-time ❑   homemaker ❑   student ❑
retired ❑   unemployed ❑

12. Do you have access to the Internet from either home or work?

yes ❑   no ❑

13. Have you ever visited eHarlequin.com?

yes ❑   no ❑

14. What state do you live in?

_____

15. Are you a member of Harlequin/Silhouette Reader Service?

yes ❑   Account # _____   no ❑   MRQ403HSR-1B

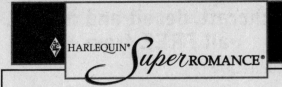

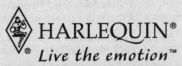

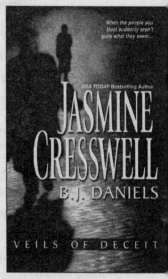